★★★
THE HOPES OF A WORLD
★★★

Five hundred men and seventy tractors: not a very large military force on which to pin the hopes of a world. At that it was twenty percent of the Rim's fighting strength. We had to be very careful not to be seen, because if Ellsworth ▨▨▨ the Rim had sent that much for▨▨ ▨▨▨▨rth, he could attack witho▨▨▨

Our agents in ▨▨▨▨ ▨▨▨▨ ▨▨▨ to foment sab▨▨▨ ▨▨▨▨▨ ng the miners: incide▨▨ ▨▨▨▨▨ ▨ns, riots, anything to keep ▨▨ ▨▨ ▨▨ edge and his troops in town. Mea▨▨▨ile our group started northwest.

The plan was to walk in—if we could. Being accustomed to Earth gravity, we could carry nearly twice as much as the old-timers and those born on Mars, but that wouldn't be enough; we could carry only three days' supplies, and we had a hundred and fifty miles to go, with a battle at the end of the trek.

—from *Birth of Fire*

FIRES OF FREEDOM

JERRY POURNELLE

BAEN

FIRES OF FREEDOM

King David's Spaceship copyright © 1980 by Jerry Pournelle
Birth of Fire copyright © 1976 by Jerry Pournelle

A Baen Books Original

Baen Publishing Enterprises
P.O. Box 1403
Riverdale, NY 10471
www.baen.com

ISBN: 978-1-4391-3374-3

Cover art by Kurt Miller

First Baen paperback printing, July 2010

Distributed by Simon & Schuster
1230 Avenue of the Americas
New York, NY 10020

Library of Congress Cataloging-in-Publication Data

Pournelle, Jerry, 1933-
  [Birth of fire]
  Fires of freedom / Jerry Pournelle.
      p. cm.
  "A Baen Books original" --T.p. verso.
  Birth of fire -- King David's spaceship.
  ISBN 1-4165-9161-3 (trade pbk.)
  I. Pournelle, Jerry, 1933- King David's spaceship. II. Title.
PS3566.O815B57 2009
813'.54--dc22

                                        2009005284

Printed in the United States of America

10 9 8 7 6 5 4 3 2 1

CONTENTS

★★★

★★★
BIRTH
OF
FIRE
★★★

★★★
CHAPTER ONE
★★★

"Here they come!" Our war leader crawled up to where I was crouched behind a garbage can. "You ready, Garrett?"

"As I'll ever be." I don't mind saying I was scared. We'd been in plenty of stomps before, but this one looked to be bad. The word was out that the Hackers had guns,

I patted my clothes to check weapons. As well as the bowie knife in my hand, I had four throwing knives, each in its hand-sewn pocket on the left side of my jacket, a chain in my regular jacket pocket, and a two-foot section of iron pipe in my belt. "I'm ready," I said.

"Good. We're counting on you." Spinny crawled off to encourage the other troops.

I was scared all right, but I felt pretty good, too. I was the hidden reserve, waiting in ambush to break some heads and show just how much better we were than those goons could ever be. I had tough comrades around me, and they depended on me. At the back of my mind I may have wished I was somewhere else, but you don't let thoughts like that up front when you're going into a fight. When this was over we'd own this part of Baltimore.

We were in a big open space under the Washington slideway. When they built the rolling roads, they left a lot of the old streets down under. There were shops and stores but not many customers wanted to go down there, so Undertown belonged to gangs and clubs. Like ours.

Our official name was Werewolves, but we called ourselves Dog Soldiers, and we were a proud lot. I was vice-president.

The first Hackers moved into the square and some of ours hit them from the sides. More Hackers moved in; I waited. When I had their guns spotted, I'd come in from behind.

Spinny had planned it that way, but it didn't go. Just as a free-for-all developed in the square, three Hackers came out of a window we'd been sure was boarded up tight. They'd loosened the nails earlier in the day. Now they jumped me from behind.

I turned and flicked a knife at the nearest one. It hit him in the arm and he dropped back. That gave me time to get my chain out and the other two backed off a step, but not for long. They had obviously worked together before. As I bent to avoid a karate-style kick from one of them, the other laid a ball bat alongside my head. It staggered me despite the surplus Federation Army helmet I wore.

Some plan, I thought. Crap. Ambush my ass! I was bigger than most of the other Dogs, and although at 20 I wasn't the oldest member, I was either the best or second-best fighter we had. I was supposed to be out there picking off Hackers from behind. Instead, I was alone and cornered. It looked like I'd end up with kicked-in ribs and a skull fracture if I was lucky—and my luck hadn't been running any too good.

I caught the guy who had the ball bat with the end of my chain. It whipped around one knee and he fell. I aimed a kick at his head, but missed. Then the other one was on me.

The last thing I remember was a gun going off, three times, and those damned sirens.

I woke up in jail. I wasn't bad hurt, but I was in big trouble. The cops had got there just as I went down, and two cops were killed in the fight. They'd been shot, and we hadn't had any guns, so it must have been the Hackers, but even if they believed us that cut no ice with the cops. They were out to make examples of us.

The problem was the cops didn't have anybody to stick it to. They had several dead bodies besides their own two, but the live crop consisted of seven juveniles—and me.

The juvenile court wasn't about to let the cops take it out on those poor children.

The cops offered me a couple of deals if I'd name some others and go state's evidence, but aside from the fact that it would be suicide, I'm no fink. Since they had only one adult to make an example of, it didn't look too good for Garrett Pittson.

I can't help my name. Garrett means "brave spear." I didn't have to look it up; my father told me. That gives you some idea of where my old man's head was when I was born. He'd just retired after twenty years in the old U.S.

Army, back before the Federation abolishèd national forces. Though he'd been in communications and couldn't have seen much fighting, he talked like he'd won all the brushfires that the U.S. had ever been in, single-handedly beating the enemy to death with his walkie-talkie.

He and my mother had great ambitions for me. I had a normal childhood, with maybe more bloodthirsty tales told me than most kids get, but nothing special. I went through a public high school where I was taught to read and write, which is more than a lot can say they learned, and got interested in electronics because my old man had the junk lying around the place, and it was fun to tinker with. It wasn't their fault things didn't turn out right.

When I got out of high school, things went to hell. I wasn't quite bright enough for a scholarship to a good college. Oh, I had decent enough grades in subjects I was interested in, but there weren't that many interesting subjects. And I liked to read, but not the books on the approved list.

Worse yet, we didn't belong to any minority groups, and we weren't quite poor enough for nondiscriminatory government aid. We sure weren't rich enough for me to go to a good college without assistance. That left the local community junior college, with plans for transfer to the state university after two years.

It didn't work. The instructors had nothing to say and weren't interested in teaching anyway. To them, it was just another job. They never talked about anything that wasn't in the stupid books they gave us, and there wasn't much in those. I could read the books and not bother with the classes. I decided I didn't want to be an engineer after all.

I didn't know what I wanted to be. The best jobs were with the government, of course. Get on civil service and stay there. It wasn't what I wanted to do with my life; I wanted to get out on my own, do something for myself. But how?

The government didn't let you do that. The government took care of you, whether you wanted to be taken care of or not. Even the dropout communes were visited by the government social workers. But if they didn't let you starve, they didn't let you get ahead, either. That's called social justice.

I wasn't interested in my classes and I wasn't interested in where I was going, and so I took to hanging around with other kids my age. At least we could earn some respect from each other; as part of proving our manhood we did some things that weren't strictly legal. Pretty soon we were in trouble with the police.

It wasn't serious, but three times my father had to come to the station house and get me out. The third time I was home just long enough to pack.

Hell, I *was* a lazy bum. He hadn't made any mistake there. I had no ambition, and while I didn't mind working—I could and did put in twenty-hour days on hobby stuff when I felt like it—I didn't see anything to work for. I wasn't going to be a rich taxpayer without graduating from something better than Francis Scott Key Community College. Any job I'd get with a degree from that joint would earn me just a little more than welfare and be about as interesting as carrying out the kitty box.

When my old man threw me out we had a hell of a

fight, and right then I decided that I was on my own. I needed no help from him. But I had no job; pretty soon I drifted down to Undertown. You can't stay alive down there unless you're part of a gang. I chose the Dog Soldiers, and before long I was proud to be part of it. Sure, I knew there was no future in it. So what? There was no future in anything else I could find, and this was a good gang.

Up to the big fight that was the story of my life. It wasn't much of a story. I thought about that a lot while I sat in the cells waiting for trial. Here I was, twenty years old, and not worth a damn to myself or anybody else.

Well, I told myself, that doesn't matter much. It looks like I've got a great future stamping out license plates, with occasional groovy variety like laundry duty and sewing mailbags.

The judge didn't like me. He was up for reelection, and the newspapers were giving him hell for turning criminals loose. The cops were pushing hard to have the book thrown at me, and the Public Defender didn't think my case was going to give him the headlines he'd need to set up a rich private practice.

They charged me with murder one, and it took the jury about ten minutes to come in and say "guilty." I read somewhere that English judges used to put on a black cap before they gave out death sentences. We didn't have death sentences and he didn't have a black cap, but if we did and he did, he would have. He socked me twenty years to life. Then they herded me back into the cells.

My deputy public defender could spare me a half hour. He laid it out for me in simple terms.

"Go to prison and you'll be a faggot inside of three years. You've seen the queens in your cell block?"

"Not me." I had nothing against homos, but I had no desire to join them.

"Yeah. Well, if you hold out, you still won't like it. Be a good boy. Work hard and they may let you out in ten years if you crawl just right. How are you at arse-kissing? Can you suck up to the parole board?"

"I'd be more likely to tell 'em to rape themselves." I never was much at the arse-kissing game.

I guess I learned more from my old man than I like to admit.

"Well, there you are," he said. He looked so goddamn smug. He wasn't on my side of the damned wire fence.

"What the hell do you mean, there I am? Why are you talking to me?"

"Don't get smart with me, Pittson. I came to offer you a choice."

"What choice have I got?"

"I can put in for a new trial. Maybe I can get one. You could get out on bail. Can you raise a hundred grand?"

"That's stupid."

"Yeah. And even if a bondsman would handle you, which I doubt, you haven't got the ten grand he'll want. So you stay inside for the new trial. And there's not a chance in hell that the verdict will be any different next time."

"Okay. So a new trial is a waste of time." So was this conversation, but it was better in the visiting room than in the cell.

"Yes. You can't stay out of prison—if you stay here. But

you've got another option: voluntary exile, transportation for life. I can arrange it for you."

I didn't have to think about it, not really. I already knew my answer. I'd read about the colony program and how they needed more men. There'd been a time or two, back at Francis Scott Key, when I toyed with the idea of shipping out as a volunteer.

It sure as hell beat what I had coming here.

Why not go to Mars? "Where do I sign up?"

★★★
CHAPTER TWO
★★★

Mars is a bleak place, but it was exciting to be there just the same. They trooped us into a clear plastic dome where we got our first look at the outside. It was a big dome, a couple of hundred feet across, and not at all safe, but they didn't tell us that.

The thing that struck me most was the stars. It was daylight outside, and although the sun looked a little small, it seemed about as bright as I remembered it being on Earth. The next thing I noticed was the sharp outline of the shadows: Mars boasted the darkest shadows I'd ever seen—although everything the sun hit was brightly lit. That was strange enough, but the stars got to me.

The sky was pink at the horizon, real pink, and you couldn't see stars there, but straight overhead they were glorious. There were more than I'd ever seen in Baltimore's smoggy nighttime skies. My old man had taken me out in the country once.

We had to drive damn near a thousand miles, and he

never did it again, but we looked at stars, and they were beautiful. Now I was looking at stars in daytime.

The camp was located at the edge of a rugged, dust-covered plain. I found out later that Hellas Basin stretched out fifteen hundred miles to the southeast, so it wasn't surprising that I couldn't see across it. Boulders were piled every which way out there, bright on the sunny side, dark as night in the shade. Anything might hide in those shadows. Once I thought I saw something moving. North and curving east rugged mountains stuck straight up into the dark sky. Some had pointed tops, but a lot more were jagged-rimmed craters, while some had flat tops like Arizona mesas. The tallest had wispy clouds stringing out from their peaks.

Two big tractors covered with little bright-blue squares were crawling out of the mountains toward us. Their treads threw up clouds of dust that fell in slow motion back onto the plain.

I don't remember much about the trip out. They shipped us in cold sleep, stacked in tubes like expensive cigars. About one in ten never woke up. That's one reason people don't volunteer to be colonists.

I hadn't been enthusiastic about the cold sleep myself, but it seemed like better odds than what I was facing if I stayed on Earth.

I looked at my fellow transportees, wondering what had made them choose to come here. Reasons much like my own, I decided. We were a pretty scruffy lot.

We stank. We didn't walk any too good, either, because we weren't used to the 40 percent gravity. Low gravity's tricky. It makes you feel light— hell, you *are* light—but you've still got the same mass. If you turn a corner fast, your legs go out from under you. Walking takes a peculiar gait, and running takes a lot of practice.

Actually, we didn't reek anywhere near as much as we should have. Not that we were clean. The air was thin. They kept the pressure lower than on Earth, about ten pounds rather than Earth's nearly fifteen. You had to shout to be heard very far away, and nothing smelled right. Food didn't taste too good—but for the moment, in that company, with no bath water for weeks and none likely, the thin air seemed a blessing.

Of course I didn't know a single person there. There'd been too little time since we were taken out of our cigar cans and put on our feet—those of us who woke up. We were dressed in welfare coveralls. We were all ages, but most were older than me. Out of the hundred of us, only six were women. The youngest one was thirty and she looked older.

The women tended to cluster. A herd of men circled around them; I didn't see any point in joining that game. Not yet. I could wait to see what choices I had. If any.

We were all white North Americans. The Federation goes through phases in its policies, and just then there was a lot of pressure not to ship blacks to Mars because it was cruel and unusual punishment. There's some chance of getting home from the Moon, but Mars is strictly a one-way trip. I thought about that, and shrugged to myself. Okay, I'm here, I thought. So I'll make the best of it. The landscape was more interesting than my fellow convicts, so I turned back to it.

The tractors were closer now. They were big boxy

things, with wings sticking out from the sides so they could carry more of the blue solar-power cells. The cells took in sunlight and gave out electricity. I knew about them; I was more fascinated with the slow-motion fall of the dust.

There wasn't much wind out there at the time, but I'd heard the Federation guards say that sometimes there were dust hurricanes, with winds of more than three-hundred miles an hour. That, I thought, would be something to see. A man out there would be blown away like toilet paper in front of a fan. For a moment I wanted nothing to do with this planet.

I'd better learn, though, I told myself. This is home. Feel the low gravity. Talking about low gravs in school didn't mean anything, but now I'm in it. I'd heard people can live to be two hundred on Mars because of that low gravity, only they don't because Mars kills them first. There are a lot of ways to die here. So learn or die.

"HEAR THIS ALL PILGRIMS. NEW ARRIVALS REPORT TO THE MAIN HALL. ON THE DOUBLE." The speaker said that three times, then repeated it in Spanish.

The guards started moving through the crowd to hurry us along. They were all a little older than me, all convicts who'd been recruited into Federation Service, with a few Federation troopers from the volunteer army. They didn't like Pilgrims. They were slaves, too, but slaves with weapons and power—the worst kind of slavemasters.

"On the double," one said. He laid his billy club against my butt. It splatted, and it hurt. I balled a fist and turned toward him. He was grinning. "Want to try it?" he asked.

"No." I turned away and headed for the main hall. No point in getting my skull bashed in for nothing, but it rankled that I had to take that.

"Always they push you around," someone said behind me. I turned to see a white-haired old man. "Always they tell you what to do. It is the arrogance of power. They think of nothing but to hurt people, to beat them, to show how important they are. Some day we will take that power away from them."

"Yeah, sure," I said. In about a million years. I could walk faster than him, and I did.

He tried to keep up. "I am Aristotle O'Brien," he said. "You may laugh at the name if you like,"

I didn't want to laugh at his name, I wanted to get the hell away from him before he got me in trouble. I didn't figure I owed him anything. As far as I was concerned the first rule was to keep my mouth shut and stay out of trouble until I knew what the score was. That lonely old man could have been my grandfather, but he hadn't learned that first rule, and probably he never would.

I put on the speed and left him. I wasn't too proud of that, leaving a lonely old man with no friends, no one to talk to, no one to help him feel human. I wasn't very proud, but I left him.

The main assembly hall, like all of Hellastown except for the dome, was underground. The walls of the tunnel leading down to it were concrete, but of a funny color— red, like the dust outside. The air stank from too many people with too little wash water. The ramp down was steep and hard to walk on. Just ahead of me was a giant, the biggest man of our group, one of the biggest men I'd ever seen. Kelso, his name was, and he was a good bit taller than my six feet. On Earth he would have weighed over two hundred and fifty pounds, no fat.

The assembly hall could have held ten times the hundred of us. It had seats and a stage. The stage was crowded with junk, such as a portable field organ like military chaplains use, a big plaster relief map, a blackboard, and a movie projection screen. Overhead were a bunch of faded streamers, old decorations of some kind.

There wasn't any wood in the room. I thought about that for a second and realized I hadn't seen any wood since I got to Mars. Even the guards' billy clubs were plastic.

The furniture was stone, concrete, iron, or plastic, none of it painted. A panel of colored glass was set high up above the stage, some kind of Mars landscape with human figures in the foreground. They were all out on the surface without suits and there was a bright blue sky all around, overhead as well as at the horizon. Idly, I wondered what it meant.

Most of the men crowded around the women. They kept pushing and shoving to get near them. Kelso plowed his way through the press until he was next to a big-chested woman with flaring hips and tight coveralls. She grinned at him. "You're a big one, aren't you, ducks?"

He started to answer, but someone shoved him, "Who the hell you pushing?" he yelled. The other guy answered, which was a mistake. Kelso reached out and picked him up. He held him off the ground for a moment, then tossed him. The guy sailed ten feet. Low gravity, but it was impressive anyway.

That's when the riot started. The guy had friends, and a half dozen of them set on Kelso.

"Break it up." The guard sounded bored. When nobody paid any attention he waded into the fight. He raised his billy club and brought it down on one head, then another. He didn't care who he hit, and I was damned glad I wasn't anywhere near that fight.

Kelso got whacked with the billy club and grabbed for the guard. But by then some other guards had come rushing over, and more came through a door into the hall. Pretty soon they had Kelso wrapped up and were beating on his head. Every now and then Kelso would get an arm free and send one flying. Everybody else stood back to watch. Kelso against the guards.

It was stupid. He couldn't win. But goddamn, what a man! I wished I had the nerve to do what he was doing. It might be worth the lumps to have somebody to strike out at. The fight didn't last long, though, and when it was over Kelso was bleeding from a dozen places, his hands were cuffed and he was sprawled out across a bench, not quite out cold.

"Was it worth it?"

A man had come onto the stage while we were watching the fight. He was about fifty, dressed in gray green coveralls with three black bands at the ends of the sleeves. He wore what seemed to be a skintight body stocking under the coveralls. "I asked, 'Was it worth it?'" he demanded. "Anyone here think it was?"

There was a lot of talk, mostly babble. One of the guards picked up Kelso's shoulders. Another grabbed his feet.

"Leave him there," the man on the stage ordered. The guards shrugged and dropped Kelso. His head banged on the bench. I could hear it all the way over where I was. One of the guards laughed.

"And the rest of you, shut up!" the man said. His voice had that quality in it: you knew he was used to being obeyed. It cut right through the babble. We were quiet.

"My name is Alexander Farr, and I am superintendent here. You might like it better if I said warden." Farr talked without using a microphone. We could hear him fine.

"You'll get more lectures, this talk's unofficial. You can go to sleep if you like. I don't advise it."

Farr reminded me of a science teacher I'd once had. The teacher used to say we could go to sleep, but he'd been willing to help you learn, as long as you wanted him to. He'd gone out of his way to teach things that weren't part of the usual program at the school. Because he didn't try to force it down my throat I'd got interested, and I learned more science than I'd thought I would.

The superintendent wasn't a very big man. He sat on the edge of the stage and his legs didn't reach the floor. He dangled them and kicked them back and forth. "Smoke 'em if you got 'em," he said. "If you're smart, you won't. Tobacco's too bloody expensive out here. Save two ways by quitting. You don't have to buy 'em, and you can sell what you've got to some sucker who's hooked."

That was no problem for me. The Dog Soldiers didn't use pot, and I'd never got interested in tobacco. One of the men handed a cigarette to the middle-aged woman in the row in front of him. He lit hers, then lit one for himself and blew a smoke ring right at the stage.

If Farr noticed he didn't show it. "You'll get the official garbage later," he said. "What I'm giving you now is the straight skinny. Hear and believe." He looked down at Kelso. "How you doing?"

Kelso grunted and tried to sit up.

"Going to behave now? Or do you like being cuffed?"

"I'm okay," Kelso said.

"Didn't ask that." Farr's tone showed curiosity but not much concern.

"I'll be a good boy."

Farr nodded. "Right. Corporal, take those cuffs off him."

"Yes, sir." The guard unlocked the handcuffs. He didn't bother to lower his voice as he told Kelso, "Next time I'll break your goddamn skull for you."

"Hear and believe," Farr said. "Okay, chums, let me give you the facts of life. Number one. Don't try to escape. There's no place to go. If you make it outside, you'll live about fifteen seconds. There's no air out there, and your blood will boil away in your veins. It's not a pretty way to go, and I'm told it's painful as hell.

"Number two. Don't try to escape. You may think you're smart and see a way to get a p-suit. You may even be able to operate it. And then what? You can't make air, and you can't carry enough to get anywhere worth going. Running out of air's not a lot better than going out without a suit.

"Number three. Don't try to escape. Sure there's a town here, and sure there are a lot of people in it. But you'll pay for everything, and I do mean everything."

He lifted an orange disk that hung from a chain around

his neck. I'd noticed that everyone except us newcomers wore one, but they weren't all the same color. "Air-tax receipt," Farr said. "Mine's orange because I'm due to have it recharged. If it turns red, that's it. Pay up or go outside. You'll need air medals, because God help you if anybody catches you in town without one."

"Why? What happens?" someone demanded.

"Outside," Farr said. "Not even a chance to pay up. Just out."

"And who's to put me out?" Kelso demanded.

Farr grinned. "Every man jack who's paid his taxes, that's who. Might take several for you, but they'll do it."

"This is not fair." I recognized the voice. Old Aristotle O'Brien. "Not fair," he repeated.

"Probably not," Farr said. "But it's the way things are." He grinned. His teeth had two gaps, and they gave him a ferocious look.

"Number four," Farr said. "Don't try to escape. We're going to give you a crash course in survival. Pay attention and you might stay alive. While you're taking the course, there won't be any Mickey Mouse crap. You'll get food to eat, water to drink, and air to breathe. The only work you have is the classes and some general crud like keeping the barracks clean and helping out in the kitchen. I guarantee you won't find anyplace you could escape to as pleasant as where you are now."

"What happens to us when we're done with this course?" Kelso demanded.

"You find a job. There's plenty of work. Company recruiters have more jobs than people. Most of 'em are pretty grim, but people do get rich on Mars, if they live long enough and find something they can do well. Most don't get rich, because the companies aren't in business to pay big salaries. And they know they've got your arse in a crack, because when that disk turns red you'll take the first offer you get. That's when they sign you up for ten-year contracts."

"Yeah, but—you mean we're just *loose?*" someone asked.

Farr laughed. "Yep. Whatever sentence you think you've got to serve, forget it. They don't give me a budget to run a prison and there are too many companies screaming for workers. Matter of fact, I erase the records when they come in. Nothing you ever did matters a damn now."

"How 'bout that?" There was a general babble. Some of the guys were laughing. "Son of a bitch, beat their asses again!" "Hell, thought I was facin' ten years in the bucket!" "But I really *am* a volunteer!"

"Now let me tell you about crime." Farr grinned. "Maybe some of you think you know something about the subject?"

He got a lot of laughs with that.

"You know nothing," Farr said. "We don't have much crime here. We live too close together to put up with people who steal from their comrades. Back on Earth you got busted, and maybe they sent you to court, and maybe they put you in the hands of the shrinks. You had parole officers, probation officers, social workers, welfare people, psychologists, and all that. Right?"

There were shouts. "Yeah."

"So they kept throwing you back until one day they lowered the boom on you," Farr was saying. "And they sent you here to work your balls off until a blowout kills you. That's the breaks. But before you think there's a better way than working, let me tell you that there's not one social worker on this whole planet."

He paused to let that sink in. "And we've got one jail in Hellastown. And no prisons. Or reform schools. Or detention hospitals. Or rehabilitation centers. Or *any* of that good crap. Give us trouble and we take off some hide. Give us more and we'll sell your contract to some awful place. Give us enough trouble and we put you outside. That's the way it is. You believe?"

Clear enough, I thought. I believed.

★★★
CHAPTER THREE
★★★

Survival training: pressure suits, because Mars has less than one percent of Earth's air pressure, and Farr wasn't kidding when he said the blood will boil in your veins. Air locks. Mining equipment. Care of plants. Communications. Local customs, including knife fights and duels. This was taught by a Federation Marine corporal who told us we'd probably lose our first fight and not live to have any more. I think I could have taught him a couple of tricks, but he showed me some I'd never seen before.

There wasn't a hell of a lot to do but study. I figured the more I knew the better chance I'd have when they dumped us out, so I studied. Funny thing was, I found most of it pretty interesting. Before long I was glad of the longer Martian day. The clocks were standard twenty-four hours of sixty minutes each, but they had stuck into them an extra twenty-fifth "hour" of thirty-seven minutes just after midnight.

I was in a barracks with about thirty other men. The

23

barracks room could have held five times that many. We'd been sent out on one of the smaller prison ships.

They gave us tests. All kinds. There were the funny games that shrinks like to play, and there were regular school-type tests as well. If you did well enough on the tests, they gave you extra goodies, like chewing gum and lollipops. It sounds stupid, but if you don't have anything else, something as silly as a lollipop is worth working for. I worked.

The school was a funny place. It was taught by a one-legged man named Zihily. He drank himself to sleep every night and had hangovers in the mornings. He talked about whatever he felt like, no lesson plan or anything, and we had to get a lot of the information out of books, although he'd answer questions if you had any.

Zihily had a few words about those books. "You will find that those texts have been charged to you. Return them in good condition. If you do not, you will pay for them. They are very expensive. It takes a long time to work off that debt."

The whole place was like that. They told us what to do, but they didn't make us do it, and they didn't give a damn whether we did it or not. If fights started nobody stopped them unless the furniture got broken. Then the ones that did the breaking had to pay. Since they didn't have money, they paid by contracting labor. One guy owed two years already.

I came into the barracks one day to find Kelso fighting again, if you could call it a fight. He was holding a character up off the ground and slapping his face. I recognized a guy I privately called Snotty, who was a real dipshit. Kelso slapped him again.

"You like making trouble for people, don't you?" Wham.

"I didn't do anything to you!" Snotty whined.

"No, not to me." Wham. "But you thought it would be fun to tear up Lefty's books. Why did you think that would be fun?" Wham.

"Good enough, Kelso." We turned to see Hardesty, who was the guard sergeant in charge of our barracks. Hardesty wasn't a bad sort. He'd told us that if we kept the place clean and didn't break up the furniture he didn't give a damn what we did, and he pretty well meant it. He didn't hassle us much. "You can put him down now."

"He ripped up Lefty's books—" Kelso said.

"I know. He'll be charged for them. Lefty won't. I said, put him down, Kelso." There was an edge in Hardesty's voice.

"Okay."

"Let's go, Snowden," Hardesty said. "Off to see the Superintendent." Snowden was Snotty's real name. He was glad enough to get away from Kelso. They left the barracks. Snotty never came back. They sold him to a thorium mine somewhere south of us.

"Thanks, Kelso," Lefty said. He was a little guy, younger than me by maybe a year, and thin as a rail. Snotty wasn't much, but he could take Lefty apart. So could nearly anyone in the barracks.

"Glad to oblige," Kelso said.

Lefty had the bunk next to me. Later that night we got to talking. He claimed to be a volunteer, and maybe he was; there wasn't any way to tell. I knew there were a couple of genuine volunteers in the barracks because Hardesty told me so, but he didn't say which was which, and there probably weren't as many as claimed to be.

After that Lefty tended to hang around with me when he wasn't helping Kelso with his math. Lefty was pretty sharp with numbers, and he helped me sometimes when things got over my head. He was good at explaining, and God knows I needed somebody to talk to.

The chow wasn't very good, but there was plenty of it. Generally it looked and tasted like mush. The only good part was dessert: ice cream. You could have as much mush as you wanted, but you had to turn in your mush bowl to get dessert: one ice cream bar.

It was something to look forward to. Lefty and I ate together. One evening we'd got our dessert and went back to our seats in the chow hall.

"Chocolate," Lefty said. Then, like it was an afterthought, "Garrett, what do you figure on doing when you get out of here?"

"I never thought. I hear the mines aren't much fun. And beginners have a high mortality rate." I didn't really like to think about it. In a way I liked the school. The lessons kept me busy, and I didn't have to worry about what to do. There was enough to eat, and after a couple of minor fights my barracksmates left me alone.

The only real lack was female companionship. Some of the others in the room were gay, but even the bad ones knew better than to be aggressive about it. There weren't any women in our room, and I didn't have any chance to get with the ones in the other barracks rooms, so the less thought about that the better. "I guess I'll just take what comes."

Lefty grinned. "I think we can do better than that. Want to throw in with Kelso and me?"

"In what?"

He reached into his pocket and came out with a pair of dice. He grinned broadly. "We'll do fine."

"Never saw you in the barracks games—"

"No point in it. Nobody's got anything to win. Out there, though—" He grinned again.

"Are you always lucky?" I asked.

"No luck to it. You watched those games? They take even money on sixes and eights. No way I can lose. Now if I can get into a game where there's some money—"

He didn't get to finish what he was going to say. A couple of hard cases from another barracks had come up behind me. I should have heard them, but I didn't. They didn't say a word. They just reached out and took the ice cream from out of our hands and walked off.

It sounds trivial. Who cares about a half-eaten ice cream bar? But when you've got nothing at all, the little you have is pretty important. Lefty was up and onto the nearest one with both fists.

They didn't even turn around. One of them put an elbow into Lefty's ribs. The other smashed him in the face. Lefty went down, and they looked at me. "Got anything to say about it?" the nearest one said.

"No." I made myself sound scared. "Nothing to say."

The guy grinned, and I kicked his kneecap in. If you get that right, the guy isn't going to do any walking for awhile. I didn't hit it perfect, but his leg buckled and he was off his feet. I moved away from him so he wouldn't be in the fight for a moment.

The other one came for me. He wasn't as big as I am, but he was ten years older. Sometimes that makes a lot of difference, even at twenty. He feinted with his hands and swung a kick to my head.

He was good at La savatte. I didn't have a chance to do anything but move with it so he didn't catch me very hard, but I acted stunned. The next kick he threw I was ready for and took his ankle, pushed it in the direction it was going already, and spun him right around. That let me get close enough to punch him in the crotch.

I don't like fights. When I was younger I swaggered a bit and started my share, but somewhere I lost the taste for that kind of thing. But if somebody does get me into it, I'm going to win if I can, and I don't care much about rules. When I saw this guy was out of action, I turned quick toward the one I'd kicked in the kneecap.

Sergeant Hardesty had hold of his collar. The guy could barely stand. "That'll do it," Hardesty said.

"Sure." I didn't figure they'd bother us again. One would limp for a week, and the other one looked like it would take a hydraulic jack to straighten him out before midnight.

"Your ice cream's all over the floor," Hardesty said. "Clean it up before you leave."

They said we weren't prisoners, but it was like a prison. We could go up to the dome in the evenings, but there wasn't a lot else to do. We didn't have any possessions, so there was nothing to gamble for. The few available women were booked solid. You could play cards, you could swap stories, and you could study.

I tried to get excited about being on Mars, but it didn't *seem* like Mars. I was getting used to the low gravity, and I'd stopped being amused over how far and how high I could jump. Except for the gravity we could have been in a cave on Earth.

Then we had p-suit training.

Zihily gave us no warning. He just announced that today would be it. "There are two types of pressure suits. The best fits only its owner. Obviously we have none of those for practice. The other variety is a general purpose Extra Vehicular Activity suit, commonly called a space suit, which will fit anyone of approximately the proper size. We have many of those. You will go out in parties often."

He called out ten names. Mine was not one of them. "You men will go out with Corporal Feinman for EVA suit training and practice."

They trooped off. They were laughing. They'd get to go outside, and it would be a break in the routine.

The rest of us listened to a lecture on mines and mining, with emphasis on laser cutting tools, until the training party came back. There were only eight of them.

"What happened?" Zihily asked. He didn't sound very interested.

"Two of 'em didn't listen. We'll have to send out a party to get the suits back." Feinman sounded annoyed, and probably was. The suits were his responsibility.

I decided I would listen very carefully when my turn came.

★ ★ ★

"Super wants Pittson," the guard announced.

Zihily jerked a thumb toward the door. "Okay, Pittson, off you go."

I followed the guard out. Superintendent Farr's office was a large cubbyhole cut into rock. There weren't any windows, but where a window would be there was a big color holo of Mars as seen from Phobos. The desk was steel and glass, and the chairs were molded plastic. Farr sat behind his desk console typing inputs into a computer and looking up at the results as they read out on a screen above the desk.

The guard waved me inside. Farr didn't pay any attention until he'd finished whatever he was working on. Then he said, "Have a seat, Pittson. How are you?"

"Fine."

"You're pretty tough, aren't you?"

What was I supposed to say? "I don't know—"

"You put two men in sick bay and you don't know."

"They had it coming," I said.

"Didn't say they didn't. You're not in the rattle." He typed something else into the console. I couldn't see the results because the screen wasn't set where I could look at it. He studied it for a moment and said, "You've done pretty well in the school, too. You were in some kind of street gang back on Earth—"

"Yeah. I thought you erased those records."

"I do. But I look at them first. Were you a leader in that gang?"

"Kind of. Why?"

He ignored my question. "I thought so. Tell me, Pittson, what do you think of your classmates here?"

"Uh?" I thought about that. "I guess most of them are losers."

He nodded agreement. "Yes. There are only three main types who come here. There are failures, men who never amounted to anything back home and won't amount to anything here. Most of them don't last long. There are broken men who used to be important and can't stand the idea of starting over. And finally there are a few who can become Marsmen.

"Which are you?"

I shrugged. "I don't know."

"You'd better figure it out. You're about done here, Pittson. You've about finished the school—now what will you do?"

"I keep saying I don't know, but this time it's for damn sure I don't."

"What do you want to do?" he asked. He seemed very serious.

"I'd like to get out on my own, but there doesn't seem to be much chance of that. From what I've seen, your school tools us up to be company slaves!" I was getting a little mad at his routine. What was his angle, anyway?

He didn't react. Instead, he grinned. "Not a bad guess. Most pilgrims are. It's all the Federation will pay for, and it's all most of them could be. But there's opportunity on Mars, Pittson, if you're willing to work. And one day we'll have the Project going."

There was a far look in Superintendent Farr's eyes. He seemed to be seeing right through the rock walls of his office out onto the red, dusty surface of Mars; and he was looking at more than desert and sandstorms.

"The Project?" The capital letters had been obvious in his voice.

He shook his head as if clearing away cobwebs. "Yeah. There's a way to make Mars inhabitable. So you can live outside without a p-suit."

"You can do that?"

"*We* can do that. Marsmen can. But not now. The Federation Council won't put up the money. The company types want quick bucks. To hell with it, it's a dream. Maybe you will catch it one day. For now, I want you to tell me about yourself."

He was easy to talk to. I rambled on, and pretty soon I was telling the story of my life. I was surprised at how much I said, and how personal it got. I suppose I shouldn't have been surprised, though; he was the first sympathetic listener I'd met since I was arrested, a hundred days and eighty million miles away in Baltimore's Undertown.

Finally he stopped me. "Are you willing to work?"

"Depends on the work."

"Reasonable. Suppose I tell you there's a job worth doing. Not company work, either. The big outfits aren't so bad, but what have you got with them? A salary at best. But what Mars needs is free men. Men who can tell the companies to roll it tightly and stuff it. Marsmen. Are you afraid of getting killed?"

"Well, sure, who isn't?"

"But you were in that gang war—"

"Yeah. It seemed like a good idea at the time."

He nodded. "Pittson, we're going to dump you out of here in a couple of days. When you're turned loose, go bum around downtown. Anybody asks you, you're waiting for a buddy. You don't have to say who, and don't. Just see what city life on Mars is like. And don't sign up with anybody until you've had an offer from some friends of mine."

"What kind of offer?" I was getting suspicious. What the *hell* was his angle?

"It'll be a good one. A chance to get out on your own, to be your own man. You'll work damned hard, but you'll have something to show for it. If you're good enough."

"How will I know it's them?" I asked.

"You'll know." Farr nodded to himself. "Now let me give you something else to think about. What do you have that's valuable?"

That didn't take much thought. "Nothing at all."

"Yes, you do. Your word. Is it good?"

I didn't understand and my face must have shown it. He shook his head and said, more to himself than to me, "It's an idea that's gone out of fashion on Earth. Out here a man's word is either good or it isn't. No compromises. Marsmen trust each other. We have to know that when a man gives his word he's not thinking about some way to weasel out.

"Pittson, nobody out here knows or cares what you did before you got here. You can start over. You can be anything you want to be. Anything you're good enough to be and will work hard enough for. Now go think about that."

He waved dismissal and I left, wondering what it all meant. It was pretty heavy stuff for a guy my age and in my situation. I began to have some hope for the first time since—since I realized I wasn't going anywhere but Francis Scott Key Community College.

★ ★ ★

CHAPTER FOUR

★ ★ ★

There wasn't any graduation ceremony. One morning after chow the speakers said, "REPORT TO CENTRAL PROCESSING" instead of announcing school call. It had been about a week since my interview with Farr. I had seen him only once since then, just passed him in the hall. He'd put his hand on my arm and winked at me, then hurried off.

It wasn't a lot to go on, but I'd built a lot of hope around Farr's promises. They were all I had, except for Lefty's offer, which I didn't think much of.

At Central Processing they charged our air tags to bright green, forty days' worth. They gave us a hundred Mars dollars, worth about half that in Federation credits. We changed our coveralls for new ones, with a choice of blue or orange.

Then they shoved us out the door. Literally—a big air-lock door. Fortunately the corridor beyond was pressurized. A hundred meters farther was another airtight door. Beyond that was Hellastown.

Hellastown was simply a lot more corridors and caves, with airtight doors at intervals so a blowout in one part wouldn't finish everybody. "Downtown" was a big five-story cavern, empty in the center. It was about half the size of a football field. It wasn't really all that big, but after the little caves and corridors of the school it looked huge.

All around the edges were openings to stores, offices, and cross-tunnels to other sections of the city. The cavern floor had been smoothed off and the holes filled in with that reddish concrete you saw everywhere on Mars. Above that were two more levels, the highest about seventy feet up. Two balconies ran around the cavern walls at the upper two levels. They had no rails, just a low wall about knee high.

On Earth some bureaucrat would have built a high fence to keep people from falling or jumping. Here nobody gave a damn.

One whole side of the square was lined with brothels, and there were lines outside each one. Everyone in the lines wore new coveralls. They seemed to be coming out about as fast as they went in.

"Son of a bitch!" Lefty yelled. "They'll spend all their money! Goddamn!"

"Uh—" Kelso pointed to the brothels. "It's been a long time—"

"We need a stake," Lefty said. "You don't want to blow it on that assembly line. Let's make some money and we'll buy a *real* lay."

"Yeah, well—" Kelso was undecided. Lefty went over to one of the lines. He started making a pitch for a dice game.

I drifted away from them. I thought about the brothels, because it had been a long time for me, too, but Lefty was right. There'd be no satisfaction in that, and my money had to last until I knew what to do next.

There were taverns, and I drifted into one. It was filled, partly with new-coveralled pilgrims, partly by men in dirty clothes and skintight underwear like Farr's. The beer was two bucks for a schooner. I looked longingly at it.

A dapper cat in creased coveralls was buying for a whole table of pilgrims. I watched as they poured it down. He beckoned for me to come join in, but I shook my head and stood, curious, because he had to have an angle and I didn't know what it was.

"You buying something or leaving?" the bartender yelled at me. He had one arm and one eye.

"Leaving, I guess," I said.

"Let him stay," somebody yelled. "Hey, kid, come have a drink." The guy was at a table with no pilgrims at all. He and seven others were pouring away the beer, and yelling stories at each other. "Come on, no hitch," he said.

I drifted over. He lifted a full schooner, drank half, and handed the rest to me. "Name's Andy Cernik," he said. "Sit down, smart pilgrim."

When I hesitated he laughed. "Go on, it's Jake. No crimps here." He named the other people at the table, but I couldn't remember any of them.

Two of the men were black, and another was Oriental. As I say, Federation policy goes in waves. They looked like they'd been on Mars for a long time.

"I'm Garrett Pittson," I said. "Crimps?"

Andy waved toward the table full of pilgrims. "Like Mister Sisson there. Your buddies'll wake up in the morning with a big head and a long hitch, wonderin' what happened to their bounty money. Hang around a couple of days, you'll get more choices."

"You guys miners?" I asked.

"Sure. Mars General. Not a bad outfit." They all laughed at some secret joke.

"What's it like in the mines?" I asked.

There was more laughing. "Goddamn hard, that's what," Andy said. "We lose maybe half the pilgrims their first year. But what the hell, it's a livin'. Could do worse."

"Sure," one of the black men said. "You could do worse by stickin' your head in a toilet maybe. Hard to think of another way."

They laughed and ordered another round. "Look, I can't pay," I told Andy.

"Yeah. Don't worry about it. Keep your stake; wish I had when they bounced me."

They didn't pay much attention to me after that. The brew was good, heavier and a lot more flavorful than Earthside beer. I found out the bartender owned the place and made the stuff himself. He'd been a Mars General miner in his day, which is why a lot of the MG crew came to his place.

The miners didn't seem to be a lot different from the Dog Soldiers: good men, tough and proud, but men with no place to go. They talked a lot about women they'd had, and which brothels were best, and how pilgrim day was the lousiest time to come to town, and how they wished the goddamn company would tell 'em when the Feddies were bouncing pilgrims so working stiffs could pick another day when the whores weren't slot-machining.

After a while somebody suggested they ought to look up an old buddy. I hoped they'd take me with them. I liked their company. But when they stood, Andy said, "See you around, Garr. If you sign up with MG, God help you, but look me up."

I went back out into the square. It wasn't like Earth at all, not topside and not Undertown. There were uniformed men I supposed were cops, but they didn't hassle anybody. The place was crowded, but not like downtown Baltimore, and except for us newcomers nobody was wandering aimlessly the way they do on Earth.

Another difference was that everyone carried a knife in plain sight. Some had big ones, broad-bladed things designed for combat and not much else. Others had smaller and more useful-looking sheath knives; but everybody was bladed. According to Zihily there were few guns on Mars, and the Federation people had them.

I saw a knife fight five minutes after I left the tavern.

Two men in blue coveralls, like ours but faded and patched, came out of a bar. They were shouting at each other. When they got outside they drew knives and squared off. A couple of cops drifted over, but they only stood and watched.

It started as a formal affair, with a lot of dodging and weaving, feints and counterfeits. They were good. Then the smaller guy made a tricky pass, thrusting up underhanded, and the big guy looked surprised as blood poured out of a gash in his lower arm.

"I'll be damned!" he said. He put his hand over the cut and drew away. "I will be dipped in dung."

"Probably."

"First blood enough?" a cop asked.

"Christ yes," the winner said. "Caz? Enough?"

"Oh hell yes." The loser looked at the cops. "I'll be at work tomorrow. No time lost."

The cop looked critically at the wound. "If you say so." He looked to his partner and got a nod. "Okay."

"Right," Caz said. He looked at his bloody arm again. "I will be dipped in crap."

"Probably."

They went back into the bar.

There were a lot of company offices around the main square, places like Peabody, GE, Westinghouse, and the other big outfits. The smaller companies had tables set up in the open space. They were all pitching how wonderful it would be to work for their outfits, but I noticed the wages were low and about the same no matter where you went.

Most of my classmates drank up their starter money, signed on with a company, drank up their bounties, and shipped off to work. They were gone within two days.

A few of us were still around. Lefty had a floating crap game that he said was making food and air money for himself and Kelso, and he was talking about opening a gambling hall when they had a stake. I didn't see much future in that, even if I'd been needed, which I wasn't.

Nobody cared about the dice games. Nobody cared about anything that didn't cost labor time or get in the way. I learned fast: you don't block the path of an armed man, and you don't break up the furniture in bars. Neither lesson came the hard way for me; I learned from another pilgrim's experience.

I found a tunnel end to sleep in. They'd been digging out to expand the city, but this project was halted for lack of a labor force. Nobody bothered me. I figured I had nothing worth stealing, anyway. That turned out to be stupid: I had a charged air tag, and that would be worth my life if there was anybody around desperate enough to cut my throat for it. Nobody was, just then.

Halfway between my tunnel end and the downtown square was a store. It was quite literally a hole in the wall, owned by a man who'd been crippled in the mines. His buddies had chipped out a couple of rooms for him, and he sold food, beer, water, and anything else he could buy cheap and sell later. He gave me a runner's job, going to the bakery for stale bread to feed his chickens, carrying chicken droppings to the recycling works, running across town to deliver beer to some old friend who gave him business out of charity. The wages were simple: two hours work for a meal with beer, and he wouldn't pay my air taxes. It was hardly a permanent job.

Everything was expensive. It cost more if it came in a can. In fact, cans were worth as much as what was in them, and some scraggly kids made a living cruising the tunnels looking for miners' beer parties where they might get thrown a can or two.

After a couple of days old Chad trusted me enough to let me sleep in the store. I worked pretty hard for him, straightening up the store and chipping out some new shelves in the rock. He needed that done, but he didn't have the tools, and he was too stove in to do it with hammer and chisel and too broke to buy plastic shelving.

I finished a little niche, not one hell of a lot accomplished for all that work. He drew a beer from his barrel and handed it to me. "Garr, I can use the help, but what are you waitin' for? I can't pay your air taxes, and that tag's going to start turning color."

"Yeah, I know. Man said to wait for a friend of his."

"You give your word?"

"Sort of."

"He give his?"

"Yeah," I said.

"Good man?"

I thought about that. Was Farr a good man? I wanted him to be. "I think so."

Chad nodded gravely. "Then you wait, that's all. It'll be okay. If something's happened, though, maybe my buddies can fix you up with a short hitch at Peabody. It's not a bad outfit, as outfits go."

I went back to chipping rock. It wasn't as hard as granite, but it wasn't soapstone either. It was red like everything else. "Mars anything like you expected?" Chad asked.

"Well, they kept saying on Earth that Mars was a frontier. I guess I expected it to be like the old western movies . . ."

"Is, lots of ways."

"Maybe." I laid down the hammer and took another slug of beer. "But you can't get out on your own. Can't live off the land."

"Farmers do."

"Sure, with a hundred grand worth of equipment—"

"Don't take that much. Work for a good outfit, save your wages, the banks will put up a lot of it if you've saved a stake. Ten years work, maybe, if you save your money. Then you're out of here. That's how most of the Rimrats got started. Wish I'd done it. Can't, now."

I thought about it. When you're twenty, ten years is a long time. Half your life. But there sure didn't seem much future hanging around here. "If this other deal doesn't come through, maybe I'll do that," I said. "Only I wonder if I can save the money—"

"That's the blowout for most, all right," Chad said. "You just stick tight a couple of days, though."

"Sure, you need the help—"

"Aah, there's that too, but maybe things'll work out better'n you expect."

"Sure." But I didn't have much hope of it. A man's word is either good or it isn't, Farr had said. It looked like his wasn't. Why had I expected anything different from a prison warden?

I'd been there ten days and my air tag was turning from green to yellow, It was getting time to move on. I figured another couple of days would do it.

A big man came into the store. He wasn't as big as Kelso, and he was a lot older, but there was nothing small about him. "Ho, Chad," he called. Then he saw me and looked me over, slowly, in a way I didn't like.

Chad came out of the other room. "Sarge Wechsung," he said. "Figured you'd show up one of these days." Chad looked at me about the way Sarge had. "Come for the kid?"

"Yeah. Pittson, I had a hell of a job runnin' you down. Old Man said to look you up next time I was in town. Had some trouble gettin' here."

"The Old Man? Oh, you mean Superintendent Farr—"

"Sure." They both talked at once, cutting me off, as if they didn't want me to say the name.

"I hear you're looking for a job," Wechsung said. "I got one. Come on, let's go, I'm runnin' out of time." His voice was raspy, as if he'd been used to shouting a lot. It didn't sound particularly friendly.

"Just where are we going?" I asked.

"I got a station out on the Rim. Windhome. Nobody watchin' the place, got to be gettin' back. Need a farmhand. You'll like it. Work your arse off, do you some good. Right, Chad?"

"Damn right!" the old man said. He rubbed his crippled leg. "Wish you'd been around when I come here. Go on. Garrett. He's a good man."

Take the word of a man I didn't know about a man I'd just met. Well, what the hell, I thought. What have I got to lose?

A lot.

"Let's go, let's go, got to get you outfitted," Wechsung said. "Chad, we'll be down at Smitty's place if you want to send down some lunch—"

"Send how? You're stealin' my runner. I'll bring it myself."

"Right." Wechsung walked out. He didn't look back to see if I was following.

I stood there a moment, then caught up with him.

★★★
CHAPTER FIVE
★★★

The suit was a tight bodystocking of an elastic weave, with metal threads running through it that fitted like it had been painted on. The outfitter chewed gum and made stupid jokes about blowouts while he literally built the suit around me. He cut the cloth, stretched it, and heatwelded the plastic threads while it was in place. Then I took off that part and he finished the welding job. When it was all done it fit snugly, not quite tight enough to cut off circulation, and looked something like a thin version of a skin diver's wet suit.

"We first came here, they didn't have thread that would stand up," the outfitter said. "This new stuff's great, though. You can gain maybe five kilos and it'll still fit. Don't put on more weight than that, though, or you'll be buying a new suit."

The pressure suit ended with a gasket at the neck. A helmet dogged onto that. With pressure in the helmet you could go outside. The skintight bodystocking reinforces your own skin so it can take the internal pressure, and your sweat glands are the temperature regulator. Marsmen wear skin-tights everywhere because if there's a blowout and you get your helmet on quick, you may stay alive.

That was quite a helmet, with lights, a radio, and hoses meant to connect to air tanks. The tanks went in a backpack. There was more to the outfit: reflective coveralls, heavy foam-insulated jacket and trousers, thick gloves, a tool kit that snapped onto a belt, boots, a knife, and another radio in a holster.

Smitty the outfitter had set up a table outside for people waiting while he worked on their gear. Chad brought lunch and beer.

"Doesn't this cost a lot, Mr. Wechsung?" I asked.

"Call me Sarge. Sure it costs."

I didn't understand and I guess my face said so.

"Think you're not worth it? Hell of a time to tell me. Once Smitty starts cuttin', I've bought it."

I didn't say anything, and he laughed. It was a cheerful laugh. He didn't sound worried about anything, but I knew it would take more than a year for me to save up what he was paying. "Let us worry about the costs," he said. He looked around. No one was listening to us. "The Skipper thinks you might make a Marsman, and I take the Commander's word for it."

"You mean Mr.—"

"Yeah."

Commander. That squared with the black bands on Farr's coverall sleeves. "Are you still in the Federation Service?" I asked.

"Hell no. Retired years ago. So did the Old Man. He went to prisoner-chasin' and I went to farming. What do they call you, Pittson?"

"Garrett's my name—"

"Fine. Garrett, you were told to think about something. Did you?"

"Yes."

"And?"

"I'll make my word good."

Sarge grinned. "Okay. And you can trust people, a little anyway, or you wouldn't have waited for me. Garrett, I have a big place out there. Lots of work. You'll sweat your balls off, and I won't pay you much, but you stick with me a Mars year—that's two Earth years—and you'll know the score and have a stake you can use to get out on your own. That's what you want, right?"

"I think so—"

"What anybody in his right mind wants."

Chad shuffled up to collect the beer mugs. Across the square a group of miners came out of a brothel. They were laughing and shouting as they got onto the jitney that would take them back to their barracks.

"What happened to the last man you had helping you?" I asked.

"Got his own place. A couple of dozen have come through Windhome, Garrett. Some got themselves killed. Some couldn't stick it and ran back here to work for a company outfit. But five have their own stations."

"And why are you doing this?"

Sarge shrugged. "You ask too many questions. Finish your beer. Your stuff's about ready and we've got to move before sundown. The tractor won't run so good in the dark."

The tractor wouldn't run at all in the dark. It had solar cells all over it—on the roof, on the decks in front and behind the passenger compartment, and on wings that could fold up when it was inside but unfolded when it was running. The solar cells furnished all the power.

It was very comfortable. The passenger compartment was bigger than I had expected and had a bunk as well as seats. This was the only pressurized part of the tractor; the rest would seal up to keep out dust, but if you had to carry cargo under pressure you put it in airtight bags.

Sarge drove up the ramp from inside the city. It went up steeply, a dark tunnel with a few lights. There were three sets of air locks at the top. Then we were outside. The sun was high in the west; it seemed very bright after my time in Hellastown.

When we got onto the plains, the motors whined as the solar cell wings extended. "Okay, watch what I do," Sarge said. "Now we're outside we switch from batteries to direct solar power. This thing develops about fifty horsepower, enough to move pretty fast and still keep the batteries charged in full sun, but you don't want to run at night. It won't go more than a couple of hours."

I looked around at the Marscape. It was bleak, and in two minutes we were out of sight of Hellastown. We drove through fields of boulders. They came in all types, from house-sized to just rocks. Red dust blew all around. "What happens if you're caught out at night?" I asked.

"You pray a lot." Sarge nodded to himself. "Pray a lot

and hope your air lasts. Then curl up and go to sleep. Batteries should give enough heat to last the night. It gets cold out there."

About a hundred below zero, I remembered from the school. But in summer daytime it was warm enough to go out without a jacket as long as you had a p-suit and air.

"The manuals for the tractor are in that compartment," Sarge said. "When we get home, take 'em inside and read up."

"Sure."

"And don't forget to put 'em back before one of us has to use Aunt Ellen again."

"Aunt Ellen?"

"The tractor. Next to your p-suit, a tractor's the most important thing in your life. Treat Aunt Ellen right and she'll take care of you."

A strong wind was blowing outside. Hellas is a low basin, formed a billion years ago when a rock the size of Greenland smashed into Mars. The impact melted the rock, and lava flowed up from inside Mars to cover the hole. Huge chunks of rock were thrown up into a rimwall, and more rocks were thrown out to make another ring of secondary craters around that.

Then for the next billion years Hellas and the Rim were pounded by smaller meteoroids. They left the basin flat but partly covered with junk. Since there weren't any hills, the visibility was terrible; we were lost in a jungle of rocks. The wind whipped the dust around so thick we could hardly see out.

"You're crazy, you know," I said.

"How's that?"

"You don't know a damn thing about me. Superintendent Farr talked to me for maybe three hours—"

"Best not mention that when anybody else is around."

"Yeah, but—"

"We have the test results, Garrett. Psych and skills both. And maybe we've kept an eye on you better than you know."

"You still don't know I'm not planning to murder you for the tractor!"

Sarge laughed. "What would you do with it? Everybody knows it's mine. And just how long would you live out here?"

"Yeah." I watched the dust for a moment. "They taught us just enough, didn't they? Just enough to know there's a lot they didn't tell us."

Sarge grinned. It was a nice grin. "See how smart you're gettin' already? Know any good songs?"

He knew a lot more of them than I did. We sang along to pass the time.

"You got to learn more songs," he complained. "Here, let's teach you 'The Highland Tinker.' We'll work up to 'Eskimo Nell'—Hey! Look, over there. See it?"

I looked where he pointed. "Nothing I see."

"Gone now. Sand cat, maybe."

I looked at him to see if he was putting me on.

He didn't look like it. "An animal? There aren't any animals on Mars!"

"That's what the books say. Me, I'm not so sure. Every now and then you see something moving. Just a flash. Some say they've seen 'em close up, about the size of a squirrel, red brown, blends with the sand."

"I thought animals weren't even possible. No air."

"Yeah." Sarge grinned again. "I'm not sayin' those who've seen 'em close up hadn't had a few. Still in all, it's a big planet and there's a lot about it we don't know."

"That's for sure." And there are plants, I thought. Plants that have the biologists climbing the walls, because they're kin to Earth lichens and can even crossbreed with some Earth strains, but they aren't the same at all. Mars plants cover themselves with a glass bubble like snail shell but more transparent.

"Wonder what'll happen to 'em?" Sarge said.

"To who?"

"To the sand cats. When we get the Project goin', can the goddamn cats live after there's air? But they do say Mars has had air before, so maybe they can. Hope so."

"Tell me about this project. Commander Farr mentioned it, but I haven't heard much from anybody else."

Sarge guided the tractor around a boulder. "The Project's a plan, a way to pump the atmosphere up to maybe a tenth Earth normal, maybe more, enough so we can go outside without p-suits. Warm the planet up. Green things growing, not just in domes, all over."

"Won't that take a long time?"

"Maybe. Not as long as you'd think, the way they tell me. Only we can't get started. Earth bastards won't let us."

We went over a ramp. This road had been used before, if you could call it a road. The only way I knew was here and there boulders had been blasted apart, or there were ramps over some of them. We topped a ramp and I got a good view of the plain and the blowing dust.

"One of these days we'll do it ourselves," Sarge said. "Only it takes things we don't have. Like atom bombs."

I shuddered. Like everyone else on Earth I had been brought up to think of atom bombs as something to kill worlds with. I said that.

"Just tools, Garrett. Just tools. We need the bombs to trigger volcanoes. There's a lot more air and water inside this planet if we can get them out. Then it'll come alive."

We topped another ramp and Sarge stopped the tractor. Without the whine of the electric motors it seemed very quiet, but then I heard the wind, howling ceaselessly, and the crackle as it blew sand against the tractor.

There was nothing out there but dust and the distant mountains. It didn't look as if it had ever been alive, or ever would be. Nothing moved but dust forming into little twisters that Sarge called dust devils.

We were utterly alone. If we got into trouble nobody was around to help us, and we'd have to get out by ourselves or not at all.

Well, I'd wanted to be on my own. I'd got that.

★★★
CHAPTER SIX
★★★

A hundred days went by. There were a lot of times when I wished I hadn't come, and twice I was ready to leave, but talked myself out of it.

We sat in the little bubble-dome at the end of a corridor into Windhome. Sarge called it his veranda. Since the dome was a hundred meters above the floor of Hellas Basin, we had a view that stretched for miles, but there wasn't a lot to see except boulders and dust devils.

Inside the dome we had a jungle of plants, and hard chairs. In Mars' low gravity you don't really need cushions anyway. I hoisted my beer and waved it at Sarge. "You weren't kidding when you said you'd work my arse off!"

"Right."

Down below, the agricultural co-op tractor snaked across the basin floor. It pulled six trailers of produce from stations along the Rim. A lot of it was ours.

That had been the first fight I'd had with Sarge: he was desperate to get production higher and higher, make bigger and bigger profits, and I couldn't understand why we couldn't take it easy and relax. There'd be plenty to eat without all that work.

"Sure," he'd said. "But how do I pay the taxes?"

"Taxes?"

"Federation bastards tax hell out of us."

There was another reason he wanted profits, but I didn't find that one out until later.

Now I sat drinking beer. It was slightly sour and I thought I knew a way to improve it. I'd been studying the tapes from the central library, and had the notion that Sarge was using the wrong malting process, one designed for big breweries with better equipment than we had. I'd found a taped copy of an old book, published in 1895, that told how they did it back then and I wanted to try it.

"Drink up," Sarge said. "We got a lot more to do before we turn in."

"Right." I was in no hurry. The work was never finished, but we were caught up for a while. We'd spent the day harvesting corn and wheat from our hydroponics tanks out in the big glass agro-domes. It had been a lot of work. Now it was getting dark out, and we wouldn't be able to work in the domes any more—so we'd do inside maintenance.

There wasn't enough power to do heavy work at night because Windhome ran on solar cells just like the tractor. Closer to Hellastown there were stations drawing power from the nuclear plant, but not out here on the Rim.

I watched the last of the sunlight. There aren't any sunsets on Mars. There's either light or there isn't, for the same reason that shadows are so dark in the daytime: no atmosphere to diffuse the light and make a bright sky like Earth's. On Mars you can be in pitch-black shadow a few feet from bright sunlight.

"You been studying that problem?" Sarge asked.

"Yeah. We can do it. These solar cells are mostly grown crystal, and the circuits to control the growth aren't that tough. Give me the right materials and we'll grow our own."

"Save a lot of money," Sarge said. "Glad you're up on that electronics bit. I never had the time to study it. Doesn't make much sense to me anyway."

I doubted that. I never saw a problem Sarge Wechsung couldn't solve if he had to. Anyway, the library has most of it laid out cookbook style. You just have to be careful to look up all the words, because what an engineer means by a word isn't always the same as what other people mean.

"You said you'll need germanium," Sarge said.

"Right. We don't have any."

"None I've found. Sam Hendrix does though, and he's only about forty kilometers from here."

That made him a near neighbor. Our nearest had a station twelve kilometers away, but I'd never met him except on the phones. I hadn't met Hendrix, either.

"We'll have to run over and buy some," Sarge said. He sat and watched dust devils for a moment. "Sorry you came, kid?"

"No." I was surprised at how easy it was to answer that. It hadn't been the easiest time of my life.

A week before I'd had a blowout. Sarge had given me Number Three agro-dome to plant whatever I wanted.

I'd put in tomatoes and squash and nursed them along until they were almost ready to harvest. Then, while I was mixing nutrients for the hydroponic food system, the joint between the glass dome and the bedrock below had gone.

Pressure went to nothing in a couple of seconds. I panicked, but remembered to yell to get the air out of my lungs so I wouldn't explode. Then I got control of myself, looked around for my helmet, found it, and dogged it onto the neck seal of my suit. I closed the face plate and reached down to the air valves, bringing air pressure into my suit. Ten seconds later I was back under pressure. You'd be surprised just how long ten seconds can be.

Then I got the shakes. Sarge had drilled me in blowout practice every day since we came. Anytime he might shout "Blowout!" and if I took more than ten seconds to find my helmet and get it on, he'd make life pure hell. I was damned glad of the practice now.

Tomatoes and squash had exploded all over the dome. Sarge was inside less than a minute after it happened. He came as quick as he could, but if I hadn't taken care of myself, he'd have been too late. We stood there and looked at the wreckage of my crop. The leaves had already wilted—everything in the dome was dead. Everything except me. We got the dome patched that afternoon and I was planting again the next day.

I'd had a blowout, I'd had screaming fights with Sarge, I'd had the blue funks from looking at that blue, bright dot near the sun, I'd worked my arse off, and I had no money at all. "No. I'm not sorry I came!"

"Glad to hear it. You do good work. We make enough profit, I can outfit you earlier than I thought."

I will be dipped in shit, I thought. So that's why he grinds so hard at it. "Thanks. Uh—Sarge?"

"Yeah?"

"One thing. Are we ever going to see any women?"

"Oh yeah." He gave me that big booming laugh of his. "I thought I worked you hard enough to keep the urges under control—"

"I'll never work *that* hard."

"Yeah, well, couple of weeks, no more'n a month."

"Oh. When we go back to town."

"Naw, not them whores. We're farmers, not labor clients. Hang on a while, kid. You'll see. You're just getting started out here."

"That's for sure." I looked at my hands. They were calloused and had the red dust of Mars ground into them. I was drinking sour beer, and my ear hurt from the blowout. There was a small network of veins coming to the surface on my right cheek, also a result of the blowout, and I knew I had enough work to fill three or four hours before I could go to bed. Tomorrow morning we'd be up at dawn to start cutting a new tunnel.

I felt terrific. I knew where I was going, and I had a friend to rely on. I wasn't a pilgrim any more.

We had the tractor loaded, and I went to the passenger side of the cab.

"Nope. You drive," Sarge said.

I shrugged and went around to the other side and we got strapped in. I wondered what to do next. Two dozen assorted dials, switches, and controls stared up at me. I looked to Sarge for advice, but he'd curled up in his seat and closed his eyes.

I'd studied the training manuals, and Sarge had checked me out. Now's as good a time for a solo as any, I told myself. Here goes. I hit the switch to activate the control panel and began the checklist.

Doors sealed. Begin pressurization, and watch the gauge. Also keep an eye on the balloon and see that it flattens out; gauges have been wrong before. Pressure to seven pounds a square inch, half Earth normal.

Sarge reached up and undogged his face plate. He still hadn't opened his eyes.

I went on through the list. Battery power on. Activate the garage doors. Back her out, slow, there's no steering wheel, there's two clutches and throttles, and if we ram something we can blow out. Or worse. We crawled out into the bright Martian sunshine. Extend the solar cell wings.

Switch to direct power. Get the course off the map.

"Damn!" I'd forgotten to calibrate the gyrocompass. Mars' magnetic field isn't reliable enough for navigation. Sarge was still pretending to be asleep.

I took a bearing on a distant peak, got a reading off the map, and lined the tractor up. I looked it over again, and everything seemed right, so I set the compass to the bearing and hit the calibration switches. It locked in, and I slewed Aunt Ellen around onto the course laid out on the map.

"Pretty good," Sarge muttered. "Wake me up if you need to and don't take her more than twenty klicks an hour."

Then I think he really did go to sleep.

Aunt Ellen wasn't as hard to drive as I'd thought she would be, and after a while I had the knack of it. I drove east along the base of the Rim, watching where I was going rather than looking at the scenery. Two hours later we were there.

"Ice Hill," Sarge said. "Sam Hendrix's place. It'd be better if you didn't say anything about germanium."

I grinned. I'd heard Sarge dicker with his neighbors over the phone. Listening to him you got the impression he had plenty of what he needed to buy and none of what he had to sell.

Like Windhome, Hendrix's station had no real form above ground, just seemingly random protrusions onto the face of Hellas Rim. But Ice Hill was a lot larger than Windhome, with over a dozen glass agro-domes, at least two bubble verandas on balconies high up on the side of the Rim, and two separate garage ramps. A dozen people milled around outside the station. To me, by now, that was a big crowd.

Suddenly one member of the crowd was different. Strange. Graceful. I stared—

"Yep," Sarge said. "Her name's Erica. Sam's number two daughter. Oldest one's married off already. Uh, Garrett—"

"Yeah?"

"Go easy. The Hendrix clan's tough, and they've got some strong prejudices."

"You mean don't seduce the daughters—"

"I mean make sure it's seduction you got in mind, and not something more forceful. Otherwise don't be too surprised if you find a knife up against your ribs."

"Hmm. Maybe I better stick with the whores."

"They're safer," Sarge said. "For the short haul, they're safer."

We entered the cleared area near the main ramp into Hendrix's pressurized garage. Windhome's garage area wasn't sealed; when we needed to work on Aunt Ellen we had to haul her into the main shop.

"They won't mind if I *talk* to the ladies, will they?" I asked.

"Christ, Garrett, don't make a big thing out of it."

"Don't make a big thing, but be careful?" I said.

"Yeah, something like that. Sorry I mentioned it."

The air-lock door opened and I guided the tractor up the ramp.

"One thing," Sarge said. "I can understand you gettin' a little excited over the prospect of female company, but I'd fold up the wings 'fore I took the tractor through that door, was I you."

Sam Hendrix was waiting for us in the garage; before Sarge could tell him my name he started talking politics. Hendrix was a wiry fellow, a bit over fifty, with steel-gray crew-cut hair, a bristly mustache, and a big scar running down his left cheek. He had some kind of accent, but too faint for me to place it.

"There is a new administrator in Hellastown. They say there will be a new charter as well. Have you heard?" he demanded.

"Reckon I've heard something about it," Sarge told him. "Sam, this is my new buddy. Garrett Pittson. Good man."

"I'm glad to meet you. Welcome to our home. Sarge, they are talking about raising taxes again. Again! Not for the big companies. Only for us. How will we live? Ah, I am forgetting my manners. Perry, show these people to their rooms. Dinner is in one hour. Glad to have met you, Garrett Pittson." He talked that way, a mile a minute, without much pause between thoughts.

Perry looked about eight Earth years old, a nephew or grandson or something. He was already wearing a pressure suit. I thought it must be pretty expensive to keep buying p-suits for kids as they grew out of them. Perry led us through a maze of twisting corridors and up some stairs. We exited into a big cavern that was the main hall, big enough to hold a hundred people or more, then walked across to another stairway. Ice Hill was a *lot* bigger than Windhome.

There were twenty people at dinner. I sat across a narrow table from Erica Hendrix. Her big brother Michael was next to me. Mike was married and had two kids already. He lived in a separate part of the Hendrix complex.

I must have talked with Mike and the others during dinner, but I don't remember any of it. I kept looking across at Erica. She had long red hair that she'd had up in braids when I first saw her; she put it up for outside work. For dinner she'd let it down in waves that reached her shoulders. It was a deep copper red, not like the color of Mars dust. She had bright blue eyes and a pointed nose. She was a big girl, not a Ukrainian tractor driver type, but big and well proportioned.

I thought she was the most beautiful woman I'd ever

seen in my life. I couldn't take my eyes off her even to eat. I think I embarrassed her, but I couldn't help it. I kept telling myself that any girl would look good just now, but I knew better.

Dinner was a huge affair. Hendrix kept pigs and cattle as well as chickens, so there was real meat, and milk, and cheese, as well as fresh vegetables and bread and *pudding*. Also, they kept the pressure higher than we did, enough so you could get the *smells* of the food as well as the taste. It was marvelous. We didn't eat like that at Windhome.

The prettiest girl I'd ever seen and the best meal I'd ever eaten. I kept telling myself it was the contrast from what I was used to. Maybe. But it was a great dinner.

Erica was my age, almost to the day. Since she'd been born on Mars it took some figuring to be sure of that. Her brother fished out his computer to check on it. Neither of them knew much about Earth's calendar—they thought all the months had the same number of days—and I had trouble with Mars' calendar with those extra intercalary days. The Martian year isn't quite two Earth years long, and has 24 months, plus extra days. It was fun figuring out what day it was on Earth when she was born.

Everybody worked at the Hendrix place. The kids served dinner and cleaned up afterward. Clearly the women regarded the kitchen work as their special preserve, but not all of them worked there. Erica, for instance, took care of an agro-dome and did power plant work on the side. Her mother said she had better marry a good cook.

There were drinks after dinner, then finally the various

subgroups of Hendrixes melted away, leaving Sam, Erica, Sarge, and myself. Sam invited us into what he called his office, which was a comfortable-looking chamber about twenty feet square filled with all kinds of odds and ends he'd made or collected. He got down a bottle of brandy and poured a shot for each of us. Erica tossed hers off like water but didn't want a second.

"Guess we ought to do some talking," Sarge said. "No point in them havin' to listen. You reckon Erica could show Garrett around? I'd like him to see what a real station looks like."

"Certainly, why not?" Hendrix said. As we left, Sam was saying, "Now this new administrator will be a problem. And they have brought in two companies of Federation Marines, did you know that? I tell you Sarge, it is getting thick."

There didn't seem to be anybody around. Since the sun was down the station was on batteries for the night, and most of the lights were off. The corridors were lit by little pools of light separated by deep-shadowed stretches.

"We're a bewilderin' lot, aren't we?" Erica demanded. She was laughing at me. I didn't mind. It was a nice laugh.

"Well, there are a lot of you," I said.

She grinned. "Father, two uncles, Uncle Ralph's wife's brother and his family, Michael and his wife and her brother—you were funny, tryin' to remember all the names. Have you been with Sarge Wechsung for long?"

"Five months. This is the first time we've left Windhome since I got there."

"They say Sarge works his recruits pretty hard."

"He does that."

"It doesn't last forever, though," she said. "Have you thought about where you'll want your own station?"

"No—we haven't talked about that much."

"But you do want a place of your own?"

"Sure. That's what makes all the work go easy."

She laughed at that. I loved that laugh. Poets talk about laughs like that one. "Wish something would make it easy for me! All of Sarge's people, the ones that stuck with it, have pretty good stations. You'll get yours." She led me through more corridors. The station was big, and I wondered about the air supply. It would take a lot to keep that large a volume under pressure—and they kept it higher than we did.

"We've hit lots of ice," Erica said. "More than a cubic kilometer of permafrost."

That explained it. With that much ice they didn't have to bother about recycling; with solar power, water can be broken into hydrogen and oxygen. Save the hydrogen for fuel—if you've got extra oxygen to burn it in— or chemical processing, or even throw away the hydrogen; it won't matter. You've got the essential part of air. Water and sunlight and oxygen, all Hendrix would ever need. That's the nice thing about planets, and the reason the space colonies never succeeded: there's nothing out there in space, nothing to mine and nothing to prospect.

"We have enough to last a thousand years," she said. "Although the way Dad keeps expandin' this place—"

As we laughed she led me up a ramp and then we were on a flight of stairs leading to another tunnel. I was thoroughly lost. "There's a nice valley on the other side of the ridge from here," she said. "Make a good station. Ice there, I think. The Rim's getting crowded, all the way from Hellastown to Big Rock Candy."

Crowded. The closest stations were seven or eight kilometers apart. Crowded. Of course she was right: the best claims, with ice and good mining, were all taken.

There was a small, airtight door at the end of the tunnel. She automatically checked the gauge for pressure on the other side—I was learning that habit, but she'd grown up with it—then opened it and we went through.

We stood a hundred meters above the Hellas Basin floor. There were flickering lights in some of the station's agro-domes down below. Phobos was almost overhead. Phobos is only about a twentieth as bright as Luna, but that's enough to show the basin floor and the rocks piled along the Rim. The little moon zips right along. You can't quite see it move, but if you look away a minute and look back you can see it isn't in the same place.

"Pretty out there," Erica said. "What's it like to stand outside under the moon, with no pressure suit?"

I tried to tell her about Earth, and about warm nights and soft breezes. I told her about going to the ocean at night. She had never seen an ocean and never would. Of course she'd read about them, but she didn't know, and I found myself getting homesick and choked up when I tried to tell her about all the things Earth has that we'd never see on Mars. Oceans and forests and whales and elephants and—

"Someday we'll have forests," she said. "And we'll go outside without these suits." Her eyes shone.

"So you're a Project nut too."

"Aren't you?"

"Don't know enough about it," I said. That was a mistake; I got an engineering dissertation. I liked her voice, and if necessary I'd have listened to her recite bad poetry in a language I didn't know, but a lecture on the Project wasn't the topic I'd had in mind for a tete-a-tete under the hurtling moons of Barsoom (actually, Deimos wasn't up yet, but never mind) with the most beautiful girl in the universe. And yet. Maybe it was earlier, maybe it was just then, while she told me about how it would be some day when there was air on Mars and it stayed warm all night in summer, and there would be green fields and forests—maybe then, maybe earlier, but I knew as well as I knew anything that this was the girl I wanted to marry.

Crap, I told myself. Garrett, you haven't seen any women for months. Anybody you met just now would be the One and Only, which is a bunch of romantic claptrap you don't believe in in the first place.

Maybe so, I answered myself. But I've known a lot of girls, and I never felt like *this* before, and damned good it feels, too. What you need, Garr baby, is a trip to Hellastown. Go away. The idea is nauseating. "We'll do it," she said. "We'll make Mars green and beautiful, the way Earth is, and it will be ours."

"Earth isn't—" I couldn't finish it. Earth *is* green and beautiful, except where people have messed it up.

We must have talked for another hour, but I don't remember what about. Finally I got up the nerve to reach for her hand. She didn't draw back. Well, here goes, I thought. I drew her to me and kissed her.

That went on for quite a while. Then she pushed me

away. "I'm no expert on this, but I think we'd better stop," she said.

"Why?"

"Because I've got the feeling we stop now or we don't stop at all—"

"And why stop at all?"

"I just think we'd better." She moved away from me and perched on a bench on the other side of the small dome. "Garrett, I am not a town girl—"

"Lord, I never—"

"Let me finish. I live on the Rim. I like it here. I know that girls in town, not whores, just girls, have plenty of affairs, and they must enjoy them. I'm damned sure I would. But then what? I intend to live on the Rim. I don't think I could stand it in town. But stations are family affairs, and I do not believe I want to get involved with anyone I'm not going to live with for a long time."

"And I'm a convict and—"

"Oh, shut up. You're just past being a pilgrim. In about a year you'll have a stake and when that time comes, if we can still stand the sight of each other, we'll open this conversation again. Until then, no."

"Yeah. Okay. I'm sorry."

"What's there to be sorry about? Didn't you enjoy it? I certainly did. I know I don't have much experience at this sort of thing, but you didn't seem too bored at the time. Now I think we ought to go downstairs, because I have work to do in the morning."

★★★
CHAPTER SEVEN
★★★

"Thinking about Erica? Pretty girl," Sarge said.

I concentrated on guiding the tractor around a small crater. The wind had come up, and whipped the dust in our faces so that visibility was bad. When I could look up, I threw Sarge a grin. "Well, actually I was thinking about the trees."

"Sure you were."

"Well, I *was*. Just then, anyway."

We both laughed. "You know, Garr, I've been meaning to grow some fruit trees myself one of these days. Fruit trees make sense. But you know what Ruth Hendrix wants? A wood table for the dining room."

Erica had told me that, but I wasn't going to spoil Sarge's story.

"Yep, a wood table," Sarge said. "Be the only goddamn piece of wood furniture on Mars. Tax collectors ever saw a thing like that, they'd break old Sam. Dah! Why'd I get on that subject?"

"Why would the tax collectors care what Sam's table is made of?" I asked.

"Property tax." Sarge snorted in contempt. "Otherwise known as a fine for improving your property. You've got a lot to learn about Mars politics, and I guess you ought to start now. The Federation runs Mars to suit the big companies."

"The only thing I've seen the Federation in charge of was the prison ship and the school—"

"Yeah. Well, the school's Commander Farr's idea. He runs it in a way that helps us out. But the rest of it's Earth types, bureaucrats, don't want anybody to get ahead. And they're bringing in marines to make sure."

"You used to be a Federation Marine."

"Sure." Sarge sniffed his contempt. "Old style. We were peace keepers, back when keeping the peace on Earth was a damn dangerous job. None of my type left. The new marines are bloody thieves in uniform, out for wages and what they can steal. That's why the Skipper retired. He wanted no part of being a tax collector!"

"What do they do with the money they collect?"

Sarge laughed. "They don't put it to anything that helps us, you can be damned sure of that! Be different if they'd finance the Project, but not them." His voice changed to an unctuous whine. "Mister Speaker, we cannot destroy the ecology of an entire planet! To humans, perhaps, a breathable atmosphere on Mars is desirable, but to Mars it is no more than pollution . . . I swear to God, kid, I heard one of the goddamn Federation Councilors say that!"

I shook my head. "Sam grows the trees and makes the

table. Why should the Federation take a cut for that? It's not very fair."

"Yeah. Question is, what do we do about it?"

"What can we do?" I asked.

He didn't answer. Instead, he sat up and rubbed his eyes, then said, very slowly, "Garrett, it's about time you started thinking about a place of your own. It's months yet, but not too early to pick out a location and study it."

"Erica said that too. She also said there's a good valley on the other side of that ridge behind Sam's place. Not on the Rim, but good mining and water ice—"

"Yeah. I know the place. Kind of remote. Have to cut a road in. Be even better if we can find a way without cuttin' a road . . ." He muttered to himself for a moment, then said, "Yeah. I like it and the Skipper will like it."

"Okay," I said. "Have I been here long enough to know, or do we go on playing games?"

"How's that?"

"Commander Farr sends you to look me up. You take me in, but we don't mention Farr's name in town. You talk about setting me up on my own, but you like the idea of my going off into the hills without a road. So will Farr. How does it all fit together?"

"Are you sure you want to know?"

I concentrated on driving while I thought about that. "Sarge, I'll do anything you want me to—"

"Didn't ask that. Do you want to know what this is about?"

"Should I?"

"It could be dangerous."

"Is Sam Hendrix in it? Is Erica?"

"Now how can I answer that, Garrett?"

"You've already answered. I think. Sarge, what's Sam Hendrix like? Would he let his daughter marry a convict? Would she care what he said anyway? Would she marry a convict?"

"What do you think?" he asked.

"I think she would. I don't know about him. You told me marriage was pretty serious business on the Rim. And the families get involved deep—"

"They do. Remember what the Skipper told you, Garrett? Nothing counts before you got here. You can be whatever you've got it in you to be. Why the hell should Sam Hendrix care what you did on Earth? You care what he did to get sent here? Or do you think he was a volunteer? Or that Ruth was? You want to marry a convict's daughter, and you ask me if he gives a damn about your background."

"I never thought," I said. I hadn't thought at all. If I had, I'd have guessed that Sam Hendrix had been here forever. And his wife? Ruth Hendrix a transportee? "Whoopeee!"

I startled him. "You gone crazy?" he demanded.

"No. Just happy. Sarge, if you tell me what's going on, will I get her into trouble?"

"Depends on what you do with the information. You don't have to join up, you know. It's a crime to know what we're up to and not report it, but if I don't tell and you don't, who's to know?"

"Okay. You've got a revolution planned. And Commander Farr is in on it."

"Sure," Sarge said. "Hey, the wind's comin' up good. You want me to drive?"

"If you want to—"

"Naw, you're doin' all right. Just watch the downwind sides of the rocks. Sometimes there's holes back there, and they fill up with dust. You can lose the tractor in one if you're not careful. There's no way to protect the Skipper, Garr. He's got to interview recruits and see they don't sign up with some company before we can get to 'em. We've got other inside men, but he's the most exposed."

"Think they suspect him?"

"Nothing to suspect him of. He hasn't done anything yet. Just selected out some transportees for us to put through Marsman training. Like you. Nothin' illegal about that, although you never know what the Feddie bastards will try."

The dust was really blowing thick now, covering the solar cells. The tractor began to lose power. We slowed to a crawl. I glanced at the charge indicator. We were running on direct, not draining the batteries, but we weren't moving very fast.

"Keep with her," Sarge said. "It'll blow off again."

"There's something else bothering me," I said.

"Yeah?"

"You're talking about me going out on my own. That takes a lot. Tractor, airmakers, solar cells, pumps—good Lord, just a lot."

"Yep."

"Damned expensive—"

"Sure is. Don't worry about it, Garrett. We'll swing it.

There's more than me on this." He sucked his teeth loudly and smirked at me. "Course, you marry well and you can save me some money. Old Sam's a rich man."

"Sarge!"

"Kids get married and start up on their own, both sets of parents help. Custom out here. Don't turn down a girl because she's rich."

"I wouldn't turn her down if she was a new pilgrim. If she'll have me. But you're not my parent. How do I pay you back?"

"Pay it forward. You'll help two more pilgrims get a start. Nothing big all at once, just over the years you kick in outfits for two. That's the way it works."

"And if I take your stuff and forget it?"

He shrugged. "Your word good?"

"I see." I thought about that all the way back to Windhome.

There were two hundred people packed into Zeke Terman's station, overflowing the main hall and packing the corridors, so many people that I couldn't see how they all got in. And more were coming. It was a Rim gathering.

I had been to one before. That had been a wake. This would be a wedding, but the atmosphere wasn't much different. The Rimrats hold a party to send off an old friend or marry new ones.

Everybody brought what he could: food, beer, wine, whiskey, musical instruments, song collections, or just themselves if things had been rough. We made our own entertainment, and talked treason against the Federation. I didn't know because I didn't have to know, but I suppose three-quarters of those at the gathering were members of the loose organization headed by Commander Alexander Farr. It had no name; it was just a group banded together for Martian independence.

I stood with Erica, not too far from the spot where the ceremony would take place. Henrietta Terman was an old friend of Erica's, and John Appleby had been recruited by one of Sarge's proteges. Appleby stood nervously at the front of the main hall. Then the Padre came in.

At least that's what they called him, and if he had another name, it wasn't used on the Rim. He was vague about which denomination had ordained him back on Earth, and no one knew why he'd been sent to Mars.

The Padre had a station of his own, filled with orphan children and rumored to hold several runaways from company labor contracts. Whenever he was needed the Padre would come, and once a month he made the rounds of the Rim stations whether he was needed or not.

He conducted weddings, spoke words at funerals, held christenings, and talked treason. He was the Padre, and he had a thousand friends.

Every one of them wanted a word with him. It seemed to take him an hour to get through the press in the Terman main hall, but finally, with John Appleby in tow, he reached his place. Then Zeke Terman brought out his daughter. He held her for a moment, then took her hand and put it into John's and clasped them together. I felt Erica reach for mine.

The Padre read from his leather-bound book for a while. The words were old; I think it was a hundred-year-old *Book of Common Prayer*, and God knows where the

Padre got it. Then he closed it and said, "Do you, Henrietta, take this man as your true and only husband, a man to stand by and work with, to have children by and grow old with, and will you remember that he's only a man and forgive him seventy times seven transgressions?"

"I will."

"Who speaks for this man?" the Padre asked.

Harry Bates stood in front of the group. Five years before he had been what I was now, one of Sarge's recruits. Now he had his own station. "I'll stand up with him," Bates said.

"And me too." Sarge had put on his old marine uniform. There was a red stripe down the trousers, and a comet with sunburst on his chest. "I'll stand with him and fight the man who says he's not a Marsman."

"Anybody dispute that?" the Padre asked.

There were a couple of laughs, and somebody shouted, "Nobody crazy here!" That got cheers.

"Okay. Will you, John, take this woman as your true and only wife, and work with her and defend her, build her a home she can be proud to keep for you, and stay away from the whores in town?"

"I will."

The Padre opened his book again. "Okay. There's some more words we need here, but I figure that's mostly what they mean and it don't hurt to put them in plain language." He continued to read, and John and Henrietta gave their responses.

The crowd was fidgety. There was a rumor that John Appleby brewed the best beer on the Rim. Nobody believed it—I certainly didn't, and I still think mine is better—but we all wanted to sample it. And Terman had set out a splendiferous feed.

Eventually the Padre ran out of words. He closed the book. "In front of Almighty God and these good people, I say you're man and wife. And if any Federation clerk says different, shove it down his throat!"

"YOWEE!" A hundred and more families yelled their approval. Then we headed for the beer.

Later, somehow, they cleared some space for dancing. I don't know where they put the people, because nobody left.

What we call dancing on the Rim isn't exactly what they do on Earth. There are some remnants of Earth square dances in it, but everything is done more violently, with lots of leaping and shouting. In 40 percent gravity that gets spectacular.

There were a lot of girls at the party. I had made up my mind: I was going to meet some of them. I was going to spend time with someone other than Erica so that I'd know it wasn't just the lack of female company in my life that made me feel the way I did whenever she was around.

I meant to, but somehow the evening was over and we hadn't been apart . . .

The main hall in Hellastown was packed: members of nearly every family along Hellas Rim, company representatives, shopkeepers, city dwellers, Federation officials; all were there—and all were talking at once.

There was a guy in natty clothes up on the stage. He kept pounding his gavel for order. His coveralls were a shiny polyester, and they had creases along the trouser legs and sleeves. He didn't wear a p-suit under it. Most of us in the room did, and we smelled, even in thin air. But not him. He was the new administrator for Hellas Region, and he'd never in his life worked hard enough to smell bad.

"Citizens, please!" he shouted. "I cannot listen to your grievances if you all talk at once!"

"Citizens, hell!" I looked over to be sure, and it was Sam Hendrix. "Slaves, that's what you're making us!"

There were plenty of cheers, but they came from the farmers and station owners. The city people were silent. The company reps glared.

"GODDAMN IT, one at a time!" Sarge yelled. He turned toward me and winked. "Let Sam talk for us."

The babble died away. Sam Hendrix got up from his bench and went to the front of the room. He stood on the stairway, but they didn't let him have the microphone. No matter. We could hear him.

"Mister Ellsworth says he has a new charter for us." Sam said. "And the first thing it means is we pay taxes on everything we do! It means ruin—"

"Come now." Administrator Ellsworth didn't have to shout. He simply turned the volume up high so that his amplified voice drowned Sam out. The dapper little creep gave us a big smile. "The charter grants you universal suffrage, and you will have representatives in the General Assembly of Mars. Of course you must pay for these benefits, but how can you object to democracy?"

Sam made a visible effort to control himself. I could see the twitching of the scar on his left cheek. I'd learned that meant he was mad as hell. He did a good job of controlling his voice, though. "Universal suffrage means the labor clients outvote us ten to one. As it is not a secret ballot, they must vote as the companies tell them, or starve. So where does that leave us? We do not require your cities and your Assembly and your rules and your laws. We can take care of ourselves, and we ask only that we be allowed to."

There were more cheers from the Rimrats, but Sam held up his hands for quiet. "Now you are telling us that before we can sell a barrel of beer it must be inspected, and we must pay taxes."

More cheers.

Ellsworth gave Sam a condescending look, the way you might look at a seven-year-old kid who wants to stay up all night to watch the dawn. "Of course we must protect the citizens from harmful products," Ellsworth said. "The new laws will assure wholesome food and drink—"

"We manage that for ourselves," Sam yelled. He was fast losing control. "Don't we?"

"Damn right!" "Yeah!" "Right on!" "My stuff's good, and there ain't a man on the Rim don't know it!" All the farmers were shouting.

Sam gestured for quiet again. "Now this Ellsworth gentleman wishes to tax everything we do. Solar cells we make ourselves—"

"We must assure quality." The amplifiers let Ellsworth break in whenever he wanted to. He sounded very smug.

"Even the caves we live in! Building codes he wants to give us! Inspectors in our houses—"

"Your children must be protected. Those stations are

not safe," Ellsworth said. His voice took on an edge. "You said you wished to present grievances. These are not grievances, they are no more than bad-mannered complaints. All these measures have the approval of the Federation Council on Earth. Now if you have nothing constructive to say, go home. I have more important things to do than listen to your grumbling. This meeting is adjourned!"

Ellsworth stalked off the stage.

After that things got worse. They held the elections, but as Sam Hendrix predicted, not a single Rimrat was elected from Hellas Region. They gerrymandered the districts so that we were outvoted by labor clients. "Our" assemblyman was a Mars General corporation lawyer.

We got word from town that some of the miners tried to stand up to Ellsworth and elect one of their own to a seat. Their votes weren't counted, according to rumor; the official word was they were outvoted by "absentee ballots." Sam Hendrix figured that there would have had to be more absentees than registered voters in that district. Ellsworth made sure that nobody else would try that trick: the leaders of the upstart group were sold. Their contracts were transferred to a mining outfit that ran its operation like a slave camp. A couple of them escaped and fled to the Rim, willing to work for shelter and nothing more.

There were now big sales taxes on everything we bought or sold in Hellastown. Federation inspectors forced their way into stations and looked for "structural defects." They turned one family out of a place that had stood safely for fifty years. A big company ended up with title.

Things weren't any better in the other colony areas. Around Marsport the independent farmers were strong enough to elect two assemblymen, but they were ignored. Katrinkadorp suffered merciless harassment. Mars Taipei was occupied by Federation troops.

Sam Hendrix tried to organize resistance among the Hellas Rimrats. "If we don't sell to the townies, they'll feel it," he said. "Boycott them. Sell no more than it takes to pay for what you have bought. It is better to drive a hundred kilometers to sell to our own people on the Rim than to go ten and sell to Hellastown."

Sarge agreed. We took our produce up into the hills, to mine camps like Inferno where they smelted iron with a big parabolic solar mirror and worked like slaves—but for themselves. We sold to other stations and made do or did without. I set up a solar cell production system; our cells weren't as efficient as those sold in Hellastown, but they worked, and the Rimrats bought them. The boycott was effective.

Even so, Sarge was way down, and I couldn't cheer him up. "I knew it would come to this," he said. We were having our evening drink on the veranda. "Knew it would happen, but goddamn, not so soon. We aren't ready for them yet. Bastards."

He drank down his beer and poured another. "Good stuff. Can sell all we make. That new malting you do is just right. Who needs inspectors? You sell bad beer, nobody buys it. Sell stuff that makes people sick, they'll force a gallon down your throat and laugh like hell. Who needs Hellastown slicks for inspectors?"

"So why are they doing it?" I asked.

Sarge shrugged. "Some of 'em may really think they're protecting us," he said. "Some. But think about it. The big outfits aren't comfortable, having us out here, taking claims they'll want some day. They haven't got the labor to work our claims now, but in twenty years—"

We watched the blowing dust for a while. "About time we had a look at your new claim," Sarge said.

"Yeah." I stared moodily at the electric fire. It wasn't a real fire, of course. It was just an electric heater, but the coils glowed a cheery red.

When I had come to Windhome it had been summer in the southern hemisphere. Now, three-quarters of a Mars year later, it was spring again, and the dust was blowing.

Winter had been hard and cold. We'd cut back to two heated domes, but even for them there wasn't enough solar power to grow many crops. On Mars, winter is a time to stay inside, with a few excursions for Rim gatherings; mostly you dig new tunnels and expand the station. But now, at last, the sun was coming south again.

Halfway across Hellas Basin was the edge of the south polar ice cap, a thin layer of solid carbon dioxide, dry ice, that was now melting off. It's cold out there in winter, but not as cold as you might think—that is, the temperature is low enough to freeze the carbon dioxide out of the air, but the air is so thin that it doesn't conduct heat away very fast. If you've got properly insulated clothing, you can get around, even at night if you're careful to insulate yourself from the ground. You've also got to watch radiation—wear dark outer covering in the daytime to pick up heat, and light colored at night to avoid throwing heat to space.

Now the dust was blowing. Winter was nearly over. It was time. I liked the idea of getting out on my own, and I was pretty sure how Erica would answer when I asked her to marry me and help set up the new station. But Sarge was my friend, the best friend I'd ever had. It was sad to think of leaving.

He must have guessed what I was thinking. "Skipper's got a new crop comin' in, and we've got to move fast now. Things are comin' apart. Skipper wants us to cycle three recruits at each of our stations. About the time I get three broke in, maybe you'll need help with your new place and I can palm one off on you."

"I see. Sink or swim time."

"You'll be outfitted pretty good," Sarge said. "Between what I can give you, and what Sam will put up."

"If she says yes."

"She will. I notice you've been to four Rim gathering now, and she puts in all her time with you. Other guys don't even ask her any more. You'd better marry her, you've cut her off from the other suitors—"

"I wish I could be as sure of that as you are," I said. But I was, really. "If you're so damned anxious to have people married, why aren't you?"

His grin faded. "Was, Garr. She's dead. Maybe I'd like to try it again, but now's the wrong time. Hey, I bought some more germanium from Sam. Closed the deal on the radio this afternoon. Tomorrow you can go pick it up for me."

"Sure. Thanks."

He nodded, but he was staring out at the dust storm. He hadn't liked the news he was hearing from town.

I was interested in politics, sure, but just then I was a lot more interested in getting over to Ice Hill.

"He has also told me that he wishes to speak to me about something rather important. As your sponsor, Garrett."

★★★
CHAPTER EIGHT
★★★

By now I had the status of a regular guest—not that hospitality wouldn't have been splendid for any Rim visitor. By custom, any traveler was welcome at any station—but in my case I got a complete discourse on politics from Sam whenever I showed up.

When he invited me into his study after lunch, I figured it was politics time again, but he surprised me. He used the intercom to send for his wife, and he asked Erica to come in as well. While we were waiting for Ruth, he poured a drink for all of us.

Ruth Hendrix was smiling as she came in.

Sam rather formally invited us to sit down. I was beginning to wonder what was happening, but Erica was grinning, so I wasn't worried.

"Well," Sam said. "Sarge tells me that you are about to go choose a location for your own station."

I nodded. I'd never seen Sam so slow at getting to the point.

"He has also told me that he wishes to speak to me about something rather important. As your sponsor, Garrett."

"Oho."

"I beg your pardon?"

"Yes, sir. He's pushing things a little, but—"

"Not pushing them at all. Now, I have had business dealings with Sarge Wechsung before. This is likely to cost me at least one arm and probably both legs. Before I go to that trouble, has anyone here an objection?"

Ye gods, I thought. I looked at Erica. She was shaking with repressed laughter, but trying to hide it from her father. Sam was trying not to notice.

"I think it's a splendid idea," Ruth Hendrix said. "And I know Erica does. Don't you, Ricky?"

Well, we got through it somehow. Nobody objected. We weren't engaged, not exactly, and wouldn't be until the negotiations between Sarge and Sam were finished and it was all announced; but as far as Erica and I were concerned, we were going to be married. Sam and Ruth even found an excuse to leave us alone for a few minutes.

The whole thing makes more sense than it probably seems to. On the Rim you can't just go off and set up housekeeping. Once in a while a Rim girl marries a town man, usually without her folks' approval, and if he's got a job she can move into town and that's that; but to open a new station requires a lot of equipment, and a lot more work than two people can do in a short time.

The parents have to help. If they've got to put up all that money, they're going to have a say in who gets it. And a new couple won't be independent, not really, for several years anyway, and if they can't make a go of it—not necessarily through their own fault, things can go wrong here despite all you can do—they've got to have a place to go. So it makes sense that the parents have to approve, and there's no point in the prospective couple getting too involved unless that approval is likely, and there's no point in all the negotiations and purchases and arrangements unless the couple approve of each other; thus the complicated formalities.

We didn't care, of course. I wasn't thinking about how it made sense. I was too damned happy to think about anything.

When Sam came back into his study he purposely made a lot of noise. "Sorry to break things up," he said. "But Garrett will have to be going. I do not like to see you travel without plenty of daylight. The dust is very thick today."

He was right. I looked around for my hat. We'd already loaded the germanium into Aunt Ellen.

"Erica, I believe you wanted to go into town," Sam said. "And there are errands you can do for me, as well. I no longer care to go there unless I must."

"Sure," she said.

"Excellent. I suggest you go to Windhome with Garrett, and take the agricultural co-op tractor into Hellastown in the morning. It comes by your place tomorrow, does it not?"

I had to think. Ellsworth had decreed that the co-op could only sell in Hellastown. We didn't have much business for the co-op any more. "Yes, sir."

"You will have to bring her back when she returns, but I doubt you will mind that."

Erica went to get her travel kit. It looked like this would be a splendid day, even if the dust was blowing up a bit thick.

We had a short delay after we were out of sight of Sam's place, but I didn't want to waste too much daylight. The dust was indeed thick, and although we had plenty of time, Sam was right: the more daylight you have ahead of you, the better off you are. Tractors do break down, and although Aunt Ellen never had, there was always a first time.

We talked about our new place, and laughed at the way Sam had acted, and wondered what we'd feel like when we had a daughter who wanted to get married. We babbled about the Project, and about Earth, and about how many kids we wanted, and what kind of floor plan we wanted when we started blasting out our home, and an hour and a half went by very quickly. Then I heard the voice on the radio. We had come into line-of-sight with Windhome, although we couldn't see it because of the dust.

"Garrett, this is Sarge. Do not answer. Garrett, Garrett, Garrett, this is Sarge. Do not answer."

"What the hell?" I said.

"Garrett, this is Sarge. Do not answer. Stop and listen carefully. Do not answer."

"There's something terribly wrong," Erica said.

"Garrett, if you can hear me, do exactly what I say. Punch the fourth channel button from the left, fourth from the left. Turn on the set and say you can hear. Say nothing else and turn it off quick. Keep the transmission as short as possible. Okay, if you hear me, go. Over!"

I hit the button and lifted the mike. "Sarge, I hear you. Over."

"Thank God, I've been calling for an hour. Garrett, Ellsworth sent the cops after me. They're trying to break the boycott. I'm holed up, but they've got me located. They may be listening to this. They'll have me in a minute. Don't come back here, they'll put you in the bucket. Look up our friends, and warn the Rim. They knocked out the photophone and our main antenna, so all I've got left is short-range. Warn 'em along the Rim. Do not answer me, they'll locate you if you do."

"We've got to do something," I said.

Erica nodded. "Yes. The first thing is to alert the Rim. Sarge is right, we've got to get the word out."

Sarge's voice came through again. "Sorry it worked out this way, kid. I wanted to set you up better, but it looks like I won't be doing that. You've got other friends, though. They'll help. You're a good man, Garrett. Here they come."

There were loud sounds like explosions, then a whistling wind. "Blowout!" I said. I looked at Erica. She nodded. It had to be a blowout, and Sarge was in it.

"They've smashed their way in," she said.

"We've got to do something. I've got to see what's happening—"

"All right," she said. "But the first thing is to hide this tractor. If we drive up there, they'll have us too."

I thought about that. "Right. We can walk from here. It's not too far." I took Aunt Ellen off the road and out into the boulder fields. We found a hollow full of dust. I drove into it, and the wind whipped more dust around us. Pretty soon the tractor would be hidden. The tracks leading in from the road were already covered over.

I switched on the pumps. By the time we had put our helmets on the air from the cabin was stored in tanks.

"We won't be able to use the suit radios," Erica warned. "They'll hear us."

"Yeah." We got out, and I looked around carefully. It wouldn't do to hide the tractor so well we couldn't find it again. There was a big split rock about ten meters away, and I looked up at the stars to get a bearing from it to the tractor. We had about three hours of daylight left, maybe a little more, but not much. When night came we'd have to be inside, either in a tractor or in a shelter.

When we were sure we could find Aunt Ellen again, we started walking for Windhome. Erica was young and healthy, but she had trouble keeping up with me. That's one advantage to being born on Earth. I was used to weighing over twice as much as I did on Mars, and even with all the air tanks and other gear it wasn't hard going. I wished we had weapons, but we didn't, except for our knives and some tools in our belt kits. I led her up the side of the Chamberpot, a tattered rimwall that stands next to Windhome. Sarge called it the Devil's Pisspot, but the official mapmakers wouldn't use that. The Chamberpot's rim has cracks that lead to Windhome, and I was sure nobody knew about them.

It was tricky climbing the side of the hill, and if you run too hard, you use a lot of air. We scrambled up the steep sides of the crater to the top, then down into the bowl. There was a ledge just inside the rim. It dropped off sheer for a hundred meters on our right, and it wasn't very wide.

Until I watched her two-step along a section not much wider than my foot, I worried about Erica. Then I worried about myself.

I couldn't talk to her because the cops might be listening. I wondered if they'd heard Sarge's message to me. If they had they'd be looking for us, but they wouldn't know in what direction I'd been coming. There's a lot of desolate area around Windhome. I decided we were safe for the moment. At the end of the ledge there was a crack through the rimwall. It was just wide enough to get through. Once inside it we were in deep shadow, but even through the dust we could see stars out above us like night. Then we were looking down on Windhome.

The station was in ruins. All the domes were cracked open, and the air-lock doors had been blown off their hinges.

There were more explosions as we stood watching. We couldn't hear them, of course, but we could see dust blow out of openings, and one of the tunnels collapsed. I stood in a boiling rage, trying to decide what to do. Mostly I wanted to kill people. A lot of them.

A group filed out of the main entrance. I had brought the binoculars from the tractor, and I could see them clearly: Federation Marines, carrying rifles. Seven of them had slugthrowers, and another had a big powerpack and laser rifle. After a short interval two more came out. One of them was Sarge. I could tell from his walk. They had him in handcuffs, but he was alive!

I grabbed Erica and pointed. She nodded. Then she held up her belt radio and pointed to the frequency dial. It took me a moment to catch on—I thought she wanted to talk, which was stupid of me. She knew better. When I tuned the receiver to the frequency she showed me, I heard voices.

"Where is he, Wechsung?"

"Go to hell."

"Look, we know your tractor is missing. Where did he go?"

"Get dorked."

One of the men hit Sarge with his rifle butt. I heard Sarge grunt, then he said, "Bielenson, you were a slimy bastard when I was in the service. You haven't changed."

"Maybe not. Take a good look, Wechsung. You men, get a lot of photos of this place. We'll show these farmers what happens to rebels. They'll straighten up."

I put my helmet against Ericas. When they touched we could talk without radios. "We've got to do something!"

"Hold on, my muscular friend," she said. "What will happen if you go charging down there?"

"Yeah." They had rifles and we had knives. There were at least ten of them, probably more in their tractors, and two of us. Three if we counted Sarge, but he was handcuffed.

"Gary, I know how you feel, but the best thing we can do is get back and tell Dad. And you've got your orders, mister. Sarge told you to alert the Rim."

She was right, but I didn't like it. I stood there trembling with helpless rage. They started boarding the three tractors. Two of them pushed Sarge into the small one and got in after him. "We could follow them," I said.

"On foot? Don't be an idiot."

"Varadd. Rogers," the radio said. "Get inside and stay out of sight. When that kid shows up, grab him."

"Sir. How long will we be here, major?"

"I'm leaving you air for two days. We'll be back for you before sundown tomorrow. Just now we've got other work to do."

"Sir." The marine sounded unhappy about being left there.

"Load up and move out."

There was a babble of voices, and the rest of them got into the tractors. They started up, the two big tractors turning eastward toward Hendrix station. The small one with Sarge and two marines turned west onto the Hellastown road.

"Come on," Erica said. She pulled away from me and ran back through the crack. For a moment I didn't move. I wanted to see what happened to Sarge, but she was right; we couldn't follow tractors on foot. By running away from me she kept me from doing something stupid. I ran after her.

We dashed along the ledge inside Pisspot's Rim. She was much faster than I on that narrow ledge, and she got a long way ahead. Then she was over the top. I caught up to her on the way down. Going down was easy—a twenty-foot drop was nothing. I had to be careful, though, because for the same speed you've got the same momentum on Mars as on Earth, you just weigh less. Still, I took that slope like it was a giant staircase. There was dust on the road below, and the faint marks of tractors.

We crossed the road and ran to Aunt Ellen. When we got inside, I brought the pressure up so we could talk.

"They're going to Ice Hill," she said. "They'll arrest my father! And Mom, too, maybe everyone there—"

"If they mean to blow up Ice Hill the way they did Windhome, they'll have to take everybody."

"We've got to warn them!"

"Yeah." I thought about the tracks I'd seen on the road. "But we've only got line-of-sight communications and they're ahead of us on the road. Just how do we warn them?"

CHAPTER NINE

Erica looked at the map, then pointed. "Take us out into the Basin. Right there."

She pointed at a rise about a kilometer from where we'd hidden Aunt Ellen. It was straight away from the Rim, not in the direction either of the Federation groups had gone. I thought of the tractor with Sarge in it getting away toward Hellastown, and the other two approaching Ice Hill. "Why?"

"Just do it. I'll tell you on the way."

"All right." I started the tractor and began picking a way through the boulder fields. There was no road or track. The map had been made by satellite photograph; I doubt that any human had ever been this way before. "Okay, why?"

"Because it will be in line of sight to Ice Hill. I think. It looks high enough."

"Dust is pretty thick—"

"If we can't get through with the photophone we'll use the radio."

"All right." I tried for more speed, but there were pits and rocks everywhere, and the dust made it hard to see. When summer comes, the dry ice on one polar cap boils off rather than melting—and blows all the way to the opposite pole. That raises big winds in Hellas. "One good thing," I said. "There's so much dust that they'll never see us out here. We can't be stirring up enough more to matter."

It took a good half hour to make that one kilometer. The hill she'd indicated was a mound about 250 meters high, a big bubble that had formed when Hellas was a lava field a billion years ago. When we reached the top, we were above a lot of the dust storm. I turned the telescope onto the Rim east of us, and searched for Ice Hill.

"There it is," I said. "I can just make out the photophone target."

Not all tractors have talking-light units, but Sarge kept Aunt Ellen better equipped than most Rimrats can afford. The sight was built into our telescope. I trained it onto the white photophone target at the top of Ice Hill, then used the joystick to get a precise adjustment. The system uses a modulated laser beam and has to be aimed just right. The advantage is that nobody can listen in unless they're in the exact line of sight, and you can see along that.

"Ice Hill, Ice Hill, Ice Hill. Mayday. Answer by photophone only. We are on Hill 252, Basin Sector Greeneight. Mayday." Erica said that several times. We waited.

"Sis! That you? I can hardly hear you."

"Perry, get Dad. Quickly."

"What's that?"

"I said get Dad. *Now!*"

There was a long delay. "The dust is interfering with the beam," Erica said.

"Just be damn glad we can get through at all."

"I am. Have I told you I love you?"

"Not often enough."

"Erica, what is happening? Why have you two left the road? What are you doing in the Basin?"

"Dad, listen!" She managed to cut him off. If we'd been using radio and had to wait for him to say "over" and switch from transmit to receive, we might be there yet.

She told him what had happened at Windhome. "And two tractors full of Federation Marines, with that officer, Bielenson, left Windhome toward Ice Hill an hour ago," she finished.

"So you think they are coming for me?"

"I don't know," I said. "But they blew up Windhome and arrested Sarge."

"It is possible. It even makes sense," Sam said. "With Sarge and myself arrested and our stations ruined as an example to others, the boycott might well collapse. Yes, I think that is what they have in mind. But it is very late in the day. There is barely enough sunlight for them to reach us in time. Perhaps they will wait until morning—"

"Dad, you've got to get away!" Erica said.

"Get away? Run? No, Ricky. If they come to destroy my home, they must take it from me."

I didn't know it then, but that very second marked the beginning of the Martian War of Independence.

We cut off so that Sam could organize his family to fight. As with Windhome there was no way we could help.

We couldn't get there; we had barely enough sunlight to get to the road.

"At least you're safe," I said. "Now what can we do? Try to follow the tractor they put Sarge in? They'll have a long start."

"Yes." She wasn't really listening to me. She was looking out at the Rim to the west.

"I suppose we'd better find a good place out of the wind. We'll be out here for the night—"

"Garrett! That's Zeke Terman's station up there!"

"Yeah. And he can see the road. At least we can find out what the cops are doing." I slewed Aunt Ellen around and aimed the telescope. It was much easier this time; we were a lot closer to Zeke's place than we were to Ice Hill.

Erica lifted the mike and went through the calling routine: "Zeke Terman, Zeke Terman, Zeke Terman, Mayday, Mayday, Mayday. Answer by photophone only. We are on Hill 252, Sector Green-eight. Mayday." She repeated it three times. We had to give our location, because the transmitting laser must be aimed at the receiver.

Finally we got an answer. "Mayday, this is Terman. What the hell are you doing out there? Who are you?"

"You'll recognize my voice," Erica said. "Are you alone? Are you all right?"

"Why the hell shouldn't I be all right? Of course I'm alone, think I've got crew to take off work and chat on the goddamn phone?"

"Zeke, this is an emergency. Please answer a silly question. It's important that we can be sure you're alone and all right. What does Henrietta call her cat?"

There was a moment of silence. Then Zeke said, "Ricky Hendrix? That you? Henrietta calls the silly animal 'Titwillow' because of something you said. What's going on?"

We told him.

"Son of a bitch! Okay, I'll relay the word down the west Rim. Where did they take Sarge?"

"They put him in a tractor and headed west on the Hellastown road about an hour ago," Erica said.

"Wait one," Zeke told us. He left the mike open, and we heard him shouting. "Bonnie, get the boys up here! Get everybody. Come running!" Then there was silence for a while, and he came back on the line. "Okay, I've got the tractor spotted, I think. Bright yellow?"

"Right!"

"Not makin' very good time with all this dust. They're still a good half hour from Iron Gap. I'll get the boys and be to the Gap before the cops get there. A couple of sticks of 40 percent and they'll not be getting to Hellastown tonight."

"By God!" I said. "We can get Sarge loose!" I took the mike from Erica. "Thanks, Zeke."

"That you, Garrett? Thanks, hell. That's my son-in-law's sponsor those bastards have in that tractor. You want in this fight, you'd better hurry to the Gap!"

Mars is at the inner edge of the asteroid belt, and has very little atmosphere. When a big chunk of rock hits, as frequently happens—frequent meaning every hundred thousand years or so—the impact raises ringwall craters that stay until another rock breaks them down, or the wind slowly grinds them into dust. There's no rain to erode the mountains.

The crater that became the Wall was formed by a meteoroid a billion years ago. Countless other rocks smashed into the old ringwall, until only one stretch was left, and that was cracked down the center. This cracked wall lies directly across the road from the eastern Rim stations to Hellastown. The crack is called Iron Gap, and it's no more than twenty feet wide in some places. You don't *have* to go through the Gap to get to Hellastown, but the quickest way around takes five hours of travel through the boulder fields, or even longer if you try to climb the Wall with a tractor.

I looked at it on the map but didn't start the tractor.

"What are you waiting for?" Erica demanded.

"Your father will kill me if I take you into a battle."

"You let me worry about my father. Do you think I'm fragile? That I can't take care of myself? I may not be as strong as you are, but you're not going to leave me out of this!"

"All right, all right. I'm sorry. But I've got about a million years of instincts that say I shouldn't do this." I started the tractor, and headed toward the Gap.

"Instincts be damned. Mars is more my home than yours! Oh, I'm sorry, Gary. I don't really mean that. We both live here."

"You don't have to be sorry. I was never very interested in the independence movement. I'm not now. But Sarge is my friend, and the Feddies won't let us get out here and live, they've got to mess everything up. And ruin the only home I've ever been happy in—"

I couldn't finish. Thinking about Windhome as I'd last seen it brought tears, and I needed to see as well as I could to get through the boulders and dust.

After we reached it, I decided to chance the road. Daylight would be gone in less than an hour, and we'd never reach the Gap across country. I'd never had Aunt Ellen going this fast before.

"Reckless Garrett, The Terror of the Martian Roadways," I said. "Whoopee!"

"You like this, don't you?" She was very serious.

"Like it? My home's in ruins, my buddy's been taken by the cops, we may both be killed, and—"

"And you love it. It's all right, Gary. But you do. You want to fight. I think all men do. I wonder if women ever feel that way? I never did. Is it something instinctual, or do you learn it, or—"

"Good Lord, girl!"

"I'm sorry. I'm scared, that's all. No, don't slow down, I'm going with you. And I love you."

"I didn't start this fight."

"No. Some men learn to control that love of combat. But you're not sorry it has started. You'll cry for Windhome, and for friends who are killed, and you'll be glad when it's over, but you're not sorry it started."

"You're a nut."

"Sure."

We rounded a curve, and suddenly the Gap was in sight, about ten kilometers ahead. I drove on. Then, 250 meters above the Gap floor, there was a startling spurt of dust from one of the straight-walled sides. Something big dislodged and fell into the Gap, sealing it.

"They'll not get through there before sunset," I said. "They must not have reached the Gap yet! Zeke wouldn't do that if they were already through!"

"I wonder how far ahead they are?"

"Don't know, but I'm not going to stop to talk," I said. The sun was almost to the Rim ahead of us. Soon we'd be in shadow, and after that we'd be on battery power.

Erica began fiddling with the radio. She didn't turn on the transmitter, but swept through all the bands, listening—

"Four Love Victor, this is One Dog Niner. Four Love Victor, this is One Dog Niner. Mayday. Mayday. Over."

"The cops," Erica said.

They went on calling.

"They can't raise Hellastown. They're in the shadow of the Wall!" I said. "They're on battery power, and out of line of sight to anywhere! The cops are cut off."

We'd run out of sun pretty soon, too. "Okay," I said. "Try to raise Zeke. I don't care if the cops hear us now. What can they do?"

"Right."

"Just a minute, Hon. Listen!"

The cop was still calling. There was a plaintive note in his voice. Then I heard it again: a big booming laugh.

"Shut up, Wechsung, or we'll shut you up!" the cop said.

"Sure." Sarge's voice was faint, too far from the mike to hear distinctly. "You boys are in big trouble. Maybe you better let me talk to my buddies out there before they roll rocks on top of this thing."

"Shut up, Wechsung. Four Love Victor, Mayday. Mayday!"

★ ★ ★

It was pitch dark before Zeke guided us to where he and his sons had stationed themselves. He had two tractors, a big pressurized trailer with a portable powerpack, and oxygen-hydrogen fuel cells in another trailer. The police would have to rely on their internal batteries, but we had power to burn. We hooked Aunt Ellen into Zeke's system and went into his trailer.

Zeke was there with one of his sons, Ezra. John Appleby was there as well. They had a coffee pot going, and food.

"Cops have been callin' us," Zeke said. "I think they're scared. They keep tellin' us how Sarge doesn't have a helmet on. We haven't answered em yet.

"Think they'd let Sarge loose if we promise to leave 'em alone?" I asked.

Zeke shrugged. "Could be. Garrett, I haven't talked to 'em yet, because they don't know I'm in this. Might be a good idea not to tell 'em. Anyway, I thought I'd wait for you and Johnny here. You two got the biggest stake in this game—"

"They already want me," I said. "May as well let me do the talking. John has a pregnant wife. No point in getting you involved, John."

"Yeah, but—"

"If you have to be, you will be," Zeke said. "I was hoping you'd say something like that, Garrett. I blew out the road, and I'll go in after the bastards if that's what it takes. But I don't mind sayin' I'd as soon not see my station blown up the way Windhome was."

"What are we up against?" I asked.

John Appleby answered. "I've seen it. The tractor's no tank, but they've got a machine-gun turret mounted on top, and they've got thick plate on it. We could take it, no question about it. They've moved off into a clear space— they're going to be damned cold by morning if they stay out in the wind—so we can't drop rocks on their heads, but we could probably get close enough to throw dynamite. But I don't see any way we can get inside that thing without killing Sarge."

"Expect reinforcements?" I asked.

Zeke shrugged. "Don't think they got a message through. Hellastown isn't going to be anxious to send out a force in the dark. Never get tanks through the Gap anyway, they'd have to go around, and they won't do *that* at night. My other boy's watchin' from up on the side of the Gap, and he'll tell us if he sees lights comin', but I think we've got till morning for sure."

"Yeah. Well, let's talk to them. Worse comes to worse, we'll offer a trade." I drank the coffee Zeke had given me, then went over and sat down in front of the radio. The trailer was big and cozy. Zeke used it as a mobile prospecting camp.

"One Dog Niner, are you listening? Over!"

"Yeah, we're listening. You bastards better let us go! There'll be two battalions of marines with tanks out here by morning!"

"This won't last until morning," I said. "You've got troubles, fellows. Now let me hear Sarge talking."

"Why?"

"Because any time I ask to hear him and I don't, I'm going to assume he's dead, and there won't be any reason why we shouldn't be throwing dynamite. Clear? We've got more power than you have. You can't run away from us, so don't waste batteries. Just put Sarge on."

There was a pause. Then, "Hey kid. You're doin' okay."

"You all right, Sarge?"

"Sure. Look, don't let 'em talk you into nothing, they're—"

"That's enough," the policeman said. "He's all right."

"Good. You keep him that way. I'll be back in a bit. Out." I switched off the transmitter.

"The trouble is," I said, "they think they can wait for sunlight and just take off. With that machine gun they know they can put any tractor we've got out of action. And there probably will be reinforcements before noon. We need a way to convince them we can disable them without hurting Sarge—"

We thought for a moment. Then I had an idea. "John, you said you can hit them with dynamite. Can you hit them with paint?"

"Paint?"

"Yeah. In a plastic bag. If we splatter paint on their windscreen and solar cells, where are they going in the morning?"

"Be damned," Zeke said. "Ezra, get on the photophone and tell your mother we need some paint down here. Paint and some bags." He turned back to me. "She won't like that. Damn bags are expensive and we can't make 'em."

"It's for a good cause. Maybe we won't need many."

"I'll throw," John said. "If I can't talk, I ought to be of some use."

★ ★ ★

It took half an hour to organize, and I let the cops stew for another half hour. We were in no real hurry. By now it would be getting cold in their tractor, even with the heaters going. Then John moved into position.

"Okay, ready," he said.

We had two radios, so we could keep John on one and use the other to talk to the cops. I called them.

"Yeah?"

"Let me hear Sarge."

"Still okay, kid."

"Good," I said. "Now. What's your name, whichever of you is in charge?"

"What's that to you?"

"I don't really care, but I ought to call you something—"

"Call him Stinky," Sarge said in the background.

"Shut up, Wechsung. My name is Larkin."

"All right, Larkin, watch close now." I switched to the other radio. "Let her fly!"

There was nothing for a moment. Then John's voice came through. "Right on target! Hit the windscreen."

"Beautiful." I called Larkin again. "Get the message? How far will you get in the morning with the solar panels covered with black paint? Oh, and don't try moving the tractor. You'll waste power you're going to need before the night's over, and there's no place you can go that we can't get upwind of you."

"He's shooting hell out of the rocks," John reported. "I wonder what he thinks he can hit?"

"Can you whap him again?"

"Sure. Here goes."

I called again. "Well, Larkin? How much air have you

got? Think your relief can get through the Gap before you run out? Ready to give up, or should we paint the whole tractor for you?"

"Damn you! It's Pittson, isn't it? You're in trouble, Pittson. Let us go and we can straighten it out. Nobody's been hurt yet —"

I laughed at him.

He was off for five minutes. We waited. Then he came on. "Okay. You win. We'll turn Wechsung loose in the morning, if you hold off the paint until then—"

"Crap. You're no Marsman. Our word's good. Yours isn't," I said.

"Attaboy!" Sarge shouted in the background.

"Shut up, Wechsung. Pittson, if we let him go, will you leave us alone? Nobody around in the morning?"

"What about it, Sarge?" I asked.

"Take 'em up on it."

"Roger."

Appleby brought Sarge into the trailer a few minutes later. We got his helmet off. "You okay?" I asked.

"Few bruises. Nothing to worry about. Damn good to have friends. Thanks."

"Sure."

"Sandwiches and coffee here," Zeke said.

'Thanks." Sarge wolfed a sandwich and washed it down with black coffee. "But we got more troubles. Erica, did you kids get through to Sam? I think they went after him—"

"Yes," she said. She told him what we'd done. "Dad said he'd fight. I'm worried—"

"He'll be all right for now," Sarge said. "By now he'll have plenty of friends there. Okay, Sam's taken care of. Zeke, can you get through to Chris Martin's place?" Martin's station was on the other side of the Gap, toward Hellastown from us.

"Sure. Want me to patch you in from here?"

"Please. And get some night traveling gear together. I have to walk across the Gap tonight."

"Tonight?" Erica demanded. "Why?"

"Only way to connect with Chris and get a tractor to Hellastown," Sarge said. "They've got the Skipper in the jug, and I've got to get him out. I could use some help. Any volunteers?"

He was looking directly at me.

CHAPTER TEN

"It's not as crazy as it sounds," Sarge said. "We always knew the Skipper would be the first one arrested when the Feddies made their move, so we took some precautions. And they don't know we're coming. They still think everything's all right out here. Last report Ellsworth heard I was in custody, Windhome was a wreck, and they were off to Ice Hill, moving on Sam at first light tomorrow, and him not knowing a thing about it. This is the right time for it."

"Well, long as it's going to be a piece of cake, I'll come along," John Appleby said.

What could I do? "Me too."

"Only need one," Sarge said. "Rather have Garrett. No offense, Johnny, but they already want him." He didn't add that Appleby already had a going station and so was less expendable than me. He didn't have to.

Zeke brought in extra clothing. Sarge used the set to call Chris Martin and arrange for him to meet us on the other side of the Gap. Martin was an old grad, one of Commander Farr's first recruits. He'd come to Mars with his whole family, and now his children were out on their own.

I asked John to take Erica to Ice Hill in the morning. The battle would be over before they could get there. "If things aren't right," I said, "let the Padre know where you've taken her—"

"Sure. Everything'll be okay. What with Sam's family and the friends he'll have coming, those Feddies won't know what hit 'em."

Sarge finished his radio call. "Won't take him long, he's got an auxiliary power trailer for night work. Garr, you about ready?"

"Just about." I felt like an Eskimo: p-suit, reflective coveralls, foam-insulated jacket and pants, another jacket, and more coveralls over the whole mess. I looked like a cartoon. I tried to hug Erica, and it was comical; with all the clothes I had on I could hardly feel her against me.

"Please come back—" She reached up through my open face plate and stroked my cheek. We could just touch lips through the face opening of my helmet.

"I'll be back."

It was cold out. The wind was up to 150 kilometers an hour, a hurricane on Earth. I'd been wrong about Martian winds. The air's too thin for the wind to have much force. It put no more pressure on us than a ten-mile-an-hour wind on Earth, but it was cold. I could feel it through all my clothes.

We didn't have far to go. Around the police tractor, then through the Gap. Zeke had blocked it good: there were three boulders the size of houses, and a lot of smaller rubble. We had to climb over.

We didn't dare show a light. Sarge didn't trust the cops. "Not that Larkin's such a bad sort," he said. "But he's scared. If he sees lights he may figure we're going to do him in no matter what you promised. Best not to take chances."

When we were through the Gap we had more light. Phobos was rising on the other side. The little moon moves so fast that it goes from west to east. I stumbled a few times, but we only had to walk about half a kilometer. The tractor wasn't there yet, and we walked on down the road. It was too cold to stand still.

Then we saw the lights, and the tractor drove up. We got in, and Sarge introduced me to Chris. He was a short, dark man who didn't talk much. There was nobody with him.

It had been a long day, and we had more to do before it was over. The motors hummed as we raced through the night. I figured Sarge would tell me when it was time, and there wasn't much to talk about. I crawled into the bunk behind the seat and tried to sleep.

"Okay, kid, we're here."

"I wasn't asleep, Sarge." I moved so I could see out the windscreen. There was a big man-made cylinder topped by a dome about a kilometer away. It looked enormous.

"Observatory," Sarge said. "Don't figure they'll be guarding it yet. It's run by some big-name scientists from all the best universities, and Ellsworth won't want the kind of trouble they can make for him if he gets in their way."

"I never knew there was an observatory," I said.

"Yep. And it's not all that far from the school. Larkin was joking about how they had the Skipper locked up in his own cells. Thought that was funny."

"As funny as bubble gum in a lockjaw ward, as the saying goes. Now what, Sarge?"

"Now Chris stays with the tractor—"

"I could—"

"Chris, I don't need heroes! If two can't get Mr. Farr out, three can't either, and I may want you to move this heap in a hurry. You know tractors better than Garr, so you stay."

"All right."

"That's settled, then. Garr, we'll climb into the observatory. The scientists won't be looking for us, and if anyone does see us, act like you belong there. They come from so many different places they can't all know each other, and they've got no reason to be suspicious if we don't get in their way."

"Right." I was getting the shakes, but I wasn't going to show it. I began zipping and velcroing myself into all my layers of clothing.

Phobos was higher now, so it wasn't quite as dark as it had been in the Gap. The little moon gave enough light to help us pick our way across the badlands. The observatory was on a high peak behind Hellastown where there wasn't any blowing dust; they'd picked the location because there was seldom any wind in this spot.

Sarge had a length of nylon line with a hook on the end made from a bent jack handle. He threw the hook upward into the dark. It fell back soundlessly, and he threw it again. This time it caught. He tugged on the line, then put his weight on it and swung back and forth. Then he pressed his helmet against mine.

"I'll go first. Come up when I give three tugs. No need to put both our weights on this thing."

"Rog."

He climbed upward and in seconds was only a dark shape against the stars. I waited for what seemed like hours. I'd worked up a sweat coming up the hill, and now, despite the still air, I felt the cold and began to shiver. Then the rope jerked three times. I began climbing.

It was easy. Despite all the gear, I weighed a lot less than I would on Earth. I pulled myself up, hand over hand, until I reached an open ironwork balcony that ran around the outside of the observatory. Sarge gave me a hand over the rail. Then he led the way around until we came to the big telescope opening, and we could look down inside.

Four or five people, bundled up the way we were, moved purposefully on the floor below. They didn't look up at all. The telescope was directly in front of us, looking as if it were staring at us, but of course it was peering at something billions of miles away. A silly thought popped into my head: what would happen if I stood on the rail and made faces into the tube?

There was another walkway around the inside of the dome, and we stepped through onto that, then climbed down an iron ladder to the floor below. One of the people down there glanced up at us, then went back to work. He may have reserved all his curiosity for the universe; I can't imagine what he thought we were doing up there. On the other hand, I haven't any idea of what he was doing either.

No one paid any attention to us as we went across to the air-lock entrance and cycled through. The corridor beyond was empty. When we'd dogged shut the door, we opened our faceplates. "Piece of cake," Sarge said.

"So far."

"Yeah. Watch for cops." He led the way along the corridor, then down another. It was steep downhill all the way. Eventually we came to a steel door set in the corridor wall. Sarge used a key to open it, showing a closet filled with janitor's gear.

"Told you we'd made a few preparations. Skipper was supposed to come out this way." Sarge did something to the shelving and the whole closet swung out on hinges. We went through, closing both doors behind us.

We had to use helmet lights in the narrow, dark passage. It went steeply downward, bending at right angles a couple of times. "Hard rock," Sarge said. "Easier to drill around than through. Here, hold on."

He stopped at a stretch of corridor wall that looked like all the rest, and examined it until he found a tiny hole. He took off a glove, reached in, and pulled with his finger. A cover plate came out revealing a cavity behind it.

"Know anything about guns?" he asked.

"I've shot them. I'm no expert."

"Yeah. Well, here." He handed me a police revolver. "There aren't a lot of guns on Mars. Keep that hid good, anybody sees you with it, they'll *know* you don't belong here." He pocketed another pistol, and a grenade. "Not much for weapons, but better'n just knives. Okay, be kind of quiet from here on. This ends up behind the shelves in the Old Man's office. There may be somebody there. If there is, we have to jump him before he can call. But we want him alive—"

"Rog."

"Piece of cake," Sarge said. He grinned. "Let's do it."

There was a peephole at the end of the passage. Sarge peered through it, then motioned to me.

The door was closed, and a man sat at the desk. I nodded, and Sarge opened the panel.

It was simple. Sarge had him by the throat while I got his hands so he couldn't touch any of the console buttons. We held him like that.

"Easy, now," Sarge said. "One peep, and you're dead." He got a knife out of his belt and held it at our prisoner's throat. "You understand that?"

He nodded.

"It's Hardesty," I said. "He was our barracks sergeant."

Sarge let him go, but held the knife in place. Hardesty gulped hard. I got his hands behind the chair and took a couple of turns of line around them. Then we wheeled him away from the desk so he couldn't reach anything.

"Where's Mr. Farr?" Sarge demanded.

"Interrogation room," Hardesty said. He was careful not to speak above a whisper. "Mr. Ellsworth was in there for a while, but he went back over to town."

"You night duty NCO?"

"Yes."

"Okay. Now I'm going to have you use that intercom to send for Mr. Farr. Before I do, I want to tell you what happens to you if you try anything funny." Sarge hitched the knife in his hand, tossing it wickedly up and down. "I won't kill you. But you'll father no more kids, and you'll live on one kidney. I'm told that hurts a lot."

Hardesty's expression didn't change. "You don't leave me much. Ellsworth will have me shot anyway."

"So which is it?"

"Neither," Hardesty said. "I've lost nothing in this chickenshit outfit. Take me with you on the way out."

"We can't trust you," Sarge said.

"Why not? I'm a convict, same as this one. Pittson, aren't you? Sure you are, put two tough creeps in sick bay. I remember you. Look, I can do some farming. After you've seen Mr. Farr, you'll know why I'd just as soon go with you. He always treated me decently, and I had no hand in what they did to him."

"Did to him?" Sarge said. "Did what?"

"You'll see. You may need me to carry him. I don't think he'll be walking."

"Jesus," Sarge said. He looked at the clock over the desk. Not much past midnight. "What do you think, Garrett?"

I shrugged. "We got much choice?"

"Guess not. Okay, Hardesty, do it. If you play tricks on us, God help you."

"And you'll take me with you."

"Yes."

"If you don't know how to work the intercom, you'll have to untie me." Sarge and I exchanged looks. Then I loosened the cords. Hardesty scooted his chair over to the intercom and punched buttons. "Carruthers."

"Yes, sergeant."

"Bring Farr up to his office. He conscious?"

"Kind of. Mr. Ellsworth said to soften him up some more."

"You'll get your fun later. I need the bastard to help find things up here. Bring him."

"Okay. Your responsibility."

We waited. "How many will come?" Sarge asked.

"Two."

"Get down behind the desk, Garrett. I'll stay by the door. If Hardesty does anything funny, shoot him in the balls."

"Right." I crouched, and Hardesty rolled up to sit at the desk. "Keep your hands in sight," I told him. We waited some more.

They knocked at the door.

"Come," Hardesty said.

The door opened, and two men pushed a wheelchair through. As they got inside, Sarge kicked the door shut. I came out from behind the desk.

"What the hell?" The guard had no time to say anything else. I smashed his face with the barrel of my pistol, got my hand over his mouth, and chopped down, twice, at the base of his skull.

Then I had time to look up and see how Sarge was doing. He was wiping his knife on the other guard's coveralls. "Mine's finished." he said. "Yours?"

"Near enough."

"Finish him."

I hesitated a moment. I'd never killed anyone before. I'd been ready to, in fights, but it had never happened, and this guy was helpless. While I stood there, Sarge came over and cut his throat. "Dead he's no problem," he said. "Jesus, Skipper, what have they done to you?"

Farr mumbled something, but we couldn't understand him. Sarge turned on Hardesty. The guard was still sitting at the desk, his hands on top in plain sight.

"Skipper, did this creep do this to you?" Sarge demanded.

"Aagh. No," Farr said. He had trouble talking, because there were new gaps in his teeth, and his lips were swollen to three times their normal size. One eye was closed, and the other bled. He tried to get up, but couldn't. Then he swallowed hard. "Hardesty is okay," he mumbled.

They had taken Farr's p-suit, and of course he had no helmet. "How do we get him out of here?" I asked. "If we could get one of the school's practice suits, we might get that on him."

"Yeah," Sarge said. "Hardesty, how do we do that?"

"Beats me. Nobody's going to bring one here. Won't be long before somebody wonders what happened to Carruthers. And I'm supposed to make night rounds in a half hour."

"Crap doodle," Sarge said. "We've got a skintight hid in the corridor, but he wouldn't live a minute, not bunged up the way he is. We've got to get one of those EVA jobs."

"Carry him in a pressure sack," Hardesty said.

"And where the hell do we get a pressure sack?" Sarge demanded.

"Kitchen," Commander Farr mumbled. "Plenty in there."

"It'll be locked," Hardesty said. "I've got the keys.

Right here." He pointed to the table where we'd put everything we'd found in his pockets.

I thought for a moment, then began peeling off layers of clothing. "We'll go together, Hardesty. You and me."

"Fine."

"Garrett, I still don't trust him," Sarge said.

"Got a better plan?"

"No."

It turned out to be no trouble at all. The night kitchen staff were used to Hardesty's midnight raids. He'd been running a black market operation in Hellastown, selling food stolen from the school kitchens and splitting with the cooks.

When we got back we dressed Farr in all my spare clothes and put him in the sack with an oxygen bottle. Then we locked the office door and went through the passageway back to the astronomy section. When we got there, Sarge went through into the dome, and came back a minute later with two prisoners.

"What is the meaning of this?" She was a gray-haired woman. I'd seen her pictures in the papers, a Nobel Prize winner. Lady Elizabeth Murray. I couldn't remember what she got the prize for, something about the shape of the universe.

"We need some outside travel gear," Sarge said. He turned to the other astronomer, a young man in his twenties. "You like that telescope out there?" Sarge demanded.

"Why, yes, of course." He didn't seem very nervous about the situation.

"What do you think a grenade would do to the mirror?"

"Good God, you can't be serious!" the man said.

"I can be. You go find us some outside gear for these two." He indicated Hardesty and me. "Garrett, you go with him. I'll keep the lady here with us. And if you're not back in five minutes, mister, that eye is going out."

"I would rather you threatened *me*," Lady Elizabeth said.

"Yeah, I thought so," Sarge told her. "Well?"

"Do as he says, Dereck," Lady Elizabeth said. "I believe he means it."

"There's a locker room just here," Dereck told me. He led me down the corridor and through a door. "I say, what is this all about?"

"I'm not sure myself," I told him. "You're in no danger. We just want to get the hell out of here."

"You're welcome to go. You've cost us a prime night of observation, you know. We're looking for a new planet. Lady Elizabeth knows where it must be, and tonight will be perfect for finding it."

He opened the door to the locker room. There was a lot of gear hanging on the wall. I grabbed stuff I thought would fit me, then more for Hardesty. "Let's go," I said.

It took more time to get the cold-weather gear on. We were just getting dressed when we heard alarm bells.

★★★
CHAPTER ELEVEN
★★★

"Into the lock. Quick!" Sarge barked.

"What about them?" I pointed to our scientist prisoners.

"Leave 'em. You two want your eye to keep looking you better pray we're out before the guards get here. Move!"

We carried Farr into the air lock. While it was cycling, Sarge reached into the sack and set the regulator to four pounds. That should be enough pure oxygen, if the bottle didn't freeze. It had no heater system like the ones in our suits. We had it inside Farr's jacket to help keep it warm. He was breathing, but we didn't think he could manage for himself.

The outer door opened and we bolted for the ladder. Technicians looked up from their consoles. We couldn't see expressions through their faceplates, but they *must* have wondered what the hell we were doing.

Sarge swarmed up the ladder, then threw down a line. I knotted a cradle around Farr and Sarge hoisted. I waved Hardesty up next. He pushed from below while Sarge pulled. Then I started up after them.

When we reached the balcony, I thought we were safe. Sarge and Hardesty carried Mr. Farr around to the big gap the telescope looked through, and went on to the outside balcony.

Then the air-lock door opened and marines swarmed through. They had p-suits and coveralls, but no cold weather gear; they wouldn't be out here long. Without all my extra gear I was feeling the cold myself, despite the exertion of climbing.

They raised their rifles and orange flashes spurted silently. I drew my pistol and fired back, also in silence. No hits for either side. Then I was through to the outside balcony. By then Sarge had lowered Mr. Farr over the side, and he and Hardesty were busy paying out line. I stopped at the slit where I could cover the ladder.

Unlike me, the marines had very little target to shoot at. I saved my ammunition until one of them reached the ladder then took very careful aim and shot him off it. Two of his buddies ran over and picked him up. They were brave men. I held my fire; they were no threat to us, and the more tied down taking care of the wounded, the better for me.

"Okay, kid!" Sarge called. The voice was loud in my helmet radio.

"Right." I waited a little longer, on the theory that the marines might have been listening. They had been. Three of them rushed the ladder. I shot the leading one and he fell, carrying the two below back to the floor. Something tugged at my right sleeve, and I looked down. There was a big rip in the coveralls and insulation, but the slug had missed me by a good two inches; that foam was thick.

I fired once more, not caring if I hit anything, and ran around the balcony. They'd be coming up the ladder any moment. It was eighty feet to the ground below. Sarge and Hardesty were running across the badlands, carrying Farr, their helmet lights dancing across the ground.

No time to go down the rope, I told myself. Eighty feet. Mars gravity is about 40 percent Earth. But it's not the same, there's a squared factor in there. No time to work it out, and the marines couldn't be far behind me.

I swung over the edge and dropped toward the ground below.

I worked it out later: I fell for almost three seconds, which seems like forever, and I hit with the same force as if I'd jumped off an eighteen-foot ladder back on Earth.

It hurt like hell. I hit and went on down, all the way, rolling, letting the thick foam padding absorb most of the force, but I still felt as if my ankles had been rammed up to my knees.

I could get up, though. It hurt, but I could run. I ran like hell toward the tractor.

We threw Mr. Farr into the bunk and Sarge climbed in with him. I put Hardesty between Chris Martin and myself in the front seat. Chris had the tractor bouncing across the rocks before we got pressure up in the cab.

"Nearest tractor air-lock is a good five kilometers from here," Sarge said.

"The marines didn't have cold-weather gear," I told him. "They've probably gone in by now." I could still feel the cold, despite everything I'd worn. "How is Mr. Farr?"

"He's alive," Sarge growled. "Chris, get us out into the

Basin. They'll never find us out there. Then head cross country for Ice Hill."

"Right. How'd it go?"

"Piece of cake." Sarge said.

They had five prisoners and one repairable tractor at Ice Hill. The other Federation tractor had been dynamited.

"Nothing to it," Sam Hendrix told us. "Their first warning that we would resist came when the leading tractor ran over ten sticks of 60 percent nitro. We had very little trouble with the second."

We got Mr. Farr inside. Erica was waiting for me. "Are you all right?"

"Piece of cake." It felt good to be able to kiss her. "And you?"

"Johnny and Ezra stopped at Windhome on the way. We picked up the two marines they left behind. Just as well for them, there was no one to get them and they would have run out of air." She took my hand. "There's a meeting in a few minutes. We're supposed to go. But we have a little time first . . ."

Commander Farr was propped up on a portable cot. Ruth Hendrix didn't want him to talk, but he insisted on having us all meet in the main hall. His voice was weak and his words tended to come out slurred, but he was all business.

"It's started," he said. "There's no turning back for any of us. Sam, did you get the word out?"

"Yes. The Rim is boiling mad. Ellsworth sent out three tanks today, but they did not go past Iron Gap. Instead they escorted the police van back, and Ellsworth has been sending messages to Marsport demanding help."

"Will he get it?"

Sam shook his head. "I do not think so. Not immediately. Some of our people in the north have begun sabotage raids. The monorail south has been cut in four places. Katrinkadorp is in revolt. They will need their marines up there for a while, I think."

"Then there's been a general revolt?" Farr demanded.

"No. Except in Katrinkadorp there is no uprising. Just our people, and sabotage."

Farr nodded to himself. "Independence. They want a meeting of the leaders. Committees and debates. Is this the proper time?" He sighed deeply. "Well, we've got no choice. We've got to do something to stir up the others."

There was a long silence. Erica took my hand. We stood, waiting for someone to say something, but no one did.

"It's too early," Farr muttered. "Everything only half planned. So we make do with what we have. The Rim is ours?"

"Yes," Sam said. "Solidly, I think. Ellsworth has done our work for us, here. We had doubters, even after the destruction of Windhome, but Mr. Ellsworth has told the Hellas Region Council that he intends to close all the stations and eliminate this rebellion once and for all. One of our people had a bug in the Council Chamber, and we have been broadcasting his speech all day. Yes, we certainly hold the Rim."

"Then we must defend it, and that means denying Ellsworth knowledge of our movements. Sarge, did you make the observations of the weather satellite?"

"Yes, sir."

"Where are they?" Farr asked.

"On a tape back at Windhome, sir."

"Send for them immediately. We need the ephemeris."

"Sir." Sarge went off to talk to John Appleby.

"Who is your best man with explosives?" Fan asked.

"Campbell, I think," Sam Hendrix said.

"Put him to work. We need something to knock down the weather satellite. Something to loft rocks into its path. It needn't be fancy."

"Yes, I think Campbell will have no trouble with that."

I thought they'd lost their minds. Knock down a *satellite*? With a homemade interceptor? Michael Hendrix explained it to me later. It wasn't really very difficult at all. We knew exactly where the satellite would be at any moment, and in Mars' low gravity it didn't take a very big sounding rocket to loft a bunch of rocks up the ninety kilometers where the satellite would be. The spy-eye was moving at better than three kilometers a second, and when it ran into a cloud of rock . . .

They knocked it out the next day. It didn't fall, of course, but the electronics were knocked to smash. It wouldn't be sending down any pictures of tractors moving around the Rim. And since we held the high ground above the Basin, we could see them coming any time, while they had no idea of what we were doing.

If the Federation could have got a big force together in the first week of the Revolution, that would have been the end of it; but they couldn't. There aren't any airplanes on Mars. Everything has to move by rail or by tractors, and although we didn't have any large force around Marsport, we had enough to knock out a rail line running unprotected for two thousand kilometers. We had only to deal with the two battalions of Federation troops in Hellas Region, and we had more men than they did. For the moment they could count on company cops to control the town; but the miners were seething, waiting for a spark to set them off, and Ellsworth knew it, so he wanted to keep his troops close to home.

We intercepted plenty of his messages. He was worried: there'd been no word from Major Bielenson's expedition beyond the return of the two cops who'd had Sarge. If we could swallow a dozen men, maybe we could beat a couple of hundred, too; he wasn't going to risk it until he had reinforcements from Marsport, and Marsport wasn't sending any until they were sure the capital was secure . . .

We got through the first week because Ellsworth was no more ready for war than we had been. During the second week he sent a force out, and we had a sharp battle west of Iron Gap: dynamite bombs against tanks and guns. We didn't try to hold ground west of the Gap; instead we made them fight for every meter.

The contest wasn't as unequal as it sounds. The ground was rugged, with almost no visibility. We had a few captured rifles, and after the first week we had crossbows powered by steel tractor springs. The steel quarrels would penetrate anything except plate armor and had a range almost as good as a rifle: no air, and low gravity.

We lost four men and two women. They took Chris Martin's station, but they paid for it with eight tanks and crews; and we stopped them at the Gap.

That night we made harassing raids. It was a nightmare

time, with us on foot in the Martian night; but we could live outside, day or night, if we had to. We knew how. They didn't. When they lost more men in our night raid than they had in the battle, they decided they'd had enough for a while, and withdrew back to Chris Martin's place.

We were holding the Rim, but we knew we couldn't hold it forever; we needed the spark that would set all of Mars afire. And we had to find it before they sent Ellsworth enough troops to roll over us.

★ ★ ★

CHAPTER TWELVE

★ ★ ★

I didn't see much of Erica after the first week of the rebellion. I was assigned to Sarge's militia company and stationed at Windhome. We were the reserve unit in case Ellsworth tried to force the Gap; the advance group was holding Zeke Terman's station.

Erica had other duties, and they kept her at Ice Hill despite her protests. She was, they said, too valuable to use as a foot soldier; she knew more about power plant operations than almost anyone else, and when she didn't have power plant duties, they could use her skills as an agronomist. Food production had to be kept up. The mine camps and refineries needed all we could grow.

Bielenson hadn't had time for systematic destruction of Windhome. He'd blown out the air locks and cracked all the domes, so that everything in the station was dead, but the electronic gear was mostly untouched. I spent my time getting the solar-cell production system back into operation. We needed all the solar cells we could get. We also built fortifications, planted mines in all the approaches, and put out patrols to watch for Feddies. It didn't leave much time for anything else.

The Skipper sent for me in the third week. He was still at Ice Hill, slowly recovering from the beating he'd got. Ellsworth had supervised that himself. They gave me a few hours with Erica, and even found someone to cover for her duties during that afternoon. Then I was ushered into Sam's study. The comfortable room was now general headquarters for Free Mars—what little there was of it. There were maps on all the walls, and extra communications gear had been moved in. The Skipper was able to sit in a chair, although Ruth Hendrix wouldn't let him stay up for more than a few hours a day.

Erica insisted on coming in with me. When one of the guards objected, she pushed him aside. "This is still my home, Brent Callahan, and if you think you can keep me out of my father's study, you just try it!"

"Let her come," Farr called from inside. "Good afternoon, Erica. Garrett. Please sit down. Drink?"

Erica looked at him suspiciously. "You want something."

Farr sighed. "Yes, of course I do. Does that mean I can't be civil?"

"No . . ."

"Very well. Please sit down and have a drink with me. Garrett, how do you think the war is going?"

"Sir? You'd know better than me. We seem to be holding on."

"Precisely," Farr said. "We seem to be holding on. But only holding on, and that is fatal. Part of Mars can never be independent. We must liberate the entire planet, towns and all, or we must give up.

I didn't say anything. He was right. Station holders, Rimrats around Hellas, the Afrikaners at Katrinkadorp, and all the other Marsmen like to say we can get along without the towns, but the truth is we need the heavy industry. Mars is just too hostile a place to live without some concentration of industry and power. For that matter, we still need imports from Earth, although not very many, and we could survive without them. Barely.

"I'd think the miners would join us," I said.

"They would, if they thought they could win." Commander Farr said. "We have only to give the word and there will be widespread rioting in most of the cities. In the confusion we might seize control. There are very few Federation Marines on Mars, and the company police cannot fight a mass insurrection. Assume we have done that. Then what? What will the Federation Council on Earth do?"

I shrugged. "Send troops?"

Farr nodded. "Probably. And worse. Send ships with nuclear weapons. Bomb one of our cities and invite the others to surrender."

"So why haven't they done that already?" Erica demanded.

Farr laughed. "It would cost too much, and for what? So far, Free Mars consists of the Rim and Katrinkadorp. The governor in Marsport is hardly likely to exaggerate how serious the situation is. It would be a confession of failure. And as long as we do *not* cause widespread rebellion, he won't ask for help."

"Then it's hopeless," I said. "We can't fight what they've got here unless we take the cities, and if we take the cities they'll send something we can't fight at all—"

"Your appreciation is correct, but the situation is not hopeless. The problem is hardly new. We planned to deal with it, we *had* to, before we could even contemplate independence. Unfortunately, events caught up with us. We cannot use the original plan. But there is a way."

"I don't like this," Erica said.

"I beg your pardon?"

"You heard me, Mr. Farr. I don't like this. There's no reason why you should be discussin' high policy with Garrett."

Farr merely nodded. "As you suppose, I need him."

"For something damned dangerous," Erica said. "Why Garrett?"

"Ricky!" I said.

"Don't Ricky me! You've done enough. Mr. Farr, there must be lots of people you can send."

"Unfortunately, there are not. Garrett has special qualifications for this job—"

"Crap!" I'd never seen Erica so angry. "What's so damned special about Garrett? Me, I happen to love the guy, but how's he special to you?"

"I can't tell you. No hint of this must ever get out. Only those going on the mission will know."

"You can find somebody else! We're going to be married, and Garrett has done enough."

I had been just about to say the same thing. I really had. Why should I volunteer? But I wasn't going to have my red-headed, blue-eyed sweetheart make a coward out of me in front of the commanding officer! Even then, I might still have told him to find another boy, but she started talking at the same time I did, and I heard myself say, "I'll do it, Commander. What do you need?"

I heard myself say it. I put it that way because it was *not* what I'd intended to say. I am not a hero.

It took another ten minutes to get Ricky out of the office.

By the time she was gone, we weren't speaking. She'd told me I was a damned fool, and I felt like one. "All right, sir, what the hell is so special about me?" I demanded.

"You're less than a Mars year from Earth," Farr said. He pointed to a big map on the wall next to him. "There is one thing we can do that will assure that Earth won't interfere, and also spark the townsmen into revolution. We must begin the Project."

I thought he'd gone off his head. I told him so.

"Not at all."

"But that takes atom bombs," I said. "Anyway that's what they tell me—"

"It does. You're going to get them for us."

"Now I know you've lost your mind. Sir."

"I assure you I haven't," Farr said. "How do you make an atomic bomb?"

"Good Lord, I don't know. That's a secret—"

"Hardly. Any high school student could find out. The basic structure of nuclear weapons has been known, and published, since 1949. An atomic weapon is nothing more than a critical mass of the proper radioactive materials. The only difficult part is obtaining the fissionables, such as refined uranium. And there is plenty of refined uranium on Mars."

"And you want me to walk in and steal some?"

Farr grinned. It wasn't a pleasant grin because of the gaps in his teeth. "How did you guess? That happens to be precisely what I want you to do. Now look here on this map.

"The Federation, not being entirely insane, keeps all refined uranium in a safe place. Specifically here, in this crater." He pointed to one of the big rimwalls in the Deucalion region. The crater was over a hundred and fifty kilometers in diameter.

"It happens that the main industrial power pile for Novoya Sverdlovsk and Marsport is also in Deucalion Crater," Farr said. "Thus, if we take control of this installation, we have the materials for atomic weapons, and also a very big threat to use against the major companies. We give the companies a choice: help us, or lose their power supply."

"That makes sense," I said. Solar power is marvelous but on the scale the big outfits operate on it takes a lot more than they can collect with solar cells. Only the big atomic power plants can furnish the kind of power Mars General and the other big industries need.

I looked at the map. The power plant and uranium storage facility were located right in the center of the crater. A monorail line ran from there to the crater rim, then branched, one branch running north to Novoya Sverdlovsk in Edom Crater, the other directly east to Yappy Crater and Marsport. There was no other way in. "How do we get there?" I asked. "They can see us coming for—"

"For about 250 kilometers," Farr said. "Obviously we

cannot take them by surprise if we use the monorails. The trains are stopped at the rim, and there is a large garrison there. Even if we could capture a train without causing an alarm, which I doubt, we wouldn't get past that garrison."

"Yeah, but if we take tractors there's no way we can get into the crater without being seen, and certainly no way to get across it. That's smooth plain, not a big boulder field like Hellas—"

"I see you appreciate the problem," Farr said. "Actually, it's worse than that. There are observation posts all around the rim. A tractor couldn't get within a hundred miles of Deucalion crater without being spotted."

He was enjoying this. "Then I don't see how we do it. Wait a minute. You said walk." I looked at the map again. "Commander, you're talking about going 150 miles *on foot?*"

"Yes."

"Can't be done. A man can't carry enough air, let alone food and water. Be generous; figure we make forty miles a day—"

"I think you would average more like twenty."

"So do I. Call it thirty. That's five days and it's just not possible."

"I sincerely hope the Feddies think that way," Farr said. "And I rather suppose they do. Most of their officials have not been here very long. Men who live on Mars tend to become Mars sympathizers, meaning they are unreliable and thus not to be trusted around the uranium stockpile. If you, with all your Rim experience, think it can't be done, then I'm sure they think that."

I looked at the map again, then shook my head. "I don't

see it. Sure, if you can guarantee us permafrost near the surface, maybe, just maybe, we could carry enough solar cells to set up airmakers and hydrolize water to get oxygen. But we'd spend one day out of two just sitting there collecting power, and it'd take damn near an acre of solar cells. It'd be easier to hide tractors!"

"Right again. Nevertheless, there is a way. Give up?"

"Yeah," I said. "I give up. How?"

He told me. I leaned back in my chair and laughed like hell. Then I stopped laughing. I was going to have to do it.

Five hundred men and seventy tractors: not a very large military force on which to pin the hopes of a world. At that it was 20 percent of the Rim's fighting strength. We had to be very careful not to be seen, because if Ellsworth knew the Rim had sent that much force to the north, he could attack without much fear.

Our agents in Hellastown were instructed to foment sabotage and rebellion among the miners: incidents, work slowdowns, riots, anything to keep Ellsworth on edge and his troops in town. Meanwhile our group started north-west.

We crossed the Rim Range by a track that led past my valley. I had never seen it except on maps, but I recognized it, a big ringwall and two small flat-top mesas, with a canyon below them. I stared at it, wondering if I would ever live there with Erica. It seemed such a short time ago that we were planning where to put our agrodomes, and where our first tunnel would be.

It *was* a short time, I told myself. Less than a month.

Yet, although it seemed that we'd been engaged only a few days, the month of war seemed like a year. Time is a strange thing, and I'm not at all sure we understand it as well as we think we do.

We went under the monorail from Hellastown to Marsport by passing through a deep canyon at night. When that was behind us we all breathed a sigh of relief. Then we plunged on across the plains, across canyon ends, over craters or around them, striving for a straight-line distance of a hundred miles a day. The way was tortuous; we often had to drive twice a hundred miles and more to do it. We had no real maps, only satellite photographs; no one had ever been here before us.

Since we couldn't possibly carry enough air and water with us, scout groups went ahead to find ice caves and permafrost. The scouts were old Rimrat prospectors who knew what to look for, men with years of experience at interpreting tiny shadows and vague marks on photographs. Without their abilities we could never have crossed thirteen hundred miles at all, much less in fifteen days.

When they found water the scouts set up solar-cell arrays to power airmakers—out here we didn't worry about being seen. Although the Federation had a manned ship in orbit, after the weather satellite was knocked out they moved it up to almost two thousand miles above the surface. Even with a good telescope aimed precisely where we were they'd have been lucky to find us, and Farr gave them something else to look at by sending meaningless expeditions out into Hellas Basin.

The landscape was bleak and empty except for the blowing red dust that's everywhere on Mars when there's wind. We crossed vast boulder-strewn plains, saw flat-topped mesas in the distance, and always there was that dark sky with wispy clouds and dust plumes rising into it, and the pink sky at the horizon. We went around craters and mountains, over rimwalls, and still we moved on.

There was one large canyon, over a kilometer wide and two hundred meters deep. We couldn't go around it, and there was no way for a tractor to crawl down inside it. Instead, we anchored a crane at the top and lowered our tractors and all but five of the men. The five took the crane apart, lowered the pieces, and climbed down. Then we crossed the canyon, and five of us climbed the opposite wall. We dropped a light line and used that to pull up a heavy cable. Then for two days we pulled up, by hand, our disassembled crane.

When it was assembled on the canyon lip, one tractor on the canyon floor was used to haul the others, one by one, straight up the side of that sheer cliff. Once the cable failed, and a tractor tumbled out of the sling to smash itself to bits on the rocks below. The next tractor went up full of men.

We went on, through sandstorms and hurricanes. Fifteen days after we left the Rim we were just under a hundred miles south of Deucalion Crater. We set up our base camp there.

The main force was commanded by an old Rimrat named Hiram Zemansky who had been an engineer on Earth; there seemed to be nothing he couldn't do. I had my final conference with him at dawn in the big pressure tent with an air lock we had set up as a command post.

His group would keep the tractors, and they were in no hurry.

My own command waited outside. There were forty of us, all young men, and all, like me, less than a Mars year from Earth. Some had been apprentice Marsmen in other stations. The rest were escapees fleeing labor contracts. They weren't devoted to the cause of independence—they weren't devoted to anything. But they said they wanted to fight, and they were young and tough. We needed them.

The plan was to walk in—if we could. Being accustomed to Earth gravity, we could carry nearly twice as much as the old-timers and those born on Mars, but that wouldn't be enough; we could carry only three days' supplies, and we had a hundred and fifty miles to go, with a battle at the end of the trek.

"Call it nine days," I told Hiram. "That leaves us a little time to get into position. If all goes well, we'll hit them at dawn on the ninth day from now."

"Right." He grinned at me, but there wasn't much humor in it. "Think you can handle that bunch?" he asked.

I shrugged. "They're not much different from Dog Soldiers. We'll get by." There was nothing more to say. I took a letter from my pouch and handed it to Zemansky. "See that Erica Hendrix gets this if I don't get back."

"Sure. You'll be back."

"Yeah. Piece of cake."

"You give the signal and we'll come a-runnin'," Hiram said. "You'll be back home in a month."

"Sure. Okay, here we go." I went out to where my command was waiting for me.

Our packs lay on the ground. They were enormous. When we'd practiced this back at Ice Hill and I'd first seen what we were supposed to carry, I thought the Skipper had gone crazy. When I got that thing hoisted onto my shoulders, I was sure of it.

"Load up," I said. We sat on the ground and struggled into the straps, then gingerly got to our feet. The camp looked very comfortable. The journey by tractor had been miserable, but now, under that load, I was already beginning to miss it.

"Move out." I waved forward, toward the north. We began the long march.

We walked in silence. I could hear grunts from the men, but even at the start we didn't have much breath to waste on conversation. Our radios were set to the lowest power, only a couple of hundred meters range, and as the column strung out many of the troops were isolated from everyone except their partners; we marched in a three-man buddy system. "One to break his leg, one to stay with him, and one to go for help."

We picked our way in single file, our three-man groups strung out over a kilometer of flat terrain broken by boulders and small craters. From the top of an occasional gentle rise we could see the rim of Deucalion ahead of us, but most of the time there was nothing but the next rock, or the helmet of the man in front of you.

Within minutes my legs felt ready to give out. Those packs were *heavy!* It takes a hundred pounds of equipment just to keep a man alive on Mars: air pressure regulator and recycler; pressure suit and helmet; insulated clothing; your share of a five-man pressure tent for shelter at night and at meal times; sleeping bag; batteries. Another 36 pounds a day per man of expendables: food, water, air, and air tankage. Three days worth is 108 pounds— 208 pounds per backpack.

In Mars gravity that's only 80 pounds. I kept telling myself that. Soldiers on Earth used to carry that much. The Foreign Legionnaires marched into battle with 90 pounds. But ours had the *mass* of 208 pounds. When you get that moving, it *keeps* moving. It's as if you had to push a washing machine across an ice pond.

We carried few weapons. We'd get those the same way we'd get our supplies. If the air and water didn't come through, we wouldn't need weapons.

I sang to myself. After a while some of the others joined in. "It's eighty-six miles to water, my lads, it's ninety-nine more to beer, if I hadn't been born a damn bloody fool, I'd not be a volunteer." Left. Right.

Break for ten minutes every hour. Across the level stretches we can make five kilometers in fifty minutes. Lie down on the breaks, you need the rest. Wait for stragglers to catch up. If you don't keep up, your break is shorter. Keep an eye on your watch; it's easy to stay down too long, and you'll stiffen up. That's it. Up again, and move on.

We were faceless men under our helmets. When we moved out we looked like huge packs with legs. I knew them all by name, but little else. Don Plemmons, my second in command. Lonny Wilson, a kid from Washington, D.C.—almost a neighbor, he'd heard of the Dog Soldiers!—who'd been one of Commander Farr's last recruits and was scheduled to move in with me when I set up station in the valley I still thought of as my own.

Left. Right. Sing again. "When John Henry was a little baby, sittin' on his mammy's knee, he said that Big Bend tunnel on the C&O road is gonna cause the death of me, Lord God! gonna cause the death of me . . ." Left. Right.

The day ended, somehow. Eight hours of marching. A little over twenty-three miles. We set up camp in a hollow out of the wind and collapsed, too tired even to eat.

If they had a chance they'd go back. I knew that. If they got together and talked it over they'd turn back. But one can't go back alone. Two can't. If any go on, all go on, because they were men and men have pride.

Wilson told me the four others in his tent were ready to quit. He didn't say more.

"And you?" I asked.

He just looked at me. I recognized the expression. It was just the way I used to look at the older members, back when I first joined the Dog Soldiers and had pride in my gang. *I am as tough as you,* the look said. He cleared his throat. "I'm game."

I wasn't. But how could I go back? I'd said I'd lead this damned-fool expedition. Erica would be glad to see me— but how could I face Sarge? How could I face me? I couldn't crawl home and admit defeat now. Not after I said I could do it. "Break camp and load up."

Wilson went out to hustle the others. The sun was an hour high when we started. We looked back longingly toward the horizon to the south, but when I turned north they followed. First Wilson, then the others, three by three.

At noon we reached the point of no return. We were a day and a half from the base camp, half our air gone. If we went on from here we were committed. An irrevocable decision. A nice word, that: irrevocable. No outs. No turning back, unless you turn back now, this minute, this second—

I didn't halt. This was not even time for a break. By the time I let them stop to rest—let us, let *myself* stop to rest—there was nothing for it but to go on. Committed. Irrevocable.

Shortly after we got moving again we came to a deep chasm, thirty meters wide, a hundred deep, stretching as far as we could see to either side. A grapnel flung across it caught on the third try. Wilson shed his pack and swarmed across handover-hand, dangling above the canyon floor, swaying in the wind—

He made it. God knows how. More lines were thrown, and soon we had a rope bridge. Wilson had to come back for his pack. No one could possibly have carried it for him. The wind swayed the bridge, and my pack was enormously heavy as I shuffled, one foot at a time, over the narrow gorge.

It was still relatively level terrain. Tomorrow will be the worst, I told myself. How can it get any worse than this?

Left. Right. Sing, damn you! "Now the Cap'n said to Johnny Henry, gonna bring me a steam drill 'round, gonna take that steam drill out on the job, gonna hammer the mountains right down, Lord God, gonna hammer the mountains right down. And John Henry said to that Cap'n, and there was fire a-flashin' in his eye, with a twelve-pound hammer and a four-foot handle, gonna beat your steam drill or I'll die, Lord God. . ." Left. Right.

Camp at dusk. Inflate the tents. Put the dehydrated food to soaking. You'll eat it cold, there's no heat. Everyone inside, into sleeping bags, before the chill sets in. Eat, and lie back on the rocky ground.

The packs were lighter the next day. We had used two days' supplies, seventy Earth pounds, almost half the weight we carried. There was another gorge ahead of us, but we crossed it easily. Sing happier songs. The rhythm of the trail, get into it, you've got a fifty-pound pack and no worries, so it's uphill now, so what? When we crossed the gorge, we were at the edge of Deucalion crater.

Like most craters, Deucalion slopes gently outward. The inner face is sheer cliff. That would be a problem when we came to it. For now, onward and upward. "And the white man said to John Henry, black man damn your soul, you're going to beat that drill of mine when the rocks in the mountains turn to gold, Lord God, when the rocks in the mountains turn to gold. And John Henry say to that white man, Lord a man ain't nothin' but a man, but before I let your steam drill beat me down, gonna die with my hammer in my hand, Lord God . . ."

Pick up the pace. This is the critical day. Today we have to climb high enough to be in line-of-sight back to Zemansky's group, or we have had it.

Damn fool stunt, Garrett. Damn fool. Left. Right. "And John Henry said to his shaker, black man why don't you sing, I'm a-slingin' twelve pounds from my hips on down, just you listen to that cold steel ring, Lord God, just you listen to that cold steel ring . . ."

We made camp at dusk. Just before dark I set up the signal laser on its tripod and aimed it precisely at the top of a flat mesa three days march behind us. I opened the focus out as far as it would go, and played it across the eastern edge of the tabletop forty miles away.

Wilson crouched beside me, his helmet touching mine. "Be like the bastards to be off playing cards."

"That'd fix us," I said. I tongued the mike button. "Big Mama, this is John Henry. Over."

Nothing. I tried again. And again.

"There." Wilson was shouting. "There, I saw it! Flash of light!"

"Maybe." Our photophone target was only a meter in diameter. I slaved our transmitter to our target and waited. Forty miles away Zemansky's troops played their transmitter across our area. When their beam hit our target, our unit sent back a response; with time they would be able to focus in, setting their transmission unit in micrometer steps until it was precisely aimed at our reflector, then narrow the focus. "Maybe."

"Cheep." It was one of the loveliest sounds I had ever heard, the tone that indicated they'd touched our target with their beam. "Cheep . . . cheep . . . cheep, cheep, cheep cheep cheepcheepcheep—Hello, John Henry, this is Big Mama. Do you read us? Over."

I stood and gave the victory signal, hands together over my head. The men around me were cheering, I knew, but I couldn't hear them. We were in radio silence.

"Big Mama, I hear you. I read you three by four, over."

"Stand by, John Henry, incoming mail at twenty-three hundred hours, I say again, twenty-three hundred hours. Godspeed. Big Mama out!"

"So we wait some more," I told Wilson.

He nodded, but there was a grin a mile wide on his face. I only then realized that he hadn't believed this would work.

I still wasn't so sure it would.

★★★
CHAPTER THIRTEEN
★★★

I was exhausted, but I couldn't sleep. Neither could the others. We had air to last until morning. The two hours until twenty-three hundred dragged on, and on.

Back at base camp they would have us located exactly. The survey laser was slaved to their communication unit; once they had it aimed at us, they had direction and range within centimeters. I lay back in my sleeping bag imagining what was happening on the mesa forty miles to the south.

Eighteen hundred pounds of supplies loaded into the rocket. Ceramic tanks of alcohol and oxygen for propellant. Everything was made of ceramic and fiberglass, everything that could be, so that when the rocket tripped the radar scanners on Deucalion rim above us, it would look to the Feddie observers like nothing more than a meteroid coming in at a shallow angle.

It would never have worked on Earth.

I wondered if it would work here. It was a bit late for

that question. Twenty-three hundred hours. We watched, and I listened.

"John Henry, this is Big Mama."

"Big Mama, go."

"On the way."

We saw nothing, of course; the bird didn't need a lot of power to fling it forty miles. It burned out a few seconds after it was launched.

We waited another minute. "It's there," Big Mama said.

We were ready. A dozen men were suited up and went out searching with radio receivers. The homing signal the supply rocket sent was deliberately weak, carrying no more than a few hundred meters at most.

Wait some more. Then one of the troops was running toward me. He came up and gestured. The victory signal.

We had supplies for three more days.

The next day was the worst of all. Our packs were full again, and we were climbing uphill. Each step was agony. Onward and upward. Left. Right. But by God we were going to make it! "John Henry say to that Cap'n, looky yonder what I do see, well your hole done choke and your drill done broke, and you can't drive steel like me! Lord God, you can't drive steel like me!"

In late afternoon we made camp below the rim. There was a Feddie observation post no more than two kilometers away. We knew that from the map, but we never saw it. We crossed the rim at night, when Phobos was up high enough to give light to the weird landscape around us. I left four men and supplies at the lip; they were our signal relay station. Then we strung lines and lowered ourselves into Deucalion crater.

We made camp after midnight, and we were up at dawn, but now we were confident. At the bottom of the cliffs we divided our already tiny force. Plemmons and nine men angled off to the right, headed for the monorail that ran from the rim to the storage area. My group kept on straight ahead.

It wasn't a smooth plain. There were rocks and boulders, and the crater floor was cracked and broken. We picked our way across, glad of the wind and dust that made us invisible to anyone above who might be looking down into the crater.

The next supply rocket was tricky: we had no direct line of sight to Zemansky. Instead we relayed through the detachment on the rim. They had survey equipment and could locate us relative to them; and they were in line of sight to the main camp. It was a simple double-offset problem, and I shouldn't have worried, but I did. I worried about everything.

The rocket almost hit us. We actually saw it fall, no more than a hundred meters away.

And on the night of the eighth day, two more: supplies and weapons. Deucalion power station was less than five kilometers ahead. We'd made it.

"Now the white man that invented that steam drill, well he thought that it was so fine, and John Henry drove in fourteen feet, and the steam drill only made nine, Lord God! and the steam drill only made nine."

★ ★ ★

It was an hour before dawn. The men were in position, and there was nothing to do but watch the second hand of my watch as it ticked toward H-hour. I watched it and recalled the last conference with Sarge and Commander Farr.

"The main garrison is at the rim," Farr had said, "The guards at the storage center itself are mostly officers, and not many of those. It has to be that way. The Feddies don't trust anyone with that kind of power. They don't think they have to, anyway. No one can get close to the depository without alerting the rim garrison. Or so they think."

"You surprise 'em, you got 'em!" Sarge had added. "Just blast your way in. You won't be fightin' more than fifty people. Don't give 'em time to organize. They'll never know what hit them."

The second hand ticked over. I turned my radio to full power. "Now!"

Two dozen rocket launchers fired shaped charges at the station in front of us: air locks, tunnel walls, any exposed place. We reloaded and fired another volley. Then we rushed forward.

Wilson's group had stripped to the minimum, discarding every metal object not needed for survival, then crawled right up to the main entrance. They rushed forward with satchel charges, and dashed away again. The air-lock doors blew off, More rockets were fired into the tunnel to blow holes in the inner doors. Again Wilson's people dashed forward, and the entrance was blown open.

We poured into the tunnels. We threw grenades into every passageway, never turning a corner without throwing a grenade around it first. There was a guard room just inside the main entrance; they were still struggling into their helmets when we got inside and shot them down.

They weren't Marsmen. Half the station personnel died because they couldn't find their helmets in time. Many of them had taken off their skin-tights when they went to bed; these had no chance at all. We grenaded their rooms anyway.

It became a nightmare. Bloody corpses lay in the corridors, in the barracks, everywhere. We blasted open more airtight doors and threw explosives through them, then dashed down another corridor, firing as we went, yelling and screaming like madmen.

The only sound was our own screaming. Grenades exploded silently. Rifles grew momentary orange flowers, but soundlessly, soundlessly; through it all we yelled into our radios.

There is a madness that takes control of men in combat, it is an ugly madness that lets you do things that later you cannot even comprehend. I remember very little of that fight.

"Wilson. No!" I shouted. We had reached the reactor control room. The door was airtight, and Wilson was placing a plastique charge against it. I had to struggle with him. If his hands had not been occupied with the explosive, if he had held a pistol in one of them, he would have killed me.

"No," I told him. "We can give them a chance to surrender. They're the last." There was a phone jack on the bulkhead, and I plugged my helmet set into it. "Hello in there."

After a moment there was an answer. "Who the—who are you?"

"Acting Lieutenant Pittson, Free Mars Army. Will you surrender?"

"What will you do with us?" the man demanded.

"Power station technicians will operate the reactor. Everybody else will be treated as a prisoner of war. We'll be glad to send you back to Marsport as soon as exchanges can be arranged. How many of you are there?"

There was no answer.

"I'm sure you can figure out a way to kill me while I stand here talking to you," I said. "And then what? My troops will blast you out of there. If you're waiting for the rim garrison to come rescue you, forget it." I sounded a lot more confident than I was. If everything had gone well, Plemmons had cut the monorail line from the rim, and Zemansky's force was racing across the plains to reinforce us.

"I give you one minute," I said.

"Can we trust you?"

"That's a dumb question," I said. "You've got no choice. You have my word as a Free Mars officer that you won't be harmed if you surrender—and my word again that we can and will dig you out if we have to."

Half the minute went by. Then: "Some of us don't have suits in here. We surrender. But how can we open the door?"

"We'll manage." After the last few days, a technical problem was a relief. "We'll rig a temporary pressure wall," I said. "Wilson, get on it."

Deucalion power station was ours.

★ ★ ★

"Garrett! I've got a relay to Plemmons!" The signalman was urgently pulling me toward his radio.

"Okay. A second." I turned to the chief of the power station technicians. "All right. None of our people understands this place." I waved, indicating the control room, with its walls covered with meters and oscilloscopes, and the three big consoles that controlled the system. "But we'll know if power is not getting through to Marsport and Edom. If that power cuts out, we have no reason to hold this place. We'll blow it to hell and gone."

I turned to one of my own troopers, a nineteen-year-old from California. I spoke loud enough so the dozen prisoners could hear me. "Kehiayan, you're in charge. If they do anything funny, put 'em outside. You needn't bother with giving them air tanks."

"Rog."

"Okay, Doug, let's go."

Communications were a problem. Plemmons was out on the crater floor somewhere, a long way out of line of sight. The only way we could talk was through our relay station up on the rim.

"Barnstorm, this is John Henry, go ahead," I said.

"John Henry, this is Barnstorm. We cut the monorail. A trainload of Feddies came out of the garrison when you attacked. We stopped the train, but there's two hundred of them headed your way. We can't hold 'em. We'll keep sniping the repair crews to halt the train."

"How far away?"

"We're about fifty kilometers from you. They offloaded some tractors."

"Tractors or tanks?" I asked.

"Both. I have to go, we're down to four men."

"God bless you—"

"Yeah, there's none like us. Barnstorm out."

"Get me the relay station," I told the communications man.

"John Henry, this is Relay One. Over."

"You monitor that call from Plemmons?"

"Right."

"Where's the main force?"

"Headed in at flank speed."

"Get a message to Zenansky. Have him broadcast to Marsport. We've got the power station. If they shell this place, or take it away from us, we'll blow hell out of it. If they leave us alone, we'll keep the power coming. Make sure everybody knows that. Get Mars Industries Association to understand it, too."

"Roger, John Henry."

Wilson had come up while I was talking. "Think they'll hold off?" he asked.

"Doubt it. Not now, not until they're sure they can't recover the bomb makings. How're you doing on the vault?"

"Blew open clean. What do we do with that stuff?"

"Get some of those transport containers out into the flatland, and bury 'em. Report where you've hidden them to Relay One, but don't make any maps."

Wilson eyed me narrowly. "It's that way, huh?

"Okay."

I took a dozen troops and went forward toward the approaching Feddies. We had to hold them until

Zemansky's group could get to us. We deployed in broken ground a kilometer from the big dome-shape of the station.

"Try to keep between them and the reactor containment," I told them. "They won't shoot heavy stuff if they think it'll wreck the power plant. They don't know how many of us there are. Keep moving, and make 'em think there's a lot."

Then we lay down and waited.

Do men love war? Certainly it is easier to fight than to think about it. What had those Feddies done to me? They were young men, like us, some with families. They'd joined up to see the world, or for the pay, or even, I suppose, because they believed in the Federation and world peace. Now they were coming to kill us, and we were waiting to kill them.

You think like that when you're waiting. You imagine a bullet tearing through your p-suit, and the blood spurting out, blood pushed by five pounds of pressure so that even veinous blood streams like a fountain. You think of what that bullet can do to you, and what the bullets in your own rifle can do to them. You wonder what the hell you're doing out here, and why you don't run like hell and let the others fight.

Such thoughts can finish you. If I had them, the others did too. "Sing, damn you," I said.

"Sing what?" someone asked.

"Anything."

Have you ever heard "The Two Grenadiers?" Why in God's name one of the troops had ever learned that, or why any of us should care about an emperor over two hundred years in his grave, I don't know; what was France to us? But it reminded us of brave men and brave deeds. We lay under the black sky of Mars, dust blowing over us, and listened.

> ". . . and under her soil to lay me,
> and when my cross on its scarlet band,
> over my heart you've bound me,
> then put my musket in my hand,
> and belt my sword around me.
> So shall I lie and listen,
> Aye!, keeping shield watch in my grave . . ."

Wilson came up behind me. He motioned out toward the horizon. Was the dust thicker out there?

> ". . . then armed will I rise from out of my grave,
> and stand as my Emperor's defender!"

"Bloody hell, what kind of song is that?" someone shouted. "I'll give you a song!

> ". . . When a man grows old,
> and his balls grow cold . . ."

I recognized the voice. Hartig, who boasted that he was the only man on Mars who knew the entire and uncut version of "Eskimo Nell." There was no tune, but it kept us from thinking about what was coming. It went on interminably.

Wilson nudged me and pointed. The dust was definitely thicker out there. We had another twenty minutes, no more. I thought about where I'd put the men. No point in moving them.

> ". . . Oh, a moose or two,
> and a caribou,
> and a couple of buffalo . . ."

I'm no expert on battles and war. After that day I never want to be. But I won't forget lying in the dust, watching the enemy column grow larger while my ears rang with the improbable exploits of Deadeye Dick and Mexico Pete.

As they started to fan out, we hit the lead tank with three rockets. It stopped, and one crewman leaped out. He ran for shelter, and for a moment it looked as if he'd make it, but then he fell. Deadeye Dick was at Number Eighteen, with Eskimo Nell looking coldly on. The song stopped. There wasn't any need for it; once the fight starts you don't think. You just do what you have to.

The dust helped; they couldn't know how many they were fighting. They tried to circle around us, but on that broken ground men afoot were as fast as any tractor. And they were not Marsmen. They had been trained to fight on Earth, where they had helicopters, where a man couldn't vanish in deep shadow and be hidden five feet from you and you never know it. We crept among them, using knives in the dark shadow, leaving them to find their comrades with their hoses cut, blood spurting from their ruined lungs.

Before long they were as afraid as we were. And we couldn't run: without the power station, we'd be out of air inside a few hours. We couldn't run, but they could—as long as they had their tractors.

I realized that and we concentrated on the vehicles. Crawl through the rocks until you can get a shot at a tractor. Fire the rocket launcher and retreat, leaving the tractor disabled; and let the Feddies wonder how they'll get out when the last tractors are gone.

They moved their vehicles out of range. Now it was hand-to-hand among the broken rocks. A concentrated charge would have broken through, but they never did that. They came in little groups, trying to infiltrate.

But they could lose ten to our one, and they'd still win. We were forced back into a tighter and tighter perimeter. I had no count on how many I had left. Twenty? A dozen? I looked at my watch. Incredibly, two hours had passed since the fight had begun.

They broke past us at two places. I had no choice now. "Into the station," I ordered. We crept in, through the holes we'd blown in the tunnels earlier in the morning, and waited. It was quiet out there.

Wilson was gone. I called my communications man. "Get into the control room and tell Kehiayan to stand by. We'll have to blow this place."

"They haven't come in," Doug said. "What are they waiting for?"

"Don't know. What are *you* waiting for? Move—"

"Kind of hate to give up just now."

They still weren't coming. We were crouched in the tunnel, weapons facing the entrance. Then there was a bright flash of light out there. I could only see the light, not what caused it. There was another. Something had exploded just at the entrance. I felt the ground shake.

There was a man at the entrance. Six rifles aimed at him, but he came in with his hands high, waving the red flag of Free Mars.

The relief force had come.

★★★
CHAPTER FOURTEEN
★★★

We brought the uranium back to Ice Hill. We were greeted as heroes. Saviors of Free Mars. So naturally when I put in for a transfer to a nice, safe, rear-area solar cell production facility, it was granted.

Like hell. The trouble with armies is the screwups get the soft jobs; do something right and they tag you for another hairy mission. To make it worse, although they did give me a couple of weeks soft duty around Ice Hill, it didn't do much good, because they put Erica on the goddamn atom bomb design project. Here I went and got their uranium and they used it as an excuse to put my girl to work twenty-three hours a day.

We got another benefit out of Deucalion: Mars-port had to talk to us. They didn't quite recognize us as a legal government, but what could they do? They had to have the power from Deucalion. The Feddie government might have thought different, but the big companies had no doubts. They needed that power. If it took negotiating with a bunch of criminals, then that's what it took.

We didn't need a big garrison to hold the power station. Sentries could see any attack as soon as it crossed the crater rim—and we made sure Mars Industries Association knew what our commander's instructions were: don't fight for the station, blow it up and run like hell. Blackmail on the grand scale, but it worked.

Our raid had been successful, and something to be proud of, but it wasn't the key event of the war. While we were taking the station, another crew had captured the Federation's orbiting spaceship. Free Mars had a navy.

That was a complicated operation, carried out by Marsmen who'd had experience in space. Commander Farr had planned to lead it himself and would have if his physician had let him go; but Ruth Hendrix wasn't about to let him expose himself to six gravities.

You must start with five pounds of fuel to send one pound from Earth orbit to Mars, or vice versa. The same five pounds of fuel is needed regardless of whether the pound sent between planets is payload or ship structure, so ship designers work like mad to keep the ships light and build in no more structural strength than they need. The ships never accelerate at more than a tenth of a gravity—so why build them to stand up to more than that? That means the ships can never land. They go from orbit to orbit, but they never touch down on either Earth or Mars.

People go up to and come down from the ships by landing boat, but fuel and cargo are sent up with laser launchers. At Marsport there's a big field of lasers, all aiming into mirrors. Those mirrors are focused onto one big mirror at the end of the field. Cargo capsules ride a track onto a platform over that mirror, the lasers are turned on, and the cargo pods are shoved upward at six gravities. The space expeditionary force rode up in cargo capsules.

It was an inside job, of course. Farr and the Marsport members of the revolutionary committee had been planning it for years, placing agents in the right jobs in the spaceport, finding out which officials could be bribed, and all the rest of it. When the time came the patriots with space experience got into the capsules, rode up as cargo, and took over the ship.

It sounds simple. I'm sure it wasn't. I've heard a dozen versions of the battle for the Feddie ship, and the tamest one is enough to curl my hair. But they took her, and we now had an operational spaceship—fueled for the trip to Earth.

"That's why we've got to get working bombs," Erica said. I'd been pestering her to take some time off from work while I still had leave.

"You're going to drop atomic bombs on Earth?" I was horrified. "It's the stupidest thing I ever heard of! They'll sterilize Mars."

"We're not going to drop the bombs," Erica said. "We're going to threaten to drop the bombs. But only if they bomb us. We know we can't do any real damage to Earth—but we can knock out a big city. And we don't have to tell them which city it will be."

"Aha." I thought about that. "So every city's got a reason to argue against Feddie interference with us.

Devilish. Only how do you know all this? You're not on the Committee."

"No, but I wouldn't work on the damned bombs until they told me what they were going to do with them. Would you?"

"I wouldn't work on the damn things at all. The whole idea gives me the willies. I want no part of atom bombs."

So, of course, I got sent out to explode one.

There are no airplanes on Mars. Can't be: not enough air. The usual means of transportation is by tractor or monorail. But Mars is big: half the diameter of Earth, meaning a quarter of Earth's surface area; since Earth is three-quarters covered with water, there's as much land on Mars as there is on Earth.

Most settled areas on Mars are in the southern hemisphere because southern hemisphere summers are a whack of a lot longer than northern hemisphere summers. It's not that way on Earth, but Earth has a circular orbit. Mars is closer to the sun during summer in the south. The growing season is longer, and the mine strikes were made here.

Most settlements are in the south, but not all. The most interesting scientific features are in the north: Nix Olympica, the big canyons, most active volcanoes. The first settlements in the north were scientific laboratories in the Tharsis Region, where the volcanoes are. Even in the north it's easier to live on Mars than to get here; certainly it was in the early days, so the scientists came to stay. They brought their wives and their students; after a while technicians and farmers and support people came out and stayed as well.

This was before the Federation. The first Mars settlements were founded by the United States in a cooperative effort among NASA and a lot of private foundations and universities. They didn't exactly thrive, but they were more or less self-supporting. Then the first wave of true colonists came, and the big mineral strikes were made halfway around Mars, near Hellas Rim and Edom and Iapygia where Marsport is located. The new colonies were linked together with monorails, but it was too far around to the earlier places, Livermore and New Chicago and Cal Tech's Pasadena East. Still, there had to be some means of getting from the old scientific colonies to the new commercial ones five thousand miles away. There wasn't a lot of traffic back and forth, but there was some.

If you don't have airplanes and there's no monorail, there is only one way to get across that much distance on Mars: a ballistic rocket. This isn't an airplane, although it looks a little like one. It is a reusable rocket ship with wings. It takes off on rocket power and is hurled like a bullet or a shell, traveling in free fall until it comes back into the thin Martian atmosphere and the wings can bite.

It still doesn't fly. It glides at hypersonic speed, until it has slowed down to where the pilot can turn it on its tail and let it fall toward the surface. Then he lights the rocket again and settles down gently—if everything is working. The first probes from Earth to Mars landed almost that way; the technique is hardly new.

It's a lousy system for short-range travel, but the only way to go long distances.

When Katrinkadorp rose and threw out the Feddies, there was a passenger rocket at Botha Field. After a complex series of negotiations, Commander Farr persuaded them to fly the ship down to the Rim. The reason was simple enough: Farr and the Free Mars Committee thought it wouldn't take much to bring the old university colonies into the independence movement. They wanted to send political agents to New Chicago to negotiate with the Regents who governed the scientific colonies. We had many allies, both student and faculty, and the Feddie garrison was small. It shouldn't take much to throw out the Feddies— but first the Regents had to be convinced that independence was possible and that the new government wouldn't cut off their connections with their colleagues back on Earth.

None of this concerned me. I'd heard that we had a ship and that some of the Rim stations were working to manufacture fuel for it—liquid oxygen was no problem, we made that every day, but rocket fuel is something else again—but I wasn't involved.

The hell I wasn't.

I'd been hanging around Erica's workshop. I was irritated because they wouldn't let me in there. Nobody but project personnel allowed. I'd got the goddamn uranium for them. They wouldn't *have* any project to work on if my troops and I hadn't given ourselves a permanent case of flat feet marching across the goddamn planet.

To top it off, Erica had been working when she wasn't asleep, and in the little time we did have together she acted mysterious, hinting that something big was coming but she wouldn't tell me what. She was worried and moody. Not much fun to be around. So we fought like cats and dogs in the little time we had together.

If I sound a little bitter, like a neglected hero, you've got it. If that sounds a little childish, you're right again. So what? It was the way I felt.

So there I stood, looking for an excuse to be near the lab in case she came out, when Perry found me. "Hey, Garrett, the Old Man wants to see you." Then he went into the lab. *He* got to go in. He was messenger and aide to Commander Farr. Ten-year-old kid brother gets in, but not old Garrett.

I wandered up to the study, wondering what Farr wanted this time, and knowing it meant a new assignment. I'd had three weeks since I got back with the uranium. To hell with the war, and independence, and—

Oh, I didn't mean it, of course. In the first place, if we didn't win, my future on Mars was a little less appetizing than the future I'd had on Earth. And I could hardly complain about Army Mickey Mouse, because we didn't have any. In theory I was an officer—full lieutenant, instead of just acting—and exempt from what little bullshit there was. Not that the rank meant much. I was Lieutenant Pittson, and Sarge was just "Sarge," whatever that meant, but he sure as hell outranked me, which was as it should have been. And if anybody had tried to get some old Rimrat like Zeke Terman to salute me, it might have been interesting for a couple of minutes . . .

No, I was just unhappy because nobody paid much attention to me. I didn't have anything to do. I suspected he was about to fix that.

"Come in, Garrett," Farr said. He looked much better:

the swelling was gone from around his face, and he could use his left hand a little, enough to hold a coffee cup anyway. You wouldn't have known what they'd done to him unless you saw him walking. "Have a seat."

"Yes, sir." Farr was the only one of us who rated a 'sir,' and he didn't insist on it.

"We seem to be winning this war," Farr said.

"Yes, sir." That was the word we had, anyway. The Federation held the cities, but now that we had Deucalion and the orbital ship and a couple of dozen other important centers, nearly every independent station owner had come out for Free Mars. The Feddies had stopped trying to take over our territory; now they were defending what they had, and getting nervous about it at that.

"Unfortunately, there are Federation Councilors on Earth who don't believe it," Farr said.

"*They* don't believe that we have the power to destroy an Earth city. Or they pretend they don't believe it. And they have not informed the people of Earth that we have the capability to make atomic weapons."

"But they must know we can—"

Farr shrugged. "Perhaps. Perhaps not. You believed it impossible. And most of the people of Earth do not know what was kept at Deucalion." He shrugged again. "There are also divisions among the miners' representatives here. Some of them are asking what is in independence for their people. Ah. Come in, Erica."

I looked around. She was a mess. She hadn't been getting enough sleep, and her eyes were red with dark bags under them. She hadn't been out of her p-suit in days, and I doubt she'd changed coveralls very recently either. Her hair was up in braids, not very flattering.

She nodded to me; we'd been fighting again.

"Well?" Farr asked.

She sank into a chair. I'd never seen her so worn out. "If the theory's right, it will work. Dr. Weinbaum says it will, anyway."

"And you think so?"

"Yes."

"Then we're ready. Do you still want to do this?"

She leaned forward, and some color came back into her face. Her eyes shone, the way they did the first night I met her. "Try and stop me!"

"I don't want to stop you. You can leave in the morning. The ship is ready."

"What's going on here?" I asked.

Farr regarded me coldly. "I'm sending Erica and one of the weapons to New Chicago. Do you want to go as military escort?"

"New Chicago?" The more I thought about that, the less I liked it. "You mean you're going to put Erica and that damned bomb into a rocket plane and blast her halfway around Mars? The hell you are!

"Garrett," Erica said. "Shut up."

"You shut up! I'm not letting you get in that stupid thing. What do they need a bomb for, anyway? What is all this—"

"Enough!" Farr shouted. "Lieutenant Pittson. The question is not whether Erica goes. That is settled, and you have no choice in the matter. The question is whether you will go, and frankly I don't think you're the proper man for the job, even if Erica has insisted that you come with her—"

"And just why isn't Garrett the right man?" Erica's voice was coldly polite.

"I think the two of you will drive me crazy," Farr said. "This is not only a technical job, it is also a diplomatic mission. You'll be working with university people, not Rimrats. Customs are different in the old colonies. And diplomacy is not precisely Garrett's strongest point."

"He'll be all right," Erica insisted. "And I want him with me. If—"

I didn't like the way she said that. "*If* what?" I asked.

Farr didn't answer immediately. He looked at Erica, then back to me, and finally came to a decision. "I see I must explain. Garrett, that weapon must not fall into anyone else's hands. And we cannot allow the Federation to capture anyone who knows how many weapons we have. That is the main reason for the security we've put on the labs. What you don't know, you can't be forced to tell—and given modern interrogation methods, don't kid yourself that you won't tell everything you know. You will. It only takes time."

He looked at his left hand and tried to flex the fingers. "Fortunately, they did not have time in my case. And Mr. Ellsworth was less interested in information than in punishing a traitor. He is not a subtle man."

"Now wait a minute," I said. "You're saying that rather than be captured, we're supposed to commit suicide?"

"No. You don't know anything important. But Erica does. I believe the Padre preaches against suicide . . ."

"No! Goddamn it, are you telling me I have to kill Erica?"

"If that is the only alternative to capture, yes." He seemed pretty damn calm about it.

"I won't do it," I said.

"I supposed you would say that. So you will not be going. Someone else will."

"With the same orders," I said.

"Of course.

"That's inhuman!"

"Perhaps." Farr looked to Erica. She had shrunk down in her chair and looked miserable. "I told you," Farr said.

"Just wait," she said. She looked at me. "Please, Garrett? Nothing is going to happen. But if—well, I'd rather you were with me."

"But I love you," I told her. "Lord God, we fight a lot, but I do love you. How can you do this? Can't they send someone else?"

"Who?" Farr demanded.

"You will not send anyone else. Garrett, I have to do this. It's for the Project! Don't you see? I have to go."

I began to understand, then. "It's a lousy choice you're giving me."

"Nothing's going to happen," she said.

"If I thought this wouldn't work," Farr said, "I wouldn't risk it."

"The hell you wouldn't," I said. "You send women on suicide missions every day—"

"But I do not send out an irreplaceable weapon," Farr said. "I do not expect any trouble at all. But the military escort on this mission *must* understand the situation. Now, are you going or not?"

It was one hell of a choice, but not really. How could I stay behind, now that I knew what the orders were? I certainly couldn't stop her from going. I knew that. "All right, damn you, I'll go."

Before the Skipper opened his mouth I knew what the next thing would be. "Sarge tells me you're a Marsman," Farr said. "Are you?"

"Yes, sir."

"I have your word."

"Yes, sir."

"You'll leave in the morning. Under the circumstances, you're both off duty until then. I'll arrange for someone to put the gear you'll need aboard the ship."

CHAPTER FIFTEEN

When the dust is blowing, Mars' dawns are more brilliantly red than Earth's best sunsets. Thin clouds form streams of pink across the horizon, while overhead the stars shine with a luster you can never see on Earth. We watched the sunrise from the lip of a small crater about a hundred kilometers from Ice Hill. Farr's people had covered the crater with a nylon net; under it stood the rocket.

The bird stood on her tail inside the crater; when they rolled back the camouflage net, I saw that she was big, as big as a small airliner on Earth. I don't know why I'd expected something smaller. We didn't get a chance to see it very well because they hustled us down and inside and strapped us into seats.

There were eight of us as passengers. My own party, aside from Erica and myself, was Plemmons, who'd cut the monorail line back at Deucalion, and Doug, my communications man. In the forward seats were Dr. Weinbaum and two members of the Revolutionary Committee.

Weinbaum had been Chief Scientist for Mars Westinghouse. All the years he'd been with them he'd been part of the Mars freedom movement. I think some of the top brass at Westinghouse had suspected—the companies are perfectly capable of playing both sides of the street. Anyway, when the fighting broke out Weinbaum fled Marsport and eventually wound up at Ice Hill. I didn't know the other two. The three of them had big powwow to make with the Regents at New Chicago.

Their escort was Kehiayan, who'd been with me at Deucalion; this was like old home week. I didn't have to ask what his orders were if it looked like Weinbaum was going to be captured. They didn't give us much time for comradely reunion, and it was just as well; none of us were very cheerful. We remembered how many we'd left at Deucalion. Once they got us strapped in they brought in a box about a meter long and half that in cross section, and strapped it into the seat next to Erica. Nobody mentioned it. I looked at it and shuddered. Okay, it's a silly reaction; but after all, the Federation was formed to keep Earth safe from nuclear wars, and every teacher in school had pounded in the lesson that there was nothing more horrible than an atom bomb. You don't easily get over that kind of indoctrination.

There wasn't any ceremony. First there was the noise of the engines, and then we felt weight. The ship accelerated slowly at first, then picked up until I suppose we were at two or three Earth gravities. That was no strain on me, but for Erica and the others born on Mars it was seven times what they were used to, and it must have been torture.

After a couple of minutes the engines cut. It was dead quiet in the cabin. With the low pressure you couldn't even hear whispers. Dr. Weinbaum took a pipe out of his pocket and tried to lay it down on the ashtray. It floated up and drifted away in a random air current. We were in free fall.

Erica let go the straps and shoved herself away from the chair. She pushed too hard and bounced off the ceiling, swam helplessly for a moment, and laughed. We all did. None of us had ever had a chance to play in free fall before. My one experience, coming down from the prison ship in the landing boat, didn't help; when I let go I pushed too hard and followed almost the same route Erica had. Eventually we swam over to the view port.

We were crossing from daylight into darkness. Mars looked cut in half, the dark portion only visible because it blocked out the stars. At the edge of the planet you could see the atmosphere, incredibly thin, a tiny thing. I pointed to it.

"There will be more," Erica said. "If this works. And I know it will." Her voice took on that glowing quality they all had when they talked about the Project. I didn't respond.

Directly below us was one of the famous wandering canyons that drive scientists crazy. If you saw it on Earth you'd *know* it was a dry riverbed. There are a lot of them on Mars, and they *must* have been cut by water, but nobody knows for sure where the water went—or where it came from. Right next to the canyon was a big crater, half a million years old, with no trace of water erosion.

Dr. Weinbaum was discussing it with his colleagues. "It

certainly didn't *rain*," he said. "So how does water cut a canyon as deep as any on Earth, and leave an enormous crater standing next to it untouched?"

Our trajectory carried us northwest, and we passed over the east edge of Coprates, the Grand Canyon of Mars. If the other canyons irritate the scientists, this one gives them the screaming willies. It's longer than the United States is wide, and four miles deep in places. The walls are steep cliffs as high as Earth's biggest mountains. The canyon is closed at both ends, so it certainly wasn't formed by water—but no one knows where all the cubic miles of material that used to be in there have gone.

We could just make out the monorail running from the east edge of Coprates to Novoya Sverdlovsk in Edom. There are several big mining colonies in the canyon, and the monorail stops there. The Federation had been talking about extending it westward another two thousand miles to the university colonies, but they hadn't done it. It would be a hell of a big project.

After that we were over the nightside, and we went back to our seats. I took Erica's hand, and she smiled softly, then went to sleep. I leaned back, and the pistol on my belt dug into my ribs.

It reminded me of my orders, and once again I shuddered.

As planned, we landed in darkness, in a crater forty kilometers from New Chicago. The Free Mars movement at New Chicago was supposed to send a party to meet us.

Unless the universities came over to the independence movement, we were probably there for keeps. There aren't very many independent stations near the university colonies, probably not enough to manufacture the fuel the rocket plane would need to take us home. The universities could do it, but only if they took control away from the Feddies. I wished Weinbaum well; this didn't look like a good place to try to set up a station. It was late fall in the northern hemisphere, and although we were reasonably close to the equator, it was cold outside. I went out first.

Tractors bathed us in light. Three figures got out of one tractor and came toward the plane. I held my submachine gun tightly. They came closer and raised their hands to show they were empty. A female voice came into my headset. "Listen my children, and you shall hear," she said.

"Of slithy toves, that gyre and gimbel in the slot machine," I answered.

"For all is vanity," she said. "Mars and Freedom. Welcome to New Chicago."

I relaxed. There were a dozen possible variations in those code words, but she'd given none of the warning signals. Her welcome to New Chicago was a bit premature: we were a long way from the universities, and Erica and I weren't going there. I went back in for the others. Plemmons, Doug, and Kehiayan were waiting near the hatch, weapons ready. Erica and the Committee people were clustered at the opposite end. They looked scared. "All's well," I told them.

Weinbaum and his colleagues got into one tractor, which drove away quickly. They wanted to be inside the university before dawn. There were three more tractors for my party. Erica insisted that we put the bomb in the cabin with her; she wasn't going to let it out of her sight. Doug and I got in with her, and I put Plemmons in another tractor behind us. All the tractors pulled power-unit trailers, and there was a lot of other gear loaded on them.

As soon as we were loaded we drove out of the crater. "My name's Eileen," our driver said. "Hi."

We introduced ourselves. She had heard about the big Deucalion raid. "That must have been exciting," she said. "It took a lot of guts."

"Mostly just hard work," I said, but I was flattered just the same.

There wasn't enough light to see much, but the terrain seemed to open up once we got out of the crater where the rocket plane was hidden. Eileen drove without maps, just following the compass; in a few minutes I was lost. I couldn't see her very well. She had her helmet on, faceplate open. In the dark that didn't show a lot, but she had a nice voice.

Erica didn't say anything, and after a while I told her, "Sweetheart, you've had it. Why don't you climb into the back and get some sleep? You'll have that damn bomb for a bunkmate, but I guess you've shared beds with worse."

"All right. I am tired." She climbed out of the seat, and in five minutes she was out. Doug curled up in his seat and began snoring gently.

"Wide-awake troops," Eileen said. There was a laugh in her voice.

"Been a long month," I said. "Doug's been on the perimeter patrol since Deucalion."

"I'm sorry. I didn't mean anything." We drove on through the night.

Dawn came about two hours later. First there was a faint pink tinge in the east, nothing like the spectacular dawn we had left behind, then the edge of the sun showed and we had full light. I looked at the landscape around us. It was not like the southern hemisphere. We were in a huge plain. There were very few rocks and craters and no hills at all. Just a flat plain, not much dust blowing, with isolated high mountains thrusting upward at random intervals. The mountains seemed enormous.

"Volcanoes," Eileen told me. "You don't have any in the south."

"No."

"What do you do when you're not fighting wars?" Eileen asked.

"Rimrat," I said. "Station owner. Make that apprentice station owner. I'd have my own except for the war, but it's not in yet. You?"

"Student. Mining engineering. My father's on the faculty Council, Dr. Hermans."

I'd never heard of him, but I supposed he was one of the people Weinbaum was meeting. "Erica's an engineer," I said.

"Oh? What school?"

I laughed at that. "TV screen. Hellastown library. She's a Rimrat. Her father's got one of the most successful operations on the Rim. We don't have schools."

"Oh. Is she your roommate?"

Now what the hell kind of question is that? I wondered. I remembered Farr's little talk about customs being different in the north. "We're engaged. My sponsor was negotiating with her father when the war started."

"That sounds like a business deal."

"Well, it's necessary." I tried to explain about Rim customs. "What's it like in New Chicago?"

She told me, but I didn't really understand. It was too unfamiliar. The university ran the town and owned most of it. There were labor clients, and a few transportees, but they didn't really count. Neither did the independent station owners. Eileen either didn't know or didn't care how they lived or what their customs were.

In the cities the university families tended to marry late, or set up housekeeping without marrying at all. Either way it was no big deal and there were few formalities. "Except for the religious types," she said. Children were raised by either parent, or by the university school system. A few students came up from Earth, but most were from Marsport and other "civilian" communities. That was her word, not mine. Faculty children tended to stay and become faculty members themselves; outsiders usually took their degrees and went back where they'd come from.

I told her about life on the Rim. It was almost an alien experience to her. She wanted to know how I'd gotten into the war, and I told her about the boycott because of Federation taxes. "I hadn't really thought about war," I said. "Independence was something we talked about in gatherings, but it was always going to happen a long time off. Then all of a sudden we were in the middle of it. How did you get involved with Free Mars?"

"Well, I told you my father's on the faculty Council. He's been corresponding with Dr. Weinbaum for years. So naturally I'm involved. We're not firebrand revolutionaries, Garrett. The Federation has treated us pretty well. But that doesn't mean we don't care. The whole labor client system is nothing more than slavery. We have to care." She was quiet for a moment. "What's going to happen after you people take control of Mars?"

I laughed. "We've got to do it first. Me, I'll go back and set up my station. The Skipper says I've got that coming. When the war's over, all the Rimrats will get together and rebuild Windhome, and the other ruined places, and help Erica and me get our station in. Won't be much different from the way things have always been on the Rim, except we won't have tax collectors to break our backs."

"Yes, but there's got to be some government," she said. "You can't throw out the Federation and not replace it."

"Yeah, but it's not my problem. I can leave that to the big brains."

"But what happens if you don't *like* what your revolutionary committee puts together?" she asked.

"Then I guess we'll just have to throw them out as well. What can they do? Collect taxes on the Rim again? Who with? What for? Why shouldn't we like what our own committee sets up?"

"You don't know much history, do you, Garrett?" she asked.

"No. What's that got to do with it?"

"Forget it. Tell me about the Deucalion raid. Did you kill many people? What's it like to be in a battle?"

"You don't think much about it at the time," I told her. "You just do it. The thinking comes later." Or before. Especially before. "I suppose you'll have your share of fighting here. If Weinbaum and your father can bring it off—"

"Not as much as you'd think. There aren't but a few hundred Federation people here, and some of them are university police who'll do what the faculty Council tells them. We won't have much fighting, except for the power plants."

Something about the way she said that bothered me. She must have sensed it, because she said, "We're a backwater, Gary. I suppose we're important to Mars, but as schools and scientists. How can the Federation force us to do anything? Can they force us to teach? So they leave us pretty well alone."

That wasn't what had bothered me. If they could heave the Feddies out without fighting, why hadn't they done it? Why were we hiding our ship out in a crater instead of bringing it into the New Chicago landing field? Didn't these people *care?*

I told myself it wasn't my problem. There was nothing I could do, anyway. Weinbaum would have to take care of that.

"Tell me more about the battles," she said. "Tell me what it's like."

We made camp out on the sands that night. The university people had brought plenty of gear, including a big pressure tent that would hold all of us. We met the others at dinner. There were about a dozen university people. The man in charge was Dr. Drury, a junior member of the engineering faculty at New Chicago. He explained that he was really a geophysicist, but he taught engineering, and he liked fieldwork.

There wasn't a lot of conversation. We were all tired

from bouncing around in the tractors since before dawn. The food was good, and there were three cooks who served it and cleaned up afterward. We weren't introduced to them.

Drury was a strange one. He kept talking to Erica about the bomb. It was obvious that he knew more about making them than she did, but the Federation had never let the universities have any refined uranium. The power plant was staffed by Federation people and guarded by marines, and the faculty weren't admitted.

"It's a breeder pile," Drury said. "They aren't getting anything like the efficiency they ought to. But they operate it themselves and take all the uranium back to that depository in Deucalion, then ship it back to Earth. Won't let us help them at all. Stupid."

"Garrett was in charge of the force that captured Deucalion," Eileen said.

"Oh? Good work," Drury said. He turned back to Erica, and asked her about implosion lenses. I think that's what he said.

I didn't think she was enjoying the conversation. "Guess it's about time to turn in," I said. "Don, you want the first watch?"

"Suits," Plemmons said.

"Thanks. Dr. Drury, if you'll show us where we sleep—"

Eileen looked confused. "You don't have to keep watches. We've got people to do that."

"Sorry," I said. "Orders. We watch that bomb until it goes off."

"I'll take a watch," Erica said.

"No. No need. We've got nothing else to do, but you've got brain work. Get some sleep."

They'd set up two separate pressure tents for our group and put my gear in with Erica's. I didn't like the arrangements. She wouldn't let the bomb out of her sight, and we had to keep watches. I wasn't about to have anyone—including me—sit outside at night. I made them move the four of us, and the bomb, into one tent, where one of us could sit up on watch. We slept in our p-suits and helmets anyway. The university people laughed at us for that. They had double-walled tents and weren't afraid of blowouts.

"Yeah, but what if the Feddies find out where we are?" I asked.

"They won't," Eileen said. "And they'd never get here without someone knowing they were coming. I keep telling you, my father's on the faculty Council."

I didn't understand what the hell that had to do with anything. But I hadn't missed that she said "you people" when she referred to the Free Mars movement. Maybe it wasn't the Feddies we had to worry about.

I got Erica tucked in, and Doug climbed into his sleeping bag to catch some rest. Don Plemmons and I had a few words before he took first watch.

"I don't like these people, Garrett," he said. "They treat me like dirt. They give orders like Feddies, and they don't even wait to find out if you've got something else to do."

"They've been all right to me," I said.

"You're an officer."

"What the hell difference does that make?" I asked.

"It does. Watch and see. These people aren't Marsmen, Garrett. Not Marsmen at all."

"Crap. They've been here longer than we have. Third and fourth generation."

"Yeah. But they aren't Marsmen."

"Don't be stupid. I'll relieve you in three hours," I said. "No point in trying to sleep for that short a time. I'll stay up. Maybe I can find some company in the university tent."

"Okay, chief!" He crawled into our tent. I'd rather have sat up with him, but Erica and Doug couldn't have got any sleep with us chattering.

Drury and Eileen were in the command tent. They acted glad to see me when I came in.

"Eileen has been telling me about your experiences at Deucalion." Drury said. "Maybe you can help us."

"How?"

"Well, we are going to have to storm that power plant," Drury said. "And we've never—well, maybe you could help. Command the assault force when the time comes. After all, you've got experience in that line."

"I do now. But only because we had a job to do and we did it. I'm sure your people—I mean, you've got to do it yourselves, you know. We can't take that power plant for you."

Drury looked serious. "I know that. People will be killed. I'm glad I don't have to decide who it will be. Perhaps we can persuade the Federation to give up without a fight."

"Could be." I didn't really believe it.

"Do you want a drink?" Drury asked.

"I've got guard duty coming up. I better pass."

"How about coffee?" Eileen asked.

"Coffee? Sure. We don't have any coffee on the Rim. Haven't had any since I left Earth."

"It's about time, then," Eileen said. "Joseph, some coffee for Lieutenant Pittson, please."

I hadn't seen the other man. He was sitting in the back of the tent, near the kitchen area. One of the cooks. He brought a ceramic mug and handed it to me. It smelled great. I held it to my nose and sniffed it, savoring it. "Thank you," I said. I meant it.

"You're welcome," Drury said.

I hadn't spoken to him. I'd said my thanks to Joseph, who'd brought it, but the cook had gone back to his seat in the back of the tent. I wondered about him. Labor client? Did the universities have labor clients? Why the hell would a man be a servant?

Drury had a nightcap, and excused himself. "We'll be there at noon tomorrow," he said. "Work to do. I'd better turn in. Eileen, will you be needing anything else from the kitchen?"

"I can manage," she said.

"All right. Joseph, you can go to bed now."

"Thank you, Doctor. Good night." They left together.

"More coffee?" Eileen asked.

"Sure. Thanks. How do you grow this, anyway?"

"I'm afraid I don't know," she said. "We've always had coffee at the university. You can ask the agriculture people when you meet them."

"Yeah, I'll have to." If I could grow coffee, I could get a good price for it. Or could I? Would the Rimrats have got out of the habit? Nobody born on Mars had ever tasted the stuff. Hell, if there wasn't a market I'd make one—Mars and coffee were made for each other. It would be worth it, though, just to have some for myself.

"What's with Joseph?" I asked. "Is he a labor client?"

"Good heavens, no." She was shocked. "He's a university cook. Part of the staff. Labor client!"

She laughed then. "There are fifty people who'd like to have his job." She moved over closer, almost touching me. They'd brought inflatable plastic couches.

She was a very pretty girl. Short, with dark hair and brown eyes, her hair cut short also, with a red ribbon in it. Erica had been busy the last two weeks, and I found myself having disturbing thoughts. Eileen seemed to like me, too.

Don't be a damn fool, Garrett, I told myself. You've got nothing in common with this girl. So what? myself retorted.

"I think everyone else has gone to bed," Eileen said. She leaned against me. I could feel her warmth. There was no mistaking the invitation.

"Guess I'd better have a look around the perimeter," I said.

"Why? You're not on guard for two hours. What's wrong with you?" She reached out and pulled me toward her. "I know damned well I turn you on."

"Yeah, you do. But I told you, I'm engaged—"

"What on Mars does that have to do with anything?" she asked.

"Erica is probably the most monogamous woman who ever lived," I said. "Look, I'd love to hop in the sack with you, but nothing good can come of it—"

"You people are all crazy," she spat. "Possessive relationships. Bride prices—that's what it is, isn't it? Bride price and dowry. Sexual repressions. You're primitives. Probably that's why you like fighting and wars."

"What the hell's got you mad? And we don't *like* wars. It's just that we won't be pushed around. I told you how I got into this—"

"You sure did. It sounded to me like you liked it. And you fight duels. With knives."

"Yeah, sometimes. But it's no big thing. Look, I'd better go."

"Go on. But you can't say you don't want me. And you can't tell me how it would hurt your precious Ice Queen—"

"Now what the hell are you talking about?"

Eileen laughed. "I've seen the way she treats you. Cold. Expects you to do things for her. If you two are in love, I'm a purple sand cat. But she owns you—"

"Bullshit. She's got the responsibility for that damned bomb, and she's worried about whether it will work, and—"

"Sure," Eileen said. "Sure. Just go on, now. Go prowl around the desert looking for Federation police! There aren't any for *two* hundred kilometers, I told you that, but you just go play soldier. I'm out of the mood, anyway."

There are times when I think women are a separate species entirely.

CHAPTER SIXTEEN

The volcano rose above a series of rocky plateaus piled on each other like poker chips of decreasing sizes stacked into a cone. The mountain jutted more than a mile above the topmost plate. On Earth it would have been an enormous mountain, but it was small for Mars.

We reached it at noon the next day. A large permanent camp had been set up at its base, and a big drilling rig was already in operation. The derrick was dwarfed by the mountain rising into the dark sky behind it.

The drill crew was mostly made up of independent station owners. The crew chief called himself Tex, and had worked for an oil outfit on Earth before he killed a man in a fight and ended up sentenced to transportation for life. He'd been sent as a labor client to work in one of the mine camps in East Coprates.

"Hard work," he told us. "Wind whistles through that damn big ditch. Not much sun down there. Colder'n Pluto's balls. And they worked us like slaves. Never anything to spend money on, no place to go, guards beatin' on your head all the time. Got sick of it. So one morning some of the gang and me stole two tractors and came here."

"You came three thousand kilometers in tractors?" Don Plemmons asked.

"Yep."

"How?"

"With great difficulty," Cal said. Cal was a black miner who'd come out with Tex. "Started with twenty men got here with nine. Took up with some farmers. Did all right."

"Are most of the station owners here for Free Mars?"

"Yeah, most of'em," Cal said.

"How do you get along with the university people?" Plemmons asked.

Tex shrugged. "Mostly we don't have much to do with 'em. The word came out that the bigdomes wanted a hole drilled. The Project, they said. So here we are. Kind of snooty lot, seems to us. Don't ever have much to say. I don't think they like convicts."

"They're on our side," I said. "These are, anyway."

"Yeah, reckon so," Tex said. "Much as they're on anybody's side. Except their own."

They were drilling a slant hole from the base of the mountain down under the crater floor. It was a big operation. In addition to the drilling rig, they had to mine ice for water. The drill wouldn't work without a lot of water pumped down the hole.

The drill was fascinating. A big derrick held pipes vertical, and electric motors run by solar cells turned them. Every few minutes the crew would connect another piece of pipe to the one vanishing into the ground. "The drill string's following a kind of soft area in the rock," Tex told us. "We're about two kilometers in already." The pipes turned endlessly, while a stream of dirty water bubbled out of the hole to run off into the sands and vanish a few feet away. Even at this cold temperature it boiled in the thin air of Mars.

We called GHQ at Ice Hill, relaying through the captured ship in orbit above Mars. "It looks pretty good," Erica told Commander Farr. "They've got the hole mostly drilled already."

"How's the cooperation with the university people?" Farr asked.

"It couldn't be better," Erica said. "Dr. Drury's a Project fanatic. And they have this huge effort, drillers, miles of pipe, everything. They're really splendid."

"I'm glad to hear that," Farr said. "Weinbaum isn't getting anywhere in the negotiations. Everything has to be referred to three different committees, and the people who have to make decisions can't be reached—I guess it's just their way. I don't mind telling you I was getting worried, but if your part's going all right, it doesn't matter."

"Doesn't matter?" I took the mike. "Skipper, if they don't get together on this, we can't get home! No fuel for the rocket plane."

"We'll get you home," Farr said, "You just see this thing goes off properly. We're counting on you. When that bomb goes off it'll be the signal for the general uprising in the cities. It will show everyone on Earth that we can make atomic weapons, and it will show the miners and townspeople that we're serious about the Project. It *must* work, and it must work on time."

"It will," Erica said. "The bomb will work, and I've been over the plan with Dr. Drury. The plug stopping up the volcano is nothing but some hardened granite. The bomb will crack it, and the pressure underneath will do the rest. It will work."

"I'm damned glad you're so sure of it," Farr said. "Because we'll have to surface a lot of our agents just before it goes. If we broadcast an appeal and nothing happens, it will set us back months. Not to mention getting a lot of good people killed. If this thing won't go, let me know before it's too late."

"The odds haven't changed," Erica said. Her voice was cold and distant. "You knew the risks when you decided to do this."

"Yes. There are always risks. This one seems the best chance of ending this war quickly. We'll go with the plan," Farr said. "GHQ out."

"We'll go with the plan," Erica said to me. "And I won't be able to rest until this thing is done. Poor Garrett, I haven't been very nice to be around, have I? I'm sorry, darling."

"It's all right," I said.

"No, it's not. But I can't help it." She came to me and we stood, embracing. "I'm glad you're here, even if you weren't needed," she said.

"That's a hell of a way to put it—"

"Oh, Garrett, I didn't want it that way. But you weren't needed, were you? We're perfectly safe here. The university people couldn't treat us any better."

"Yeah—"

"You sound suspicious," Erica said. "Why?"

"No good reason," I told her. "It's just that this is such a damned big operation. Drillers, miles of pipe, the rig, an acre of solar cells spread out on the mountain side, tractors, permanent buildings— it's too much. They couldn't have kept this hidden from the Feddies."

"But they did. We haven't been bothered."

"Yeah. All the same, I'll be glad to get back home." I pulled her to me and kissed her. Then again. Then— "Not now," she said impatiently. "Please. I want to check some figures—"

"I sort of had figure checking in mind myself," I said. I looked at her to show what figure I had in mind.

"I have to work. And we've got to make an early start in the morning. Dr. Drury is taking us to the top of the volcano. I want to get some sleep." She pulled away. "Good night, Garrett. I love you."

"Yeah. Sure. I love you too—"

She went into her room and closed the door. They'd given us a concrete blockhouse, with an air lock, and a big main room, and three smaller rooms. There was even running water, hot water in the daytime. I had the bomb put in one of the rooms, and one of my troops was awake and in the blockhouse at all times. Erica thought I was silly; when we first came she wouldn't let it out of her sight, but now she said I was making a fool of myself, and insulting our hosts as well, by insisting on guarding it with our own people rather than let the university staff take care of it.

I thought she was probably right, but the Skipper had

made it clear that the damn thing was *ours,* and we would set it off at the right time and place. I went over to the desk and sat down to take the first watch.

It's soft duty. I told myself. And there's coffee to drink. Relax and enjoy it.

Drury had instruments set up all around the area. Every now and then he'd blow off a dynamite charge and needles would squiggle as the shock waves passed. By feeding the squiggles into a computer he got a picture of the rock and gunk under the volcano. The bomb had to be placed just right so it would crack the rocks that plugged up the lava and gas flow. If everything went right when we blew the weapon, there would be a big gusher of water vapor and gas.

We drove up the side of the mountain the next day. I left Doug and Don Plemmons sitting on the bomb so I could stay with Erica. It took most of the morning to drive up the side of the big mountain, even though the university had blasted out a road years before.

"This one volcano won't do much," Drury told us as we drove up. "But if—no, when—this works we'll have others. I'll show you, up on the rim."

When we reached the top we got out and looked over the edge. The volcano floor was far below. It was flat and smooth. "This was active not a thousand years ago," Drury said. "An instant, geologically speaking. It's still got plenty of pressure underneath. A single bomb should do it. But come look here."

He led the way up a series of steps cut into a big rock at the rim edge. There was a flat place on top where you had a view of the plains all around us. "Look out there,"

Drury said. He pointed northeast. "We're standing on a little baby, but look at that."

He was pointing to an enormous, cone-shaped mountain. Its base was beyond the horizon, over a hundred miles away, but still it was huge, like Manhattan Island standing on end, ten miles high. "When we set *that* off, you'll know it! And it's not the biggest we have, either." He pointed northwest. "You can't see it, but over that way is Olympus Mons, the granddaddy of them all. Biggest mountain in the solar system. Fifteen miles high, higher than from the bottom of the deepest sea on Earth to the top of Mount Everest. They could see it from Earth before the spacecraft ever got here. Nix Olympica, they called it. Snows of Olympus. You can see the cloud cover over it."

There were thin white clouds out where he pointed.

"One day we'll wake him up," Drury said. "That will really be something to see."

I still made rounds at night. It seemed silly and I knew it, but I couldn't get over the feeling that an operation this big couldn't be hidden. The Federation still controlled everything in this part of Mars. Even the station owners were careful to hide their revolutionary sympathies. And there might not be very many Feddie cops out here, but there were enough to roll over us.

I couldn't help thinking how safe the people at Deucalion had thought they were. So every evening I went out and made rounds, just before sundown, and then later, in the dark, watched for any signs of movement out on the plains. I never saw anything, of course.

I made night rounds and went into the cook shack to find some coffee. I got a cup. The place was deserted, so I sprawled out and relaxed. Then Eileen came in and took off her helmet.

"I wasn't very nice to you the other night," she said. "I'm sorry—"

"It's okay."

"Sure." She got herself a cup and sat next to me. "Ice Princess all bedded down?"

"I wish you wouldn't talk about Erica that way."

"Sorry, but she is and you know it. She have a headache or what?"

"Eileen, for heaven's sake—"

"What are you so nervous about?" she asked. "Look. We're adults, we're the same age, and we turn each other on. Why shouldn't we do something about it? Like this." She leaned toward me and kissed me.

We set the coffee cups down and tried that again. After a while she reached for the tab on the big spiral zipper on my pressure suit.

"Maybe we better open the inner door to the air lock," I said.

"I already left it open."

There wasn't any conversation for a long time after that.

I didn't like myself very much the next day. I kept telling myself there was no harm done. Erica hadn't lost anything. I still loved her. She had no use for me. Nothing was changed between us. And the rest of it. Every man has his own set of excuses, and mine weren't very original.

The work went on. Erica and Drury worked every day, getting the drill string sent down just right, making certain the bomb would fit in the drill casing and go smoothly to the proper place. The drill could only work when the sun was up, of course; there weren't enough batteries and fuel cells to power it at night. But from before dawn to that last bit of sun, the crew was working, and so was Erica.

It left me a lot of time with Eileen. She'd look me up, "just to keep me company," she said, and sit with me on guard watches. When I was on watch we just talked. She'd never been to Earth, of course, and I found myself telling her a lot of things I'd told Erica. Eileen was a good listener.

Then came the day: the hole was finished. Erica lowered the bomb into the shaft. It took all day and part of the night to get it placed right. Then the drill crew pumped mud in on top of it to seal in the blast.

"It's topped up," Tex said. "Our job's done."

Erica brought in her detonator. It was built into a radio chassis. "I suppose there ought to be some kind of ceremony," she said. "Here goes." She threw two switches, and three lights glowed on the box.

"It's armed," Erica said. A broad grin broke out on her face. "It really works! Nothing can stop it now. Let's tell the Skipper!"

It took an hour to set up the relay link. Erica told Commander Farr what we'd done.

"And you're sure everything is set?" Farr demanded.

"Yes, sir," Erica told him. "The responder worked, and that shows we have communications with the device.

Now it will detonate when I send the right signal. The bomb can't be disarmed unless you know the proper frequencies and codes, and I've allowed no one to examine the detonator. I didn't even choose the final frequencies until this morning."

"And you've got the detonator under guard?" Farr said.

"Certainly."

There was a long pause on the other end. Then Farr said, "Okay. We'll go with the plan. I want that thing to go off exactly at thirteen hundred Mars Zulu the day after tomorrow. That's 5:00 A.M. your time. Not tomorrow, the day after, at 5:00 A.M. your time. Understood?"

"Yes, sir," Erica said.

"Good. That will be late afternoon at Marsport. We'll start broadcasting the message four hours before Go. An hour later we'll have to reveal your location. You run like hell as soon as she goes. That okay with you?"

"Yes," Erica said.

"All right," Farr said. "There's a lot riding on this. The big uprisings will come when the ship gets telephotos of that volcano going up and broadcasts them all over Mars. We're telling the miners and the other labor clients that the Project will be the first thing Free Mars will do. We're telling them their kids will be able to go take free land and live on it without all the expensive equipment they'd need to set up stations. And we're telling Earth to look close, because this could be what happens to your city if the Federation ever bombs one of ours."

"The big push is set for when we detonate the bomb?" I asked.

"Yes. Make sure it's on time. A lot of our people will have to surface, and if that thing doesn't go on time, we'll lose them."

"I understand," I said. "We'll sit guard on the detonator until it's time. How's Weinbaum doing with the negotiations?"

"Still delays. He thinks the Regents are waiting to see which way the wind blows. They'll come over if there's a general uprising, and if Earth doesn't look like bombing us out. Your little stunt ought to convince them. But you've got your secondary contacts just in case, right?"

"Yes, sir," I said. We'd been given the names and locations of some friendly station owners who'd hide us if the university people couldn't take care of us.

"All's well, then," Farr said. "This is it. In a couple of hundred hours it should be all over except for mopping up. GHQ out."

We carried the detonator into our blockhouse. Erica put it in her room.

"It seems too good to be true," I told her. "The war over—"

"Maybe," Erica said. She looked at the box with its glowing lights. "Anyway, my job's done. Nothing left to do but push a button at the right time. Until then, there's nothing I can do. It's over."

"Over for us." I thought about my buddies back at the Rim. Sarge would be leading an attack on Hellastown. I wondered how many would be killed.

"Garrett, I don't know how you've stood up to all this," Erica said. "I'm exhausted." She came over and put her arms around me. I held her close. We kissed, then again.

"I thought you were exhausted," I said.

"Not *that* exhausted. Who's outside?"

"Don's in the main room—"

"Close the door. Then come here."

For a moment I thought about Eileen and I felt like a bloody heel, but then I wasn't thinking about anything at all.

CHAPTER SEVENTEEN

We got our gear packed up and ready so we could run. After that there was nothing to do but wait. Erica and I stayed in the blockhouse. We had decided we wouldn't leave until the bomb went off. Later, Dr. Drury came in to have supper with us, while Doug sat in Erica's room with the detonator. "It will be a magnificent thing," Drury said. "Magnificent. Making over a whole world. We can all be proud to have been part of it."

"It will take a long time," Erica said. Drury nodded. "But we can speed it up. Melt off the polar caps—"

"They melt every summer anyway," I said.

"Not all of them. One melts, the other forms. But there are ways to keep them melted. And there are layers of both poles that never melt at all. We've studied this extensively. The Project can be speeded up enormously— and will be, when the Federation gets out of the way."

"I'm glad we've got you people on our side," Erica said. She waved at the blockhouse. "This would be a building to be proud of back home. Here it's just a temporary thing at a research camp. You've got enormous capabilities at the university."

"Thank you," Drury said. He raised his glass. "To the Project!"

We all drank to that.

"Of course," Drury said, "not everybody at New Chicago U is a Project enthusiast—"

"I'd have thought they would be," I said.

"Well, some think we don't understand Mars yet. They want to study it the way it is. They have a point; there's a lot to learn, a lot we can learn about Earth by studying Mars. We'll lose most of that information when the atmosphere begins to build up."

"How long do they want to wait?" Erica asked.

Drury shrugged. "They don't say. But have you ever heard of a research project being *finished?*"

We laughed at that. I had two glasses of wine, then switched to coffee. "I still won't feel right until that damn thing's set off and we see the gusher," I said.

The party broke up about eleven. Drury went to his quarters and I got a nap. I relieved Doug about 2:00 A.M.

"One day and night after this," I said. "Get some sleep. I'll catch Plemmons for the next watch."

"Right."

I made sure the inner door of the air-lock was open. I was wearing my suit, and had my helmet beside me. With that air-lock door open nobody could get in without blowing out the blockhouse, and we could still trigger the bomb. It would go off early and spoil the Skipper's big speech, but it would still show Earth we knew how to make nukes—and show Mars that we were serious about the Project, too.

The Project was the big thing with the labor clients. All our agents told us that. With the Project under way there was hope for anybody. A lot of workers would probably choose to stay with the big companies. We were telling Mars' industries that if they didn't help the Federation against us, we'd let them keep everything they had except labor contracts; if they could hire workers, and they probably could, they could go on mining, refining, selling to Earth, and making big profits.

Actually we were going to need the companies. If they closed down there'd be no employment for most of our people.

I'd been sitting in the main room, thinking about what I'd do with my valley and wondering if I could get coffee beans to grow. After about an hour the air-lock speaker was activated.

"Garrett?"

Eileen. I didn't want to see her. I felt ashamed of myself for ever getting involved with her.

"I couldn't sleep," she said. "Let me in."

Oh hell, I thought. I couldn't argue with her while she stood out in the cold, and I did owe her something—I could hardly tell a girl I'd been sleeping with to get lost. I closed the inner air-lock door and waited for the lock to cycle.

"Cold out there," she said. "Hi."

"Hi yourself."

She sat down on the other side of the room. "It's a long night."

"Yeah. Tomorrow will be longer."

"This one's long enough." She bounced up. "I'm restless. Got any coffee?"

"Sure."

"Here, I'll get yours too." She took my cup and filled it and one for herself. "Everybody asleep?"

"Yeah. If you're going to drink that, you'd better take your helmet off. It dribbles inside if you try to drink through the faceplate. Or it does for me.

"In a minute. I almost froze out there." She sipped at the cup. As I'd warned, she spilled some inside her helmet. "That's good. Aren't you having any?"

"In a minute. I'm about coffeed out."

"I guess I will take off this helmet. Give me a hand?"

"Sure." I went over to help with the thing. As I got to her, she raised a little cylinder, about the size of a lipstick, and a small cloud of spray came out into my face.

"Wha—" I tried to shout, but I couldn't. My face was paralyzed. My vision began to go, not so much dark as that nothing made sense. I vaguely saw that she'd slammed down her faceplate and was sealed up.

I couldn't do anything. I gradually felt my knees giving away and knew I was falling, but I couldn't do anything about that, either. I tried to get a deep breath but nothing happened, and now things began to get darker and darker, and she was going back into the blockhouse toward Erica's room and there was nothing I could do about it, nothing at all

I thought I was back in Baltimore Undertown, because I heard sirens and gunshots, and I tried to fight the

Hackers who'd jumped me but I couldn't move. Then I passed out.

"Garrett! Garrett, O God let him be all right! Garrett!"

Someone was shouting in my ear. Part of my mind knew it was Erica and wanted to answer, but I couldn't answer because I couldn't control my lungs. I felt my chest expand and contract. It was a curious feeling, because I hadn't told it to do that. I opened my eyes. They wouldn't focus on anything. There was a big white blur above me. The blur had blue eyes and red hair. It moved away and there was another blur that looked like Doug, only his face was clearer, and after a moment things swam into shape.

Doug was bending over me holding an oxygen mask over my mouth and nose. He was manipulating an oxygen bottle to force air into my lungs, then he'd turn it off and shove hard on my chest. He kept doing that.

Don Plemmons held guard on the air-lock with an automatic rifle. The inner door was open. On the other side of the room Eileen stood flattened against the wall, as Erica alternately slapped her and shook her.

"What have you done to him?" Slap. "Tell us!" Shake. "If he dies, I'll—" It went on like that.

She said some horrible things. I don't remember most of them. I don't *want* to remember them. I didn't know Erica knew that much physiology.

Eileen was white with fear. She tried to talk, but Erica kept slapping her. Finally Erica let her alone. "I don't know what it was," Eileen sobbed. "It was some kind of gas, they told me it wouldn't kill anyone, just paralyze him. I don't know!"

"Nerve gas," Doug said. "Don, there's stuff for that in the med kit. Get 'em and a hypo."

Don vanished. I couldn't turn my head to see where he went, but after a while he was back again.

I felt a stabbing pain in my thigh. Then another in my neck. "Maybe that'll do it," Doug said. "It's supposed to be a remedy. All we got, anyway." He kept on working with the mask. "Can you hear us, Garrett?" he asked.

"Awugll!" I was surprised that I could say anything at all.

"Maybe he'll make it," Doug said. "Erica, if she don't know, she don't know. You can stop shaking her."

"Yes." She came back over to me and knelt beside me. "Please be all right, Garrett. Please."

"Urk." Something was happening. I tried to help the breathing process. After about three tries I was able to inhale. Then exhale.

"What the hell do we do now?" Plemmons said.

"Watch that damn box," Doug said. "Stay close to it and trigger the bomb if it looks like we've had it. But wait as long as we can."

"Maybe we ought to set it off now." Don Plemmons said.

"Think we should wait," Doug said. "Erica? It's your baby."

"We wait. How is he?"

"Tryin' to breathe," Doug said. "I think he is going to make it. Maybe we ought to shoot that bitch now and get it over with?"

"No," I managed to say.

"So you can talk," Erica said.

I got in a deep breath. "Need to find out why," I said. "How many in on this."

"Good thinking," Plemmons said. "Lady, unless you like breathin' Mars air without a helmet, you better tell us what this is all about."

Eileen was crying.

"I can't believe Dr. Drury knew," Erica said. "He's all for the Project."

"No Marsman," Plemmons said. "He don't give shit about Free Mars."

"No, but he is for the Project," Erica insisted.

"Drillers," I managed to say. "Drillers are patriots. Get help."

"He's right," Plemmons said.

"Sure, and how many of this chick's friends are out there waitin' for her to get through killin' us all in our beds?" Doug asked. "Go out that air-lock, and maybe you face a couple dozen Feddie cops."

"We've got to do something," Erica said.

"First thing is we beat shit out of that chick," Plemmons said. "She'll talk.

"No," I said. "We don't work that way." I took a deep breath. Then another. I flexed my fingers and legs and they responded. One side of my face seemed paralyzed, and it took a conscious effort to breathe, but I could see and hear clearly, and nothing seemed wrong with my mind—nothing that wasn't wrong to begin with. I tried to sit up.

"Easy," Doug said.

"What's it about, Eileen?" I asked. "Why did you sell us out to the Feddies? You did, didn't you?"

She was still crying. "Because you'll ruin everything," she said. "Your horrible Project. We're learning what causes ice ages on Earth, we're learning what makes planets, and you'll ruin all that! You can't, you just can't do it."

"Are there Feddie cops outside?" I asked.

"Yes. University police. My father sent them."

"And Dr. Weinbaum? Did you betray him, too?"

"I don't know—"

"You know Kehiayan's orders," Doug said. "They didn't get the Doc alive . . ."

"Worry about us. We've got to stay alive a little over twenty-five hours and blow that thing off," Plemmons said. "Got any suggestions, Lieutenant? I guess you're in charge again." His voice was heavy with sarcasm. I had that coming.

"I think I can get up," I said, and did it. "Okay. We've got to get help. The only help I know of is the drillers. If they haven't been arrested. And the only way we can find that out is to get out of here. How many air bottles have we got?"

"Enough."

"Get packs together and fill the water tanks in the suits. We need twenty-five hours worth of air and water. We'll skip food. Then we've got to figure a way out of here."

"I got a way," Plemmons said. "Blow out a wall with shaped charges. Stands to reason they're watchin' the airlock, not the back of the blockhouse. Blow it and run like hell."

"Will a blowout hurt the detonator?" I asked Erica.

"No. Are you really all right?"

"I'm going to live. I—"

"We'll talk about it later," she said.

"Yeah. Just what happened? How did you—I mean, why didn't she get the rest of you, too?"

Erica's eyes narrowed. "Because Don told me you'd been seeing her," she said. "And I heard her voice out here, and I watched her. And don't say I was spying on you, because I've got a right to know what my fiancé is doing! I'm not giving you up to some school-educated snob! So when she sprayed you with that stuff and closed up her faceplate, I came up behind her and knocked the can out of her hand and batted her head against the wall."

"I'm amazed you didn't kill her," I said. I said it to myself, but I must have been talking louder than I thought.

"I would have, but I thought we ought to find out what she'd done to you."

Lord save us, I thought. "Don, set the charges in the back wall of your room."

Plemmons nodded and went back into the block-house. "What do we do with the bitch?" Doug asked.

"Put her helmet on her, tie her up, and leave her," I said.

"Maybe I should spray inside the helmet with some of that gunk," Doug said. "Erica?"

Eileen's face went white. "You can't! You aren't— you can't?"

"No," Erica said. "But I'd like to. Wait a minute. What did you put in Garrett's coffee?"

Eileen didn't answer.

"Would it have killed him?" Erica demanded.

"No! It's just a knockout drop—"

"Drink it," Erica said.   She brought the cup over. "Now, and every drop, or I swear I will use that spray can on you."

"But—"

Erica got the spray can.

"All right!" Eileen drank the coffee. They put her helmet on her and closed the faceplate. She sat still for a minute, then her head slowly nodded over.

"She could be faking," Erica said. "Tie her up, Doug."

"Right."

I got up and moved gingerly around the room. I could walk all right. My face still felt funny, the way it does after a jawful of novocaine, but otherwise I seemed okay. A little light-headed, maybe, but that could have been from the shots as much as anything. "I'll function," I said. "Okay, let's get ready."

We got our packs and weapons. Erica carried her detonator. "All set?" Plemmons asked.

"Yeah," I said. "Let her fly."

We heard the explosions, then whistling air, and then silence. Half the wall was blown out. We leaped through, and Doug and Erica ran off toward the derrick. Plemmons and I ran to either side and wheeled around.

Someone fired at us from the dark. There were the silent orange flowers I remembered from the Deucalion battle. A figure moved toward me, and I swung the sub-machine gun like a hose, cutting him down. I fired another burst, then ran off after Erica.

Plemmons dropped down behind some rocks. "Move, Chief," he said. His voice was loud in my headset.

"No heroes," I ordered. "Need all of us—"

"Be along in a minute." He fired a burst with his automatic rifle, and I ran on, wondering if I'd ever see him again.

We'd let the drillers guard the wellhead because, short of drilling out the hole again, there was no way the bomb could be disturbed. They'd been taking the rig apart and stowing it for travel, so we weren't too worried that anybody would drill for the bomb.

It was a kilometer to the well site. About halfway I felt woozy. This looked like as good a place to make a stand as any. I found a boulder and got behind it.

A figure came running toward me out of the dark. I sighted on it. "Don?" I called into the mike.

"Yeah, Chief, don't get nervous."

"Leapfrog," I said. "Move on."

He slowed and looked around but couldn't see where I was.

"Go." I ordered.

He ran past, and I waited. My eyes were getting accustomed to starlight, and Deimos, the outer moon, was up. Deimos doesn't give much light; it's not even a disk, just a very bright star, but it was something. I thought I saw movement in front of me and fired a burst.

More orange flowers answered me. At least a dozen. I tried to remember where they'd been, and fired at a couple I was sure of. More answering fire from out there.

I didn't think I'd hit anybody. We stayed that way, trading silent shots for several minutes, and then I decided it was time to get the hell out of there. I crawled into a deep shadow and began to move toward the drill site.

Something bumped against me. I grabbed it, and we rolled over in the dark, tearing at each other. My weapon was tugged out of my hands. I reached back onto my belt and got my knife and thrust it, then again. Again. I felt him go limp, and hoped I hadn't run into one of my friends. Then I felt around for my submachine gun and crawled farther into the shadow. Finally I got up and ran.

"Garrett!" It was Erica's voice. I wished for air, so I could tell where she was.

"Coming!" I called.

"Hurry. We've got a tractor—"

"They're listening," I reminded her.

"I know that. Hurry."

"Sure. Count off!"

"Plemmons."

"Barston."

So Doug and Don had both made it. And Erica. I was breathing hard as I got to the well site. There wasn't anyone around that I could see.

"To your left," Erica's voice said.

I ran off into the darkness and almost fell over them. There were four drillers as well. "This way," a voice said. One of the drillers moved off, and we followed. He went around a boulder the size of a palace, and there was a tractor behind it.

"Get on," the driller said. We climbed on top of it, and it began moving off, upward, up the side of the volcano. It made sense; the cops were down below, and we couldn't go that way, but I didn't much like the idea of climbing that hill. Suppose we were still there when it was time to set off the bomb?

I moved toward Erica. There was something bothering me. It had for a couple of days, but I hadn't needed to know before. Now I did. I took her shoulder and moved my helmet next to hers. "Radio off," I said.

"Off. What do you think you're doing? Let me go."

"Damn it, save being mad for later—"

"I will. Believe me."

"I believe you. I have to know something. That bomb's a couple of kilometers underground. There's no radio signal can go through that kind of rock. There must be a wire connection, something like that."

"Something like that," she said.

"What? Can they get at it and disable it?"

"It's a transponder. A receiver picks up the detonator signal and sends a sonic pulse through the ground," Erica said. "It's well hidden."

"Does Drury know about this?" I asked.

"Did you? He's a scientist, so he knows there has to be one—but he has no more idea *where* than you do."

"All right. But you had to have help. Who does know?"

"Tex. The Skipper said we could trust him. And he's driving the tractor."

"Okay." Now I had time to pay attention to what was happening to us. We were driving, without lights, at maybe twenty kilometers an hour, which doesn't sound very fast until you think about it. The road was narrow and getting narrower, and we were headed up the side of the mountain. I didn't think we were likely to be coming back down.

I pulled Erica closer to me. "Sweetheart, I'm sorry—"

"I don't want to talk about it."

"All right."

"You damned fool."

She did want to talk about it. She had a lot to say while we went up that mountain, up a goddamn mountain that we were going to turn into a volcano in about twenty-four hours. Boy did she want to talk about it.

★★★
CHAPTER EIGHTEEN
★★★

We stopped about two kilometers from the drill site. When dawn came we'd dug in. Nobody had bothered us. There wasn't but one way up, and we had that covered, with the tractor's lights shining down on the road below.

"We in range for your gadget?" I asked Erica.

"Yes."

"Then there's nothing for it but to wait," I said. "Doug, have you got anything we can raise the Skipper with?"

"No. Not with us."

"That worries me," I said. "They'll try to get to him and tell him it's all off. Or something—"

"Won't matter a lot," Plemmons said. "Plan's movin' now. Agents have gone up front. Skipper won't call it off, too much at stake now. Not unless you tell him yourself."

"Maybe. I'd sure like to get through to him," I said.

I looked around at my tiny command. Tex and Cal and two other drillers. Don and Doug. And Erica. Eight of us. I wondered how many Feddies were down below.

"I'll have a go," Doug said.

"No," I told him.

"My job, Garrett. I'm communications. And you're needed up here—"

"I'm not needed at all."

"You got a job to do," Doug said. "It won't end when that bomb goes unless—" he turned toward Erica. "Anyway, it's your job, not mine. Mine's communications, and I know where the sets are. Maybe I can sneak through. These aren't Marsmen, you know. University cops. Townmen. No good out in the open. I'll be safer than you are."

"All right," I said. "How will you go?"

"Around west and down the draw. Cross the road when I think I can. Hell, it's a piece of cake." Doug waved and was gone.

We waited. Nothing happened. The sun got higher.

"Did Eileen know when H-hour was?" Erica asked.

"Not from me. Did Drury?"

"Of course. But I don't think he would tell them—"

"He will if they ask right. The way you asked Eileen what she'd done to me. Did you mean any of that?"

"I don't have to say."

"I believed you," I said.

"I wish they'd do something," Erica said.

"Maybe they think they can wait us out. Have you heard any chatter on the radios?" She had been tuning back and forth across the different bands,

"No. But they could be using very low power."

"Probably are."

We waited some more. The sun got higher, and it warmed up a bit. It was going to be damned cold out there for the night, with only the tractor as a place to warm up.

"I'm getting hungry," I said. "I could—"

"Hush. Listen." She showed me the frequency. I tuned to it.

"Pittson? Can you hear us?"

I thought about whether we should answer. Why not? "Yeah, I hear you. Who is that?"

"Captain Moncrief, Federation police. Your rebellion has been called off, Pittson. Your Commander Farr has been broadcasting that the big push is not on after all. You may as well give up."

"Bullshit."

"It's true."

"I don't care if it is. I've got my orders."

"What do you think is going to happen to you when you detonate that weapon?" Moncrief asked,

"I try not to think about it. But I'm gonna do it, Guess when?"

"I know when."

"Good for you."

"Pittson, give us the detonator and we'll send you home. Back to Hellas. You and all your people. We don't want you. But what you're doing is insane."

Trouble was, he was probably right.

"I'm getting something else," Erica said. "Here."

I changed bands. There was nothing but static, then: "Blowhole, this is Highguard. We know your status. Your orders are unchanged. Garrett, if you're listening, we have the message. Hope you can hear this." The message repeated several times.

"The ship," I said. "Doug must have got through. Hope he's all right."

We waited some more.

They rushed us just before dark. It was stupid. They had no chance of knocking us off before we could set off the bomb. They could make us trigger it twelve hours early, but they couldn't stop us.

They didn't even manage that. We cut down five of them as they came up the road, and I think I got another in the rocks off to our left. It wasn't much of a battle. They didn't have any better weapons than we did.

An hour later they tried something else. First they called and got me to talk, then they let us hear a man groaning.

"That's your communications man," Moncrief said. "We don't like hurting people, Pittson. But there's too much at stake here. Give up, and we'll let him go. And you, too. All of you. We'll send you home."

"Bugger yourself."

There were more groans and a couple of screams.

"I think that is Doug," Plemmons said. "Bastards. Dirty bastards."

"Can't take that," Cal said. He moved off before anyone could stop him. A few minutes later we saw gunfire below.

"Cal," Tex called. "Answer me, you black bastard!"

"Got a couple, gettin' more." His voice sounded pinched.

"He's losing pressure," Tex said. "Oh Goddamn."

There were more shots and a grenade went off below. Again no sound, only the flashes. Then nothing.

A sniper hit Plemmons about midnight. We got him

into the tractor so he wouldn't freeze and left him to care for himself if he could. He'd been hit on the right side, just below the rib cage. It didn't look good.

"Pittson's Last Stand," I told Erica. "Come on." I led her away from the tractor, a little higher up the mountain and off to one side. We kept the radios off. I had a sleeping bag from out of the tractor, and we managed to get that around us. There was a wind whipping past, but it was very thin, not any real problem.

We huddled together, helmets touching. "I've been thinking," Erica said. "I want a wood table. Why should mother have the only wood table on the Rim? Will you make me a wood table, Gary?"

"Have to wait for the tree to grow," I said.

"Sure. No problem. They say people on Mars can live to be two hundred. We've got plenty of time."

"I love you."

"I hope so. I wish we weren't all sealed up in these suits and stuff. I wonder how Eskimos manage to be affectionate? There are Eskimos on Mars. Did you know that?"

"Sure. I met the Greatstars at a Rim gatherin'. Be good to see them again. Wonder how the Skipper's making out with his speech? Wish we could hear it."

"Garrett, what time is it?"

"Five minutes later than the last time you asked."

"O God. I was sure I'd waited three hours."

There were flashes out to the left, where the tractor was. They were firing again. The fools. It went on for a long time.

★ ★ ★

There were twinges of light in the east. "Two minutes to go," I told her. "You ready? Box didn't freeze?"

"No. I designed it to take this. Or almost anything else."

"I damn near froze my balls off—"

"I hope not," she said.

"Yeah. I haven't heard anything on the radio for hours—"

"No. Is it time?"

"Coming up. I love you. Five. I always did. Four. Three. Two. One. Go"

She pressed the keys. Almost immediately we felt a sharp whump! and the ground shook beneath us. Then we felt rumbling. When we pressed our helmets against the rocks we could hear it, a long rumbling sound like thunder that wouldn't go away.

The rim of the sun came over the horizon. The plain below us was still dark, but there was light shining on us and on the mountain peak. The sky above us was still dead black velvet with stars against it.

The rumble went on, then the stars began to fade, and there was a peculiar color to the sky above. White clouds shot upward toward the stars, white cloud with red tinges, then solid chunks of red.

"It worked!" Erica screamed. "Garrett, it worked! The Project! It worked!"

"Yeah." It sure had. Streaks of fire shot upward and the entire mountain shook. The white vapor climbed higher and higher into the sky, then condensed. Snowflakes and hail began to fall around us, mixed with red-hot rock that flew out of the rim in a much lower arc.

Fire and ice. I stood and threw back my head and roared laughter and defiance and every other emotion. "Fire and ice. A new world born in fire and ice!" I was fascinated with the image. It was the first poetic thought I'd ever had. I liked it. I said it again, "A new world born in fire and ice."

Sanity came back almost too late. "We've got to get the hell out of here—"

"The Feddies—" Erica shouted.

"Bugger the Feddies. They're running too. Let's go!"

We dashed down the mountain toward the tractor. When we got closer we saw bodies around it. Tex, his faceplate smashed open. Another driller. The door of the tractor stood open, and there was a body there, too. A Feddie cop with a knife in his chest.

Don Plemmons lay inside the tractor. He was stiff as a board, and there was a huge icicle of blood on his chest. His hand was still curled, as if he were gripping the knife he'd thrust into the Federation policeman.

"There's nobody alive here," I shouted. "Help me get Plemmons out—"

"We can't leave him! He should be buried—"

"He will be!" I pointed up the mountain. A red glow was pouring over the edge. "He will be! It's his monument, his and Tex's and—" I tried to remember the driller's name, but I couldn't. "Come on."

We dragged the stiffened corpse out of the tractor. I had time to lay Don so that his enemy was at his feet. Then I prayed, silently; the tractor started.

There was enough sunlight to move it. I got the wings extended and there was more power. We drove down the road. A chunk of rock hit the deck of the tractor, destroying some of the solar cells. It slowed but went on. We rolled over boulders that had fallen in the road or pushed them aside. Once we went off the road and up onto the side of the hill to get around a big one.

Then we were in the flat below. Fire and ice still fell around us, but not so thick now. We drove on, across the plateau to the road down to the next level. When we turned off, we faced three tractors.

We had no armament except my submachine gun.

"They've got us," Erica said. "I—you're not— they can't take me. I—"

"Crap. By now the revolution worked or it didn't. I don't care if they know how many bombs we have, or how we make them, or—"

"But—"

"But nothing!" I picked up my weapon and worked the bolt. "Well, General Pittson strikes again. Pittson, hero of Pittson's Last Stand, Pittson's Disaster, Pittson's Retreat, Pitt—"

"Shut up and listen!" she said. "Look, those aren't Feddie tractors!"

The tractors had stopped. A man got out of the lead vehicle and stood with his arms waving at us.

"It's Doug," I said. "He must have gone to our station contacts for help." I tuned through the frequency band until I heard him.

"We did it," Doug was shouting. "We did it! They're rioting in every city! Mars General Company has declared for Free Mars! We've won! Garrett, Erica, we've won! Goddamn it, we've won."

★★★
EPILOGUE
★★★

We were married a month later. Sarge stood up for me. He had some new medals for his uniform When Commander Farr offered to fight the man who said I wasn't a Marsman I couldn't help crying. Best of all, the Padre told Erica never to mention Eileen again. But she didn't give her word . . .

★ ★ ★

KING DAVID'S
SPACESHIP

★ ★ ★

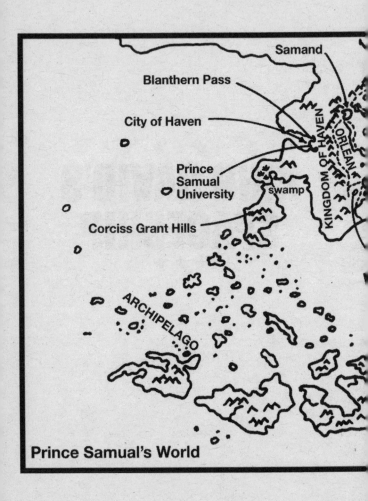

Samand

Blanthern Pass

City of Haven

Prince
Samual
University

swamp

Corciss Grant Hills

KINGDOM OF HAVEN

ORLEAN

ARCHIPELAGO

Prince Samual's World

Startford

tates

ECHFELD

ding
blic

arch

OR SEA

EASTERN KINGDOMS

SOUTH CONTINENT

Duane (after Pournelle)

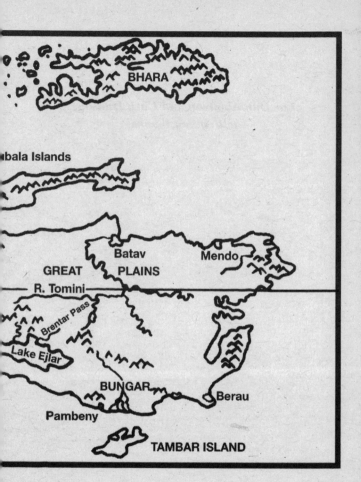

For Dan Alderson and Gary Hudson,
with many thanks

★★★
CHRONOLOGY
★★★

1969: Neil Armstrong sets foot on Earth's moon.

1990: Series of treaties between United States and Soviet Union creates the CoDominium.

2008: First interstellar drive tested.

2020: First interstellar colonies. Great Exodus begins.

2110: Coronation of Lysander I of Sparta.

2111: Formation Wars begin.

2250: Leonidas I proclaims Empire of Man.

2250-2600: Empire of Man enforces interstellar peace.

2273: Prince Samual's World becomes Member Principality of Empire.

2603: Secession Wars begin.

2627: Prince Samual's World drawn into conflict.

2632: First bombardment of Prince Samual's World.

2637: First battle off Makassar.

2640: Secession Wars continue. Dark Ages in many systems. Effective termination of First Empire.

2658: Second battle off Makassar; remnants of loyalist fleet take refuge on Prince Samual's World.

2680: Battle of Prince Samual's World. Loyalist officers deposed.

2681: Brief occupation of Prince Samual's World by secessionists.

2694: Loyalist-engineered coup on Prince Samual's World.

2711: Bombardment of Prince Samual's World; effective end of high-energy civilization.

2723: Last starship visits Prince Samual's World; many loyalist families evacuated by remnant of Empire.

2740: Prince Samual University founded to preserve knowledge.

2748-2770: Local independent cities and petty states battle for possession of Prince Samual University; townsmen defend University

2770: Treaty establishes independence of University under protection of coalition of local city-states.

2791: Plague Year on Prince Samual's World.

2800: Interstellar trade ceases. Piracy and brigandage. Dark Ages throughout former Empire of Man.

2810: First Hundred Year War begins on Prince Samual's World.

2864: Petty kingdom of Haven begins expansion, consolidates gains.

2870: Effective end of Secession Wars in Old Empire.

2903: Leonidas IV of Sparta proclaims the Second Empire of Man.
The Oath of Reunion is sworn.

2915: Fifty Year War begins on Prince Samual's World. Many petty states eliminated

2917: Plague Year on Prince Samual's World.

2990: Haven begins new campaign of unification.

3013: Prince Samual's World discovered by units of Imperial Navy.

★PART ONE★
COLONY
★ ★ ★

★1★
THE BLUE BOTTLE
★ ★ ★

The crowd was noisy in the Blue Bottle, although it was early in the evening. Tavern girls squealed as customers pinched them, gaily clad waiters brought round after round of drinks, and throughout much of the room everyone was shouting merrily.

The reason was not hard to find, for in one corner of the crowded room three officers of the Imperial Navy held court, buying drinks for anyone on Prince Samual's World who would sit with them and laugh at their jokes. Some of the regulars held back, their distaste for the enforced association more evident with every round, but for each of them there were four others from Haven City more than willing to share the Emperor's humor and liquor. Before the night ended the officers would doubtless have new recruits for the Royal and Imperial Marines, young lads suddenly sobered to find themselves in an iron service out among the stars, never to see their homes and discovering that Imperial officers were not such jolly good fellows when you were under their command.

For the moment the whiskey, brandy, and grua—distilled from a cross between a berry and a peach grown only on Prince Samual's northern continent—flowed freely, the jokes were new to the locals even if they had been told a century before in the barracks at New Annapolis, and His Imperial Majesty's crimson-and-gold-jacketed officers were relaxed, feeling as at home as they ever did on a barely civilized planet.

The three of them were classmates, not six years out of the Academy, the gold and silver stripes of lieutenants only recently sewn on their sleeves. Closer inspection would have revealed that one of them was a year younger than his friends, a school prodigy admitted early to midshipman status as much because of his talents as his family influence, and that young-and-only-just-lieutenant Jefferson was very, very drunk. His classmates had discreetly opened the top clasp of their stiff tunic collars, but Jefferson's was half unfastened, revealing a none-too-fresh shirt and a tiny breast-pocket computer beneath.

His natural shyness overcome by countless thimble-sized glasses of grua, Lieutenant Jefferson basked in the esteem of the flatlanders. He had almost forgotten that they were barbarians, and that he and the tiny Navy outpost on Prince Samual were the only representatives of true civilization within ten light-years. The others were singing, and when his turn came he added a verse so obscene it shocked the tavern girls. He grinned and looked about for approval, then tossed off another glass.

Across from Jefferson a young native, browned by field work, too young to be in the Blue Bottle if he were not sitting with the Emperor's overlords, beamed at his new friend and shouted approval of the song. "Great, Lieu—uh, Jeff, great. Tell us more about what it's like out there. Tell us about other worlds. Are we the most backward place you've ever seen?"

Lieutenant Jefferson belched loudly, murmured an automatic apology, and focused dizzily on his admirers. "Oh hell, no, Simom, not by a full broadside. Samual's got guns, and factories, and—and long-distance communications, and hydroelectric power; man, you've got nothing to be ashamed of. You've got no world government, and those wars you're always in stomp you down or for sure you'd be Class Two status in the Empire instead of a colony. When I think how bad you got torn up in the Secession Wars, it's amazing you got this far in a few centuries . . . standard centuries, that is. You're doing fine here. That right, laddie?" he asked, digging his elbow into his classmate's ribs.

Lieutenant Clements turned his black face to Jefferson and grinned, his teeth sparkling. "Sure that's right, Jeff, you tell 'em this is the best duty we've had since we left the capital. Maybe better," he shouted, turning back to the tavern girl beside him.

"Hear that?" Jefferson asked his companion. "Simom, we've been to places where they don't even have hydro-carbon power, no electricity, no pellet guns, nothing but horses and men running around in iron pants the way you see—well, the way we see in Imperial history books, books about the time when Earth was all there was to it. Friend, you almost have space travel. Another hundred years, another fifty years even, you'd have found us instead of the other way around. Too bad you didn't," he added, his voice changing. "Been better for you if you had. Class Two status for sure, maybe Class One, if you'd had real space flight before we got here. Not your fault; the survey ship just happened by looking for a gas giant to scoop some fuel from and decided to look you over. A real pity." He looked at his empty glass. "Host! Host! More grua!"

Two of the regulars of the Blue Bottle made a point of walking past the officers as they stamped out of the tavern, their kilts swirling, but Jefferson did not notice them. As the headwaiter brought more drinks, Simom asked, "What was it like, that place where they wore iron pants? Is it far from here? Have you colonized it? Can we go there?"

"Ho, one at a time," Jefferson shouted. "Far? Not more than twelve light-years, one jump from here, I think. Let's see, yeah, there's nothing between the two suns and theirs is a big one; hell, it's that thing you people call the Eye of the Needle; you could see it right now if you went outside. And no, no colonies there, not enough to make it worthwhile yet. And we're spread so thin. Keep a little observation post there to watch for outies, a first lieutenant and a couple of middies, few Marines. Not even a ship in orbit. Detection gear, observation satellite, that's about all. Nothing important there, except, of course, their Temple."

Jefferson had allowed his voice to drop for a moment, a note of weariness creeping in as he thought of the immense task of the Imperial Navy trying to reclaim the pieces of an Empire lost and shattered in the Secession Wars, the capital itself only reaching for the stars decades ago. His Majesty hoped to knit together the fragments before another war could send mankind staggering back to primitive conditions. There had been no winners of the last war, and the next would be worse. There must not be a next one, he said to himself. Never again. Then he brightened as the raucous humor and obvious friendship of the natives washed over him. Best enjoy it now, he thought. They wouldn't be so friendly to the Navy after the colonists arrived—but that was years away, and the night was young.

"The funny part, Simom, is that the Temple is worth more to them than the whole bloody planet, if they only knew it! They were right to make it a holy place and preserve it, but if they only knew! Why, there's a whole Old-Empire subsection library in that rabbit warren they've built up around what used to be the Viceroy's Palace! The Service librarians almost went out of their minds, some of the history books and things they found there. Even a few science books, operating manuals for old Imperial Fleet stuff; you name it, it's there, or bits and pieces of it are.

"They don't even know what it all is! Wouldn't do them any good if they did, no technology to understand it anyway. And my sweet Savior, how they guard that stuff! Thought we'd never get any of it copied for the archives. If we'd taken just one of those cubes out—yeah, cubes, the library was geared to a computer. Not much like your books. Took a lot of work to get *that* fixed, I'll tell you. And those priests watched every second we were there. Never did make copies of most of the stuff; we'll get it some day. Be a great job for some historian. We had to sneak in, convince their bishops we were from the stars— they still haven't told the people in the city about us. And the chaplain had to get in on the act, convince them we were religiously orthodox, gave them some song and dance about how we, too, believed that God spoke from their archives. The chaplain said it was all right, the first thing they copied was a Bible, so he didn't lie about it. Couldn't harm a thing copying the stuff or they'd have boiled up so thick it'd take a battleship to kill them all. Can't do that, they're good people. We'll need everyone in this sector one day. Whoosh, I talk too much, pour me some more. That grua's the best thing about this planet. Well," he added, looking at the tall blond girl who stood at his elbow, "*one* of the best, anyway."

Lieutenant Jefferson was not the only drunken officer in the Blue Bottle, but he would hardly have recognized the gray-eyed man in a plain kilt two tables away as a member of the officer class. Colonel Nathan MacKinnie, lately cashiered from service to the Committee of Public Safety of Orleans, preferred whiskey in large glasses, and had had almost as many of those as Jefferson had of grua. MacKinnie was tall, centimeters taller than usual for Samualites, but without the remarkably broad shoulders typical of the planetary dwellers. With his straw-colored hair silvering at the temples, he looked more akin to the senior Imperial Navy officers than the natives. He sat quietly, motioning effortlessly for a new drink from time to time, and smoking countless pipefuls of 'robac. At intervals a particularly loud shout from the Imperial table would bring a grimace to his face, but for the most part he sat emotionlessly, giving no sign of the enormous quantities of whiskey he poured down his gullet.

Hal Stark, MacKinnie's one-time sergeant, now servant, companion, and comrade, watched his colonel anxiously, mentally computing the amount of whiskey Nathan had drunk, the time since they had eaten, and the earliness of the evening, before he turned to his own drink, his second of the day. He was allowing the amber grua to roll back over his tongue when MacKinnie snapped his pipe against the heel of his hand so hard that the stem broke.

"Damn!" he muttered. "Hal, look at those drunken excuses for officers. And those sots are the rulers of Prince Samual's World, the 'representatives of civilization' as they call themselves, the men who can decree what will be done and snuff out the independence of Orleans like a candle in a hurricane. Babbling, shouting, the overlords of everything we've ever known."

"Yes, sir. Begging the colonel's pardon, but I seem to recall a young lieutenant some years ago couldn't hold his liquor no better than them, if it's all right to say so." It was difficult to tell just how much of Stark's apologetic air was genuine.

Colonel MacKinnie frowned for a moment, then burst into a loud guffaw. "I sure didn't, did I, Hal?" He looked at the ruined pipe in his hands, then signaled for the barmaid and bought cigars of genuine Earth Stock tobacco for a price he couldn't afford. "There were a few times when you had to roll me back to barracks, weren't there? You never missed, either. What are you best at, Hal? Batman, sergeant, or unemployed striker to a colonel with no command?"

"Best at whatever the colonel wants me at, that the right answer? Where are we going next, Colonel?"

MacKinnie shook his head slowly and looked around the room as if there might be some answer to the question. "They haven't stopped the fighting on South Continent. Maybe we can pick up something there." He reached into his pouch, and added, "We'd better find something soon, or we starve. But it won't be the same, Sergeant. Just something to fight over, get the bills paid. What we do won't matter anymore. The future here belongs to them." He waved his cigar at young Jefferson, who held the blond girl on his lap, her hands deep inside his open tunic, while he tried to force a glass of grua between her body and his lips. She squealed.

"Worse for you than for me, Colonel. I never did know what we were after, not really anyway, not the way you did. Long as you know, it's good enough for the troops." Stark tossed down the last of his drink, then looked back at his officer. "Drink up, Colonel, there's plenty to do somewhere. We could raise up a fair-sized regiment of men who'd follow you to hell. Tomorrow, I'll round up some of the old headquarters company and we'll go show the Southies what war's really like."

MacKinnie grinned momentarily as he methodically warmed his cigar before lighting it. The bar was pleasant, the company was good, and for a moment he forgot the hopelessness, even ordering a small grua to dip the end of his cigar into. He inhaled the strong smoke and leaned back in his chair, his feet stretched out under the table. Stark looked at him again, saw the lines leave Nathan's face, and ordered another round.

It was no good, MacKinnie thought, but there was no point in upsetting the big man next to him. He'd have to play the game out to the end, but, by all the Saints, he was tired now, tired in a way that the sleep and rest and soft duty they'd had for the last weeks could never cure. It was strange, he thought. Colonel of his own regiment at forty local years, a full citizen of Orleans, inevitably to be senior colonel and then general before his last parade. Not bad for a wandering mercenary soldier whose city-state had been extinguished only months before his graduation from its tiny war-academy, set to wandering in search of a living until he'd ended in the ranks of Orleans's army. Promotion, merit, recognition, citizenship, a good career. And it was all over when the landing boats came down from the ship that still whirled in orbit above Samual.

Ten years of brilliant campaigning had ensured that Orleans would not suffer the fate of his native Samand. No power or likely combination of powers could annex the Republic—but in a week the Imperial Navy had accomplished it, so that Orleans was now the Duchy of Orlean, subject to His Majesty King David Second of Haven, and no Orleanist officers wanted in the Royal Service, thank you. Honor, of course, and an inadequate pension to the hero of Blanthern Pass whose regiment had defeated the best that Haven could put in the field. Well done, old chap! Of course His Majesty has his own colonels, but we have a pension for you sir. No hard feelings, and of course no retaliation against the Orleanists. Well, not much, anyway, and only against a few of the political officers. You were never in politics, were you, Colonel? No, of course not. Too good a soldier. Yes, you can go now. And Colonel Nathan MacKinnie was suddenly an old man, feeling his campaigns and ready to drink far too much. He had left the palace and walked aimlessly before he noticed that Stark was behind him.

He could have fought, of course. Even after the Committee bowed to the inevitable power of the Imperial Navy, he could have taken MacKinnie's Wolves to the fields, wandering in the forests, cutting down Haven soldiers, fighting tiny actions with formations too small for the Navy to find and blast out of existence with their space weapons. But for how long? And what would the Imperials do to Orleans? How long would the people of the Republic have supported him? How long before the romantic gesture turned stale and the admiration of the citizens turned to hatred and disgust as town after town was bombarded from space, turned to a blackened cinder as Lechfeld was? MacKinnie inhaled his cigar, letting the warm smoke drift over his tongue, out his lips, and into his nostrils, tasting the incredibly pleasing combination of real tobacco and grua before destroying the delicate flavors with the harsh tang of whiskey.

Across the next table, a couple rose and staggered toward the door, leaving him a clear view of Lieutenant Jefferson. The young naval officer was telling an admiring peasant about a strange planet, a place where they had no guns, only swords, and they worshiped Christ in a temple which once was an Old Empire library. Both of us drunks, MacKinnie thought. But the boy's one up. He's going somewhere, and what he does won't be undone by something you couldn't fight, couldn't understand. Stark was right. The young man did resemble the old Nat MacKinnie, but not this one. The old one was going somewhere, and what he accomplished would be his. And so the same would be true for that boy. Cursing bitterly, Nathan MacKinnie realized that he felt envy for the young men who had conquered his world.

★2★
GENTLEMEN ROBBERS
★ ★ ★

The evening wore on. The first round of entertainers finished their acts. It was too early for the late performers, and for many of the customers it was several drinks too late for anything else. The room became less noisy as the early festive crowd departed, leaving the Blue Bottle to serious drinkers and tavern girls. Only the voice of Lieutenant Jefferson, punctuated by the giggles of the girls at the Navy table, was heard above the low buzz of conversation. MacKinnie decided that it was time to go.

He stood in sudden decision, but when he swept his hand behind him for the cloak he had left on a nearby chair he lost his balance and lurched heavily into a small, round-faced man with a tiny mustache. The little man jumped backward with rabbit agility and began to mumble apologies.

"Not at all, sir," MacKinnie told him. "My fault entirely. No offense intended," he added unnecessarily. The little man was unarmed, and the thought of his issuing a challenge to Colonel MacKinnie was humorous. With an effort Nathan suppressed the laugh that the image generated.

"None taken, of course," the man said. "Would you join me in a drink?" He extended his hand. "Malcolm Dougal," he said apologetically.

The grip was firmer than MacKinnie would have expected. He took a long look at the chap. He saw nothing out of the ordinary. A kilt of some family plaid, a muted version of a much bolder tartan no longer worn in public, well suited for business. Expensive jacket, minor jewelry in excellent taste, a heavy signet ring on his left hand, probably Prince Samual University although there were other places that copied the design. Except for his small stature you could see a hundred like him in businessmen's dining clubs anytime you cared to.

On closer inspection, though, Dougal wasn't really so small. He just appeared to be such a rabbit that you took him for a small man, and of course anyone standing next to Stark would seem tiny. There was something else about Dougal, an air that was faintly threatening when you looked at him closely, but that was ridiculous. MacKinnie shook his head to clear it of whiskey.

"Thank you, I've had more than enough," Nathan said. "Nathan MacKinnie. I'm sorry, I'm forgetting my manners. Too much whiskey. No offense intended."

"And none taken. Perhaps we'll meet again. Good night."

"And a good night to you, Citizen Dougal." MacKinnie bowed and faced the exit, leaving Stark to collect their cloaks and pay the bill. Outside, they turned toward the harbor, walking slowly to the waterfront hostel where they had rooms more compatible to MacKinnie's meager pension than the brick and stone district around the Blue Bottle. MacKinnie had no objection to staying in cheap lodgings, but he was still sufficiently a colonel to want to drink in a gentleman's tavern.

A light rain began to fall, causing the few citizens out on the street to scurry for cabs. An alcohol steam car whirred quietly by, slowing momentarily as the driver gazed at their faces before deciding they would not be customers. Then a horse-drawn two-wheeler clopped alongside.

The coachman shouted at them. "Good rates, sirs. Anywhere you want to go. Anything you could want to find in Haven, I know where it is. Good rates. You'll get wet out there, sirs, you will."

MacKinnie nodded, and the coachman jumped from his bench to hold the canvas doors open for them. "Where will it be, sirs? Blackfriar? Hellfire? Want to meet some ladies? Not like the ones in the Blue Bottle, though there's plenty that likes them, too, but I mean real ladies, maybe not welcome back home no more but well brought up, you know." Examining Stark with an expert eye, he added, "And my ladies got real handsome young maids live right there in the house with them for your man there, sir."

MacKinnie snapped his fingers, ending the chatter, and the coachman climbed back to his seat. He started the team and leaned down to the window. "Where to, sirs?"

"Waterfront," Stark answered. "Imperial Landing

Wharf." He was damned if he'd give this garrulous old coachman the name of the cheap hotel they were forced to live in and let him someday say he'd taken Iron MacKinnie to a flyblown flophouse.

The rain came down harder, forcing the old man to raise the dodger on its elaborately carved wooden braces. "Wonder if he gets many customers in this rig?" Stark mused.

The old man leaned down and cackled. "More than you might think, chum. Lots of gentlemen want to visit my ladies. And lots of real ladies still think cabs are better than steam buggies. We aren't as fast as those things, but plenty of people remember the good old days when there weren't nothing but us and they don't forget old Benjamin, no, they don't."

MacKinnie snapped his fingers again, and the coachman turned back to the road, muttering to himself, but after a few moments he again leaned down to his passengers. "Even those Imperial Navy lads, they like the cabs. You hardly see nothing else around Empire House but cabs. Oh, they keep a few steam cars waiting by just in case they're in a hurry, but you watch, them young officer kids, they never rode in a cab with real horses before. Get the biggest thrill out of it, so they tell me."

"I expect so," MacKinnie said absently.

"Been a big lift for the cabbies, the Imperials," the coachman said. "Just them being here, that's better than taking over Orleans, not that the Kingdom's not going to do right by itself out of the Duchy, no, sir." The old man whistled to himself and looked to the road again, guiding the team through the twisting, narrow streets of the old waterfront town until they emerged on the broad Dock Street, deserted except for a few drunken sailors reeling perilously close to the water's edge.

Across the narrow protected bay which had given Haven its name, brilliant lights, brighter than anything seen on Prince Samual's World for three centuries, played on Empire House and the hundred-meter-long landing boat the Imperials used to ferry their people from the destroyer in its orbit. Another city block housed a complex of strange machinery the Imperials used to support their base. Pipelines extended into the harbor. Their power plant had warmed Haven's waters, making fishermen happy with their catches, but outraged at the rapid growth of ship-worms and other vermin.

The brilliant lights also played across the hemisphere that was Marine Barracks, but none was reflected from that sheer black surface. Imperial Marine Barracks was protected by what the Navy people called a Langston Field.

MacKinnie knew little about the Field. Artillery shells fired at it were slowed to a halt, and the explosion was absorbed by the black shield, or perhaps by the metal walls beneath; certainly they did no apparent damage. The Navy proclaimed that resistance was useless: nothing short of an Imperial cruiser would be able to penetrate Marine Barracks. MacKinnie had reason to know that whatever weapons a cruiser might carry, nothing MacKinnie's Wolves had been able to fire would harm the fortress. It was one reason the Wolves surrendered.

The landing boats were vulnerable, though. In the short fight around Lechfeld he had damaged one badly and killed several of the Marines aboard—then fire came from the skies, a flaming death that scorched the village and baked half a battalion of Wolves in an instant.

But the Imperials could be hurt. They were only men. If they hadn't had Marine Barracks . . .

Wishful thinking, MacKinnie told himself. Even if he captured the barracks and destroyed the last of the landing ships the destroyer up there in the sky was safe from anything the entire population of Prince Samual's World could do. Some of the professors at Prince Samual University were experimenting with rockets which might, built large enough, go so fast they would never come back to ground. They might get to the destroyer. The professors had built one great war rocket which used liquid fuels and went more than two hundred kilometers, but there had only been the one—and even if they had another, how could they make it hit the destroyer?

The Imperial Navy said the destroyer was also protected by a Langston Field. Even if the rocket hit, there would be no more effect than MacKinnie's howitzers had had on Marine Barracks. The Imperials were right. Resistance was useless. A feeling of helplessness settled over Nathan MacKinnie. He closed his eyes and felt the whiskey reel his head around and around.

He was awakened by shouts. He had no idea how long he had dozed miserably, hoping to get to a rest room and then to bed before the full effects of all that whiskey did their worst. It could not have been long, he knew, because they were not yet around the bay to Empire House.

It took MacKinnie precious moments to rouse himself

from the stupor of half-drunken sleep and realize that the coach had been stopped by several men. Robbers? Here in Haven, near Empire House? Bold robbers, then, desperate men indeed.

He snatched open the door and tumbled out in a fighting stance, his pistol in his hands for a moment before a heavy cane struck his wrist and sent the big service pistol spinning into the dark. On the other side of the coach he heard Stark growl deep in his throat, the enraged sound of a deadly fighting man, and he heard the sharp *chunk!* as his big sergeant's hand, arched into a blade that could easily crack baked clay, snapped into flesh. Someone over there would not get up for a long time.

He hoped Stark was giving a good account of himself. Whatever Hal could do, MacKinnie was helpless. A pistol pointed at him from the shadows, and on either side were men with shortswords. With a shrug, MacKinnie raised his hands. There was nothing else to do.

He heard Stark strike again, then a dull sound which he could not recognize. Moments later three men carried his sergeant around the coach. One dangled a sandbag from his fingers and looked to the dim figure of the man with the pistol. "He's only out for a little while as you ordered, sir. I wish I could say the same for two of my men. They may never get up again."

"That will do," the voice from the shadows said. It seemed strangely familiar to MacKinnie, but he could not recall it. "Bring Colonel MacKinnie and the others with us, if you please." The figure vanished into a side street.

MacKinnie felt the point of a sword at his back. The weapon was similar to those carried by the Haven police, and as he thought about it, MacKinnie remembered that shortswords had been standard equipment for Haven soldiers until the present king had increased the length of the bayonets his troops carried and relegated swords to dress uniforms. The men at either side of him seemed quite familiar with their weapons. Very useful skill, MacKinnie thought. Very useful indeed if you wanted quiet work.

They walked on in silence for the better part of a kilometer, twisting through deserted streets and getting soaked by the rain until they entered a multi-storied building no different from the others they had passed. They descended two flights of stairs in utter darkness before one of the men struck a light and another produced an electric torch, and MacKinnie could see three more men carrying Stark.

They had to be military, MacKinnie thought. Their discipline, silent and efficient, was excellent, and it was obvious that this was no simple robbery. There had been ample opportunities to cut their throats and take what little remained of his monthly pension. Besides, the leader had known MacKinnie's name and rank, and had even insisted on personally examining Stark before they started off. Thieves did not take such good care of their victims.

At the bottom of the stairs they entered a dank stone tunnel which seemed to stretch nearly a hundred meters before it turned, twisted, and ended at the bottom of another flight of stairs. MacKinnie was now genuinely interested in where he was being taken, and needed no prodding from behind to climb vigorously, each step working off more of the whiskey until he was better able to handle himself. Without the fog of drunkenness he felt more in control of the situation, ready to take any opportunity to free himself.

He was halted in a wood-paneled hallway. The only light was from the small electric torch of the guard behind him. They stood for several minutes before a door was opened from the inside and bright light spilled out to blind him. Then he was ushered into a large office. Around the walls hung red drapes of rich material, and over the desk was a large painting of King David Second.

Sergeant Stark was draped on a woolsh-hide couch along one wall of the office, his shoulders so broad that nearly half of him was spilled over, one arm dangling to the elaborately patterned carpet. MacKinnie saw that his companion was breathing steadily, although he was not yet conscious.

Under the copper-edged painting of the king was a rich wood desk, fully two and a half meters by two, its gleaming top bare of papers or any other object, and behind the desk stood Malcolm Dougal, still resembling a rabbit, a nervous smile on his lips as he spoke.

"Welcome, Colonel MacKinnie. Welcome to the headquarters of His Majesty's Secret Police."

★3★
CITIZEN DOUGAL
★ ★ ★

MacKinnie looked slowly around the room. Two young men dressed in kilts as plain as Malcolm Dougal's stood against the door behind him, their pistols held carefully across their chests in a guard position. Plain kilts or no, they were soldiers, and under their dispassionate expressions MacKinnie detected a slight twitch, nervousness perhaps, at the presence of the secret policemen, or, more likely, hatred for Nathan MacKinnie who had defeated their army three campaigns running.

The room gave the general impression of opulence. The only furniture was the desk, two chairs, and the couch, but there might have been anything behind the red drapes which ran from floor to high ceiling along two walls. When Nathan said nothing, Dougal motioned toward one of the woolsh-hide chairs. "Please be seated, Colonel. Can we get you anything? A drink, perhaps? No, I suspected not. Something else? Earth Stock coffee, or chickeest?"

There was a visible tightening to Dougal's lips as he offered Earth coffee, something which told MacKinnie the offer was a test. Without hesitation Nathan said, "Chickeest, thank you. Black, and lots of it."

Dougal relaxed. He waited until MacKinnie was fully seated, then motioned to the guards. "That will be all, Corporal. Remain on call." MacKinnie heard the door close quietly behind him. "They will bring the refreshments in a moment, Colonel," Dougal said. "And now, you are wondering why you are here."

"I'm more interested in who you are. I've never seen or heard of you before, and I know of most of His Majesty's officers."

"The two questions are not unrelated. Malcolm Dougal is actually my name. My position is rather vague in the budgets presented to Parliament, but as it happens, I am the Director of His Majesty's Secret Police Service."

MacKinnie nodded. "I suspected that Lord Arindell was too stupid to operate as efficient a service as Haven's. So Inspector Solon reports to you when he wants his real orders."

"Yes. You see, I am being honest with you, Colonel. I expect you to be so with me. Had you taken my offer of a drink at the Blue Bottle, I might have brought you here in a more pleasant manner, but I could not take the chance of your refusal. Or of the Imperial Navy noticing either of us. Everything depends on their not becoming suspicious. Everything."

He leaned forward and regarded MacKinnie intently. "I now ask your word of honor that nothing said here tonight will ever be repeated to anyone without my permission except as it may conform to duties I have assigned you and you have accepted. Please," he said urgently.

MacKinnie longed for a cigar, but thought better of displaying the Earth tobacco he had in his pouch. The warning had been plain in the way Dougal had pronounced the words "Earth Stock" when offering the coffee. Dougal leaned back in his chair, but his manner was alert, expecting an answer. MacKinnie said the only thing he could under the circumstances. "You have my word, Citizen Dougal. My word of honor."

"Thank you." There was a tap at the door, and one of the guards brought in a platinum tray with copper pots of chickeest, pewter mugs, and cigarettes of a popular Haven brand. MacKinnie noticed that everything he had seen since he entered the room was native to Samual.

Behind the guard, the tall, thin figure of Inspector Solon, dressed in the midnight-blue undress uniform of the Royal Haven Police, stood silently in the doorway. He made no move to enter, and Dougal did not speak to him. When the guard left, Solon went out behind him, closing the door.

"You saw the inspector, of course," Dougal said. "There are two reasons for his being here. First, I wanted you to see that he obeys me so that you know I am who I say I am. But more important, I trust no one else to guard that door until we are finished." He smiled pleasantly. "I trust I have impressed you sufficiently. Enjoy your chickeest; you will be here for some time."

"What about my sergeant?"

"He has already been examined by Inspector Solon,

and the man who struck him was an expert. There is no permanent harm. He should be joining us in an hour, perhaps less."

"Then get on with it." MacKinnie sipped the bitter stuff, never as satisfactory as Earth Stock coffee. Only a few things were that you found among the stars. Men had colonized Prince Samual's World nearly a thousand standard years ago, but they had lived on Earth for millions.

"Tell me what you know of the plans the Imperial Navy has for Prince Samual, Colonel MacKinnie."

"Precious little. They appeared less than a year ago, and almost immediately settled in Haven. At first they didn't interfere with the planetary governments, but then they made an alliance with your King David—"

"Your king also, Colonel," Dougal interrupted.

"With King David. They helped you conquer the other city-states around Haven, and finally did for you what no Haven army had ever been able to do. They gave you Orleans. I don't know who's next, but I presume this goes on until Haven takes all of North Continent. After that . . . who knows, the Southies, I suppose."

"And then what will they do, Colonel?"

"Your newspapers keep telling us they'll help us, give us all kinds of scientific marvels, but I've yet to see any of them. You Havenites have kept them all."

"We haven't, because there have been none. Every assistance the Imperials have given us has been direct, with their Marines operating the weapons and none of my people even allowed to see their new technology. Go on, what after that?"

"Once you have conquered the whole blasted planet, I guess they take you into their Empire, with David Second as planetary king."

"And you find that unpleasant?" Dougal smiled.

"What do you want me to say, Citizen Dougal? You've told me you head the secret police. You want me to say treason out of my own mouth?"

Malcolm Dougal poured more chickeest, carefully, not spilling a drop, and took a long sip before replying. "Appreciate your situation, Colonel. If I meant you harm, it would happen to you. I need no evidence, and there would be no trial. No one knows you're here but my most trusted men, and if you never leave this room, why, who will know it? I'm interested in what you think, Iron Man MacKinnie, and it's damned important to Haven and the whole planet. Now stop being coy and answer my questions."

It was the first spark of emotion MacKinnie had seen in Dougal save for the slight tightening of the lips when he mentioned Earth. MacKinnie paused for a moment, then answered.

"Yes, I find that unpleasant. I can think of more unpleasant things, such as domination of the planet by one of the Southie despots, but after what you've done to Orleans, damned right I find it unpleasant."

"Thank you." Dougal was speaking in his normal tone, an apologetic note to his voice, but the resemblance to a rabbit was gone. Now he merely looked like a businessman. "Would you find absolute domination by an Imperial Viceroy even less pleasant?"

"Of course."

"And why?" Dougal waved in an imperious manner. "I know why. For the same reason that you drink chickeest, bitter as it is. Because he is an outlander, a foreigner, not of Samual at all, and we belong here. This is our world and our home, and I tell you, Colonel MacKinnie, that we will never be slaves to that Empire. Not while I live and not while my sons live."

"So you hope to escape that by using the Imperial Marines and Navy to conquer the planet?"

"No. I had hoped to do so, but it won't work. Colonel, once their colonists and viceroy land here, King David will have no more influence over this planet than your sergeant. I thought you knew little of them. Few know anything at all." He reached under the desk for a moment. Within seconds, MacKinnie heard the door open behind him.

"Yes, my lord," a flat voice said. Before he turned to look, MacKinnie knew it was Inspector Solon. The voice fit him perfectly, cold and toneless, like a voice from a tomb.

"Bring that book, Inspector," Dougal said quietly.

"Yes, my lord." The door did not close, and seconds later Solon crossed the room carrying a sheaf of papers held in a strange clasp.

"Thank you." Dougal dismissed Solon with a wave and pointed to the papers. "This is the only Imperial artifact we have been able to obtain. It appears to be some kind of work of fiction, about the adventures of a naval officer on a newly settled planet. But it also gives us much information about the structure of the Imperial government, just as one of Cadace's best-sellers would tell them a lot about the government of Haven even though there's not a line in it intended to do so. Do you understand?" MacKinnie nodded.

"Then," the policeman continued, "understand this. The Empire has several kinds of planetary governments within it. There is Earth itself, which is the honorary capital, but is mostly uninhabitable because of the aftermath of the Secession Wars. For their own reasons they keep some institutions including their naval and military academies there, but the real capital is called Sparta, and is in another planetary system entirely. After the capitals there are what they call Member Kingdoms, which are planetary governments strong enough to give the Imperial Navy a good fight if the Empire tried to interfere with their internal affairs."

"All monarchies?" Nathan asked.

"There is at least one republic. Many are monarchies." Dougal sipped at his chickeest. "Then there are Class One and Class Two worlds. We can't tell the difference between them, but they have less authority over their own affairs than the Member Kingdoms. They do have representation on the capital in one house of a multi-house advisory council, and some of their people are officers in the Imperial services. The two classes refer to some differences in technology which we do not understand, but the relevant factors are the technology levels when admission to the Empire takes place. They both seem to have something called atomic power which fascinates the physicists at the University, and their own spaceships."

MacKinnie nodded, recalling some remarks made by the drunken lieutenant in the Blue Bottle. He mentioned this to Dougal, who nodded.

"Good," Dougal said. "You are here because you overheard him. You see, Colonel, after the Class One and Class Two worlds, there's nothing left but colonies. And that's what we'll be."

"What's the status of colonies?" MacKinnie asked.

"They have none. Imperial citizens are imported as an aristocracy to impart civilization. A viceroy governs in the Emperor's name, and the Navy keeps a garrison to see that no trouble develops. The colonists end in complete control of everything, and the locals do as they're told or else."

"How can they govern a whole planet against everybody's will? What good does it do them to burn half the world to ashes like Lechfeld?" MacKinnie drank the last of his now cooled chickeest, then answered his own question. "But of course they don't have to fight their own battles, do they? There's always a local government ready to toady to the Imperials. Someone to do their dirty work for them." He looked significantly at Dougal.

Malcolm Dougal pretended not to notice. "Yes. There is always one. If not King David, then one of the Southie despots. But it won't happen, MacKinnie. I've found a way to win this fight and get Class Two status for Samual. I've found a way, a chance, but I can't do it alone. I need your help." Dougal leaned across the desk looking intently at Nathan MacKinnie.

Colonel MacKinnie stood, slowly, stretching to his full height before lifting the copper pitcher and pouring another mug of chickeest. Still moving very carefully, he strode to the couch, examined Stark for a moment, then returned to his chair. "Have you a pipe and 'robac, my lord?" he asked. "This promises to be quite a night . . . Why me?"

"I hadn't intended it to be you until tonight. I had no real plan before, merely studied a series of actions I might be able to take, made preparations for an opportunity, any opportunity, but now that young fool has told us how to save the state. You heard him, of course."

"If I did, I didn't understand. What are you going to do?"

"But you must have heard him. You were there when he babbled about the Old Empire library on a planet at the Eye of the Needle."

MacKinnie thought for a moment, then said, "Yes, but I don't see how that can help us."

"You haven't thought about this for months, as I have. We found that book not long after they landed, Colonel. It took only a few weeks to understand most of the language. It's not all that different from ours, at least the written forms, which is why the Imperials get around Haven so easily."

The policeman lit a 'robac cigar, leaned back in his chair, and glared at the ceiling. "Ever since I could read that thing, I've thought of little else but ways to escape this trap. There's no way to avoid being part of the Empire, but by the Saints we can make them take us in as human beings, not slaves!"

"If you had the book so early, you must have understood what they wanted before Haven made the alliance with them."

"Of course. It was on my advice that His Majesty entered the alliance. Unless we consolidate Prince

Samual's World under a planetary government, we have no chance at all of escaping colonization. And unless it's under King David, I won't have any influence over the planetary government, and you will pardon me if I think I may be better at this kind of intrigue than some of the, shall we say, more honorable men of the other city-states?"

"All right," MacKinnie said. "So you're a master of intrigue. I still don't see what we can do."

Dougal laughed. "You've drunk too much whiskey, Iron Man MacKinnie. Tonight and other nights. You're not above a bit of duplicity yourself. You used several very clever dodges on us. Your record, Colonel—I have it here—your record says you are more than just a simple combat soldier. But it's pleasing to be able to instruct you."

Dougal poured more chickeest. "That library is the key to it all. If we had the knowledge that must be there—our people at the University, and the industrial barons of Orleans and Haven, and the miners of Clanranald—what couldn't they do? We could build a spaceship. A starship, perhaps. And by their own rules the Imperials would have to admit us as a classified world, not a colony. We'd still have to knuckle under to them, but we'd be subjects, not slaves."

MacKinnie took a deep breath. "That's quite a plan."

"It's the only possible plan."

"I don't know— Look. Suppose it's true. With knowledge, construction plans even, with a planetary government to bring together the technology of North Continent and the resources of South Continent, perhaps it could be done. Perhaps. But we haven't the time. It would take years."

"We'll have years. The Imperials won't move until we

consolidate the kingdoms. They're in no great hurry. They've made it clear they want as little bloodshed and destruction as possible. I can see that it takes time to bring in all the city-states. That will give us time to build the ship. It won't be easy, building a thing like that under their noses, but they won't have very many people on this planet, and they won't suspect a thing until it's done."

MacKinnie shook his head. "I don't see how you can keep them from finding out, but you're better at that than me. But you can't get at the library without a ship, and we can't build a ship without the library. Even if we had one, we couldn't operate it. There's been nobody on this planet who ever saw the inside of a starship for hundreds of years. Until the Imperials came, most of the population thought that history before the Secession Wars was just a lot of legends. How in hell do you propose that we get to the Eye of the Needle?"

"That's the simplest part of the plan, Colonel. The Imperials have already offered to take us there." He smiled at Nathan's startled look. "They're not all Navy and Military, you know. Some Imperial citizens are Traders. There's one batch of them right now negotiating with King David over the rights to grua. They think our brandy will be worth a fortune on their capital.

"They want platinum and iridium, too; those metals seem to be very useful to them and in short supply. But there isn't much they can give us in return, because the Navy won't let them sell us what we really want— technology. The Navy rule is, you can't trade anything more technologically advanced than what your customer already has without special permission from the Imperial

Council. We offered to buy those little devices they all carry around like notebooks. 'Pocket computers,' the Navy men call them. They seem to be machines. They can't sell those."

"What can they sell?"

"Not much, it appears. But they have offered the king transportation to a world less advanced than ours, some-place where we can try our luck at selling. They suggested a planet at the star we call the Eye of the Needle as the closest, and we are already discussing an expedition to go there and try to organize trade. . . ."

"The Navy will permit this?" MacKinnie asked.

"Under conditions. Stringent conditions, I might add. We can't take anything more advanced than the natives already have. The Navy inspects our trade mission and goods before we go to the planet. But they will let us go. It appears that the Imperial Traders Association has a good-sized block of votes in the Imperial Council. I don't pretend to understand capital politics, but the ITA seems very influential. They can force the Navy to let us trade with that planet, Makassar, it's called."

"Won't they be watching to see that we don't get near the library?" MacKinnie asked. The whiskey fog was gone from his mind now, but more than that, he felt useful again, as if there were something he might do which could not be taken away by a whim of fate. He listened to Dougal with keen interest, not noticing that Sergeant Stark was stirring on the couch to his right.

"They have never mentioned the library," Dougal said. "Until that young lieutenant babbled about it in the Blue Bottle, I never knew it existed. I think the library's an anomaly in their records, not listed as an advanced artifact because it's so old and the people on Makassar don't know how to use it. That's only a guess. I do know they've been willing to let us go there."

Dougal paused and again looked intently at MacKinnie. "That leaves me with the problem of one Colonel MacKinnie, who knows about the library. I decided when I heard about it that we'd have to try to get the knowledge there, and since you know about the library, I'd either have to kill you or send you on the expedition. I don't know how to get those books, and I'm not sure that anyone on this planet does know. But I'd rather have you on our side than dead. You were very resourceful against Haven, Colonel. Will you swear allegiance to King David and work for Haven now?"

★4★
TRADER
★ ★ ★

MacKinnie woke to the stale taste of 'robac and the sick feeling of whiskey in his stomach. He lay for a few moments on the caltworm-silk sheets, slowly recalling where he was. There were no windows to the room, and the only light was from a soft glowplate on one wall. To his right there was a rest room with marble appointments, and through it was a connecting door to a room similar to the one where he was lying. He knew it was there, because Sergeant Stark had lumbered unsteadily into it when they left Dougal's office. They were in the same building, but beyond that MacKinnie had no idea of his location. The only doors leading outside the suite were locked, and he had no doubt that Dougal's guards stood watch in the hall.

He raised himself on one elbow. To his left a closet stood open, revealing racks of rich clothing. His own kilt and jacket, freshly cleaned and pressed, hung neatly on the door, and with them hung his service pistol.

MacKinnie wryly slipped from the bed to examine it, not surprised that there were no cartridges. His watch was in the pouch hanging with his clothes, but it had stopped. He had no idea of the time.

Now that he was up, he decided he might as well stay up. He took his time in the rest room, using luxurious shaving equipment and treating himself to a double dash of the most expensive lotions and powders he had ever seen. If all guests of King David's secret police fared as well as he, there would be long lines of people hoping to be arrested for high treason, but he suspected there were more dungeons in the building than guest suites.

As he finished shaving, Stark knocked at the door, then waited for MacKinnie to finish. The sergeant had shaved and dressed by the time Nathan had put on his kilt and was buttoning his coat. Stark seemed no different from the hundreds of mornings they had spent in garrison as he expertly straightened MacKinnie's jacket and made tiny adjustments in the kilt and fall.

"What have we got ourselves into, Colonel?" Stark asked. As he spoke he made tiny signals with his hands, indicating the walls, then his ears.

MacKinnie nodded. "I'm not sure, but it beats chasing Southies. This could be a job worth doing. Tell me, can you round up some of the Wolves who can keep their mouths shut and act like Traders' guards?"

"Many as you want, Colonel. How many do you think we need?"

"All of them, but I don't think the Imperial Navy will let us take a regiment to Makassar."

"We'll get as many as you want. Going to be funny

calling you Trader, but I reckon I can get used to it." Stark looked around the chamber, noting the carved wooden furniture, and the crystalline rock formation patterns in the parts of the floor not covered by carpets woven in the Archipelago. "Fancy quarters, uh, Trader, sir."

"Yes. Well, I suppose we might as well get on with it. We wouldn't want to keep Dougal and Inspector Solon waiting."

"Yes, sir. Begging your pardon, sir, I hope he won't go with us to that crazy place. Going up high like that, off the world even, that's enough without that walking corpse to give me the creeps."

"He won't be coming along. Nervous, Hal?"

"No, sir, not if you say not to be. But I am having a little trouble getting used to the idea."

"That's two of us. All right, Hal, tell them we're ready for breakfast."

"Yes, sir." Stark found the speaking tube in a small recess under the dim light, uncapped it, and whistled. After a second there was an answering note. "Our respects, and the colonel and I are ready for breakfast." Stark listened for a few moments, then returned to MacKinnie. "He says someone will be with us in five minutes, sir. Seemed polite, anyway." When there was no answer from Nathan, Hal capped the tube.

Four guards were visible when the door opened. At least two of them were from the party which had captured MacKinnie and Stark the night before. Their weapons were holstered, and they were extremely polite as they invited MacKinnie and Stark to accompany them, but Nathan noticed that as one led the way the other three fell in well behind, eyeing Stark nervously as they walked stiffly along. They were ushered into the big office MacKinnie had seen the night before. The curtains were drawn back along one wall to reveal a walled veranda beyond where Solon and Dougal sat at a glass-topped table sipping chickeest. As MacKinnie approached, Solon stood, nodded to Dougal, and left without speaking to them.

"Good morning, Trader," Dougal said. He stood, waited for MacKinnie to be seated, and indicated a place at a table a few feet away for Stark. "Your breakfast will be here shortly. I trust you enjoyed your sleep?"

MacKinnie smiled pleasantly. "A great deal more than I thought I would when I was first invited here."

Dougal nodded. "There have been others who did not enjoy their stay in this building at all." He dismissed the guards with a wave, then turned back to Nathan. "The subterfuge starts this instant, Trader MacKinnie. We will use your proper name, although we will change your first to Jameson. MacKinnie's common enough in Haven, and there is a great Trader family by that name."

"Are you sure the Imperials won't recognize me?"

"Reasonably. Besides, they aren't looking for a dead man. Colonel Nathan MacKinnie was killed at Lechfeld. Died of his wounds a few weeks after the battle. Tough old soldier, too proud to say anything when he turned over his sword to the Haven General Staff. The records already show that."

"But there was a young officer who interviewed me . . . and the paymaster will know my pension has been paid for months. Then there's the landlady at our flop."

"There *were* those people, Trader. Unfortunately, they all died last night in a series of tragic accidents. The Blue Bottle had another accident, I'm afraid. It burned to the ground, everyone in it killed shortly after the Imperial Navy men had left. Nothing the Watch could do, the fire was so fierce. It almost seems as if someone deliberately set it, but I'm sure His Majesty's Police will catch the scoundrels if that's true. More chickeest?"

"And my men? My former officers?"

"They're being recruited for an expedition to the Archipelago, with offers so generous I'm sure no one will turn them down. If anyone does, well, Traders' expeditions have been known to have reluctant members in the past."

Before MacKinnie could reply, the corporal arrived with their food, and Dougal insisted that they eat before resuming the conversation. When they had finished, the policeman signaled, and the corporal brought MacKinnie a pipe. It was one of his own from the rooms where he and Stark had been living. It did not seem necessary to comment on it.

"You haven't been very active since you left the Service," Dougal said. "It won't be difficult to cover your tracks, at least enough to keep the Imperials from looking too closely at you."

"All right, what's the drill for today?" MacKinnie asked.

"Mind your aphorisms, Trader. We wouldn't want your military background to show through, although we will have your records show that you served honorably as a company commander in His Majesty's Home Guard during the Theberian War. You won't have to play a part for long; I intend that you leave as soon as possible. We'll send for the other members of the expedition now. Remember, this is a trading mission, and you are Trader MacKinnie. You've met none of them before. Here." Dougal held out a small box. On opening it, MacKinnie found it full of rings, brooches, and other personal jewelry, all in good taste and the kind of thing he might have worn if the military habit were not so strong in him. He selected a ring, brooch, and earring and put them on.

"Now you look more like a Trader. I have more for your man." Dougal held out gaudier jewelry, flashier but less expensive than Nathan's, and waited until Stark had put it on before beckoning to the corporal.

As the others approached, MacKinnie asked quickly, "What are you to these people?"

"A high officer of the secret police. They are all trustworthy servants of the crown, but they do not know the real purpose of this expedition." Dougal stood, smiling expansively. "Welcome, gentleman, freelady. This is Trader MacKinnie, who will manage King David's shares of this expedition. He has financed much of it, I might add. Trader, here are your crew and advisors."

They sorted themselves out and stood expectantly, waiting to be presented. The first was broad-shouldered, of medium height, and stood stiffly erect. Dougal said, "Trader, this is Shipmaster MacLean of the Royal Merchant Service. He is qualified in both sail and motor vessels."

"Honored," MacLean mumbled, looking straight ahead. His grip was firm, testing MacKinnie's, and Nathan was

pleased to note the surprise in the officer's eyes before he
let go. The man was so obviously from the Haven Navy
that MacKinnie could not understand how the Imperials
would be expected to be deceived, but he said nothing.

"And this is Academician Longway, who studies social
organization and primitive cultures as well as ancient
history." MacKinnie studied him closely. The man was
broad and short, typical of the people of Prince Samual's
World, dark hair and light eyes, and could have been a
miner if it were not for the thick spectacles. His kilt was
scholarly, dark with a thin red stripe, but the grip was firm
and the voice steady.

"Honored to meet you, Trader, and I must say, pleased
to be selected for an expedition as important—important
and rare—as this. It's not often a scholar gets the chance
to visit a really strange culture. I've been to the Archipelago,
to many of the islands there, but of course it isn't the same.
I can't say how pleased I am to be going with you. It's an
historic event."

"Let's hope you feel that way when we return,"
MacKinnie said. He kept his voice as pleasant as possible,
and found that easier than he had thought it would be. He
had never liked men who chattered, but the enthusiastic
friendliness of the scholar was infectious all the same.
Longway motioned to the man who stood behind him.

The man was young, not more than twenty local years.
He stood shuffling his feet nervously, his long gangling
arms hanging loosely at his sides. He was of very slight
build and stood with a stoop that made him seem even
shorter than he was. He also wore thick spectacles, and
his kilt was plain, smudged with ink and food stains. He

carried a large book under his left arm, and the end of a bulky notebook protruded from his pouch.

"This is my assistant, Scholar-Bachelor Kleinst," Longway said. "Most brilliant student at the University, I might add. Does very good work."

"Honored, Trader," Kleinst mumbled, holding his hand out perfunctorily and withdrawing it limply as soon as possible. His voice matched his appearance, and MacKinnie instantly disliked him. Nathan turned expectantly to the last member of the group.

"Allow me to present Freelady Mary Graham," Dougal said. "She will serve as your assistant and secretary. I might add that she is a graduate of the University."

MacKinnie hid his surprise. There were few women in the universities, and fewer still graduated.

He had seen lovelier girls, the city of Haven being noted for the beauty of its women, but there was nothing wrong with Mary Graham's appearance. She had the typical brown hair and light eyes of the Haven population, but she was considerably smaller than most of the city women; not so small as to be tiny, and well formed for her height. She wore rather severely tailored clothes which did not quite hide a pleasing figure, and Nathan noted that she stood attentively, waiting for him to speak, her nervousness betrayed only by a slight motion of her fingers drumming against her skirt. Nathan guessed her age at something more than twenty, but almost certainly below twenty-five.

"Honored, freelady," he said, nodding slightly.

"My honor, Trader."

Her voice was not unpleasant, MacKinnie decided.

But her presence annoyed him. There was no need for women in an expedition as important as this, and he was surprised that Dougal would suggest it. In Nathan's world women were divided into two groups: freeladies to be protected, and camp followers who served no less useful a purpose but who were more or less expendable. Mary Graham did not seem to fit into either category.

He was certain that he was again being tested, because a more unlikely group for saving the state would be hard to imagine. Dougal had explained the night before why MacKinnie himself should command the expedition. The Imperials were likely to know of any of Haven's really competent officers, yet a military background seemed required if anything were to be accomplished on Makassar. Still, MacKinnie did not look or act exactly like a Trader, and the crew assembled here contained an obvious naval officer, a talkative scholar of uncertain abilities, a weakling of almost effeminate appearance, and a girl. Surely, he thought, the Imperials would suspect— but even if they did not, what would be gained by sending this group to Makassar?

Dougal ushered in two more young men wearing battle dress without insignia. "MacReedy and Todd, guards," Dougal explained.

MacKinnie looked them over carefully and decided they were the most authentic in appearance of any of his expedition. He indicated Hal. "This is Stark, your guard leader. We'll have a few more guards for the expedition when we find out precisely how many we can take. Guard Leader, please take your men to your table and get to know them."

"Yes, Trader." Stark led the men to the other side of the veranda.

MacKinnie turned back to the policeman. "My lord, I am sure the others will excuse us a moment while we discuss the cargo. There are some difficulties about financing which I am sure would only bore them, so perhaps they can be working on equipment lists while we discuss finances in your office?"

"Certainly, Trader." The others bowed, and MacKinnie led Dougal through the veranda doors to the office beyond.

Once inside, MacKinnie exploded. "How in hell do you expect the Imperials to be stupid enough to pass that crew? This is a thin enough plan to begin with, Dougal. I can't begin to accomplish the mission if you saddle me with incompetents. My Saviour! You give me an obvious naval commander itching to learn anything he can about their starships, a weak-eyed little intellectual, and I don't know, maybe the Academician will do, but where did you find that girl? In your freshman spy classes?"

Dougal held up his palm briefly, stopping Nathan's tirade. "Sit down, Trader, and have something to drink. Calmly, now."

Still fuming, Nathan sat and stuffed his pipe. "And another thing. I don't appreciate murder. How many people did you kill last night, anyway?"

"As many as necessary, Trader," Dougal said coldly. "Think of them as martyrs to Prince Samual's World, and we'll erect statues for them when this is over. If it works. What would you have had me do with them after they heard the most important secret on this planet?"

"Swear them to secrecy—" MacKinnie was stopped by the policeman's laughter. "I suppose not," Nathan said. "Hide them? Lock them up—"

"So that if one escaped we would really have lost the secret. Tell me, Colonel Iron MacKinnie, do you recommend that the military do things by half measures?"

"No—"

"Nor can we. I am not proud of what was done last night, but in my judgment it was needed. Tell me, did you ever consider guerrilla war against the Imperials? I know that you did. Would not innocent lives have been lost in your war? How many more will be killed in futile resistance to the Imperial colonists if we fail? I wish to hear no more about it." He lit a cigarette, calmly inhaled, and continued.

"As to your crew. First, of course MacLean is a naval officer. The Imperials will know we intend to send a spy on the expedition. It might as well be a clumsy try so that they don't suspect you. They will probably be careful to keep MacLean away from their ships' engines and controls, but I doubt they will object to his going.

"Academician Longway has been on several expeditions to the Archipelago, and he knows as much about primitives and ancient civilizations as any man on this planet. He has fought his way out of tough situations in the past, too. He may be more use to you than you think."

"All right," MacKinnie said. "I didn't object to him anyway. What about the scholar? A strong wind would blow him away."

"Kleinst is just what he appears to be, except for one small deception. He's not an historian, he's a physicist.

The best we have who isn't prominent enough to be known to the Imperials. The boy is sharp enough to learn Longway's patter sufficiently well to fool anyone not an expert. I admit his appearance is against him, but we can't be choosy. You'll need someone who understands what science we know if only to tell you what to bring back."

MacKinnie lit his pipe. "And the girl?"

"The daughter of one of my officers. She really is a graduate of the University, she's reliable, and no one expects a girl to be intelligent. She may have an opportunity to learn something you don't. Pretty girls often do; they have methods not available to men."

MacKinnie started to interrupt, but Dougal gestured him to silence. "You may keep your shocked proprieties to yourself," the policeman said. "She is loyal and reliable, if somewhat young, and secretaries are not that uncommon on trading expeditions. We know that among the Imperials women often accompany men. There are even women officers in the Imperial Navy—oh yes, I'm quite serious."

MacKinnie tried to digest that thought, but couldn't. It was just too alien. "And which one is your agent watching me?" he demanded.

"All of them. But you won't betray us. I have enough information on you to fill a small library. The Service has had you in mind as a possible servant to King David since we took Orleans. When you overheard that conversation, I already had more than enough to act on. I don't waste good men, MacKinnie. Haven will need everyone we can find for the great task ahead of us. We're saving a planet from slavery! You won't violate your oath."

"Thank you for the confidence." MacKinnie stood. "Just how much do they know?" he asked, indicating the group on the veranda with a wide sweep of his hand.

Dougal smiled faintly. "Enough. They know this to be an expedition to a primitive world, with the ostensible purpose of establishing a trade mission, and an ostensible secret mission of filling the war chest for planetary conquest. They think the real purpose is to learn all they can about Imperial science, customs, military power, and that sort of thing—that this is a straight intelligence mission. They've been ordered not to violate Imperial regulations without specific orders from you, but to keep their eyes open whenever they're around Imperial ships. You and your sergeant know about the library. You can tell them about it when you've reached Makassar." Dougal lit another cigarette.

"I suppose they'll have to do," MacKinnie said. "All right. Now what about my cargo?"

"Primitive weapons, in large quantities. Axes, swords, and the like. Armor. Some gold and platinum, but not much because we can sell those to the Imperials directly. Cloth. Good tartan woven from winter-sheared woolsh. Grua. Spices. Some trinkets. You'll have the list soon enough, and if you think of something primitive the Makassarians might buy, or something you will need, let me know. But don't try to smuggle in anything the Imperials would object to."

"Not likely," MacKinnie said. He sighed and stared at the ashes in the bowl of his pipe. "Ever head a military force?" he asked.

"No. Only police. Why?"

"Old maxim. No plan survives contact with the enemy. This one won't either."

"Probably not, but what else have we?"

MacKinnie shrugged. "I don't know. But it's insane. Oh, it's probably the best we can do, but you'd better have a Plan B, because I think your main battle plan has about as much chance of working as I have of swimming the Major Sea."

★5★
EMPIRE HOUSE
★ ★ ★

MacKinnie sat alone on the veranda. The others were off on their various errands, leaving him as the only member of the expedition with nothing to do. He had finished his chickeest, and was wishing mightily for a good cup of coffee when Stark arrived.

"Find any of the Wolves?"

"Yes, sir. We can get our pick of the noncoms. The officers are a little harder to find. But are you sure you want any of the men? Being as how you're supposed to be dead? They're good at fighting, but they aren't so long on keeping that kind of secret. Don't know how good I'll be, for that matter."

"What about those two that Dougal furnished? Any use?"

"MacReedy's typical, si—uh, Trader. Served a hitch in a trading expedition-guard unit on South Continent, another on a sea passage through the west end of the Archipelago. He'll do. Todd's another case. Officer cadet,

I expect. Seems a good lad, probably make colonel someday, but his speech and manners don't come from the barracks. Keep him from talking too much and he'll pass."

"About what I expected," MacKinnie said. "No point in complaining. Dougal has his own ideas of how this ought to go, and we won't be able to change anything until we're off-planet. Maybe not even then. I'm not completely sure who's in command."

"I am," Stark said.

MacKinnie grinned. "Well, let's be sure of it." He thought for a moment. "Hal, get us Dunston and Olby, and pick a couple of available corporals. I have a hunch we may need some steady noncoms, and I'd as soon not have all the fighting men come from Haven. Uh—there's no need for them to advertise that they're Wolves."

Stark grinned knowingly. "Yes, Trader." The grin faded. "Think we'll have much fighting?"

MacKinnie shrugged. "I don't know. Dougal does, or he wouldn't be sending me. I don't do a lot else. I'll find out more when I meet the Imperial Traders Association reps, I suppose."

"Yes, sir. When do we get rolling?"

"Soon as possible. There's nothing to wait for. Not enough time for proper training of the troops, and not much idea of what to train them for anyway. There's one hell of a job waiting for us if we do get back with what we're after, but that's Dougal's problem. His and Solon's, and the Magnates." He looked up to see Mary Graham and Academician Longway approaching.

"That was prompt," he told her. His smile was forced.

Graham gave a thin answering show of teeth and said, "As soon as you approve the cargo list, Trader, I'll have the goods taken to the Imperial wharf for loading. It's all in the warehouses. Have you any other instructions?"

"Yes. Get someone who knows how to make body armor and find out what dimensions are needed. I want a full suit of chain mail for each of us, and that includes you, freelady. And have a variety of swords of the best quality obtainable, all types available, brought for our inspection. We'll want to choose personal weapons. Guard leader Stark will instruct you on how he wants his men equipped."

"Yes, sir." She took a notebook from her pouch and wrote with tiny precise motions. "Is that all?"

"No. Join me for lunch."

"Yes, sir," she said in the same tone, then turned to follow Stark to his table.

MacKinnie turned to Longway. "Academician, is there any special equipment you will need?"

"I'm afraid not, Trader. There are many items we could use, but they are all technological and forbidden. I would suggest you have breastplates made for yourself and your men. If the Makassarians have developed archery to any extent, you will need them."

"An excellent suggestion." MacKinnie lit his pipe. "Of course we don't expect to fight pitched battles. I hope we'll only need armor to protect ourselves from thieves and the like. Still, some decent plate might be useful, if it can be made in time. I'll tell the freelady."

"As for the rest," Longway said, "we know so little about Makassar that it is hard to tell what we should take with us. Notebooks and paper, of course. A few drafting instruments for making maps. Some standard reference works would also be useful. Do you think the Navy will allow books? Does Makassar have movable type?"

"No books," MacKinnie said. "And don't ask the Navy about them. Take only handwritten material, and don't ask the Navy about any specific item without my permission."

Longway nodded thoughtfully. "If you say so, Trader. I still have some of my personal clothing and trading items to assemble. Am I excused?"

MacKinnie nodded dismissal and went to the table where Stark sat with his men. Todd and MacReedy were quietly drinking ale while Stark issued instructions to Mary Graham. She wrote furiously in her book as he spoke.

Hal had a look of concentration and drummed his fingers against the table as he spoke. "I'd like crossbows, freelady. Good spring steel ones. There's an armory sergeant, Brighton, in the Orleans garrison who knows how to make them—he used to supply them for our special forces teams. Thirty of those, I'd reckon. They ought to have that many in stock somewhere."

"Crossbows," Graham said. "And quarrels?"

"Yes. As many as they have." Stark paused thoughtfully. "For underneath the armor we'll want suits of woolsh-hide with the hair left on, good thick stuff. If a man's going to pound on me with a sword, I want some padding under the chain mail. You go order all that, and I'll have more for you by the time you get back."

She nodded and left. MacKinnie sat at the table and poured ale for himself. "She seems to get the job done," he said. "Maybe she'll be useful."

"Never had much use for women on campaign, Trader," Stark said. "But she doesn't miss much. I'll make up my mind when I see the gear, but she's got it all down in that book of hers and seems to know where to find things in a hurry."

"Why are we in such a hurry, sir?" Todd asked.

"The Imperial Trader ship is leaving soon," MacKinnie answered. "We have to be on it or wait for another."

That's the official reason, MacKinnie thought. But there's a better one. If those Navy kids start talking about that library again, to the post commandant, or the Traders, or anyone, eventually somebody's going to connect us and the library. The sooner we get out of here the better.

It's a fool's errand, but it's worth a try, and the quicker we get back the quicker the Magnates can work on that ship. If we can get them anything, and if they can build one at all.

He knew that Dougal had already suggested that some of the University scientists work on life-support technology, using hints from the stolen novel to guide them. Others could investigate hull designs. But first Dougal would have to secure their loyalty; Prince Samual University was located in Haven, but had been independent, its independence guaranteed by treaties, for centuries. Now that Haven had conquered so many neighbors the University's independence wasn't likely to last long, but the rector would hardly take direct orders from King David's secret police. . . .

That would be Dougal's job.

But none of it would mean a thing until the secrets of the engines and their energy sources were discovered.

And that's my job, he thought.

Mary Graham returned for her luncheon engagement, her notebook bulging with subsidiary lists and scraps of paper. MacKinnie held her chair, then examined her with frank curiosity.

She's pretty enough, MacKinnie thought. And she knows how to dress so as not to emphasize her looks. She gave a lot of thought to that outfit, which means she wants to make a good impression. Why does she want to go on a tomfool expedition like this? There's only one way to find that out. "You look as if you have some sense," he said. "Why do you want to come on this insane trip?"

"I think it's my duty, Trader." It was obvious that she was choosing her words carefully. If that was an act, she was very good at it. "Citizen Dougal says this could be one of the most important missions in Haven's history, although he wouldn't say why."

"You're a patriot, then?"

She shrugged. "Not a vehement one. I would like to be part of something important. There's not much opportunity for that. Not for women."

True enough. Which was the way things should be. Women on campaign were a nuisance. Although there had been one—he quickly pushed that thought away. He couldn't think about Laura without pain and anger, and he'd brooded too much anyway. Now he had a job to do, and it was important to keep his mind clear. "And just what do you think you can do for us?" he asked.

"I don't know, whatever is necessary, I suppose. Many

trading expeditions do have secretaries, and my education may be useful to you."

Nathan laughed softly. "I doubt it." And I doubt further if you'd do the only thing I think of that might really be useful, he thought. Or will you? She could be a highly trained agent. Haven was said to employ women in their secret-police forces, but the few that Orleans's security forces had encountered had been obvious, lower class women pretending to be from good families. This girl wasn't like that. She had the manners of the aristocracy. Like Laura. And Laura had been small, like this girl— Once again he pushed that thought away. "Just what was it you studied at the University, and for that matter whatever possessed you to go there in the first place?"

"I studied a little of everything, Trader. Since there are so few girls in the University, I could study almost anything I liked. My professors didn't know what to make of me, anyway. Such serious old men, you could almost hear them clucking their tongues when they discovered they were expected to listen to a girl read them papers. But since they didn't take my efforts to get an education seriously, I could study what I wanted to and go to the lectures that interested me. Really, it's a wonderful way to study."

"You still haven't said why you went, freelady."

"Please call me Mary. After all, I do work for you. Don't I?" She sipped cold wine, and MacKinnie noticed that she did so gingerly. A telling point; girls of her class wouldn't be accustomed to drinking wine in the afternoon. "Now. Why I went there," she said. "I don't know, it just seemed the thing to do. Shocked all my friends . . .

the few friends I had, anyway. They're all married now, and I'm a terrible old maid. You can just hear them, 'Poor Mary, she can't catch a man and hold onto him!' But I wasn't interested in that. There's so little for girls in Haven, anywhere on North Continent, I guess. No adventure. It was explained in one of Academician Longway's lectures, that the war left so few women on Samual that men kept them at home so no one would see them, and it's only recently we were allowed to go out on our own. I don't know if I believe it, but that's what he said. Certainly I'd like to do something more than just raise children and help my husband get promoted by flirting with his superiors. I thought the University would help, but it just made people think I was a frimp. That's why I wanted to go on this expedition so badly." She stopped, out of breath, and smiled nervously.

"So you have no romantic attachments?"

"Not now. I was engaged once. To the son of one of my father's friends. But that's all over."

"What does your father think of your entering the Service and going off to another planet?" MacKinnie appeared to be relaxed, but he watched the girl closely. He was fairly sure that she was just what she seemed to be, which meant that she would probably be more hindrance than help. By her own account, her education at the University didn't seem to be anything useful to the expedition.

"He gave his approval, Trader," she said stiffly. "I have all the necessary permissions duly notarized. Are you afraid he might challenge you?" Her eyes flashed briefly, then she thought better of what she had said. "Oh, I didn't mean that. Please don't be angry with me, but I get so tired of having to ask Father's permission for everything I do."

"I take it you would prefer some such equality-of-sexes nonsense like Therean."

"Not that equal, Trader. I've no wish for the life of a camp follower or a tavern girl. But—surely there's a place for us in some honorable work. Not all of the secretaries in Haven were born in the charity wards. If freeladies can manage affairs for Magnates and Traders, why can't they own property themselves? Academician Longway says they did in the Old Empire. Why, there were even women in Parliament and nobody thought anything of it."

"Do you believe that?"

"Well, it seems a little strange, but why not? We're not brainless, you know. Not all of us, anyway. Who managed the estates when the men were off on campaign? You know as well as I do that not all of the wives and companions had guardians . . . if they could manage their property as long as the men were alive, even when they were away for months, why couldn't they do it after their men were killed?"

MacKinnie laughed and turned his attention to his pipe. "Management is one thing, ownership is another, freelady Mary. If you own something, you can sell it." And there were city-states where women owned property. Often enough, given the casualties in war, the result was that most of the land was owned by heiresses, and the men sought good marriages as a route to wealth.

None of which was important. It was obvious that Dougal was sending Mary Graham for reasons of his own, so MacKinnie might as well make the best of it. She might even be useful. "How far along is the cargo?" he asked.

She reached into her pouch and shuffled through papers until she found a bulky sheaf. "Here is the list. The items checked off have already been moved to the Imperial landing dock."

"And the armor?"

"Citizen Dougal has arranged for the Haven armory to prepare the chain mail. They seem to have found something which works, and one of their people will measure us this evening. The tanners will be along to measure us for the underpadding as well. And Duncan and Larue are forging swords to various patterns, and have sent over all the varieties they make. We've located crossbows, and they're making bolts for them."

"Duncan and Larue," MacKinnie mused. "I can remember when I was younger, there were whole regiments of cavalry armed with sword and pistol. Battles decided by them." But then, he thought, everything changed. Suddenly there was a new military technology, new tactics based on self-loading rifles and quick-firing guns with multiple barrels, breech-loading field pieces light enough to be towed at a gallop. The whole manner of war changed, to become more impersonal and a great deal uglier.

I learned the new ways, he thought. Learned them well, when a lot of my brother officers wouldn't. They couldn't change. Insisted that elan and military spirit were more important than weapons and tactics, and they got their regiments butchered for their pains. I learned the new ways, but I never liked them. He looked up from his reverie. "That's one company that will profit by this expedition. Assuming we find something worth importing."

Dougal arrived an hour later. "You will meet the Imperial Traders shortly," the policeman announced. "We have fresh clothing ready for you in your quarters. When you get changed, we'll go to Empire House." The policeman fell in beside MacKinnie, walking with him to his suite. "Be careful with these Imperial Traders. There are two of them, and they both look soft. Don't believe it; they didn't get rich by being stupid. Of the two, Trader Soliman is probably the actual leader although they claim to be equals. There is antagonism between the Imperial Traders and the Navy, but I wouldn't count on it too much. We don't know the real story, but the Traders seem to be with us against the Navy."

"Yes," MacKinnie said. "You told me that the Navy wouldn't let us go on this trip if the Traders hadn't pushed them into it."

"Exactly. The Traders are eager for us to go. Quite generous in their terms. I'm not sure why."

"When a businessman wants to do you a favor," MacKinnie said, "I've found it a good policy to watch your pocketbook." They arrived at the door to his suite, and Dougal waited outside.

MacKinnie found a dress kilt, doublet laced with gold and silver piping, and jewelry in the style of the great merchant princes of Haven. When he lifted the clothing, he found cartridges for his pistol had been laid discreetly on the bed. With something approaching relief, Nathan loaded the large-caliber revolver and buckled it on before he realized how out of keeping it was with the rest of his clothing. A quick search of the small leather case he found on the bed with the clothing revealed a smaller dress pistol, its dragonwood handles inlaid with pearl and jade and thin copper strands. He unloaded it and squeezed the trigger several times, pleased with the smoothness of its action. The proofmarks showed it to have been made by the Brothers of St. Andrew, reputedly the best gunsmiths on Samual and certainly the most expensive. Although he hesitated to carry a weapon he had never fired, MacKinnie buckled it outside his doublet, sadly leaving the big service pistol hanging in the closet.

Two sets of guards were on watch at Empire House. Outside the large, walled courtyard, soldiers of King David's personal guard stood rigidly at attention. A junior officer in a tiny office inside the gates examined their passes, collected their weapons apologetically, and directed them across the lava stone courtyard to the building itself.

Two huge doors swung open as they arrived. The Imperial Marines inside the entryway wore full dress, scarlet and blue uniforms with gold trim, a blaze of color; but the weapons the sentries carried were incomprehensible to MacKinnie. Their rifles looked very functional, but the knobs and dials along the stocks were meaningless—and there were no visible openings in the barrel ends.

MacKinnie expected to be searched again, but instead the Marine noncom looked at a panel of lights and meters and a screen that showed shadowy figures; MacKinnie got only a glance at it, but he thought he saw the outline of his cigar lighter on the screen. In some way the Marines could see through the leather of his pouch . . . .

They waited in silence while the noncom spoke into a handset.

Very efficient, MacKinnie thought. It would be difficult to penetrate this place. Not that it would do any good to take Empire House. The fortress would still remain, and so would that ship in orbit above Prince Samual's World. No. Dougal's way was best—except that Dougal's way doomed Orleans to rule by Haven. . . .

An inner door opened and a young naval officer came in. He had small badges made of a curious substance, not metal but not anything else MacKinnie had ever seen. He gave one to MacKinnie.

"You are to wear these at all times inside Empire House," the officer said. "My name is Lieutenant Akelian, and I will take you to your appointment."

"This has my picture," MacKinnie said.

Lieutenant Akelian looked up in surprise. "Of course. We take photographs of everyone who visits Empire House. This way, please."

MacKinnie glanced at Dougal. The policeman's lips were set in a tight line. And no wonder, MacKinnie thought. Akelian was one of the three who had been at the party in the Blue Bottle. But he doesn't seem to recognize us. Given the amount he drank that night, it's no wonder. . . .

Akelian led them through brightly lit hallways. MacKinnie had never seen an inside room so well lighted. Electricity, someone had told him. Electric lights. But not from a carbon arc like a military searchlight. The professors at Prince Samual University were experimenting with a new kind of light, as they had experimented with long-distance communications using electricity, but electrical equipment took miles of wire, too expensive to be very practical on copper-poor Samual. They were ushered onto a moving stairway, then at the top led to another door. Akelian opened it to show them a large room.

Two fat men in plain clothing, wearing trousers rather than kilts, undecorated coats, and only a few jewels, their almost drab appearance contrasting strongly with MacKinnie and Dougal, rose languidly as they entered a large, plainly decorated room. Akelian waved MacKinnie and Dougal in, looked sternly at the civilians for a moment, and left without speaking.

As soon as he had left the room, one of the Imperials laughed. "God bless the Navy," he chuckled. "But may He grant that their lieutenants come of age soon. Good evening, gentlemen."

Dougal returned the greeting, then said formally, "Imperial Trader Soliman, I have the honor to present Trader Magnate MacKinnie, His Majesty's servant and manager for this expedition. Trader MacKinnie, Imperial Trader Soliman of the Imperial Capital, and as I understand it an officer of the Imperial Traders Association."

MacKinnie watched them narrowly and noted that the fat man made no movement to offer his hand. MacKinnie bowed slightly, was rewarded with an even smaller bow, and turned to the next man.

"Imperial Trader Renaldi, I present Trader Magnate MacKinnie," Dougal purred.

"My honor," Renaldi said. When Nathan began his bow, Renaldi matched him, bending to within a degree of MacKinnie but not quite as deep. The difference might have been measured with calipers.

"Gentlemen," Soliman said, "this room is at our disposal for the time. Let us sit and enjoy ourselves like civilized beings." He indicated couches drawn up in front of an open fire. As they sat, he continued, "Remarkable how peaceful it is to have a fire in the room with you. We haven't used them in the capital for a long time now. There are very few houses with fireplaces, and I can't remember when I last saw one lighted. I will have to have one installed on my return, a great aid to contemplation. Right, Chasar?"

"It would be pleasant," Renaldi said.

"They are not quite so pleasant when they are your only source of heat," Dougal said.

"No, I suppose not," Soliman said. He looked thoughtful. "When the Navy permits trade in such things, Imperial Autonetics will bring factories to make better heating systems, I expect we could sell many of them." He sighed. "But the military departments never act quickly. It will probably be some time yet."

MacKinnie noted that both men spoke the language of North Continent almost perfectly, but with the careful pronunciations that indicated that it was a recently learned foreign tongue. Having never heard the Imperial language, he was not sure how close it would be to that used on Samual, although it would obviously be similar if Dougal were able to read the book his agents had stolen. Still, it must require some study, he thought, and therefore it followed that the Imperials either had some method of learning languages quickly, or that the Traders thought it important enough to spend the time and effort learning the local tongue. Either alternative seemed interesting.

Soliman hovered around them, offering refreshments which he poured himself at a small stand at one side of the room before finally joining them before the fire. They sipped chilled wine from one of the islands of the Archipelago, and Soliman praised it highly. "I hope it travels well," he told them. "This will be worth a fortune on the capital. It is as good as real Earth wines, or nearly so, and they command a price you would never believe. This is a very fortunate world, gentlemen, your wines and brandies can make you rich. And your grua—do you think the peach plant would grow elsewhere? Ah, but it would never thrive as it does here. If only Earth had not been so devastated in the Secession Wars."

He lowered his voice confidentially. "That is why the Navy is so stern, you know. Their academy is there, and they grow up with the results of the wars. They are determined that it will never happen again, even if they must enslave the entire galaxy to see to it. And now that it is traditional for the Emperor to send the heir apparent to New Annapolis, the whole government is infected with their dedication." He sighed deeply.

"Have you visited Makassar yourself, Traders?" MacKinnie asked.

"Briefly, briefly," Soliman replied. "A desolate place, with little value to us. Yet I am certain you will find many useful things there," he added quickly. "Not so desolate as all that, and of course we are accustomed to more comforts than you. Copper abounds there, but perhaps the costs of shipping will prevent you from importing it on any really large scale. There may be little for us, but we believe you will find the voyage profitable. And of course we did not venture far from the city where the Navy has its base."

"Has the Navy decided on the details of the voyage?" Dougal asked. "Will Your Excellencies accompany us? A naval officer perhaps? Who will command the ship?"

"I have business beyond Makassar, but I will go with you there," Renaldi told them. "I am looking forward to the voyage, and Trader Soliman will guard my interests here." Renaldi's tone had indicated that he and Soliman had tossed coins for the privilege, and Renaldi had lost, although he was attempting to act in good humor. "As Soliman and I own the ship, it will be commanded by our own merchant captain and crew. One of the Imperial Navy officers will be aboard as observer, to ensure that none of their silly regulations are violated. We must caution you, Trader," he said, turning to MacKinnie, "they are very stern about their rules. Do not attempt to violate them, or you will never see your charming planet again. The Imperial prison world is not a pleasant place."

"No need to speak of such depressing matters," Soliman interrupted. "Better to think of the profits that can be earned. And, of course, this will be the first time any of your people have been off this planet since the days of the Old Empire, will it not?" His offhanded manner could not conceal his interest in the question.

Before MacKinnie could answer, Dougal asked, "and

the language of Makassar? Will Trader MacKinnie find it difficult to deal with the natives?"

"The language is much like your own, or ours," Soliman answered. "Degenerate forms of Old Empire, with some local words. It requires study, but there will be no great difficulties. Tell me, Trader Magnate MacKinnie, are you looking forward to going off-planet?"

"With some anticipation," MacKinnie answered. "It will be a new experience for me." He emphasized the last word slightly, receiving an approving nod from Dougal. "But what are the conditions on Makassar? Are they likely to be friendly? Will we be allowed to wander about their cities, or must we remain in one place and let them come to us?"

"The Navy has no objection to your traveling about," Renaldi replied, "provided you take nothing more advanced than they already have on Makassar. Journeys on the planet with primitive equipment can be dangerous, you understand. The planet has no political system as even you on Samual might know it. Here, you have a few strong governments and many city-states in a complex of alliances—at least on North Continent. On Makassar, there are dozens of kingdoms, free cities, small republics, leagues, and such, none very large by your standards. The kingdoms themselves are more fiction than fact, with independent baronies scattered about them. No doubt this is the result of their lack of technology, coupled with their primitive military organizations. All of this is huddled together on the coast of the one large continent. But it all comes to an end on a great grassland plain that stretches east for over three thousand kilometers. You will find none but barbarians there. No one knows how many of them there are; they move around at will and raid the edges of the civilized lands. There are also island kingdoms of barbarians off the coasts of the civilized regions, and these stage raids on even the largest cities. You are welcome to wander the countryside, Trader MacKinnie, but do not be surprised if you are killed. The only safe place is in one of their large cities, and they are not entirely safe. The Imperial Navy maintains a fortified observation post, but no warships, so that even if you were able to signal the Navy, there would be little they could do to rescue you. Makassar is not altogether a healthy place."

"Ah, but there are never profits without danger," Soliman purred. "And who knows what you may find out among the kingdoms of the east? The Navy post is on the western coastline, and we know so little about the planet."

MacKinnie nodded. "We will be very careful if we leave the Imperial fortress. Gentlemen, what I do not understand is why Makassar is so primitive. Why did they not retain any basic technology at all?"

"Ah," Soliman answered, "that is something we have speculated about without final answer. From our records, it was relatively unpopulated when the Secession Wars began. The planet seems to have served mostly as a rest area for the Old Empire Navy and Civil Service . . . a park world, kept uninhabited and unspoiled. Little machinery. Few power installations. Then, as the wars continued, for some reasons of strategy we do not know, parts of the planet were fortified. The fortifications were destroyed, and with them, much of the only city, although the old palace seems to have survived. Then the wars boiled on past Makassar. Perhaps there were not many people left on it. Many of them would be civil servants. Few artisans, and of the native inhabitants most would have been dedicated to service professions. Pleasure-house operators. Prostitutes. What kind of civilization would you expect them to build, given the destruction of most of the machinery?" He paused thoughtfully, sipping his wine.

"And then, too, much of the vegetation on the planet is native to Makassar. Not edible by us. Hardy stuff. A form of our wheat grows across the plains, but it is straggly and more fit for horses and cattle than men. Most of the crops of Makassar are Earth Stock; they have a very wide variety of such foodstuffs but getting an edible crop takes constant attention. How natural for some of the population to become raiders, living off the cultivators! And so the cultivators divert part of their efforts into maintaining a warrior class. The warriors become an aristocracy. The warriors must have something to do in times of peace, and they will not toil in the fields. . . . Indeed, they can't, because the barbarians may sweep over them at any time, and the warriors must know their business if they are to do their job. The planet has known constant warfare, between the civilized people and the barbarians, among the warriors within the civilized area, between civilized cities and baronies. At least, we think that is what happens. Certainly they are fighting all the time."

"There was a period much like that on old Earth," Renaldi observed. "It would seem to have been ended by the development of scientific farming, which was a discovery of the Church. But Makassar has developed its own ideas of a church, not altogether to the satisfaction of New Rome."

"Ah, yes," Soliman added. "In addition to yourselves and the Imperial Navy observers, you will find one other group on Makassar. His Holiness has sent a bishop and a small group of missionaries to win these people back to the state religion. They are not having notable success."

Dougal finished his wine and set the glass down. In an instant, Soliman hauled his great stomach off the couch and gathered the other glasses on a copper tray, taking them to the cabinet to fill them. As he did, Dougal observed, "I am sure that Trader MacKinnie will be careful not to fall afoul of His Reverence the Bishop. May we here on Samual expect a similar visit soon?"

"Doubtless," Renaldi answered. "Of course, you seem to have developed along more orthodox lines than the people of Makassar, although the Church will find the multiplication of sects distressing. Still, you will find New Rome tolerant and willing to compromise. Do you anticipate much resistance to unification of the churches?"

"Not much," MacKinnie answered. "We had religious wars, over a hundred standard years ago. Not much zeal left on Prince Samual's World. The orthodox churches have been proclaiming their obedience to New Rome since the Imperial Navy landed, and the others don't know quite what to make of it. How much will the Empire interfere with local matters like religion anyway?"

"Oh, hardly at all, hardly at all," Soliman assured them. He served the wine carefully, and MacKinnie caught a stern look which Soliman passed to Renaldi. The latter quickly changed the subject, and the next half hour was passed discussing trade goods and the proposed cargo.

They were interrupted by a knock at the door and, when Renaldi answered it, two Imperial Navy officers entered the room and walked stiffly over to stand in front of MacKinnie. Their manner was anything but friendly.

★6★
REGULATIONS
★ ★ ★

The contrast between the two officers could not have been greater. One was young, tall, of slight build, his hair an indescribable brown something like damp straw. The other was much older, with lines of care etched around his expressionless eyes, his hair gray where there was hair at all. He was heavy and short, but he had in common with the younger man a look of hardness and dedication; yet, again in contrast to his junior brother in service, there was none of the air of expectancy and anticipation the boy displayed.

"Trader MacKinnie." The older man said it factually. "I am Captain Greenaugh of His Imperial Majesty's Navy. I command the garrison here and *Tombaugh* up there in orbit. This is Midshipman Landry, who will be my observer on this stupid voyage of yours."

MacKinnie stood and bowed slightly to Captain Greenaugh, even less to Landry, making no move to extend his hand when the others did not.

"Won't you sit down, Captain?" Soliman asked softly. "Some wine, perhaps? Grua?"

"No. Mr. Landry and I are on duty." The midshipman's face was impassive; or had there been a hint of a smile? It was hard to tell.

"Then please be seated," Soliman insisted.

"I prefer to stand." He turned his attention to MacKinnie. "As you are to be the local in charge of this expedition, sir, it is my duty to caution you that any infringement of Imperial regulations on the part of any member of this expedition will result in trial and punishment of both the crew member and you personally. Is that understood?"

"Yes, Captain," MacKinnie said. He elaborately inspected the large ring on his left hand, then looked up. "I understand perfectly. Tell me why you are so unhappy with me, if you would, please."

"I am not unhappy with you, sir. It is understandable that you would wish to travel in space. I am unhappy with Mr. Soliman for browbeating me into letting you do it."

"Browbeating, Captain?" Soliman said in an amused tone. "Why, I merely indicated—"

"You merely indicated the relevant passages in the Imperial regulations and reminded me of your influence. I don't give a damn about your influence, but I can't ignore the regulations. However, I warn you, MacKinnie, if Mr. Soliman can be sticky about regulations, so can I. You'll get a copy of the pertinent sections before you go, but I decided to see you personally to try to talk you out of this venture."

"If you please, Captain," Dougal asked, "why are you

so opposed to our simple trading expedition? I thought it was Imperial policy to encourage trade among the worlds of the Empire. Your ambassador promises that Prince Samual's World will profit highly through joining the Empire."

"Sir—" The captain paused and snapped his fingers.

"Citizen Dougal, sir," the midshipman answered. "In the service of King David."

"Citizen Dougal, I have all too few officers on this station. I am responsible for the protection of this world from all interference with its development and assimilation into the Empire. There's a nest of outies not twenty parsecs away; your King David is in one hell of a hurry to unify this planet against stiff opposition; the survey team keeps borrowing my people; and thanks to this expedition I have to send a junior officer off for the Saints alone know how long. There'll be reports to file, inspections to conduct. And for what? So Mr. Soliman here can add another mega-crown to his bank account, and you people can bring some kind of gimcrack new luxuries to absorb what little capital there is on Prince Samual's World. I don't like it and I don't have to like it."

"Sorry you feel that way, Captain," MacKinnie said. Inwardly he knew all too well the plight of a military man caught up in the details of government. He would have felt sympathy for Greenaugh, but the memory of Lechfeld was too strong. The Imperials were the enemy. "But you have admitted that you understand our motives for wanting to go. I hope we can get our work accomplished without causing you any trouble."

"You're damn right you will," Greenaugh snapped.

"But before you make your final decision, let me acquaint you with the regulations. Item: you will be supplied with a basic naval study of the planetary languages found in the chief city of Makassar. You will at no time teach any native your own language or Imperial speech. All negotiations will be conducted in one of the planetary languages. Is that understood?"

MacKinnie nodded, suddenly realizing why all the Imperials he had met spoke a variant of the language of Haven. If you used a man's own language, you weren't likely to tell him anything he didn't know about. He wouldn't even have the words for most advanced concepts.

"Item: as Imperial subjects," Greenaugh continued, "you would ordinarily be entitled to protection from barbarians and arbitrary imprisonment. In your case we can't extend it. The garrison on Makassar is too small and there's no ship. If you get in trouble, you're on your own."

The captain took a small notebook-sized object from his pocket, touched a stud on the side of it and glanced at its face before returning it to his scarlet tunic. MacKinnie recognized it as one of the tiny Imperial computers, supposedly equivalent to hundreds of the best mechanical calculators in use in Haven's banks; equivalent and more. The Imperials used them for everything, as notebooks and pocket clocks, for communications and diaries.

"Another thing, MacKinnie. Any technical innovation traced to you directly or indirectly can result in a charge of interference. If it results in any severe disruption of the development of that planet, you can get life imprisonment. Assessment of the effects of innovations and your responsibilities for them are up to the Emperor's Lord Judges."

"Why are the regulations so severe, Captain?" Dougal asked. "It is our understanding that the Empire intends only peace and friendship for its member worlds."

"Damn right. And sudden technical changes destroy both. I've seen worlds where some smart guy used a little technology and a lot of guts to set himself up as a planetary king. Half the population out of work, the other half in a turmoil. Took the better part of a fleet and a division of Marines to keep order on the place. Mister, it's not going to happen in my sector."

"The regulations are severe for a purpose," Renaldi added. "There is no telling what the effects of even the most innocent technical revelations can be. Even something as inherently benign as medicines can change the whole pattern of life. There is a famous case, from the early days of the New Empire. The Church went in and with the best of motives taught practical medicine to primitives. The missionaries were particularly concerned with saving children from infant diseases. They intended to give them some new agricultural and industrial techniques, but the people were not ready for them. They rejected the agriculture and industry, but they adopted the medicine. Within fifty standard years, there was famine all over that world. The results were horrible."

Greenaugh nodded. "Still were when I was young Landry's age. I served a hitch on an escort vessel convoying a provisions fleet. Silliest thing you ever saw. You ever think of how futile it is to try to ship food to a whole world that's starving? If you took every ship in the Navy and merchant service and put them on it, even if the food was free and waiting in the same star system, it wouldn't do any good. But the Emperor's sister got interested in the place and they had to have a try at 'helping.' Did no good at all. Population's thinned out a bit now on Placentia, but the planet'll never be the same."

"So you see," Soliman said softly, "it is important not to interfere. No matter what the reason. You can always say that things would have been worse if you did not interfere, but you can't know." He sipped his wine. "Besides, people will have adjusted to the evils they are accustomed to. Your attempts to help may introduce evils they don't know, which are always worse to bear and will probably retard their natural development."

"Thank you," MacKinnie said. "We will be very careful. What else must I know?"

"Still determined," Greenaugh said. "Thought you would be. Well, if I can't persuade you to give it up, I can't. Bring your crew here tomorrow for inspection. Midshipman Landry will tell you the rest of the details." He strode to the door, then paused and turned back. "Just remember, MacKinnie you were warned. The hell with it." He went briskly out, followed by his midshipman.

MacKinnie started to speak to Dougal once they were in the cab and drawing away from Empire House, but Dougal motioned him to silence. They returned to the Royal Guest House, where Dougal invited MacKinnie to shower, insisting that he do so in a manner that told MacKinnie it was an order. When he finished, he found fresh clothing, the elaborate Trader's kilt and doublet gone. Dougal joined him as he finished dressing, and MacKinnie noted that the policeman had changed as well.

"Sorry, Trader," Dougal said, "but we have found by bitter experience that the Imperials have devices, so small you would hardly notice them, which in some manner allow them to hear over long distances. Our engineers did not believe it at first, but I tested the hypothesis by feeding them false information when we had reason to suspect. I proved it, and now my people have found one of the things. Not as big as the end of your thumb."

MacKinnie whistled. "Was there one attached to our clothing?" he asked.

"No, not this time. But the cab stood outside Empire House while we were there. They had ample time to do as they liked."

"Any idea of the range of those things?" MacKinnie asked.

"None. And as we do not know how they work, there is no guess. Some of our best physicists insist they have a theory how one might be built, now that they know it is possible, but they say any such device would have to be very large and use much power. Still, it is a start." Deprived of a place to sit, the policeman locked his hands behind his back and paced the room nervously.

"By the way," MacKinnie asked, "what will our churches really do if their New Roman Church decides to take over here? I notice King David's bishops are thick as flies in Orleans."

"Better ours than the outlanders'," Dougal snapped. "And all the more reason for the success of your mission,

MacKinnie. Perhaps they are not as severe on the Classified worlds."

"Yeah." Nathan stood against one wall, patiently watching Dougal stride back and forth. "But after that interview I don't know any more about how to get those books—but they aren't books, are they? That Navy kid, the night he babbled about it all, said they were spools, whatever that might be. That they could be made to print books, if we knew how to do it. Only we don't know how, do we? We don't really know much of anything."

"Giving up?" Dougal asked.

"No, by God!" MacKinnie grinned. "And the sooner we start, the better chance we'll have. It's still a fool's errand, but at least I can feel useful again, win or lose!"

THE BURDEN OF EMPIRE

★★★

Lieutenant Alphonse Pavlovnicek Jefferson was in love. It had happened very suddenly, but he had no doubts about it; he had all the signs he'd been led to expect from romantic novels. His previous affairs seemed laughable or disgusting in recollection; he had no desire at all to go tavern-crawling with his classmates; he wanted only to get back to Elaine. It had to be love.

He'd met her on the street when he'd lost his way and asked for directions. Of course he'd been glad for an opportunity to speak to a local girl; getting acquainted on Prince Samual's World wasn't as easy as it was on more civilized worlds. Since he was more lost than he'd thought, she had to draw a map, and it seemed natural to offer to buy her a coffee at a sidewalk restaurant that seemed so conveniently located that it made Jefferson believe the fates approved of his meeting Elaine. She said later she'd accepted because she had never talked with an Imperial before. Her parents didn't encourage that.

Hours went by. He couldn't remember anything significant they'd said. It was just talk, at the coffee house and then walking in the park and along the waterfront, a pleasant stroll on a pleasant afternoon, with nothing important said, but there it was: he wanted nothing more than to see her again, and she'd agreed. Of course he would have to call for her at her home, and meet her father, and ask his permission to see her. He'd been warned that local customs were very strict, and Captain Greenaugh had made it clear that any officer causing problems would be handed his head.

Jeff wasn't exactly looking forward to the interview with Elaine's father, but surely all would be well. Fate couldn't play him such a trick as to let him find Elaine and then be forbidden to see her. Her father was a Haven civil servant, and the Empire was allied with Haven. He couldn't openly dislike Imperial officers, and he might even welcome the opportunity to get to know one. Jeff told himself that several times.

For the moment, though, he had another appointment. High Commissioner Sir Alexei Dmitrivitch Ackoff was holding his weekly seminar on colonial government, and it was strongly suggested that all junior officers attend. Presumably there was a difference between a strong suggestion and an order; if Elaine hadn't already been late getting home for dinner, this might have been the day Lieutenant Jefferson found out. However, she had insisted on going home, and even in his euphoric mood Jeff knew it wouldn't be a good idea to test Ackoff's patience.

He was very nearly late. The others had already gone into Ackoff's spartan conference room. Jeff hurried inside and as he did the opposite door leading into the Commissioner's office opened and the others stood respectfully. Sir Alexei nodded and waved them to their seats around the big conference table as he took his place at its head. He was not a tall man, nor was he large; from his looks no one would have guessed that he was the most powerful man on Prince Samual's World, the only man there who could give orders to the Navy and make them stick. He did have an air of importance, of speaking in a tone that indicated he expected to be obeyed, but even that wasn't permanent; he was, after all, a diplomat, skilled in persuasion. This was his first assignment as top authority on a planet, but he'd been deputy commissioner twice before, and was said to be highly competent.

Jeff's father knew Ackoff slightly, and in his last letter to Jeff had mentioned the Commissioner as an excellent example of the best—and worst—of the Imperial Civil Service. "Give him a policy, and he'll enforce it. Even have sense enough to grant exceptions. But you have to give him a policy. He's not likely to come up with one on his own." The dry voice went on to suggest that Jeff erase that portion of the letter, lest Sir Alexei find it. "Your brother will inherit the family title, my lad," his father's image had said with a wink. "And you'll need friends like Sir Alexei if you intend to found your own branch of the family. You might even think about staying on Prince Samual's World. Not a bad place from what I hear, and they'll want colonists. Shouldn't be surprised if you managed a barony out of it. So it's worth keeping Sir Alexei happy. Besides, he's not a bad sort if you deal with him on his own terms."

"Gentlemen," Ackoff began. "I find myself falling further behind in necessary work, so we will have to cut this short today."

Midshipman Landry was seated across the table from Jeff. Landry looked relieved. Jeff hoped that his own face wasn't quite as obvious, but it probably was, because Ackoff looked directly at him.

"You are amused, Mr. Jefferson?"

"No, sir."

"You shouldn't be. As of tomorrow you will be assisting the survey team. So will most of the rest of you. And you needn't groan, gentlemen. The work is important."

I suppose it is, Jeff thought. But . . . "Sir?" he asked.

"Yes?"

"I—do you know where I will be assigned?"

"Near Haven for the moment," Ackoff said. "At the University." His lips curled slightly, perhaps in a smile, perhaps something else. "We must fully understand the capabilities of the industrial base here. Get a total picture of their energy budget. Assess their ability to maintain complex technologies. Without that information we can't know what to license for import."

Midshipman Landry raised his hand.

"Yes?" Ackoff said.

"Trader Soliman says he already knows what he wants to import, and if he's wrong the market place will show him up soon enough."

"Yes. He would say that," Ackoff said. "I don't suppose he gave you the benefit of his thoughts on what he would import?"

"No, sir."

"You may be certain that Mr. Soliman's ideas will be considerably different from mine," Ackoff said. "Luxury and convenience items, no doubt. And imbecile acts like this expedition to Makassar. It's quite natural that Mr. Soliman wants profits for Imperial Autonetics, and it doesn't take genius to imagine ways to accomplish that. Our task is to bring this planet smoothly into the Empire, and that may be a bit more difficult. Consider our situation, how very few we are, how expensive it will be to bring *anything* here. We cannot afford mistakes. The market may show up Trader Soliman, but the worst disaster he faces merely costs money. Our mistakes will cost lives— and do not deceive yourselves, we *will* make mistakes."

The officers around the table looked at each other significantly. This was Ackoff's favorite lecture, and once started it was unlikely that he'd change the subject. More importantly, he wasn't likely to ask many questions. You could safely relax and daydream when Ackoff took that tone and spoke of the burdens of Imperial office. . . .

"For example," Ackoff said, "any fool knows that energy systems are the key to industrialization. Make energy cheap and plentiful, and people will figure ways to use it. But what energy systems? Satellites? This planet hasn't the industrial base for that, and we haven't the personnel to build either the orbital or the ground components. We're unlikely to get enough skilled people. Scratch power satellites for a generation or more.

"Small fusion plants? Who will operate them? Who will maintain them? How many engineers do we bring in, and who will train others here? And how is the power to be distributed on a world where metals are dear and copper so scarce it's used as jewelry? We'll have to use organic conductors. That's a very sophisticated technology, far too complex for a world this primitive, but I suppose we'll have to do it even so.

"And once we begin, when we've made electricity cheap and plentiful—how do we control industrial developments? No matter what we do, we're going to change the class structure of this planet. Power relationships will shift and flow in unpredictable ways. Mister Jefferson. What is our primary mission?"

"Sir?" Jeff looked up with a start and tried to recall the question. "To keep the peace."

"Precisely. Which means that when this planet does develop an industrial base, it *must* be governed—*well* governed—by people loyal to the Empire. Governors both able and popular, at least popular enough to retain their offices without constant revolt. Yet consider this. If we are to bring them industry, we must bring in the personnel to build and operate the primary systems. How do we induce them to come here? What can we offer highly skilled people so that they will colonize a primitive world?"

"Wealth," Landry said.

"Precisely," Ackoff agreed. "Wealth. Opportunity. The chance to found an aristocratic family. Power indeed. But whenever you bring in an alien governing class you will inevitably breed resentment among the population. Breed enough and you can't govern. You lose control. Whether we like it or not, Prince Samual's World will within a few generations have the capability of building modern weapons. When that time comes, the planet must be loyalist. The alternative is almost unthinkable. Remember Istvan and Kutuzov's choice. . . ."

Jeff shuddered. Admiral Kutuzov had bombed an entire planet into the stone age. The alternative was the revolt of a whole sector; the alternative would have been another Secession War, Imperial planets destroyed, all of the horrors of the war years. Kutuzov had made the right choice, but it was one no sane officer wanted to face.

And, he thought, it could happen here, too. To me. Or, the other side of the coin, if I decide to become a colonist. Perhaps not to me. But to my children. Mine and Elaine's—

The thought startled him. Was he really thinking of marriage? He barely knew her. But he didn't want to be away from her, not for an hour, and—

It wasn't unthinkable. She came of a good family. Imperial policy encouraged colonists to marry locals, and send down roots into the world they chose to live on.

"Hard choices, gentlemen," Ackoff was saying. "And the decisions we make will change the history of this world. For the moment the local government cooperates with us. Even welcomes our help. We have encouraged them to believe that once they have established a planetary government, the local dynasty will remain in control. You ladies and gentlemen will naturally continue that deception as long as possible."

"What happens when they find out we've been lying to them?" a consular officer asked. Her tone made it obvious that she did not approve.

"It is not precisely a lie, Miss Neville," Ackoff said. "More a diplomatic truth—"

"Whatever we call it, they'll find us out, and what then?" she asked.

" 'Find us out,'" Ackoff repeated. "You young people can afford phrases like that. I can't. What will they find out? That no matter what our intentions, the experts we bring in will be more important than even the most influential locals? That the Traders and technicians and diplomatic personnel and civil servants will have the knowledge and skills to rise high during the inevitable turmoil of change to a modern society—and their traditional leaders will not? That is the real truth, far more influential than any legalities we may impose. Try as we will—and we do try—there will be no way to avoid a change of ruling elites here. For obvious reasons we must see that the new ruling class is loyalist. Sometimes that requires shoring up traditional leaders long after they have lost the ability to govern. Sometimes it requires replacing them. Sometimes—"

"Why can't we just leave them alone?" Sirica Neville asked.

Ackoff shrugged. "Would that be kindness?" he asked. "Suppose we do as you suggest. Leave them alone, let them develop as they see fit. Quite aside from the fact that the inevitable revolution here could as easily cast up monsters as saints for their leaders, what are we to do if they move away from the Empire, make alliance with outies, become a threat to this sector?"

Kutuzov's choice again, Jeff thought. There's got to be a better way than that. . . .

"So I leave you to contemplate our burden," Ackoff said. "We must not fail." He glanced at his pocket computer. "And now, as it is getting late, I'll let you go. Please stand for the pledge of allegiance. . . ."

They all turned to face the portrait of Leonidas IX, Emperor of Humanity.

★8★
THE VIEW FROM SPACE
★★★

Despite Dougal's frantic desire for haste, getting the cargo inspected and loaded took three more days. Eventually it was accomplished, and MacKinnie met Dougal for the last time before departing.

"We must thank Trader Renaldi for his help," Dougal said. "Without his assistance we'd still be dealing with Imperial clerks."

MacKinnie chuckled. "He wants to get back to civilization."

Dougal snorted contempt. "He would say that—"

"He didn't *say* it."

"No, but it was obvious." Dougal shrugged. "Well, we can be thankful for his impatience. Also that Imperial bureaucrats are no different from our own."

"It should be fairly obvious to them that we're far too primitive to be a threat to the Empire—"

"Or more to the point, to their files. And their careers," Dougal said. "It's fortunate that they didn't assign this task to that young blabbermouth from the tavern."

"Yes. This Midshipman Landry is competent enough, but he's never been on Makassar. I'd have thought they'd put one of the chaps who's been there on this—"

"They can't spare anyone higher-ranking than a midshipman," Dougal said. "That boy, Lieutenant Jefferson, is supposed to be quite competent."

"We must have seen him on an off night," MacKinnie said.

"Possibly. At any event, they have him working at the University, reading our engineering textbooks, and looking at the research laboratories."

MacKinnie frowned. "Are they suspicious? And of what?"

"I do not know. He says he is part of a survey to determine what Prince Samual's World needs. Certainly there are enough of them looking in odd places, but we know more about Jefferson than the others. He has become friendly with the daughter of one of King David's officials, and they report his activities to me. So far he has not again mentioned Makassar, but I'll be happier with you away."

"Yes. And speaking of that, I'd best be leaving for the harbor," MacKinnie said.

"Nervous?"

"A bit."

"You've done all you can."

"Sure," MacKinnie said. "And that's little enough. God knows how I'm going to bring home those books."

"Or whatever they are."

"Yes. Or whatever they are." He shrugged. "One thing at a time. Take what comes and do what you can." And that, Nathan thought, was what I was told by my tac officer back in the Academy. An Academy that doesn't exist. . . .

"You won't fail us." Dougal hesitated a moment, then put out his hand. "Good luck."

"Thanks. I expect I'll need it."

The merchant landing boat was ugly, a squat, winged cylinder nothing like the slim Navy landing ship that floated next to the main pier of the Imperial docks. The boat's gangway was a slice out of one side which lowered to match the height of the dock. The compartment inside was bare steel.

"Built to lift mass," Landry explained as they boarded. "There's no need to maneuver in atmosphere. Not like a Navy boat."

The others didn't answer, although MacLean listened with evident interest to every word Landry said. They went down a short corridor to a compartment filled with padded seats. "Find a place," Landry said. "I'll help you strap in."

"Why the straps?" Longway asked. "If this falls, they won't help much, will they?"

"Not a lot," Landry admitted. "But these boats are quite serviceable. Not much happens to them."

"I hope not," Mary Graham said. "I—where are the Traders?"

"They lifted off hours ago," Landry said. "With their own cargo. Not as big a load as we're carrying—"

MacKinnie could draw his own conclusions from that,

and he didn't much like them. There didn't seem to be much to do about the situation, though. And at least Landry was aboard. . . .

There were warning tones from somewhere, three repeated notes, then a series of shorter tones that blended with a sudden roar from behind them. The landing boat lurched and began to move across the water.

"What pushes this?" Kleinst asked.

"Steam," Landry said. "Distilled water flows through a nuclear heat source—"

"Nuclear?" MacLean asked.

"Sorry," Landry mumbled. "It would take too long to explain. I don't know if I'm supposed to tell you anyway—"

"The Empire is our ally," Mary Graham said. "Why can't you tell us?"

"A good question, freelady," Landry said. "I don't really know the answer. But I have my orders . . . lean back, here we go."

The acceleration increased suddenly, and they were pressed back into their couches until they weighed far too much. MacKinnie gritted his teeth and fought to stay calm. He couldn't see out but he was certain they were flying now, the first natives of Prince Samual's World to fly in a heavier-than-air machine for centuries. Nathan glanced across the aisle toward Mary Graham. She gripped the chair arms unconsciously, but there was a set smile on her lips. MacKinnie couldn't see any of the others.

The feeling of too much weight went on for a long time. MacKinnie estimated it at about twice normal;

uncomfortable but not painful. He had carried companions on his back for much longer. But he wished it would stop.

When the engines quit, the silence was terrifying. Worse yet was the sensation of falling.

Mary Graham was the first to speak. Her voice was quite calm. "The engines have quit. Are we going to crash?"

There was a confused babble from behind, and one of the guards shouted "Goddam, we *are* falling!"

MacKinnie grimly faced death, reviewing the silly prayers the chaplains said over the dying. Somehow they did not seem silly at all.

"No, no," Landry protested. "I'm sorry, I should have warned you. We are in orbit. The sensation of falling is natural, but it's false. In fact, we *can't* fall. Without power we'd never leave this orbit, because we're falling *around* the planet—oh, hell, I don't expect you to understand. But we're quite safe."

"I'm glad to hear that," Longway said grimly. "But you might have told us—"

The incident served to reassure MacKinnie about Kleinst. The young scholar had evidently known they were safe, but made no move to assure the others and thus break his cover as social historian. MacKinnie did not care for weaklings, but the young man seemed to have common sense as well as educated intelligence.

The landing boat's engines started again, this time far more gently than before. For nearly an hour they experienced accelerations, now forward, now sideways, then finally there was a resounding clang, followed by other sounds. Midshipman Landry glanced at his pocket computer. "Good time," he said. "Couldn't have matched up quicker myself."

"Do you pilot these craft?" MacLean asked. "Your pardon, but you seem young for such a task. It must be very demanding."

MacKinnie listened with amusement. From his interviews with MacLean he knew what an effort MacLean must have made to be polite to a mere midshipman.

"I have been a qualified landing-craft pilot for nearly a standard year," Landry answered proudly. He glanced at Mary Graham as if seeking approval. She smiled. "It's not *that* difficult," Landry continued. "The computers do most of the work. The fact is, we couldn't fly these ships without them."

The compartment door opened and two men in coveralls came inside. One wore gold piping on his sleeves, and both were dark men, with eyes that seemed to slant. There were no orientals on Prince Samual's World, and MacKinnie and the others stared at the crewmen.

"My name is Taka," one of the crewmen said. He floated through the compartment, not touching the decks, and began loosening the straps holding MacKinnie in his seat. When they had everyone loose they gestured toward the opening.

Mary Graham stared openly at the newcomers, but MacKinnie couldn't tell if it were their strange eyes or the way they levitated through the compartment that interested her. Kleinst had a bored look, but under it MacKinnie thought he detected keen interest. The pale young scholar seemed relaxed, but whenever the crewmen spoke he tensed slightly.

"Come aboard," Landry said. "We should not waste time. . . ."

They floated gently through the connecting passageways between the landing craft and the main ship, gingerly following the towlines the ship's officers had strung for them, everyone quiet and awed by the experience. We've left our world, MacKinnie thought. And I'm supposed to bring back the knowledge so we can *build* one of these. He shook his head grimly. The more he saw of the ships, the more he was convinced that they had taken on an impossible task.

Their staterooms proved to be minuscule cubicles, sparsely furnished at first sight, but when buttons were touched, various utilities such as beds and tables unfolded from the walls. MacKinnie sat in a chair and held himself in it while he looked at the various gadgets, but learned nothing.

Weight slowly returned.

A ship's officer led him into the lounge, where some of the others were already assembled. The room was completely alien to MacKinnie. It was splendidly furnished, but in addition to couches, chairs, and tables on the deck beneath him, one large, circular wall was also covered with carpeting and furniture, all bolted into place. The wall was not a complete disc, for a large central tube ran through it well over Nathan's head. More strange than the double furniture was the deck, which curved up both in front of him and behind him, yet, when he walked around it, always felt as if it were down. After a few strides, he looked back to see that where he had been was now well above him. A few more steps brought him around the central column "overhead" to reveal Renaldi apparently hanging from the ceiling, relaxing in a large chair, a drink in his hand.

"Ah, Trader MacKinnie, please be seated. The others will be here shortly." Renaldi sipped his drink. "Pleasant to have weight again, is it not?"

"Yes." MacKinnie sat, again noting the eerie sensations in his inner ears whenever he made a sudden movement. "How have you accomplished this, uh, giving us weight?" Renaldi looked startled for a moment, then smiled. "You truly don't know, do you? I'll wait until the others arrive and explain. Have a drink, Trader. We can only enjoy this for another hour before the captain gets under way, and we will all have to be in our staterooms for the transition."

MacLean, Longway, Kleinst, and Mary Graham joined them within moments. Midshipman Landry arrived a few minutes later, and explained that the guards and their leader were quartered on another deck with a lounge of their own. When all were seated, Renaldi told Landry, "The Trader is curious about our weight, Midshipman. Surely the Empire will not fall if we explain it to our guests?"

"No, of course not, Trader," Landry said. "You see, gentlemen and freelady, the captain has caused the ship to rotate about its long axis. Thus, you are thrown toward the outside of the ship. When we begin our voyage, however, the ship will accelerate for long periods of time, and the rotation will cease. While we accelerate, you will feel weight, but 'down' will be that deck in front of you, and this deck will become a wall." The boy paused for a moment, then said suddenly, "If you have never been off-world, you have never seen your own planet. There are ports at that bulkhead there; allow me to open them for you."

Before any of the others could rise, Kleinst had charged across the deck, eagerly waiting until the port was uncovered. With a shrug, Landry uncovered several more, and the others took turns looking out. No one had the heart to remove Kleinst from his post.

They saw Prince Samual's World, although it did not appear to them as a sphere, as the orbit was not that high. Although it was partly obscured by clouds, they could see much of the great mass of North Continent, a portion of the Major Sea, and several of the larger islands of the Archipelago. Except for the fleecy clouds, it looked exactly like globes and maps they had studied in school. The world below them appeared to be moving across their field of vision, however, and after it passed they would see the black of space, stars shining more brightly than they had ever believed possible.

For long moments there was no conversation. Finally, slowly, one by one they filed back to their seats, except for Kleinst, who stayed at the port until they were ushered to their staterooms for the beginning of the voyage.

MacKinnie was not allowed off the lounge deck except to go down a ladder to the deck below where Stark and the guards were quartered. His troops had far less luxurious quarters than his own, but somewhat more open space, and Hal was using the time to best advantage, training the men in unarmed combat, and experimenting with swords and shields from their personal baggage. The men seemed cheerful enough, and MacKinnie ordered a small daily ration of brandy for each man to relieve the monotony. He returned to his own quarters for the same prescription.

The days flowed by with a monotonous quality, relieved by their constant efforts to master the language of Makassar. MacKinnie and MacLean sent for wooden swords and put in an hour of practice daily, resulting both in bruises on their persons, and considerable respect for each other. They also trained with their men.

Longway and Mary Graham seemed to have a knack for languages, particularly the Academician, who passed from the main dialects to lesser ones he found in supplementary sections of the loose-leaved books the Imperial Navy had supplied. They were informed that the books would be collected before they made planetfall, and MacKinnie held his breath at the mention, but nothing else was said about them.

Eleven days out from Samual, they were again strapped into their chairs in their staterooms, experiencing another hour of weightlessness before normal weight returned. By constant pestering of Landry whenever the boy joined them, MacKinnie induced him to tell them that during the first part of the journey they had accelerated, and were now decelerating in order to enter faster-than-light travel. When he received only quizzical looks from the others, Landry explained further.

"There's two kinds of drive, normal space and hyperspace. In normal space, the fusion drive works into a

Langston Field releasing photons which propel the ship. Never mind, I'm not allowed to explain it to you anyway. But this pushes the ship right along, and we experience acceleration from it. The hyperspace drive works on a different principle. It works along the pseudo-nuclear force path between two stars. I don't suppose that means anything to you. There are force paths between the stars similar to the forces that hold atomic particles together. Unlike the atomic forces which fade off rapidly in an exponential relation to distance—oh, hell, that doesn't tell you anything either. What's important is that the drive won't work if you're near a sun or a planetary body. You have to get to the precise Alderson point to get into hyperspace. Otherwise nothing happens when you turn on the drive. Navy ships have better equipment for locating Alderson points, so they don't decelerate as much as a merchant ship. Eventually we'll arrive at the right place and we can get into the hyperspace path between stars. In there we can go faster than light."

Landry glanced about him, and Kleinst quickly assumed the blank stare typical of the others. The midshipman scratched his head, muttered that that was all he was allowed to say anyway, and asked for another drink. MacKinnie noted that the boy would usually have exactly three drinks, and would always leave their company as soon as he had consumed the third one. He also noticed that the midshipman seemed to be a great deal more talkative when Mary Graham was present.

Days were measured by the ship's clocks, which were geared to a standard day somewhat shorter than that of Prince Samual's World, as Samual's years were slightly shorter than those of Earth. MacKinnie noted that the Imperials tended to use many expressions and physical devices traditional from Earth.

On the twenty-second day, they were once again warned to go to their cabins, and later each was personally inspected by Landry. "Don't panic, no matter what you think you see or hear," he warned each. "The Alderson drive affects different people different ways. It's very usual to feel disoriented. Just be calm and everything'll be all right."

An hour after the boy left them, MacKinnie was in a cold sweat, waiting with nothing to do. He hoped that the others would remember their instructions. As he inspected his mechanical watch for the twentieth time, there was a strong thrumming sound which seemed to permeate the ship. This went on for several minutes, then there was an imperceptible lurch, as if intolerable acceleration had been applied for a time so short that it had no chance to affect them.

At once, Nathan was aware of a sensation of intolerable wrongness. He looked at the walls and other now-familiar objects, and they seemed the same in every detail, yet somehow different. Strange sensations crawled across his scalp. The thrumming sound was gone, but something of it lingered, and it did not sound like anything he had ever heard before.

Then there was a moment of silence. It was too brief to be completely perceived, but it seemed to be a silence which had a tangible quality, a deadening effect that sucked up sound, and perhaps heat and light and every-thing else. Then there was the sound again, which rose and died away, and after that weight returned, oriented toward the circular section which MacKinnie had come to think of as the walls of his cabin. With weight, his universe returned almost to normal, although somewhere inside his brain there was a tiny terrified awareness that everything was wrong.

★9★
MASKASSAR
★ ★ ★

They were in a new star system. MacKinnie tried to comprehend that, but it was impossible to believe. Yet it must be true. The stars outside the ship were subtly different, some constellations remaining as before, but others altered.

The journey to Makassar took another twenty-four days, with the transition from acceleration to deceleration taking place in the middle of the night. They were gathered in the main lounge, with Stark acting as a serving man, on the "afternoon" of the last day, when the hatch opened and they were joined by Landry and Renaldi.

"We have nearly arrived, gentlemen," Renaldi announced importantly. "I have requested Midshipman Landry to allow you to see the object of all your attention, and he has graciously consented. It will be visible through the ports over there." As Renaldi spoke, Landry removed the locks from the observation ports and opened them.

Makassar was a tiny ball, hanging in the dark of space. The most prominent feature, easily visible even from their distance, was a pair of enormous ice caps. Much of the world between them was water, with a single continent, mostly in the Southern Hemisphere, swimming westward like an enormous whale. Two large islands, almost continental in size, hung above it in the Northern Hemisphere, and the shallow seas were dotted with smaller islands. There were two distinct colors to the seas where the sun shone upon them, and Kleinst remarked that it must be due to a dramatic difference in depth. Deep water was mostly in the Northern Hemisphere, with the continent surrounded by the pale blue marking much shallower depths.

"It's a lovely world," Landry remarked, standing next to MacKinnie and pointing out some of the more visible features. "Smaller than Earth. Gravity is about eighty-seven percent of that of Earth, which makes it about, oh, let's see." He withdrew his small computer and wrote directly on one face of it with an attached stylus. "I make it seventy-nine percent of the gravity you're used to, Trader. Your men are going to be very strong compared to the locals down there. That might be useful."

"It might be indeed," MacKinnie muttered. "Are those ice caps normal in size? I seem to recall our maps of Samual show much smaller ones."

"Makassar is a bit colder than Samual. Orbit's more eccentric, enough to make some climatic differences. The inclination of the planet is also greater. Turns out it's summer—by planet inclination—in the Southern Hemisphere when the planet's farthest from the sun. I don't know, but I wouldn't be surprised if the two big islands in the north were uninhabitable, or nearly so. It would be pretty cold there. You're arriving in the middle of spring on the main continent."

MacKinnie recalled the maps they had been given. Except for a few sea trader towns, the entire population of Makassar was concentrated on the main continent, at least as far as the Imperials knew. The maps weren't very accurate, but at that they'd be the best obtainable.

They watched the planet grow larger and larger as the ship approached. Each member of the expedition stood in silence, lost in his particular fantasy, dreaming of other worlds. Then the alarm sounded, and they scrambled for the landing boat.

The Imperial base was located in a small trading town by a great bay at the western end of the planet's single continent. A scattered chain of islands led across the shallow seas to a series of large islands from which trading ships and sometimes pirate raiders came. Because of their depredations, the area around Jikar was largely uninhabited, which suited the Imperials well. Their presence in the town was disturbance enough; they had no desire to be seen by any large number of the people of Makassar.

A light rain was falling as they left the landing boat. They stood on the stone dock and stared about them in silence.

"Another world," Mary Graham said. "It's hard to believe."

"It is that," MacKinnie said. He sniffed the air, but could smell nothing. The rain had washed away any alien odors, and kept them from seeing very far. He turned back to Graham. "This is the first chance we've had to talk alone," he said. "What was the long heated conversation you had with Renaldi yesterday?"

"It was nothing—"

"Your pardon, but I do not believe that."

"He wanted—I tell you, it was nothing."

"The Trader invited her to dinner," Longway said.

"Alone?"

"Yes. Of course I refused," Graham said.

MacKinnie looked at her grimly. "You should have told me. I am—"

"My guardian," Graham finished for him. "Yes, and what good would that have done? You would have challenged him. He would have been horrified and thought us barbaric. Nothing would have been accomplished—"

"But—"

"She's right," Longway said. "By his standards there was nothing improper about the invitation." He put his hand on MacKinnie's sleeve. "I know," he said. "The invitation implied that she might accept it. Since freeborn ladies would never visit a man in his quarters, he implies that she is no more than a tavern girl. But he does not know that, Trader MacKinnie."

"And who will explain this to her father?" MacKinnie asked.

"He is not here," Longway said carefully. "Nor is there any reason to explain to him. Trader, Imperial ladies are, I think, no more immoral than our own, but they are their own mistresses. Not under guardianship. The Empire is as shocked by our customs as we are by theirs. More, I think. And remember where we are. You can hope there will be nothing worse than this to endure."

MacKinnie turned away without answering. Longway was right, of course. Even on Prince Samual's World there were cultures which did not so thoroughly protect their women as did the North Continent civilizations. There were even places where men did not go constantly armed. He had adjusted to those, and he could to Makassar.

Navy House was crude, a stone building constructed by the locals, and there was no Marine fortress. Whatever defenses the Imperials had installed were not obvious to MacKinnie as his group approached the Imperial headquarters.

Many of the locals were small men, brown and dark, reminding MacKinnie of the officers aboard the trading starship. Their clothing was crude, some of the men wearing trousers, others dressed in long, gownlike robes which hung to their knees. In sharp contrast to the passengers of the starship, everyone seemed to have a beard of some kind, although many of them were not well developed. Their hair was long, and it was obvious at a distance that they did not often practice bathing.

In the hundred yards from the docks to Navy House MacKinnie's party was approached by at least ten beggars, some of them proudly displaying truly horrible disfigurations. They shouted and pleaded, and MacKinnie was pleased to see that he was able to understand them reasonably well. The practice aboard the ship had been useful for learning the language, even if he did not care much for his first encounter with it. Stark tossed out a few copper coins, allowing them to escape as the beggars cursed and fought for the money.

They were permitted to stay in Navy House for a few days only, and MacKinnie's officers eagerly explored the small town, talking to the inhabitants and investigating the possible marketable goods for sale. At the end of the third day on the planet, they assembled in the one large room of the headquarters building. Renaldi, as usual, sat by the fire, a glass in his hand.

"Your Excellency, we have been unable to find a single thing worth transportation to Prince Samual's World. We are beginning to think there is nothing here," MacKinnie began. "Where are the spices, and exotic cloth, and the rest that you and your partner described?"

Renaldi laughed. "For all I know," he said thickly, "there may not be another valuable thing on the planet. Soliman cleans a place out pretty good when he gets the chance."

"But—but," stammered MacKinnie, "if there's nothing here, we're ruined. You've charged us an enormous price for transportation to this place. Surely there's something worth buying. How are we going to recover our expenses?"

"You probably won't. We never promised you a profit, Trader." Renaldi pronounced the title as if it were an insult. "In our business, you have to take chances. Perhaps you took an unwise chance."

"But we took it on your advice!" MacKinnie snapped, then changed to a pleading tone. "Surely you know of some way we can make this profitable for King David. Surely with your experience you can help us."

"Unlikely." Renaldi drank deeply. "But whatever it is you are to do, be quick about it. The ship leaves in three days."

"Three days! Why, that's impossible. You promised us sufficient time to arrange for trade, even to organize a permanent company here. We can't begin to arrange for trade in three days. You knew that before we started." MacKinnie looked down at the impassive face and had an urge to tear out the small mustache by the roots. He restrained himself and said, "I'm going to complain to the Navy. They'll make you honor your contract."

"Our contract, Trader, says that you will be brought here, and returned at a time mutually convenient. The ship leaves in three days. That's convenient to us. And you've nothing to complain about; we're going to two other star systems before we go back to your miserable planet. You won't be permitted out of your quarters while we're there, but think of the broadening travel you'll experience."

"It is not mutually convenient if one party does not agree," Longway said softly. "We may have few rights, Imperial Trader Renaldi, but I suspect Captain Greenaugh will enforce those we have. He did not seem to be overly fond of Imperial Traders, Your Excellency. We will not leave in three days."

Renaldi shrugged. "Suit yourselves. The next ship we could schedule through this miserable system will arrive at this port in something over a standard year. If you wish to wait for it, I will have the Navy compute the exact number of local days before it arrives. You can wander this poverty-stricken ball until you tire of it." He got up with an effort and filled his glass from an open bottle on the great table which dominated the room. MacKinnie noted that the bottle was handblown, and crudely at that, but of an interesting color. Renaldi seemed to be fond of the local liquor.

"Three days or over a year," Nathan observed. "Neither is very convenient."

"Those are the times convenient to us. Which do you choose?" Renaldi backed away from MacKinnie nervously as the soldier approached him, fingering his belt as if grasping for a weapon which was not there. He managed to get back to his seat, where he regained his composure. "Come, now, we never promised you more. And think of the adventures you can have, wandering about on a planet of swineherds." He laughed for a moment, saw MacKinnie's face, and stopped short.

Nathan turned to MacLean and said, "Go get the lieutenant in command of this post. We may as well find out just what else this man can do to us." The group waited in a strained silence for several minutes before MacLean returned with Midshipman Landry and another officer.

Lieutenant Farr was a short, dark man who resembled the planetary locals. MacKinnie wondered idly if he had been chosen for the post for his ability to blend in with the rest of the population. Nathan explained the situation, and Farr and Renaldi conversed in the Imperial language for several minutes, speaking too rapidly for even Longway to understand. Renaldi became more and more excited, but the lieutenant spoke with a deadly calm. Although he did not have the intense, dedicated look which MacKinnie had noted was common of the Navy men, he never seemed to smile either. Instead, his manner was coldly official with perhaps the merest trace

of relief from the boredom of being commanding officer
to a post without a mission.

When the conversation was finished, Farr turned to
MacKinnie, speaking very slowly. "If he is correct about
the details of the contract your king signed, then he can
legally do this. We could examine it for you if you'd like,
but it might take some time. There are no legal officers on
this post."

MacKinnie canted his head to one side, realized the
gesture was meaningless to the lieutenant, and said,
"Thank you, no. I'm sure they drafted it carefully
enough." He seized a glass, filled it, and drained it off. "Is
there any chance of our finding a decent trading community on this planet, Lieutenant? And will we be allowed to
go and search for one?"

"The only place I can suggest is the main city, Batav.
It's said to be wealthy, although what the locals mean
by wealth is not likely to impress you. It is all you will
find."

MacKinnie nodded. "Then I suppose we must go
there. I can't return to King David without something to
show for his investment."

"There are difficulties," Lieutenant Farr said slowly.
"The Empire cannot transport you there. The entire
countryside is in a state of war, and it is not likely you will
survive to reach Batav. We can give you no protection. . . ."
The officer paused. "But if you must go, perhaps you will
find another party of Imperial citizens who set out for
Batav. A group of churchmen defied our advice and
departed months ago. We have not heard from them, and
His Holiness will insist on knowing what became of his

missionaries. If you find what became of them, it will make the job easier."

MacKinnie looked at the officer, realizing that if the Navy could not send troops to search for missionaries, it would never attempt to protect a group of colonial Traders. Prince Samual's World seemed far away, lost in the swirl of stars above them, and he knew he would never see it again. One thing, he thought; at least they would have no way of knowing what he intended doing at the old library, if he ever reached it.

"We'll look for them, Lieutenant," Nathan said. "Now, I suppose we must find quarters in the town, so that we can organize our expedition. I dare not return to my own world without a profit until I have done everything I can do." He turned to Renaldi. "As for you, I understand that the Empire preserves local customs insofar as this is possible. I will live for the day when you return to Prince Samual's World and I meet you on a field of honor. Presuming, of course, that you have any." When Renaldi made no reply, MacKinnie stalked away.

★10★
JIKAR
★ ★ ★

The tavern reminded MacKinnie of the Blue Bottle. Even the name was translatable into something close to Blue Wineglass, and it reminded MacKinnie of home. Although it was only an hour past noon, the place was full.

Blatt, Master Tanner, and Hoorn, Master of Drapers, were glad enough to enjoy MacKinnie's hospitality. They finished the first bottle of wine in silence, savoring the richly flavored concoction the tavern keeper made from the sour local product. It sold at a price almost no one in the village could afford, making MacKinnie a popular man. Nathan watched the two men, once pleasantly stout but now disfigured with the folds of flesh which marked malnutrition. Other townsmen sat in brooding silence, many of them at tables empty of bottles. The tavern keeper had served his tithe, and they had no more credit; but there was no place else to go.

"Is Jikar often like this?" Nathan asked when the bottle was done at last. "Your pardon, Masters, but it would seem that no village could survive long in this state, even one blessed with harbor and fields."

Hoorn cleared his throat and glanced suggestively at the bottle, too proud to ask for more. MacKinnie signaled with a careless wave and was rewarded with a burst of activity from the tavern keeper. Except for a small boy of no more than eight years, MacKinnie had seen no one in service to the tavern, yet it was a large place, obviously once a prosperous one. As the new bottle was poured, Hoorn sighed deeply.

"Since *they* came," he whispered. Then in more normal tones, although still keeping his deep voice low, he added, "Our war fleet was destroyed when *they* landed. The pirates will not accept tribute from Jikar; we have killed too many of them in battle. Our city is small, Trader, but we were once proud. Now what is there for us? The harbor is closed by the pirates, and the barbarians ravage our fields. Yet *they* will do nothing. They cannot interfere, they tell us." The Draper's voice rose to a shout tinged with tears. "In the name of the Immortal God, have they not interfered already? They have been the ruin of Jikar!"

"Aye," Blatt muttered. "Our fleet and our army were the same. Both lost. The pastures are burned off, the fields trampled. Oh, we are safe enough within the walls. *They* will not allow the town to be sacked. We could wish that they would. Then our young men might take courage and be ready to fight again instead of huddled at the steps of the church to receive alms they once gave, or drinking the tavern keeper's tithe before it can reach the priest. A curse on outlanders." He lifted his glass to toast damnation before he realized who his host was. "Pardon, Trader. You do not seem like one of *them.*"

MacKinnie nodded absently and considered his predicament. On the next day, the landing ship would rise, leaving his crew stranded on the planet, but he had yet found no way to leave Jikar. Just outside the city walls barbarian hordes prowled, ready to plunder anyone foolhardy enough to take either road, north or south. Outside the harbor, patrols of pirates based on the islands across the great shallow bay called the Sulawa Sea enforced the blockade of the port, demanding not only tribute but the head of the Master of each Guild in Jikar. It was to the credit of the people of the town that no one had ever been heard to speak in favor of dealing with the pirates, except two ancient Guildmasters who claimed they had few years left anyway. Their own councils refused to consider the proposal.

The barbarian incursion into what had once been civilized territory had created chaos in lands which had never been well governed in the best of times. Many of the warrior families which had maintained at least the illusion of peace and order were no more; others had fled. No one could answer for the safety of a small party setting out to the Old Empire city nearly three thousand kilometers away.

The Imperials had very little information about Batav. In hopes of finding a local who had journeyed there, Nathan approached the Guildmasters who ruled Jikar, only to find that few townsmen had ever traveled farther than a few hundred kilometers at best, and most of those had died in the brief, futile resistance to the Navy. To the

Navy, the loss of three hundred and ninety locals was a regrettable incident. To Jikar, it was ruin.

"God is angry with you, Trader," Hoorn said. "A few years ago, Jikar was the busiest port on the coast of the west. Out here we don't have large cities as they do in the east, but there were over five thousand souls in our town, and as many more on the lands around. Trading was good. We had no need of lordlings to fight our battles for us. We were free men, bound to no one, our own protection. The Guilds rule here, not some bonehead warrior capable of nothing but mounting with sword and lance."

"You speak too hard of the men of iron," Blatt said. The wine was warming him to the conversation, recalling pleasanter times he had been in the tavern. He lifted a blue-tinted blown goblet, the kind which gave the place its name, and drank deeply. "They do nothing but fight, true, yet I think Jikar would never have been free if there were not the marshlands to our east. It was our curse that the iron men died in plague, their strongholds fell, and hordes swept past. Before that we had only to fight the few raiders who passed the great houses like thieves in the night. When their full force fell on us we knew it."

"Knew it and won!" Hoorn shouted. "Ah, Trader, had you seen it. Our young men, the sailors from our fleet and the boys of the Guilds, standing with pikes leveled, never giving ground, while the barbarians dashed themselves against us. Glory to the Lord, the field was red with their blood. We took a hundred horses and many ayuks for our own." Evidently horses and cattle had been brought to Makassar by the Old Empire. Now both ran wild across the plains, hunted by local predators unless protected by men, but managing to survive.

Some of the barbarians also rode the ayuk, a native beast that resembled a moose with long, semi-prehensile claws and an elongated prehensile snout. It lived on the hive-rat, warmblooded egg-layers about seven inches long which lived in great colonies with only a few retaining active sexual powers. The hive-rat was one of the most dangerous creatures on Makassar, although it was not carnivorous. It ate the stone-hard local woods with ease, burrowed in the ground, and found any plant life edible by humans quite nourishing. It would fight when trapped, and when one was wounded, hundreds of them came to its aid in blind fury. More than one man had died through being caught by them in the open.

"A great victory." Blatt nodded. "One which Master Hoorn could tell you more of, for he commanded for the Guilds that day. Aye, we broke them, but we could not pursue them. Most escaped. Had we forty of the mounted iron men to give chase, the victory would have kept the barbarians from our gates for a hundred years."

"Ah." Hoorn drank again. Then he smiled and shrugged. "We can agree the warriors know how to fight. Yet I have in my day seen them turned back from the gates of a city like ours. In open battle. The young men stood to their pikes, and the iron men Master Blatt is so fond of split about them on both sides, afraid to attack. They took no tribute from that city." As Hoorn finished, a young man, dark of hair and tall for Makassar, one quite muscular but now thin like the others, strode arrogantly across the room, his head high in contrast to the locals

MacKinnie had seen. He could have been twenty-five Earth years, but he looked younger, and his clothes were subtly different. His trousers were of the rough-texture cloth worn by the villagers, but the jacket and cloak were of finer stuff, and Nathan noted that there were discolored lines at the collar, as if it had once been trimmed with something now lost. He recalled that cloth-of-gold collars and bands were the marks of the Guildmasters.

The tavern keeper gave the newcomer the glass of cheap wine and thick slice of bread which he served to all daily in lieu of his tithe to the church. The man began to eat without speaking to anyone.

"That's who you should talk to," Hoorn told MacKinnie. "We should send for him. If there is a man in Jikar who can tell you what you'll find beyond the river and forest, Brett can. Or that warrior friend of his."

"Who is he?" MacKinnie asked.

"His name is Brett," Hoorn said. He lowered his voice. "He is said to have come from far away, some say the eastern coast. He comes carrying tales and songs, and will not discuss his ancestry. As for me, I believe he was born a barbarian."

"Yet he speaks many civilized tongues," Master Blatt said.

"Aye." Hoorn pursed his lips in thought. "The barbarians do not come here often, so it is a thing not done here. But I am told that in parts where the plains riders are more common, the townsfolk often capture young plainsmen and keep them as slaves."

"And you think Brett was one of those?" MacKinnie asked.

"It is possible," Blatt said. "Although I do not envy anyone who would be master to the singer. I would rather have him as a friend."

"Aye," Hoorn agreed. "There have been other singers in Jikar, but none came as Brett, Most are on foot, but Brett rides a great war-horse, and has for companion one of the iron men with armor and lance and sword. Vanjynk his name is. He was driven from his lands to the south and now wanders as Brett to sell his abilities to any purchaser."

A wandering mercenary, MacKinnie thought. As I once was.

MacKinnie studied the dark features of the man in question and approved. He might be down on his luck, Nathan thought, but he wasn't defeated. Despite his youth he was more akin to the Guildmasters than the tavern loafers. "Call him over," he said in a moment of decision.

"Singer," Hoorn called. "At your pleasure, join us. Our noble friend is a willing host."

The singer came to the table and bowed as Hoorn performed introductions.

"I am told you know of faraway lands," MacKinnie said. He poured a glass of wine and pushed it toward Brett. "If you have the time, perhaps you can tell me of your travels."

Brett made a wry face. "I have little but time." He drained his wineglass at a gulp.

"You do not travel alone, singer?" MacKinnie asked, pouring more wine.

"Not for a yir. I teach Vanjynk poetry, he teaches me to fight. Now we are both good at both trades and the living is better." He stared ruefully about the tavern. "Or was. But we will not leave our bones here for Master Blatt to put to earth."

"You would like to leave Jikar, then?" MacKinnie asked.

"Trader, we would pay the man who allowed us to fight for him, be it only that he had sufficient men to cut through the maris. But the maris will stay until they have eaten and burned everything they can find, and as they are not so stupid as the Guilds hope, that will not be before the snows. Then they will leave. At that they will bring you a blessing, Guildmasters."

"What blessing could a horde of barbarians—maris, you called them?—what blessing can they bring?" Blatt stood, his wide shoulders almost blotting out the younger man, his great hands, hardened with brine and tanners' liquor, on his hips.

"Calmly, calmly, you will alarm our host and the wine will stop," Brett said softly. There was a hint of threat to the voice, a tone one did not take with Guildmasters. "I call them maris because that is what they call themselves. And the blessing is the destruction of the hive-rats. There will be few enough of them when they move on—in fact, that is why they will move on. The ayuks must eat many of them, which keeps the maris moving about the great plains. When the ayuks don't eat, the maris don't eat. Even here they'll finish off all your Earth crops before the ayuks are done with the hive-rats."

MacKinnie listened with interest. "The maris live off their ayuks?"

Brett looked at him in puzzlement. "Your speech is

unlike any that I have heard in any land," he commented. "Yet you are not native here, where the maris have not been. Where have you lived that you don't know about them? Ah, the cities of the mountains of the north. Well, know, northman, that the plantain of the great flatland is as poisonous to us as most of the other plants on Makassar. It must be true, as the priests say, we came here from another star long ago, else why would God have put us where we cannot eat? But the ayuk can eat the plants, and men can eat the ayuk, and drink her milk, and, even as the maris do, drink the blood of their steeds. Their horses fare better, eating grasses which grow among the plantain, and some maris live from their horses alone, but the ayuk is better. It is not enough, though. Fed nothing else, they waste and die, even as these men here. In your north, you can eat the tallgrass, which they say came from Earth, and you eat the grotka. But did you eat nothing but grotka, and the swimmers from the sea, you would die also."

MacKinnie nodded. The Imperials had told him of the dietary problems of Makassar. Most of the animal life was edible, but not all of it, and little of the plant life except that which came originally from another planet. The local plants stored up various metals, which gave them their hardness, but also made them deadly. The local animals separated out the metal, although some, like the hive-rat which ate not only fruits and grains but woody stems, were deadly. All lacked essential vitamins. Listening to the singer, he had an idea.

"I wish to return to the mountains of the north," Nathan said. His maps showed that Batav was nestled on the side—the wrong side from Jikar, of course—of the mountain range which ran down the great peninsula jutting from the north edge of the continent. The mountains then curled east before they dwindled away to hills, still high enough to form a natural barrier to the great plains.

"North?" Brett asked incredulously. "How long has it been since you came from there? But you must have come by ship. The land route has been closed for two years, Trader. The High King of the Passes is dead, and the others fight for his place. No life is safe, no judges sit, and the people make do as best they can. With your wealth, you might hire enough men to take you south. With me to show the way you could fight through the maris and come to the city-states and kingdoms of the Kepul. But not to the north, Trader. We could never pass the Sangi." Brett tossed off the glass of wine, then waved at a smaller man, fair-haired and contrasting with the singer in every dimension, yet bearing the same manner of confidence. The newcomer came forward slowly.

"Trader," Brett said, "this is Vanjynk, the best friend a wanderer ever had, tragedy as it is that he must roam the lands." Brett poured his friend wine without asking.

Vanjynk nodded to MacKinnie and sat in silence. MacKinnie noted that he was younger than Brett, possibly by as much as two of the local years. Yet he was born of the nobility, while whatever Brett's origin it had not been in an iron and stonewood fortress. The relationship between the men must have been complex.

The others explained to the young warrior what MacKinnie had in mind. "But there is no way through the Sangi," Brett finished. "Or none that I can see."

"Nor I." Vanjynk drank slowly and deliberately, as he seemed to do everything else. "You will not find enough men to take the trail through the forest. The coast is closed. I do not know the sea."

"The sea," Blatt snorted. "Were there a way by sea half the town of Jikar would be off trading. All your gold will not pay the pirates, Trader, and there is but one warship left in Jikar."

"There is a ship here?" MacKinnie asked. "Is it for sale?"

"For sale?" Hoorn thought slowly. "It belongs to the Ironsmiths. There is little in Jikar that is not for sale, including our daughters' virtue. I could save you money in the purchase, for a fee to my Guild."

"Not allowed." Blatt spoke positively. "To sell a man that which sends him to his death is not allowed. Go back to your clothing, Hoorn; the Guilds cannot plunder this man from the stars."

Nathan noted the sudden look of interest Brett tried to hide, then turned to Blatt. "I buy it willingly, Master Tanner." Although he said nothing to show it, the man's honesty affected him more than MacKinnie wanted to admit to himself. "To return to our homes with nothing would be not only our ruin, but that of many others. Go with Guildmaster Hoorn and buy that ship for me, and we will do well by both your Guilds. Freemen Brett, Vanjynk, I will pay you for your advice, whether you come with me or not; but we are taking that ship out of the harbor of Jikar if every pirate on Makassar is lying in wait out there."

★11★
SHIPFITTER
★★★

MacKinnie and his party were inspecting their ship when the landing boat rose from the harbor and vanished from sight in the low clouds above. Nathan was not sorry to see it go. He had far too much work to waste time playing a role, pleading with Renaldi or demanding rights from the Navy. The ship was not in condition to be launched.

There was an additional blessing. Midshipman Landry had left with Renaldi. When Lieutenant Farr was told of MacKinnie's plans he decided that the Navy could ill spare one of its young officers for a year, especially since it was more than likely that MacKinnie's party would never be heard from again. Landry was ordered to go to the next port and report to headquarters for further instructions.

Before Renaldi left, the lieutenant had made it clear that the Navy was displeased with his treatment of MacKinnie, and would insist that no matter how remote Nathan's chance of survival was, Renaldi was obligated to

provide transportation back to Prince Samual's World.
MacKinnie was privately convinced that the lieutenant
was more upset about Landry's wasted time than the
injustice of the situation, as Greenaugh had been led to
believe that the boy would be gone only a few months.
However, he was now guaranteed passage home if he
could return to Jikar.

Mary Graham remained on Makassar. She pointedly
refused to be on the same ship with Renaldi without
MacKinnie's protection, and she was legally correct by
Haven law and custom. This was upsetting enough, but
Nathan found she also insisted on accompanying the
party on its expedition to Batav, and nothing MacKinnie
could say would convince her that she could not go.

"What did you expect me to do here?" she insisted. "I
knew there would be danger."

"Freelady," MacKinnie replied coldly, "Citizen Dougal
sent you without my request. We had thought to establish
trading offices in the Imperial port, where you would
remain as our agent."

"But there is no need for offices here," Graham
protested.

"True. But you cannot come with us. You will be a
great inconvenience aboard ship. How can we provide
you proper quarters? To be blunt, what of sanitary
arrangements? This is madness."

"Madness, Trader? Is it less mad to leave me here, in a
city besieged? I may yet be of use to you."

"No."

"You say no. You had better reconsider. If I am not
reliable enough to go with you, how can you trust me to

remain silent for a year? You leave me here with the Imperial officers—"

"I did not say that I do not trust you."

"Would Dougal leave me behind? Think on that. Dougal would have me killed rather than risk it."

He would, MacKinnie thought. Yet—what does she know of our real mission? I haven't told her or any of them. Kleinst knows. Perhaps Longway. Does Mary Graham? One of them may well have told her.

"Please," she said. "Trader, I was told this mission is important, to Haven and to Prince Samual's World. Will you deny me the chance to show that I—that the women of Haven—are no less bound to duty and honor than you? Do you think only men can be patriotic?"

I hadn't considered it, MacKinnie thought. More importantly, though, dare I leave her here? She's right, Dougal wouldn't. I can't think how she can help, but—

"Very well."

"Thank you. You won't regret it."

I regret it already, MacKinnie thought, but he said nothing.

And now she was busily clambering about the dockyard, following MacLean and hastily scribbling notes as the seaman happily inspected the craft. A gang of young locals, glad of employment, stood by under the supervision of the Shipwright Guildsmen. The Shipwrights had lost heavily in the brief and pointless battle with the Imperial Navy, and were willing to allow anyone in the town to work on MacKinnie's outfitting provided that they paid dues to the Guild and worked under its Masters. From the crowd inside and outside the dockyard,

MacKinnie thought half the able-bodied men of Jikar were hoping for employment.

The boat itself was hardly impressive. Only about thirty meters long, it was drawn up out of the water on a primitive ways. MacKinnie saw a round-bottomed boat with a small skeg running her length. The stem and sternpost were carried up high out of the water, and a great platform was constructed across the stern. On top of that was a cabin. The rest of the boat was undecked, with platforms for rowers along its sides. Over a hundred men could sit on the two sweeps halfdecks, but there was no chance of hiring that many for a long voyage, even if the pirates were not outside the harbor. At present, MacKinnie had no crew at all except his original expedition, although Brett and Vanjynk were on his payroll and would come even though they thought there was little chance of getting through.

After MacLean inspected the vessel, MacKinnie took him to a sheltered space to hold a conference. Hal Stark stood by to be sure they were not overheard, and MacKinnie wasted no time. "Can we make it? It's vital that we get to Batav, if we have to swim."

MacLean sucked on a pipe casually for a moment. Smoking did not seem to startle the villagers although they were never seen to smoke, but MacLean's lighter was far in advance of anything on the planet. MacKinnie wondered how he had got it past the thorough inspection Mr. Landry conducted before they were allowed to unload their goods from the landing ship. The pipe gurgled for a few moments before MacLean said, "Need some modifications to get that far. From what I've heard, this is sheltered water around here, but after we've gone north a ways there'll be nothing to the west for four thousand kilometers. Big waves will come across there in a normal westerly. Sure as hell be bad in a storm."

"So we could make it?" When MacLean nodded, MacKinnie went on, "How big a crew will you need?"

"The way I intend to modify her, no more than twice the number we already have, but everyone will have to lend a hand. A few locals would be useful if you can hire them.

"I'm going to make her sail, Trader. She's got that damned stubby mast on her; I'll yank that and put in a taller one, then stay it properly, deck the boat over and put some iron ballast in her. Nothing the Imperials can object to. And I'll mount leeboards."

The term meant nothing to MacKinnie, but he'd find out soon enough. "Sail up high will tip it over, won't it?" he asked.

MacLean shook his head. "Ballast will fix that, I hope. She's beamy enough, should be good form stability. I like the hull sections. They've ridden out some mean storms in those things. That big iron ram on the prow goes back almost amidships; it's the closest thing they've got to a ballast keel." He sucked on his pipe. "You can tell there's a lot of shallow water here, and with those weird tides from the two moons, they must run aground a lot. That's why the boats have nearly flat bottoms. Beach them for the night usually, I expect. We can get there, Trader, but I don't know about the pirates."

MacKinnie nodded. "Suggestions?"

"Just fix the boat and hope we can outrun them. Sure

as hell can't outfight them. Oh, and this is a bigger boat than most of the pirate stuff. Faster. Warship, one of the best on the planet, I'm told. But there's a hell of a lot of pirates. Without a full crew, if one of their ships boards us, we're dead."

"Yeah. Well, we cross that when it happens. How long to get the work done?" Now that Nathan was no longer watched by the Imperials every moment, he had control over his actions again, and the new sense of purpose drove him impatiently. He glanced about himself, took out his pipe, and borrowed MacLean's lighter to fire it. "How'd you get this past?" he asked.

"This?" MacLean looked at the lighter as if he had never seen it before. It was an ordinary flint and steel device, not as elegant as the flameless units the Imperial Navy carried. "I just walked out with it. Landry saw it, but he didn't say anything."

MacKinnie nodded slowly. By Empire standards, the lighter was primitive enough to be classed with Makassar technology. He wondered how many more Samualite devices were strange to Makassar but would be overlooked by the Navy; it was a point to remember.

"How long until we can sail?"

MacLean scratched his chin. "With luck, a few days. Decking's the hard part. There are a lot of hands to do the work, but they've never done this kind of thing before. Still, by the time you get the goods and provisions on board we should be just about ready to get under way."

It took two of the local weeks. Although the Makassar day was somewhat longer than Samual's and quite a bit longer than the standard Earth day, MacKinnie noticed that he and his crew soon became accustomed to living by local time, which was measured by sundials or not at all.

One reason the work went slowly was that the local church insisted on Sabbath-keeping, and in addition seemed to proclaim at least one Holy Day each week. These, and the inexperience of the locals with the construction methods MacLean insisted on, caused the first delays. Then when the ship was completed, another week was consumed in obtaining cloth suitable for sails and having the Drapers sew it.

MacLean was the only man available to design the equipment needed. He designed and cast anchors more advanced than anything seen on Makassar since the war; installed windlasses and winches, cast in bronze by the Ironsmiths; and had the Drapers lay up ropes and cables from local fibers. It all had to be done, and MacLean had to see to each detail personally. The days dragged on and on.

MacKinnie watched nervously one day when a party of Imperial sailors led by the junior lieutenant of the planet walked around the dockyards, but they evidently saw nothing to disapprove of. Anchors and winches were things for primitives, and the Navy men did not even understand the purpose of some of MacLean's devices. As a precaution, MacKinnie had taught Brett the use of most of them, so that if asked he would appear familiar with the equipment. The Navy might think it in common use elsewhere on Makassar.

By the time the ship was ready for launching, the trade goods and weapons they would carry were piled on the docks. A light drizzle driven by the strong westerly winds thoroughly soaked the party as they stood watching the locals launch the ship. The primitive ways did not permit much sophistication—half the young men in the town simply lifted and strained until *Subao* was in the water, then fell to carrying aboard the iron ingots MacLean had selected for ballast. MacKinnie expected to get under way immediately, but found that there was more to do.

"What now?" he asked MacLean.

"Masts. Stays. Running the sails up to see how they fit. Securing the ballast. Trader, that ship may be on her ear in a storm one of these days, and you'll hardly want the ballast shifting around down there. And we still have the leeboards to install. You can save time by getting your gear aboard today, but don't plan on leaving for at least three days more."

MacKinnie cursed, silently so that MacLean would not hear him. There was little else he could do.

That afternoon MacLean gave instruction on how to sail the boat. He discovered that young Todd had sailed small boats in the Haven harbor, and, under MacKinnie's questioning, the boy admitted to being a military cadet from one of the wealthier families of the kingdom of Haven. MacLean immediately appointed him midshipman and quartermaster.

They learned the language the locals used aboard ships, although MacLean had to adapt several local words for terms they would not be familiar with. Then he had Todd drill everyone on the names of lines and gear on the ship. MacKinnie noted that Brett seemed very adaptable, learning faster than the outworlders, although his friend

Vanjynk was almost uninterested. Stark, as usual, soon learned his tasks and drove the guardsmen to theirs, not a bit upset by Todd's sudden promotion over him. That night Stark and MacKinnie sat in MacKinnie's small room at the inn overlooking the water.

"Best we get the men some action, sir," Hal said. "All that drill with sword and shield's fine, but they get restless carrying stores and driving nails. Got some good pointers from that Vanjynk fellow, he's gifted with this armor and stuff. Reckon he's in the same business we are."

MacKinnie nodded. "From what I can see, it was all he ever learned until he lost his lands and had to go wandering with the singer. What do you make of Brett?"

"Don't know, sir. Takes my orders right enough, better than Vanjynk, but there's no understanding him."

MacKinnie nodded. "He's a tough one. That's a pretty strange partnership he's got with Brett. Vanjynk seems to be one of the iron men Blatt forever tells us about." He hoisted his glass and winked at his sergeant. "Iron MacKinnie's new troops. Few enough of them. Had any success at recruiting?"

"That's what I wanted to talk to you about, sir. There's a shipmaster I've been drinking with, man named Loholo. He claims he can get us a crew for a price. Part of the price is he wants to go with us. Mr. MacLean wasn't too interested in having a native shipmaster aboard, said there was enough command problems already what with nobody knowing who ranked who. He's not happy with you being in charge, sir. But I can't tell about Loholo; the Guild people seem to think a lot of him. Should I send for him? He's in the Blueglass tonight waiting to hear."

"No harm in talking to him. Sure, why not?"

Stark nodded and went to the door. He spoke briefly in low tones to one of the guardsmen outside. "Be here in a couple of minutes, Trader. Be best if I were on duty when he came in." Stark took his glass to another table across the small room.

Captain Loholo was a short, dark-brown man, stocky and strong-looking, with a distinct slant to his eyes, reminding MacKinnie of the starship officers he had seen. He had seen many others of his type on Makassar, in sharp contrast to the tall, blond men like Vanjynk. Loholo wore a golden skull ornament in his left ear, and carried a large curved knife in his belt. His clothing was of finer material than was usually seen on Jikar men, and everything he wore was freshly cleaned. He stood self-confidently in the doorway, coolly eyeing the star men.

"Trader," Hal said, "I want you to meet Captain Loholo, shipmaster and merchant. I'm told he's the only captain left in the port."

"Please have a seat, Captain," MacKinnie said, pouring a glass of wine. "My guard chief tells me you can raise a crew."

"Aye." Loholo fingered the glass, looked at MacKinnie for a moment, and drank. "Not a very good crew, Trader. The good men are at the bottom of the sea or run off to join the pirates. But there's men here who can pull an oar. Not seamen. Apprentices from all the Guilds, boys on tithes who'd like to be men again." He spoke so rapidly that MacKinnie had difficulty following him, and had to have Loholo repeat his words.

"I've seen them," MacKinnie said. "But Captain MacLean has not been able to recruit anyone."

"Nor will he." Loholo touched the wine bottle and looked at MacKinnie, who nodded. The brown man filled his glass and drank before continuing. "Your Captain MacLean is a strange man, Trader. He puts decks over the ship so that oarsmen can't breathe properly. He has taken out most of the rowing benches. What's left is up too high for proper leverage. You couldn't row that ship a hundred klamaters. And all the iron he put in the hull is no more than dead weight to be carried along. The men won't sail with him because even though they aren't seamen, they can see your man is no seaman. The ship will be too slow to escape pirates, and it won't sail properly if it does get past them." He shrugged. "Your pardon if I speak bluntly."

"But you're willing to come? And bring a crew?"

"Aye."

"Go on. Why?"

"You're not a beached captain, Trader. If you had the seawater in your blood, you'd know. My ship went out to fight with me ashore laid out by plague. She never came back. Everything I had was in that ship, Trader. Nothing left to buy the Ironsmiths' vessel. Even if a warship is no good for trading, I tried to buy *Subao*, for a ship's still a ship. I figure you'll all come to your senses about the ship when you see it won't work. And you'll need a man who knows how to sail these seas. I expect to be your shipmaster a week after you leave port. If you live that long. But the chance is worth it to me."

One way or another, MacKinnie thought. The dagger

at the man's belt had once had a jeweled hilt, but it wasn't meant for show purposes. With his own crew aboard, Loholo could make himself master of the ship if he were that kind of man. He looked over at Stark, who obviously had the same thoughts. Still, there was a way to make use of the man, and perhaps he was honest.

"Your own crew went down with your ship?"

"Aye. Every man. It won't be real seamen I can get you, Trader, but they'll be willing."

"Why?"

Loholo grinned. "I'm well known as a captain who comes back. Rich. And I'm said to be lucky."

"Still, how will you get them to join, with the pirates outside the harbor?"

"Tell them the star men will protect them. They know what happened out in the harbor the day *they* landed. They'll believe."

"And you don't?"

"If the star men will help you, you don't need to have the guard captain out giving free wine to find men, Trader. So they won't."

MacKinnie nodded. "What of the pirates?"

"There are ways. I know these waters, Trader. When the moons come together, there's deep water over the reefs. It goes down fast. Get over them at the right time, ahead of anybody chasing you, they never catch you. I doubt the pirates know my waters as I do. We'll have a chance. That is, if you can row the ship. Got to put the benches back in."

"What if I told you," MacKinnie asked, "that after we have returned to Jikar from where we are going, we will make you master of the ship and our trading agent, with gold every month and part of the trading as well?"

Loholo looked at MacKinnie closely. "Do not tempt a desperate man, Trader. Do you mean what you say?"

"If you serve me faithfully. The first service is to find a crew of twenty men who can fight. Say that we are insane, but that you, Loholo, will get the ship past the pirates. Get us a crew without talk, and have them ready to come aboard by dark tomorrow."

"And you'll give me the ship when you return? Mine to sail and command?"

"Yours to sail and command. And the chance at carrying trade from starships all over Makassar. You will become the owner of many vessels if you like."

Loholo grunted. "One is all I need. You'll have your crew, Trader. But this man of yours commands this voyage?"

"Yes. He commands. He has a young apprentice who will be a ship's officer. And there is my guard captain. But if MacLean wants you as an officer, he'll tell you so. I expect he will."

"I was a crew master once, Trader. I can be one again. Until you need me."

★12★
RIPTIDE
★★★

They sailed at dawn. Loholo, now crew master, had brought twenty young apprentices, all well armed. The stores were aboard, and MacLean had fitted the lee-boards, huge, fan-shaped, wooden boards pivoted at the small end of the fan and fastened nearly amidships of the vessel. When raised they were like giant shields. MacKinnie got the crew and passengers aboard the night before they were to set out, and watched with interest as MacLean and Loholo helped the crew sling hammocks, cursing the men into place in the narrow space below decks.

MacLean had placed the quarters in a traditional manner, his own cabin right aft with smaller staterooms to each side for MacKinnie and Mary Graham. Just forward of them, Longway and Kleinst had even tinier compartments, really not much larger than bunks with doors to close them in; then Hal and his guards slung their hammocks in a compartment which stretched from one side of the ship to the other. MacLean insisted that two of Stark's men be on duty and armed at all times, posted on the quarterdeck near the great tiller which steered the ship.

In the first light, mist still rising from the water, the crew was turned out from their hammocks to man the sweeps.

Loholo clucked his tongue at the arrangement. There were no rowing benches; instead the men walked the decks with great oars dipping down to the water, two men to an oar. The ship moved slowly away from the shore out into the bay.

"Wouldn't it be better to go at night?" MacKinnie asked. They stood on the quarterdeck with the other Samualites, Hal and his guards in full armor. Armor for the rest of the crew was secured with rawhide lashings in convenient places about the deck. Just forward of the quarterdeck Brett and Vanjynk stood at the ready, also in armor. It was impossible to make Vanjynk man a sweep, and MacKinnie decided that it would be senseless to require Brett to do so, so the two were carried as guards. Their mounts were stabled in the hold with the cattle *Subao* carried as part of the food supply.

MacLean eyed the distance to the slowly vanishing shore, then peered through the mists ahead and astern before answering. "No, Trader. The night would not keep the pirates from seeing us, and the wind dies away then. By midday there should be a strong wind. The sea breeze and the prevailing westerlies lie together on this shore. It will take a strong wind to outrun the pirate ships."

"If you say so," MacKinnie said with a shrug. And if the

wind doesn't come up? He shrugged again. "It's the only chance we have, anyway. Carry on, Captain MacLean."

"Aye, aye, sir." There was a note of the contempt seamen have for lubberly owners in MacLean's voice, but Nathan saw no reason to make a point of it. He needed MacLean to reach Batav.

He went to the rail and stared overboard. Around him the dawn was already turning the dark water clear. Small fishlike creatures swam lazily near the boat, looking at it before they darted away, easily outdistancing the men at the oars in spite of Loholo's shouted oaths. The crew master counted strokes in a tireless voice, keeping a steady rhythm not interrupted when he fell to cursing one of the men: "Sweep, step, back, back, Fool, step, back, back, Pull, you, stinking, filth, Sweep . . ."

MacLean left MacKinnie to stand near the tiller, his eyes on the compass mounted on the small mast just forward of the helmsman. Another mast, well forward, towered above the ship, and on both the sails were laced around the booms, their covers removed and stowed below decks. The sails were ready for instant action. MacKinnie could already feel the morning breeze coming from the south before it shifted to the west in the afternoon.

Mary Graham and Longway made their way over the slowly rolling deck to stand at the starboard rail with MacKinnie. Loholo's calls were clear and slightly musical. "Stroke . . . step . . . back . . . back . . . Stroke . . ."

"Point to starboard, Mr. Todd," MacLean said softly.

"Aye, aye, sir."

"We should see the land over there as soon as it gets

light," MacKinnie told his companions. "I understand Loholo thinks we should hug the shore. There are reefs and rocks only he knows, and he swears he can get us through them without the pirates being able to catch us."

"Interesting," Longway said pensively. "Then why did he not take some other ship through there? Why has the pirate blockade been so effective?"

"You're not supposed to ask that," Nathan replied. "But MacLean thinks it's worth trying anyway. Add something to our chances, and the farther we get before the pirates intercept us, the better chance of coming ashore where there aren't any barbarians." It was getting light faster now, and the shoreline could be seen dimly ahead. Above the fog, fifty miles away, the peaks of mountains flashed whitely in the morning light.

"If we can get to those, the barbarians won't matter," MacKinnie said. "All we'll have to worry about will be the pirates. We could even beach and run for it."

"It would be a long walk," Longway said.

"True. But what else can we do?"

Kleinst stood quietly at the rail, and MacKinnie thought he noted a slight tinge of green to the scholar's complexion. If the young fellow couldn't manage in the gentle swell they were experiencing, he was in for big trouble when the real wind came up. Kleinst had kept out of the way the whole time they were on Makassar, although he seemed to have developed a strange friendship with Brett. Nathan had more than once noted the scholar and the singer conversing over wine in the physicist's quarters at the dock-side inn.

"Where are these pirates, Trader?" Longway asked.

"As a practical matter, should we be getting the oarsmen in their armor?"

"Not for hours," MacKinnie replied. "They stay well out of the harbor itself, probably afraid of the Navy boys. But they're out there, all right, just over the horizon. You'll see them soon enough."

"Sooner than I'd like," Longway muttered.

It was fully light now. The Eye of the Needle had cleared the eastward landmass to send its rays slanting across the sea. The early morning mists vanished rapidly as the ship moved quickly along, and there was no sound but the commands of Loholo, who had lowered his voice until he could barely be understood on the quarterdeck. "Stroke . . ."

The harbor had dropped well out of sight when the sun burned off the last of the mists. The water was an incredible light blue, the bottom visible not more than three yards below the surface. Long, thin fish darted about, pursued by tentacled monsters nearly a meter in length, green eyes glaring after their prey. Larger creatures of the same general form swam into view to look intelligently at the humans on the boat before swimming lazily away. MacKinnie wondered idly what they were when MacLean shouted from his post at the mizzenmast.

"Hands make sail!" he ordered.

MacKinnie watched with interest as the Samualites gathered in the waist.

"Man the mizzen halyards," MacLean called. He turned to the helmsman. "Turn her into the wind, Mr. Todd. Put the helm over."

"Helm's down, sir."

"Stand by mizzen halyard. Get those gaskets off, there."

Hal and one of the guards took the lacing from the sail, then seized the halyard. "Make sail," MacLean ordered. The big gaff rose jerkily, the men on the throat halyards pulling too fast, but eventually the throat and peak rose together. "Take a turn around the winch. Haul, men. Tauten it, that's it. Haul, you bastards! Now belay it all." The gaff sail flapped in the wind, and the boat slowed noticeably.

"Now forward to the main," MacLean ordered. "Get it up, smartly now." The men ran forward, and the big main, almost twice the size of the mizzen, was hauled up almost as quickly as the smaller one had been. "Man the sheets," MacLean ordered. "You fool, that line over there," he added to a guard who stood looking blankly about. "Stand by to trim the sheets, Mr. Stark."

"Yes, sir," Hal answered. He gave MacKinnie a quizzical look and turned back to his soldiers now turned afterguard. The ship was barely moving through the water now, the men straining at the oars, and Loholo stood silent with his hands on his hips looking at MacKinnie as if to say he had told him so.

"Put the helm over, Mr. Todd. Bring her four points to starboard."

"Aye, aye, sir. Helm's to weather." The boat turned, and the wind caught the big sails and pushed them off to the right. "Trim those sheets," MacLean ordered. "More. Bring them in. Strain, you blackguards. Belay. Mr. Stark, I'll have the starboard leeboard down."

The boat was skidding sidewise now, moving to leeward

as fast as it was going ahead. The oarsmen struggled to keep steerage way, Loholo back to counting the pace when he saw no response from his silent appeal to MacKinnie. Stark cast off the line holding up the great fan-shaped lee-board, and the heavy wood splashed into the water. An iron shoe along its lower edge sank it quickly.

"Mr. Loholo, get those oars in," MacLean ordered. "Quickly, man, and get your crew set." The boat heeled sharply to a gust of wind, almost tumbling the starboard crewmen over the side. "Any man can't stay aboard gets to swim ashore," MacLean said. "Stark, get those jibs up."

The gust heeled the ship, and the leeboard bit into the water. The boat began pulling ahead, slowly gathering way, until it was apparent that it was rushing along, faster than the oarsmen had been able to pull it, and still it gathered speed. A white, creamy wake appeared at the bow, and two quarter waves angled off from the stern. It seemed to MacKinnie that the wind picked up noticeably, and the boat was headed into it. *Subao* rose gently over the waves, rushing along until Loholo stood looking over the side with amazement before making his way aft.

"Yes, Mr. Loholo?" MacLean asked.

The former captain stood looking at his new master in silence, then brought his hand to his forehead in an awkward salute. "She's faster than oarsmen have ever been able to push her, Captain. This may be the fastest ship on Makassar."

"Let's hope so, Mr. Loholo. Faster than the pirates, anyway. Get your men to lookout stations, if you please."

"Aye, aye, sir." Loholo turned to his crew. "Banta, up those shrouds. Move along there, lad, and keep your eyes open. Fast as we're going, we'll be in pirate waters soon." He strolled along the deck, expertly keeping himself erect, as he placed crewmen in the bow and sent the rest to the waist.

"How does she sail, Captain?" MacKinnie asked quietly.

"Well enough, Trader," MacLean answered. "A little better to windward than I'd thought she might. Doesn't point as high as a proper keelboat would, but with a full keel we couldn't beach. As it is, we can go closer to the wind than anything the pirates have got. That's how I expect to outrun them. They'll have to use sweeps, and I don't think they can catch us going to windward. We'll leave the bastards behind . . . uh, your pardon, freelady."

"Don't apologize on your own ship, Captain MacLean. I think it's wonderful what you've managed to do with this primitive boat." She looked up at him, then at MacKinnie. "Can I get you anything, Captain? Trader?"

"Chickeest," MacKinnie said. "If you can cook in this."

"If she can't we'll have cold food the whole voyage," MacLean snapped. 'This is perfect weather, Trader. By afternoon we'll face some real waves. I'm not looking forward to the tide either. You may not have noticed, but we had the aid of a strong tidal current going out. It should be even worse when it turns. Best get some practice in the galley now, freelady. Take young Brett down to help you."

"All right, Captain." She stumbled across the deck, looking for handholds, then let Brett take her arm to guide her to the companionway. The ship was heeling sharply, the deck standing at perhaps forty degrees off the horizontal.

It took her nearly half an hour to heat last night's chickeest, and she spilled part of it bringing the pot and cups up to the quarterdeck, but Mary Graham seemed proud of her achievement even so. Now she had the same slightly green cast as Kleinst, and MacKinnie looked around to see the scholar grimly holding the rail and staring at the distant shore to starboard.

"Sail ahead," the lookout called. "Two sails."

Loholo scampered up the shrouds like a monkey, shading his eyes and staring off where the lookout pointed. He bounded down to the deck and trotted panting to MacLean. "Pirates right enough, off the port bow, Captain. Under sail."

MacLean nodded. The pirates were to windward, using square sails to run down toward *Subao*. "Steady as she goes, Mr. Todd. Mr. Loholo, it might be best if you stood with Todd at the tiller. Steering to windward's trickier than just watching the compass, and we'll need more experienced helmsmen. Have you any of your crew who might have some ability?"

"None, Captain. They're all landsmen. Willing lads, but no sea legs."

"You'll have to do it, then. Take your post, mister." MacLean cupped his hands to shade his eyes and stood easily on the pitching deck. True to his earlier promise, the sea was running higher now, and *Subao* heeled farther, making it impossible for anyone but the three sailors to stand without something to hold on to.

"Best tack now and get sea room," MacLean said.

"Stark, get your hands to the jibsheets. The gaffs will take care of themselves. Snap to it, man, we haven't all year." Hal and his guards ran to the foredeck, motioning to some of the oarsmen sitting idle in the waist to join them.

"Stand by to let those sheets go," MacLean shouted. MacKinnie was surprised to note that the Navy man's voice carried easily into the wind, although Brett repeated the order from his post at the mizzen.

"Put her helm down, Mr. Todd." The ship swung into the wind, through it, the booms snapping across the deck. One of Loholo's men scrambled to get out of the way, flinging himself to the deck to allow the main boom to pass over him, while the quarterdeck crew, copying MacLean's example, ducked low. The jibs backwinded, pulling the bow around. "Let go the jibsheets," MacLean shouted. "Now trim them in on the port side. Snap to it. Man the leeboards! Smartly, men!"

The port leeboard was pushed down, and tackles strained to raise the starboard one. MacLean stamped with impatience until the task was done, then turned to MacKinnie. "She's lively enough. Bit slow, easy to get caught in stays. If I end up out of action, remember that. Leave the jibs cleated until the bow's well around, or you'll be in irons." Nathan fervently prayed he would never have to work the ship himself. At least there was young Todd if MacLean were killed.

Now they were approaching the pirate ships rapidly, and the lookout called down, "Five sails beyond the two ahead, sir."

"That'll be more of the pirate fleet," Loholo said. "Beg

your pardon, sir, but the reefs are over there." He pointed off to starboard and ahead.

MacLean nodded coolly. "We can't make that course yet, Loholo. When we've sea room, we'll try your advice." He gauged the distance to the rapidly closing pirate vessels. As they watched, the enemy ships extended their oars, the sweeps working rhythmically, rippling down each of the vessels. The pirate ships were much like *Subao* had been before MacLean's modifications, with more beam to weather storms in the shallow sea but generally resembling her. On the bow of each was carved one of the large tentacled creatures MacKinnie had seen in the water, the stays to the stubby masts running into the nest of arms which jutted forward and upward.

"Idlers below," MacLean ordered. "Freelady, Professor Longway, Mr. Kleinst—go below and stay until you're called, if you please. Mr. Loholo, I can spare you from the tiller until you get your men under arms."

"Aye, aye, Captain." Loholo padded forward to the waist to arm his men.

MacKinnie watched Hal break out crossbows, handing one to each of his Samualite guards and posting them along the waist. The pirates had noted that *Subao* was going to windward without oars, and adjusted their courses to intercept well forward of their present position, so the ships were not closing as rapidly now, but slowly they drew up to three crossbow shots away to port and as many forward.

"I doubt there will be a battle," MacLean said quietly. "Unless they are very much faster with those oars than I think, they cannot possibly catch us."

As if to make his captain a liar, the lookout shouted, 'Three sails off the starboard bow. Three sails ahead, sir."

MacLean shook his head. "If they adjust to our strange antics as quickly as these did, we'll have to fight after all." He eyed the distance to the nearest pirate ship. "Mr. Stark, I'll thank you to go forward and stand ready to bring the ship about again. Don't cast off that jibsheet until I tell you. And give me five men on the leeboards."

"Aye, sir." Hal took his men forward, carefully seeing that each man stowed his crossbow along the rail on the low side. MacLean shook his head. "Put them on the starboard side, Stark. I don't need loaded weapons clattering about my decks when we go about.

"Stand by, Todd. I want to cut this as close as possible without letting them ram us." The pirate ships drew closer now, angling in toward *Subao's* bows in a staggered line. "Fall away a point," MacLean said softly. The ship gathered way, leaping through the water. "Stand by . . . Put the helm over!"

Subao brought up into the wind sharply, hung for a moment, and fell off to the starboard tack. "Let go the jibsheets. Now get them sheeted in. Haul those leeboards, you sons!" MacLean was icy calm as he watched the armored prow of the nearest pirate approaching. The sweeps on the enemy vessel were moving faster and faster, and they could hear a drum amidship beating the count.

Zing! MacKinnie heard something snap over his head, and looked up to see a round hole in the mizzensail. Then there was a chorus of sounds, the bolts thudding into the bulwarks. "Get down!" MacKinnie called. Stark, crouching low, half ran the length of the ship to seize his crossbow. All they could see was the great bow of the enemy thirty yards away, white water curling from each side and the beak of the ram protruding slightly from the water in front of it.

The pirate ship bore ahead. MacKinnie stood in silence. There was nothing to do but wait. The Iron ram grew larger and larger. Then it seemed to slip behind slightly.

Subao gathered more way, and the pirate ship was no longer aimed amidships. "Hold your course," MacLean said quietly. As MacKinnie watched, the pirate ram fell farther behind, tried to turn more toward *Subao*, and caught her sail aback. "Steady as she goes," MacLean murmured.

The pirate ship passed astern so close they almost touched the oars. A cloud of arrows flew from it toward them, and Stark replied with his own volley of steel bolts. There was a shout from the pirate, then it was gone.

"He'll have to get that sail down before he can row to windward," MacLean remarked casually. "Never catch us now. Masthead! Where are those other ships?"

"Off the port bow ahead, sir!"

"They're directly to windward," MacLean said. "Let's see if they have any sense. Mr. Loholo, you can come back to the quarterdeck now."

"Aye, aye, sir." As Loholo approached, they could see blood on his hands. "One crewman dead, sir. Arrow in his throat. Some holes in your sails, too."

"Yes. Where are those reefs of yours, and when will the tide be out?"

Loholo pointed to a cleft in the hills along the shoreline. "Right off there, sir. Tide's full now. Going out starting in an hour."

"Excellent. Todd, steer for those reefs and get the picture of them from Loholo. We may make use of them yet. Mr. Loholo, how many men does one of those pirate vessels carry?"

"Seventy, maybe a few more, sir. Not all of them sailors."

"How many of them can fight?"

"Most all, sir. That's why they're aboard."

MacLean nodded. "As well they can't board us. Mind your luff there, Mr. Todd, you're too close." MacLean looked along the coast, then thoughtfully tossed a light line over the stern and watched the angle it made with the centerline of *Subao*. "Making more leeway than I like," he remarked to MacKinnie. "And that fellow out there seems to have some sense. The others are trying to close with us, but he's standing well out to keep to windward of where we'll be. This could be rather interesting."

They sailed on. The afternoon sea breeze brought a shift in the wind, backing it around to nearly directly offshore, as the tide turned, running little trails of bubbles out to sea. The first group of pirate vessels was lost behind them, and they were easily outdistancing the second, which made the mistake of closing with *Subao* and ended up under her lee before trying to stroke back to her in the heightening seas. Although they gained at first, the effort was too great for them, and they soon fell farther and farther behind. Now only one enemy vessel remained between *Subao* and open water.

As the chase went on, the shoreline fell away to north-ward, bringing the wind more directly off *Subao's* beam, and increasing her heel. The animals in the hold below screamed their protest, a shrill, keening sound unnerving to anyone not familiar with it, causing Brett to rush below to comfort his horses. The pirate ship ran along the shore-line parallel to *Subao,* slowly drawing closer but taking no chances of losing her prey as the others had done. Her captain had trimmed the great lateen sails the boat car-ried, and kept only a few men at the oars. MacLean stood anxiously at his post, with Loholo now holding the tiller. The crew master learned the task far more easily than MacLean had thought he would, and now held the huge wooden bar easily, balancing himself against the rolling of the ship and watching the shoreline.

"Where are we now, Mr. Loholo?" MacLean asked.

"In shoal waters, Captain. With the tide running out, we'll come to ground in a quarter hour."

"Yes." MacLean looked out at the pirate vessel. "Nothing for it but to work out some more, even if it lets him get closer. Hands forward to trim sheets," he called. "Take her a point closer to the wind if you would, Mr. Loholo."

"Aye."

On the new course they closed more rapidly with the pirate ship, the tide helping to cancel their leeway. In minutes, the current was running so strongly that the line over the taffrail stood off to a sixty-degree angle from *Subao's* stern.

"Going out fast, Captain," Loholo remarked.

"Mr. Todd," MacLean ordered, "get forward with a

lead to call soundings."

The cadet perched himself at the shrouds, leaning out to cast the lead line and calling back in a clear voice. "Three meters . . . and a half two . . . three meters . . ."

"He's closing with us now, Trader." MacLean looked at the pirate thoughtfully. "Guards in armor, please. He may be able to board." *Subao's* ability to point higher than the pirate vessel was almost negated by the strong tide off the lee bow, and the longer waterline of the enemy ship gave her an advantage in hull speed. MacKinnie looked around the horizon. There were no other ships in evidence.

"As good as we could expect, Trader," MacLean said softly. "We expected to fight a dozen enemies, now there's only one."

"And a half two . . ." Todd called. "Mark two . . . and a half one . . ."

The tide was racing out now. MacKinnie had never seen anything like it, and asked MacLean how the current could be so strong.

"Those two close-in moons make for strong tides," MacLean answered, "and this big shallow basin doesn't really hold much water. Won't take a lot of vertical rise and fall to empty it." The captain looked carefully at the current. "We're going aground in a few minutes, Trader. If we try to run with the tide to keep afloat, that pirate will have us. At least if we're run aground, he can't ram the ship. Might be quite a fight when he sees us high and dry. Or he might decide to run out with the current and get his friends. You'll have to decide whether to go ashore in that case."

MacKinnie nodded. It seemed to him the enemy ship

was staying close to *Subao*. The pirate might be trapped as well. If they really didn't know these waters all that well, they might think *Subao's* crew intended to stay afloat.

The leeboard scraped bottom, heaving up ponderously before settling back to its position, then hit again.

"Hands to the halyards!" MacLean shouted. "Get those sails down. Move, damn you!" Then in a calmer voice, "Mr. Loholo, put your helm to weather if you will . . . ease her against the current . . . steady . . . Sergeant Stark, get your men's backs into it!"

The sails were hauled down, the men pulling desperately. Heavy canvas billowed across the decks, and the Makassar crewmen leaped to subdue it. It was bulkily piled on the booms and lashed in place. The ship swayed, blown against the current by the strong wind, held in place until there was no way on her at all, then began ponderously to make sternway. Loholo balanced off the helm without orders, obviously accustomed to taking ground with ships in the shallow seas of Makassar. As the tide raced away, she settled bow first, straightened, and came to rest on the sandy bottom, angled toward the shore.

"We're fast," MacLean said. He looked out at the pirate ship three hundred yards away. "By the Saints, he's caught! He can't make it against the wind."

The enemy crew was straining at the oars, while others gathered the lateen sail against the mast, but even as they watched, the stern touched bottom. The tide race was incredibly swift, and within seconds the pirate was stuck as fast as *Subao*.

Brett ran to the waist of the ship. He struggled with the

hatch cover until Vanjynk rushed up to help him. MacLean shouted from the quarterdeck. "What in hell are you doing?"

"We must get our mounts up from the hold," Brett called. "Master Vanjynk and I would fight on our horses, Captain."

"Let them," MacKinnie told MacLean. "We're outnumbered, and having a cavalry force can help. Look there." He pointed to the pirate vessel. Men were boiling off its decks, but instead of rushing toward *Subao*, they formed ranks on the hard sand alongside their ship.

"My turn," MacKinnie said. "You men see to your armor. Hal, help Brett sway those animals up out of the hold."

The hatch cover was already off, and using the main boom held at an angle by the peak halyard, the two chargers were lifted by bellybands, swayed over the side, and set in place on the sand. Brett and Vanjynk scrambled to saddle their beasts and cover them with chain mail skirts.

"What are they waiting for?" MacLean asked, pointing at the pirates.

"They don't know how many we are, or if we have star weapons," Loholo said softly. "They will listen to their leaders tell them of rich loot, and the insults they have endured from Jikar, and finally they will attack. It will be best if our men are already on the sands unless you intend to fight from the ship."

"Not from here," MacKinnie said. "They've got axes. Give one of them a few minutes unmolested and we won't float off here with the tide. Hal, form the men on the sand behind the ship so the enemy can't see what we've got!"

"Right, Colonel." Pleading and shouting, Stark managed to get the native crew into a semblance of order while his Haven guardsmen took places in a group at one end of the line. Shields glinted in the sun as the men stood nervously.

"Serve out those pikes, Mr. Longway," MacKinnie ordered as the Academician appeared at the companion-way. "Then you and the others stay below."

"If you order us, Trader," Longway said. "But I can fight." He came fully out on the deck, and MacKinnie saw that the scholar's portly figure was cased in mail over leather. Together they took the pikes from their racks along the bulwarks and handed them over the sides to the waiting troops. Each of the Makassar natives wore a breastplate and greaves, a metal cap, and a shortsword, and held a round shield on his arm. The Samualites had mail as well. With their pikes in hand, MacKinnie's small force seemed more disciplined, ready to face an enemy.

"They can fight well if told what to do," Loholo said. "They are young men, but the Guilds begin their training early."

MacKinnie eased himself over the rail to join the small group, leaving MacLean and Loholo on the ship. He turned to face his men.

"The important thing is to preserve discipline," he said. "If you stay in ranks, there's not much they can do to you. Keep your shield wall up as long as they aren't close, so they can't bombard us with arrows, and advance when I tell you. I want to hit them with a solid force, not a ragged group of individuals. Hal, have your Haven men form a reserve group behind the main body, and keep their javelins and crossbows ready. I want a solid volley from the crossbows as soon as the pirates get in range, and keep that up until they're too close to reload. Then hold those javelins until I give the order to cast."

"Yes, sir."

"Then wait for my orders. Brett, you and Vanjynk stay with me until I give you the word."

"It is not proper that we stay behind and allow these groundlings the honor of opening battle," Vanjynk said slowly.

"Proper be damned. Vanjynk, if you or Brett start a charge without my orders I'll have Hal shoot you out of the saddle. I ask nothing dishonorable, Master Vanjynk, nothing save winning this battle."

"We have agreed to serve the star man," Brett said, "It is proper that we take his instructions, my friend." He clapped Vanjynk on the shoulder. "Besides, what honor have pirates? What is propriety to them?"

"Here they come!" Longway shouted from the quarterdeck.

MacKinnie strode to the bow of the ship and looked around. The pirate group, nearly a hundred strong, was moving slowly and in good order across the sand toward *Subao*. "Hal, get your crossbowmen out at the stern and stand by. Fire when you think they're in range."

"Yes, sir. Guardsmen, right face. March." Stark took his tiny group to the stern and deployed them just beyond it. This put them closer to the enemy than MacKinnie's detachment at the bow.

Nathan eyed the advancing ranks of pirates, now broken up by small tidal pools until there were definite gaps in the formation. There seemed to be no effort on the part of the pirate officer to re-form his men. From what MacKinnie knew of similar groups on South Continent, it was a masterpiece of tactics for the pirates to have formed at all before starting a wild charge.

They came on, and Hal shouted to his men. "Ready! Fire!"

Several fell to the volley of crossbow bolts, but the rest came on. MacKinnie watched, but gave no signal. Behind him Brett and Vanjynk talked calmly to their animals, but their voices were rising in pitch. Their eagerness to join the battle sounded through the soothing words.

A second volley cut down more of the pirates, and the ragged army of brightly colored natives, armed only with swords except for a few with axes and shields, curled around toward their tormentors, presenting their flank to MacKinnie.

"Now, men. March out. Follow me and stay in good order. Brett, you and your companion remain behind the shield wall until I tell you."

The pirates were now caught between the two small detachments. Their leader shouted orders, and they broke into smaller groups and hurled themselves toward Stark and his men.

"With me, troops!" MacKinnie shouted. "Keep your ranks. Watch the men to either side and stay next to them." He trotted his group away from the bow, angling away from the ship but moving sternward, keeping the pirate group between the two parts of his army. Some of the enemy turned to face him now. Others continued their charge toward Stark.

Hal fired one more volley of crossbow bolts and his men dropped the weapons. They bent to seize their javelins. As MacKinnie's group closed with the pirates, Nathan shouted, "Now, Hal." Stark's group ran forward, casting their slender weapons, tearing holes in the ranks of the pirates, and then MacKinnie was upon them, his pikemen thrusting their weapons forward, as Hal and the Samualites fell on them with sword and shield from the other side.

On either flank a group of pirates now fought MacKinnie's troops, but the main body held back, unwilling to enter the dangerous area between. Then they suddenly broke directly toward MacKinnie's force, charged forward, ducking under the spear points, closing rapidly with the unarmored men, slashing with shortswords. Two of the young Jikarian sailors fell, opening a gap in the line of pikes.

On the other side of the formation the pirates made no headway at all against Hal and his Wolves. Unarmored, with inadequate shields, they did well to hold Stark back, but by sheer numbers were able to do so. A third group darted forward to leap for handholds along the ship's railing.

MacKinnie charged into the gap in the line of pikemen, his sword slashing, shouting to his men to hold firm. A shortsword thrust at him, and he parried, beat hard in quarte, following with a cut to the pirate's neck. His enemy fell and Nathan brought his sword in a whistling moulinette to drive back a second attacker. The gap was too wide to hold with his saber alone, and another enemy tried to circle to his left, only to be impaled by the pike-men, his last stroke falling weakly on MacKinnie's mail. Nathan frantically shouted orders to close the line.

The Jikarians awkwardly moved closer to each other. "Shield to shield!" MacKinnie shouted. "Close it up!" When they had filled in the gap he was able to turn his attention to the group which had charged the ship.

The pirates were stopped at deck level by Longway, who stood sword in hand, thrusting at the face of a pirate who had managed to raise himself almost to the level of the thwarts. MacLean stood with him, while Loholo, shouting in mad fury, jumped to the sands below with an enormous two-handed sword. The native captain sent the weapon whistling around his head and screamed oaths.

"*Subao* is mine!" he shouted. "Filth, slime of the sea, spawn of unwashed carrion eaters! . . ." He lopped off a pirate's head at a blow, then stood with his back to the ship, holding the rest at bay with the fury of his attack.

The pirate chieftain, his rank marked by bright gold bands around his neck and ankles, shouted commands to his men, breaking them away from combat to re-form and make use of their superior numbers.

MacKinnie waited until they had broken off the battle. Then he signaled Brett. "Now!" he shouted.

Brett screamed strange curses. He and Vanjynk spurred their mounts forward and thundered toward the pirates, wielding their great swords to crash through feeble attempts to parry as the enemy tried to avoid being trampled by their mounts. The beasts themselves fought, rearing up to strike with sharp hooves, crashing down to crush men to the sand. A group of pirates broke and ran as Hal and his shieldsmen closed swiftly in a disciplined formation from the other side to hew down the outer ranks. MacKinnie held his own detachment in place, their spears held out toward the pirates, forming a wall of points, while Loholo continued his mad rush, his great sword singing. The last of the enemy turned to run toward their ship.

Brett and Vanjynk pursued the enemy across the sands, but when a group aboard fired on them with cross-bows, MacKinnie shouted them back. He re-formed his little command behind *Subao* again and left them to rest easy in ranks while he surveyed the battlefield.

He had lost two native troopers, killed when the pirates broke ranks. Several others had deep cuts, and one had a throwing knife through his shoulder. In addition, MacLean had caught a wicked cut across the back of his hand from the dying efforts of a pirate Longway spitted. The others were unharmed. The Haven detachment had been always on the attack and the pirates had little chance of closing with them, nor were their weapons heavy enough to do much damage through chain mail unless given more time than Hal had allowed them.

There were thirty-four bodies on the sand between the two boats. Some wriggled feebly. Most lay well away from *Subao*, cut down in flight by Hal's men or the cavalry in pursuit.

"It's always like that," he explained to Longway and MacLean as he climbed back on board. "I've never seen a battle where at the decisive moment the loser didn't have enough strength to turn the table. Once they lose the will to fight, they're finished. More men are killed in pursuit than battle every time."

"But it seemed so easy!" Mary Graham said.

MacKinnie turned, surprised to see her on deck. "I told you to stay below," he muttered. "As to easy, it wouldn't have been if they'd caught us on our decks. If they'd swarmed aboard with our troops not in formation and no room to maneuver, they'd have won. They were fools to fight on our terms. What can you serve my men for lunch, freelady?"

She swallowed hard before she replied. "Will they come back?" she asked. "It will take time to prepare."

"I doubt they've the stomach for it." He turned to Loholo. "Will they try to attack again after we're afloat?"

Loholo shook his head. "We'll both have enough trouble staying off that shore, Trader. There won't be much time for fighting when the water wall comes."

MacKinnie noted that while they had been fighting, the officers had broken out one of the ship's anchors. MacLean had it carried out and laid in the sand on the seaward side of *Subao*. "We'll need that," he explained. "Without it, the ship might be washed ashore when the tide returns. This ought to hold us until we can sail off."

"Will the pirates have one out?" MacKinnie asked.

"If they have any sense."

"I see. That gives me an idea. I'll have to speak to Brett."

There was no further action, but Nathan kept his crew in ranks on the sand. They ate in place. An hour before the tide was due in, Vanjynk's horse was swayed aboard, and the rest of the crew then took their places on the ship, leaving only Brett and his mount on the sand behind the ship. A few pirates approached to within a hundred yards, but the sight of Brett thundering around the side of the ship toward them put them to flight, and Brett returned to his post as Vanjynk fumed in the waist.

"We'll have need of you, Vanjynk," MacKinnie said. "You stand by to carry out your orders." They waited.

"I see it!" Loholo shouted from the masthead. "The tide's coming."

MacKinnie waved to Brett. "Now!" he ordered.

The mounted rider galloped toward the enemy ship. He stayed well out of arrow range, going around until he found the anchor the pirates had laid out beyond their boat. He cut the anchor cable with a quick slash of his sword, then rode furiously back toward *Subao*. His armor and that of his mount had earlier been put aboard, and as Brett reached the ship, Vanjynk was ready with a belly sling. Rider and animal alike were swayed aboard, as the thunder of approaching water grew louder.

MacKinnie climbed partway up the shrouds and stared seaward. He saw a dark line not more than a kilometer away, and as he watched it advanced at incredible speed, a wall of water three meters in height boiling furiously toward them. The pirates screamed, one standing in the stern of his ship and shaking his fist at *Subao*. There was nothing they could do; by the time they could reach *Subao's* cable, the wall of water would be on them, and it appeared that no pirate was willing to give his life to make trouble for MacKinnie. Their ship was carried relentlessly toward the rocks as MacLean gave the order to raise sail and prepare *Subao* for her long voyage.

★ PART TWO ★
LOYALTIES
★ ★ ★

★13★
THE HUNTING LODGE
★★★

Twelve light-years from Makassar Malcolm Dougal cursed as he followed a winding road uphill through thick forests. The forest had been a game preserve for all the centuries since the Secession Wars had devastated Prince Samual's World, but Dougal ignored its loveliness, as he ignored the bird songs and the calls of the corkborers.

He did not know that the trees themselves had been imported from Earth. If he had, he would have cursed them, as he cursed everything of Earth.

He wore plain kilts. His round face, always rabbitlike in appearance, was screwed into a grimace that made him look less harmless than he usually did, but still few would have guessed his occupation. He considered his appearance an asset; as he sometimes said in rare moments when he could relax with his friends, what should a secret policeman look like?

A corkborer fluttered past, and Dougal actually lashed out at it, although he usually enjoyed the antics of the small flying mammals. Others darted near in curiosity, but Dougal took no notice. As he neared the lodge he muttered more curses.

Twenty years, he thought to himself. No. Be fair. More like fifty. Damn the Empire of Man! Where was the Empire when we *needed* help? When we were trying to rebuild a civilization out of radioactive ash and ruined cities? And now, with our own spaceships not more than fifty years away, the Empire has come—and they won't give us fifty years. They won't give us any time at all. They've come, and I must meet the king in secrecy in this lonely place. . . .

It disturbed Dougal's sense of majesty. Instead of walking up this wooded hill to a lonely log cabin, he should be approaching his sovereign across a purple carpet, or meeting him privately in the working office behind the Audience Chamber. Now those rooms could not be trusted. Nothing could be trusted. The Empire had ears everywhere.

They'll not learn this secret!

But they might. Fear warps us all, he thought. And so I meet King David out here, and not even the royal guardsmen know where His Majesty has gone.

The king's instructions were explicit: Dougal was to tell no one of this meeting, and His Majesty would be alone. No one, not even the guardsmen, were to know the meeting had taken place. Only two men in the universe were to know that Dougal and King David were meeting here.

More did, of course. Malcolm had provided men to cover the hunting lodge. But they were reliable men, absolutely reliable, men who could be trusted to—

"Halt!" Two men stood in the deep alcove of the lodge doorway. Dougal recognized them as guards officers out of uniform. They carried both pistols and rifles, and they stood alertly. One eyed Dougal coldly, then nodded. "Pass, my lord."

But—why? Dougal wondered. As he entered the lodge he had an even greater shock, for the king was not alone under the high-beamed ceiling.

"Our greetings, my lord," David said formally. "We trust you are well."

"Thank you, yes, Sire." Dougal bowed to the king, then to the other man.

In contrast to King David's handsome youthfulness, the Prime Minister was old. His face was wrinkled, and his belly spilled over his waistband. Malcolm Dougal was quite aware that he would probably look much like Sir Giles Og in thirty years—except that he did not expect to live thirty more years. His occupation made that highly improbable.

"I had understood this meeting was to be secret, Majesty," Dougal said.

King David nodded. "It was and it is. Tell me, my lord, how many of your secret police do you have outside?"

Malcolm Dougal said nothing. The king nodded again. "And as I knew you would not let me come here alone, I saw no harm in bringing a few guardsmen as well. Trustworthy guardsmen."

"And Sir Giles?" Malcolm asked.

"He's the reason for the meeting. Malcolm, the budget's no good. Sir Giles must have more money or the administration is going to collapse."

"Raise taxes," Dougal said.

Sir Giles's voice was quite clear and steady, unlike his appearance. His orator's voice and timing had been a major reason for his rise through Parliament. "I cannot in good conscience ask for higher taxes, my lord. We have the highest taxes in our history at this moment. Yet, between the wars, the mysterious expedition to—" He hesitated over the name. "To Makassar, and the growing amounts the secret police absorb, more than half the kingdom's revenues have vanished. With such high taxes we should not have financial problems—but we do. I must know why."

"No," Malcolm said.

"I think we must tell him," the king said.

"Sire! Your promise—"

King David shrugged. "I gave you my word, Malcolm. I won't break it. Here, let's sit down and end the formalities. There's a lot to talk about. Get us a drink, will you, Sir Giles?"

King David sat in a rustic armchair before an open fire and waved the others to join him. He was not large, and although his features were handsome in shape and design, his face had been disfigured by an early disease, so that the gentlemen of the bedchamber had their work cut out before public appearances. He had not bothered with makeup for this meeting. The small scars gave him a rugged appearance, adding to his look of determination.

"His Majesty has told me nothing," Sir Giles said. He brought small glasses and a bottle of grua and set them on a table near the king's chair. "He told me only that it is vital to the realm that the large sums spent by your office continue." Sir Giles paused. "I am a loyalist, and I appreciate the necessity for police to consolidate our new acquisitions, but I am not prepared to pay for my own enslavement, by the crown or by anyone else."

Dougal laughed. "I do not have in mind enslaving the citizens of Haven, Sir Giles. Quite the opposite—"

"You will pardon my saying that as we do not know where the money goes, we have no evidence of your intentions—"

"The work is vital to the entire planet," King David said. "My word on it."

"And mine," Dougal added.

"Not enough," Sir Giles said. "Not enough at all."

"I see." Dougal regarded the Prime Minister coldly. "Neither my word nor the king's is good enough—"

"Of course not." The older man lifted his glass. "Your health." They drank. "I am loyal to the dynasty, but I am also loyal to the Constitution. If you cannot entrust me with your secrets, I belong not in the government but in opposition."

"Sir Giles has brought his resignation," the king said.

"I see." Dougal stared into the crackling fire. Without Sir Giles the coalition supporting the government would collapse. The coalition was needed.

Or was it? Could the king rule without a government? Malcolm dismissed the thought sadly. The secret police were efficient, but they would be unable to hold on against an enraged populace. The rights of Parliament had been easily won from King David's father, but won easily or not they would not be lightly surrendered.

And government by terror would never produce what Prince Samual's World needed.

Would anything?

Malcolm quickly reached a decision. "I'm going to tell you a story, Sir Giles. After you've heard it, you will never be far from one of my men. If you ever betray us—"

"Spare me your threats."

"They are not threats. I hoped to persuade you not to ask to hear."

Sir Giles sat quietly for a moment. "I almost believe you have a good reason for what you're doing—"

"I do."

"But I will not give up the Constitution for an unknown reason. Tell your story. But I promise you only that I will keep your secret. I do not promise to help in whatever—"

"You'll help once you know," Dougal said. "My only problem is knowing where to begin." He stared into the fire. "In King John's time Haven became the largest single state on Samual. He consolidated a number of petty princedoms and city-states, and it looked for a while as if the old dreams of a single government on this planet would be realized. But the next step was Orleans, and the Orleanists wouldn't join. The wars went on. Eventually we developed new industries, and unification looked possible again. Except that everything was wasted on wars. Every effort at conquest of the Orleans Republic failed."

"We nearly had them beaten," King David mused. "One more campaign—"

"Almost," Sir Giles said. "Until that damned Colonel MacKinnie of theirs beat us at Blanthern Pass. Iron Man MacKinnie—my lord, I am familiar with our history. What has this to do with the budget? Orleans is our duchy now—"

"It is our duchy because the Imperials came and their Marines helped us defeat Orleans," King David said quietly.

Malcolm nodded. "Precisely. The Imperials allied with Haven, and they are helping us establish a unified government on Samual. There's nothing on the planet that can stand up to their weapons." He laughed bitterly. "So after ten generations of dreaming about it, we're getting unification handed to us."

"But we're getting it," Sir Giles said. "More slowly than I like."

"It goes slowly and it costs money," Dougal said. "Both for a reason."

"Yes." The young king's voice was hard. "Our goal is to unify the planet, not enslave it. The Imperials will do that soon enough."

"Sire?" Sir Giles carefully set his glass on the table. "The Imperials are Haven's ally. How can they enslave us? They've fewer than fifty people on the planet."

"Allies." Dougal was contemptuous. "Everyone assumed they would be allies, Sir Giles. And they did help us with Orleans. But my agents have found out why they did. They intend to use us to unify the planet, then bring in colonists from other worlds. Traders. Petty bureaucrats who want to be aristocrats and who'll become *our* nobility. We will have damned little say in that government."

The Prime Minister was silent for a long moment. The only sounds came from the forest, and from the popping of the logs in the fireplace. "I would not have thought it of them," he said finally. "The Navy officers do not act like conquerors. They do not seem such villains."

"They're more dangerous than villains." Dougal spoke rapidly now. "They're fanatics. The Imperial Navy intends to unify the human race so it can never again fight an interstellar war. If they have to kill off half of mankind to justify Lysander's title as 'Emperor of Humanity' they'll do it."

"Just as we were willing to unify Samual by conquest," David said.

"I see that well enough," Dougal said. "I know what motivates them. The same goal motivates me. If I'd been an Orleans citizen I hope I'd have had sense enough to see that unification was necessary, and worked to gain some status in the union. Which is what we must do for Samual within the Empire." The policeman's voice rose in angry tension. "And by God we'll outwit them yet!"

Sir Giles leaned forward. "What—what are you doing? We can't fight the Empire—"

"No. The best we have couldn't win a single battle," Dougal said. "But despite that, we can be our own masters yet. They have laws, Sir Giles. They have a Constitution. We can exploit that. One of their rules is that worlds that have space travel enjoy a far higher status than those that don't. Worlds with space travel control their own domestic affairs, and have representation in the Imperial Parliament—"

"Space travel? But that's impossible," Sir Giles protested. His eyes widened in sudden comprehension. "You are using the secret funds to build spaceships? How? We know nothing of spaceships—"

"That is the real secret," Dougal said carefully. "And I would very much rather it remained a secret even from you. It will be the strangest secret you will ever hear, and even a hint—a hint—to the Imperial Navy would destroy all our hopes."

"I see." Sir Giles sat again and rested his chin on both hands. The veins on their backs showed darkly against his neat white beard. He turned to the king. "I suppose, Sire, that this hideously expensive expedition to Makassar has something to do with this? That you expect those men to spy out the secrets of spaceships from traveling in them, and bring that knowledge back to us?"

A good cover story, Dougal thought. "Yes."

"It can't work," Sir Giles said. "Sire, my lord, you have not a technical background. I am many years away from my training as an engineer, but I can tell you this: there is not a factory on Prince Samual's World that could build such a thing even were the Imperials to give us free run of their ships. We haven't the basic tools, we don't even know what the problems are. This scheme is madness!"

"There is more," King David said. "We have hopes for more. We have hopes that our expedition to Makassar will return the most priceless cargo ever to come to Prince Samual's World. A cargo of freedom."

"How?"

"Our secret is fragile," Dougal said. "Worse, the Imperials themselves know Makassar's secret—"

"This talk of secrets," Sir Giles said. "You don't understand at all. Your expedition is no secret. The Navy knows your men went there. As to their orders to spy out the 'secrets' of the Navy ships, were you to tell the commandant he would be no more than amused. My lord, you do not appreciate the difficulties involved! It will be a hundred years before we are able to build spacecraft—"

"Perhaps," Dougal said. "And perhaps not." There was an ominous silence as Dougal coldly studied the Prime Minister's face. "You are determined to have it all, aren't you? You leave me few choices. Either I must tell you the rest or have you killed."

"Lord Dougal, I forbid it!" The king's voice was sharp and loud. "I have deliberately turned away from learning of many of the things your police have done in my name, but by Christ you will not sit here and threaten my Prime Minister!"

Dougal spread his hands. "I said I had two choices, Sire." And another behind that, he thought. My men are outside, and the king has few guardsmen here. . . .

"I had not known you were disloyal," the king said. "Your thoughts are obvious to one who has grown up at court."

"I am loyal, Sire," Dougal protested. "Loyal to Prince Samual's World, Haven, the dynasty, and you."

"In that order."

"Yes, Sire. In that order." He stood, a small man in plain kilts, unarmed, his rabbit features almost comical, but the room was filled with menace. "Majesty, Sir Giles, there is nothing I will not do to keep this world free! We will not be ruled by outlanders! Prince Samual's World has been our home for centuries, and what claim has Sparta or Earth itself to rule us?" He visibly fought for control of himself.

"The secret, Sir Giles?" Dougal's voice rose. "It is simple enough, so simple that a careless word will doom our great plan." He smiled wryly. "And I needn't shout it, eh?" He sat again, and lowered his voice. "There is a building on Makassar, a building which the locals believe to be no more than a temple. But inside it is an old library. . . ."

Sir Giles listened with growing horror. It was obvious that neither Dougal nor the king appreciated the magnitude of the problem they had set themselves. When the policeman had finished talking, Sir Giles poured a drink and thought furiously. How could he tell them?

Simple enough. He couldn't.

"There. Now do you understand? Will you aid us?" King David asked anxiously.

"Sire, your cause is noble and just," Sir Giles said. "And certainly the knowledge that your expedition may bring back to us could change our world. But—" He paused, and felt Dougal's cold stare. "There is more to building spacecraft than knowledge," Giles said. "You will grant that I know more of our technical capabilities than you. And I do not think that even with detailed plans we will be able to build a ship."

"We can try," Dougal said.

"And this is where all the money has gone."

"Much of it went to finance the expedition," Dougal said. "The rest is being invested in expansion of the Haven shipyards, and in establishing a secret military base in the Corliss Grant Hills. We have sent many young scholars there. Always there have been legends of communications without telegraph wires . . . and already we can do that. The devices are crude, but they work. In the shipyards we are studying metal working, ostensibly to build metal craft that will travel under the sea—but if we can make them watertight we can make them airtight as well, to withstand the ether of space. Sir Giles, we are doing all we can—"

And worth doing, too, Sir Giles thought. But not for the reasons you think. There is no possibility of a spaceship. Yet, if I say so, they will kill me. The guardsmen and Dougal's secret policemen would cooperate on that. There is only one way I will leave this lodge alive.

He rose and went to the desk. "This is my resignation," he said. He took it and threw it into the fire. "I will help you. But you will forgive me if I am not certain that you will succeed—"

"None of us are," Dougal said. "We cannot even be certain that MacKinnie will return. But without him there is no hope at all."

★14★
BATAV
★ ★ ★

The harbor at Batav was lined with stone steps leading to the waterfront, and patrolled by great warships flying the Temple flags and banners, saffron-robed acolytes standing in the bows to challenge newcomers. The harbor entrance was closed by a massive chain stretching between huge rafts at the ends of a log boom.

Loholo explained to the guard boats that they were from Jikar, but at MacKinnie's orders did not tell them the ship was commanded by men from the stars. One of the patrol boats escorted them past the chain. *Subao* moved slowly, sails furled, the crew working the sweeps. The bottom was visible below the ship, and gangs of men stood in water to their waists to scoop out mud from the main channel.

"Convicts," Loholo said. "You don't want to run afoul of the priesthood here. But they do keep the harbor open. Finest harbor on Makassar."

They were shown to a gray stone dock, a niche cut into the harbor sea wall and lined with log rafts so that the ship could be tied up without concern for the enormous tides on Makassar. Nearby another crew of convicts strained at pumps to force silt into barges. Another barge had been filled and was headed out to sea.

"The Temple priests run everything here," Loholo said after they made *Subao* fast to the raft. "There'll be one of their junior deacons along in a while to make you an offer on your trade goods. You'll do best to stall him until you find what the local merchants will pay for part of the cargo, but you'll have to sell some of it to Their Holinesses. If you don't, we'll never leave this harbor."

MacKinnie stood on the quarterdeck of *Subao* and watched the traffic along the harbor street in front of him. In contrast to Jikar, there was activity, but not as much as Nathan would have expected for a large city like Batav. There were not many ships moving about in the harbor, either. Draymen unloaded a cargo vessel four rafts down from *Subao*, but the intervening slips were empty, and there was another large space before the next ship.

High above the harbor stood a chalk-white building, flying the banners of the Temple, great red and blue crosses on a field of black, with a stylized portrayal of the Temple itself at the fly. The old Imperial Library had been built of native granite, and had formed a part of the Vice-regal Palace. Gargoyles and cherubim were carved in stately rows around its cornice, while Corinthian columns held the four porticos at the cardinal compass points. MacKinnie had seen nothing like it on Prince Samual's World, and found the massive strength of the building impressive despite its ugliness.

"That's the Temple," Brett said quietly. He was standing

on the opposite corner of the quarterdeck from MacKinnie, with Kleinst and Longway eagerly asking him about the city. "God Himself built it before the Fall, when we were all star men here, and He put all wisdom and knowledge in it. But the men of Makassar were proud, and said that since they had all knowledge, they didn't need God. In wrath, He struck at the Temple—see, you can see on the side there where part of it was rebuilt. But before He could destroy it, the priests reminded Him of His promises to our people, and He spared the Temple, but took from us the knowledge of how to use the great wisdom in the Temple. Only the priests know, and they don't know how to translate the words of the angels when they can make them speak at all."

Brett sniffed loudly. "That's what the Temple priests will tell you. There was a time when they had believers in every city, and their deacons and acolytes controlled whole duchies and kingdoms. In most places, the true Christians like those in Jikar were a little band forced to hold meetings in secret. But now the Temple people don't control much more than Batav, and it's their followers in other cities who meet in secret and fear for their lives. All that happened in two men's lives, or so I am told."

"But what would have caused such a rapid transformation of the religious values of a whole society?" Longway asked with interest. "My observation has been that such changes take a long time unless they come with technological changes. We experienced a comparable collapse of the established church on Prince Samual's World, but gunpowder and discipline and money were more at the root of it than anything else."

"Star man, I don't know," Brett answered. "But strange things have happened to us for many years. The summers are shorter, and the winters colder, and the plainsmen move to the coasts and attack the cities because there is less and less to feed them and their herds in the plains. The people say that God has turned His face from Makassar."

"Ah," Kleinst said. Everyone turned to look at the thin-faced scholar, who appeared nearly normal for the first time since going aboard the ship. "Of course. The orbit of Makassar is highly eccentric, and its axial tilt is also high. The two have produced reasonable weather in the Southern Hemisphere for generations, but now they are getting slowly out of phase with each other. The winters will be worse and worse here, until it is the northern part which is inhabitable. Naturally the barbarians flock toward the equator."

"And of course as they move into the more temperate areas, they destroy the civilizations there," Longway added. "But this often produces an internal strengthening of the ruling church. Yet I have heard of cases where when there was already schism, the eroding of the civilization would cause many to turn away from the churches, or look to new ones for salvation. Yes." They stood silently for a moment and watched the guard ship take convicts aboard.

Mary Graham brought wine and chickeest. One of the guardsmen carried the heavy tray for her. During the voyage she had developed amazing skill at producing hot meals, even when the ship was running before gales which MacLean estimated to be over sixty kilometers an hour in strength. She had trained several of the young Makassar guards to assist her, and quickly became absolute mistress of the commissary department of *Subao*.

"Is that the Temple?" she asked, pointing to the huge structure dominating the city.

"Yes, my lady," Brett answered. "Five hundred priests and deacons, and two thousand guards are all quartered in the cells carved in that building. Not that their army has done them any good against the plainsmen."

"But what can the barbarians do against Temple guards?" Mary asked. "You tell me they have no equipment, and the Temple must be wealthy if it has so many soldiers."

"They will not fight the way the Temple wishes," Brett answered. "The plainsmen run before the heavy-armored men, and when the Temple horses tire, the chiefs bring their clans back with ropes and many of them ride around the iron men, lacing them to their steeds, pulling them to the ground. Or the plainsmen move aside and let the iron chargers thunder past, then attack from behind."

"Mobility against heavy cavalry," MacKinnie muttered. "And the Temple guards are drawn away from the walls so they have no place to rest and re-form their troops." He nodded. "But, Academician, I am concerned about the Temple. Can the priests hold this city and their relics against the enemy?"

"Not for long," Longway answered. "If my experience on South Continent is useful, the people of the city will be weary of the fighting, now that their church is no longer thought to be the voice of God. The priests will never be able to rally enough men to hold those walls if the enemy stays at the gates."

MacKinnie nodded. "I've seen the will to fight collapse before. They become concerned with their comforts and neglect their lives, and soon they will lose both. We may have arrived at a critical time."

"But how dreadful," Mary said. "All these people. What will happen to them?"

Brett drew a long breath before he answered. "The men will be killed. The prettier of the women will be carried off and if they are fortunate will find places in the herds of one of the warriors. The youngest boys may be taken in by a clan to be raised as plainsmen. The rest, those who would not fight when the walls were taken, will die to amuse the women of the tribes."

Mary shuddered. "Trader, is there nothing we can do here?" she asked MacKinnie.

"I would not weep for all of the city people, my lady," Brett said. "You have not seen what they do when they find a small band of plainsmen. Life is hard out there, and men do what they have to do."

They were interrupted by Stark and two guardsmen who had been posted at the end of the pier. "Company coming, sir," Hal said. "Not what I expected, not those deacons you told me to look out for. Civilians, I'd say." He pointed to the end of the pier, where two obvious magnates approached. They were guarded by half a dozen well-armed men. "Should I turn out the guard, sir?"

"No, but get as many men as you have ready at the hatches and keep these here on deck. Then come back up when you get the troops posted. Quietly; I don't want to start trouble if there's none coming." MacKinnie watched the group move slowly down the stone pier.

The leader of the group was tall and thin, like a cadaver. He raised his hand, palm toward MacKinnie. "Greetings," he said. "I hope you had a pleasant journey."

MacKinnie frowned. He knew what the man was saying, but—suddenly he realized what he had heard. The stranger was speaking the Imperial language. "Are there any here who understand me?" He switched quickly to a local dialect. "Peace and greetings."

"Welcome aboard," MacKinnie answered in what he hoped was the Imperial speech. "And what may I do for Your Honor?"

The man turned to his companion and said something quickly, then looked to MacKinnie in obvious relief. "Thank the Savior, the Navy has come to find us. Our prayers have been answered. When we heard there was a ship from Jikar, we hardly dared hope."

MacKinnie stared at the small party. The two leaders were both tall and dark, looking nothing like the locals MacKinnie had seen. Their guards, by contrast, were all obviously natives, probably hired swordsmen.

"Come aboard, please," MacKinnie said. "May we make your guards comfortable with wine and something to eat?"

"Thank you."

MacKinnie nodded to Todd, sending him scurrying below to find Hal and arrange for refreshments for the guards. The two star men were helped aboard and led to the owner's cabin below. When they were seated and wine brought, they introduced themselves.

"I am Father Deluca, and this is His Lordship Auxiliary Bishop Laraine. We are representatives of His Eminence the Archbishop Casteliano, Missionary ruler of the Church on this forsaken planet. It is a miracle you have found us."

"I do not understand, Your Reverence," Nathan said. "Surely you have means to call the Navy whenever you wish?"

"No, my son," Bishop Laraine said sadly. "The barbarians have destroyed our transmitter. Brother LeMoyne might have repaired it had they not been so thorough, but in fact we were fortunate to escape with our lives. Two other members of our mission, a brother and a priest, were not so favored, God rest their souls. We made our way to this city, and here we stay, besieged by barbarians, with little gold, no communicator, and afraid even to allow these heathen to know our true mission. They burn heretics here, and they believe us to be such. Not that martyrdom is so frightening, but it would hardly accomplish anything for the faith under the circumstances."

"I would not contradict His Reverence," Deluca said, "but in reality these are not heathen. They believe all of the doctrines of the Church except submission to the authority of New Rome. But they also believe they have a divine inspiration, holy relics, enclosed in that Temple of theirs, and that God speaks to them from their Temple. They even have records showing that their bishops have a direct continuity with the first bishops of Makassar. I believe New Rome might rule that they could be accepted in the Church without new ordinations would their hierarchy only submit to authority."

The bishop shook his head sadly. "What Father Deluca says is true enough, but there is no way to dispel them of their illusions. They truly believe these artifacts of theirs contain Holy Writ, which no doubt they do, there being copies of the Bible in the library, I am sure, but they believe their Temple to be a source of continuing and everlasting revelation."

"I see," MacKinnie told them. He drained his glass while he pondered what to tell them. Nathan had no experience at lying to the clergy, his contacts with the priestly orders being limited to one or another of the many varieties of military chaplains who had served with him, and he was vaguely disturbed. He decided on a compromise. "I don't like to tell you this, Your Reverence, but only part of your problems have been solved by our arrival. We have no transmitter either." He used the unfamiliar word cautiously, but no one responded. "We do have gold and we can make your stay here more secure, but it will be some time before we can get you back to Jikar. The storm season is coming on, and my native shipmaster tells me there is no way to sail westward during that part of the year. We ran before one westerly gale coming in here, and the seas were dreadful. I am told they get worse."

Laraine showed no emotion at the words, but Father Deluca half rose from his seat, only to strike his head on the low deck beams above him. He sat back down with tears in his eyes, as much from disappointment as the blow. "Then we must stay here in this awful place for another year." He sighed heavily.

"As God wills," Laraine said sharply. "Your offer of

money is generous, my lord. His Eminence will be pleased. Will you come with us to tell him?"

"They tell me I should wait until the Temple people come to inspect my cargo," Nathan answered. "After that, I will be honored to meet His Eminence. What does the local priesthood think you are?"

"Merchants despoiled by the barbarians," Deluca answered. "We thought of fleeing to the nomads and trying to win converts among them, but there are few of us, and the barbarians never listen before they kill. Even the Temple has ceased to send missionaries among them. His Eminence ordered us to remain with him until we were sure there was no chance to win over the Temple hierarchy before sacrificing ourselves."

Nathan nodded and filled the wineglasses again. It was, he thought, as well that they had lost the device they used to communicate with the Navy. If they hadn't, he would have had to destroy it himself. The Navy must not be reminded of the library at the same time they thought of Prince Samual's World. But perhaps these Imperials would be useful. At least he might learn something from them. "You have had no success at convincing the Temple people that their holy relics are nothing more than leftovers from the Old Empire?" he asked.

Deluca shook his head. "We brought Brother LeMoyne, who is both a librarian and trained in physics, hoping to show them, but they will not let us near their sacred relics. No one but the priesthood can touch them. And we, the representatives of the True Church, are turned away like Philistines."

The bishop smiled. "There is a certain, ah, humor, in

the situation, my lord. That we are turned away from the center of this planet's religion. Or what was once their center, because their authority is fast going. I think now it would have been better had we worked in Jikar first, but of course we couldn't know that."

Hal knocked at the doorway. "Sir, those deacon people are here to examine the cargo. They say they want to talk to the master of the ship, and also the owner. There's fees to pay for using the harbor, and they want to buy all our food and wine."

Nathan stood, stooping carefully to avoid the deck beams. He had learned that after several painful experiences during the voyage. "If you will excuse me, I will speak to the Temple representatives," he told them. "Please feel free to enjoy any of the facilities or refreshments. Your Excellency," he added, bowing.

"Drive a hard bargain with them," the bishop growled. He waved dismissal.

There were three of the robed Temple deacons on deck. There were also two uniformed guard officers, while a rank of ten swordsmen stood at rigid attention on the pier below. The guard uniforms were blue and crimson with silver decorations, the officers' hats plumed, and the sergeant of guards carried a gold-headed baton. The discipline of the men, and their weapons, made MacKinnie realize that the Temple commanded a trained fighting force. Or at least they could obey orders. He wondered why, with their discipline, they had not destroyed the barbarians. Too rigid in their tactics, he thought, remembering Vanjynk and the battle on the tide sands.

One of the officers stepped forward from the group around Captain MacLean and Loholo. "Are you the owner of this vessel?" he demanded.

MacKinnie nodded. The officer continued, "I present you to His Excellency, Sindabaya, Junior Archdeacon of the Temple of Truth."

"Peace and greetings," one of the gray-robed men said. "It is customary to bow to me when receiving blessings, Trader. Are you ignorant of the proper forms, or merely a heathen?"

"Your pardon, Excellency," MacKinnie protested. "My thoughts were on the plight of our civilization, and not the more important things at hand." He bowed, receiving another blessing for his trouble.

"It is well. We have not seen you in Batav before, Trader, and when we last saw your shipmaster he had his own ship. Why is this?"

"Pirates, Your Excellency. In all Jikar, there are few merchant ships remaining, and few merchants to buy them, because the army of Jikar takes all the goods for the great expedition. They intend to fight their way through the barbarians before sending the fleet to destroy the nests of pirates."

The officer who had spoken looked up hurriedly, then conversed in low tones with another robed figure before speaking. "Jikar is not large enough to put forth such an army or fleet," he said flatly.

"Oh, this is true, sir," MacKinnie said. "But the Guilds have made alliance with other cities, and many of the people of the plains and hills have fled to Jikar for assistance. Then, the fleet captured many pirate vessels by surprise when they dared sail too close into the harbor and were left by the tide. The water ran red for two changes of the tide after the battle on the sands, and the Guilds had a large fleet, but few with whom to man it. But when their war on the land is finished, they will turn to training the young men to be sailors, and there is talk of bringing the fleet north, east perhaps, bringing many merchant ships under the protection of fifty galleys of war. But, I thought, what use to go in such a number? Prices will be low, when there are so many goods for sale. But if now, when there are no ships from Jikar, if now I sail to Batav, and east, and south, why, then trading will be better, and my friends will remember me when the great fleet comes. . . . Or so I thought. And I was told that the great Temple, the home of wisdom itself, was in need, and thus I brought my cargo, and my foodstuffs; I will sell them to the Temple saving only what must remain to feed my men, and I ask no more than a pittance beyond what it has cost me to bring the goods."

The gray-robed men muttered among themselves, and their spokesman said, "Your piety is noted. What have you for the Temple?"

Despite MacKinnie's intent to be generous, it took hours to agree on the price of the cargo. The deacons were so accustomed to haggling with traders that even when it was not necessary they bargained. Meanwhile their officers inspected, poking into the holds and looking in the deck boxes.

The priests noted the amount of food aboard and heatedly disputed MacKinnie's estimate of what he would need for *Subao's* own consumption. They insisted that more had to be delivered to the Temple. MacKinnie knew from their concern with foodstuffs that the siege was more serious than the Temple would admit.

"They have to be desperate," Longway whispered. "I've spoken with one of the guards. They're taking everything edible from any ship that calls here—and there are fewer ships every month."

Eventually the bargain was struck, and a gang of Temple slaves swarmed aboard to carry away what the Temple had purchased. The soldiers stood guard over them and searched each for stolen food or weapons. The deacons watched the soldiers and noted on wooden-backed slates what was taken and what was left aboard, how much was owed to MacKinnie, how many slaves came aboard, and how many left.

As the last of the goods was taken ashore, Sindabaya joined MacKinnie and his staff on the quarterdeck. "We guard more than the true faith," the priest said. He waved his hand to indicate the city and the harbor. "For all time that we record, the Temple has been the source of wisdom and hope for the people of this world. When other cities fall, we hold the means to build them again. If the Temple falls, what will be the source of knowledge? When God brought men to this place from the stars above, He set the Temple to watch over them and give them truth. That is our burden, and we will not fail."

MacKinnie watched an officer drive one of the slaves into his place in the ranks, and said nothing. Sindabaya noted Nathan's expression and grimaced. "The world has changed. Once they went singing to their tasks. Ships brought wealth to be laid at the steps of God's Temple.

Now few ships come, and the barbarians wait outside the walls, and my officers beat the convicts as I watch. But there is no other way! They will not work without blows, and the work must be done! The Temple must be saved!" He turned to the group on the deck and raised his hand in blessing, watched them narrowly for a moment, and left the ship.

Deluca climbed carefully to the quarterdeck as MacKinnie watched the Temple party drive men and ayuks, both overloaded, down the stone streets toward the warehouses.

"Now that they have inspected your ship," Deluca said, "it is lawful for you to leave it. Will you visit the Lord Archbishop?"

MacKinnie nodded, selecting Longway, Kleinst, and Todd to accompany them. Deluca assured them that his own merchant's guard would be sufficient, and would escort them back to the ship after their interview.

"But you will need our guards," Deluca told them. "The streets are no longer safe. Thieves have banded together in great numbers, and attack even armed men. Our own guards are trustworthy only when together, yet there is nothing to steal and no place to buy food with what gold can be found. The city feels no hope for the future. Only the Temple has the will to fight. The people of this city once ruled the world, but now they are ruled by the Temple."

They walked along the broad waterfront street. MacKinnie noted the empty dockyards, warehouses with the doors standing open, and everywhere the beggars and crowds of surly men who had once been longshoremen and sailors, owners of shops, landholders of small farms outside the walls of the city. It was little better away from the waterfront. They moved through a series of narrow, twisting streets overhung with buildings, lined with nearly empty shops. Men lay in rags even in the center of the smaller streets, and often they blocked the way.

They emerged from this maze of alleys to broader streets, each with a stone-lined ditch running down its center. The ditches were partially filled with refuse, but surprisingly little for so primitive a system.

"The men on Temple charity carry away the garbage," Deluca explained, "and bring barrels of water to wash the sewage away in the few dry weeks of the year. There is heavy rain in this city almost daily, but it never lasts long. This is the cleanest city on Makassar."

MacKinnie remembered Jikar, which was swept daily by the Guild apprentices, but said nothing. Batav was cleaner than he expected a primitive city to be, certainly more so than the garbage-strewn warrens of South Continent.

There were people in the streets. Some wandered through the ground-floor shops, although there was little to buy. Every shop had a large crucifix at its door, and a wind chime whose major feature was a replica of the Temple from which various shells and other sounding materials hung. Most of the population was small and dark, although there was a fair number of the taller, fair-haired men like Vanjynk. The tallest were still smaller than MacKinnie and the two clergymen, and here and there someone would turn to watch the group before staring off at nothing again.

Once, MacKinnie saw a group of uniformed Temple guardsmen, with a bright-yellow-robed official walking in their midst. He asked Deluca who the man was, and was told, "A tax collector. Some of them have taken minor orders beyond the deaconate, but are not full priests. They don't allow the priesthood to work directly on squeezing the population, but a lot of them have served a trick in that occupation before they take final vows."

They arrived at a small courtyard, behind which stood a massive stone and log house. Two swordsmen stood in the courtyard, and opened the iron gates when they saw the bishop, then went back to their posts, lounging carelessly against the gate pillars.

"Two weeks arrears in their pay," Deluca told Nathan. "It is strange. Many men in this city have nothing to eat, and you would think they would be glad of duties where they are well fed and have at least some money, but more and more throw themselves on Temple charity, work in the streets when they work at all, and refuse honorable employment. The city has lost its heart."

MacKinnie nodded. The barbarians were at the gates, but the men of the city either thought themselves lost already, or refused to think about it at all. Only the Temple kept the enemy at bay, providing whatever spirit Batav had been able to muster. Nathan doubted that even the iron-willed Temple believers would be able to hold things together for long.

The inside of the house was sparse, showing both the lack of funds which had furnished it, and, perhaps, the austere temperament of the Archbishop. MacKinnie was shown into the great hall, where His Eminence sat in ragged splendor, staring at the dying embers of a fire which was not really needed to heat the room.

"As we supposed, Your Eminence," Laraine said, "the ship was from the west. And more than we dared hope, it is owned by men from the Empire, although by their accents they are from a part I have never visited. A colony world?" he asked, turning to MacKinnie.

"I didn't ask your origin when I offered to help you, my lord," Nathan replied. "Is it necessary to discuss mine? The Empire contains many worlds, and the citizens of some are more fortunate than those of others. But despite the contempt the Empire feels for my world, it is my ship and my gold which can save your lives. We may even be able to help you in the work you came to do."

Deluca gasped, but before he could speak the Archbishop said, "He speaks well. Let him continue, for God often sends help in strange disguises. Our work is with the souls of all men." The old man waved toward a chair. "I gather that you have no way of calling the Navy to assist us?"

"We were not permitted such devices, my lord."

The Archbishop nodded. "A colony world." He nodded again. "The Navy could do nothing even if you could call them. Once we are dead, they will send a punitive expedition, and the Imperial Traders Association will be the loudest voice in demanding vengeance for the deaths of the priests of the Lord. The Church has more than once been used as a pretext for Empire."

"I do not understand, my lord," MacKinnie said.

"The Emperor has no wish to conquer these worlds." At MacKinnie's puzzled look, the old man halted. "Bring our guests something to drink." He turned to MacKinnie. "You know nothing of Imperial politics. Are you a member of the Church?"

"New Rome has not yet come to my world, my lord. We are Christians, more or less. I was baptized into the orthodox church, which I am told is acceptable to New Rome."

"Forgive my curiosity; it was not idle. It follows that you know nothing of Imperial politics. What are you doing on Makassar?"

"My king has sent me to head a trading mission, my lord. He rules the largest civilized country on my home world, and is allied with the Imperial ambassador. The Navy is aiding him in the subjugation of the planet."

The Archbishop nodded. "But you are not a Trader. Nor are any of these with you. Please, do not protest. You cannot deceive a man of my years. You are a soldier, and these others, what are they, spies? It does not matter. And here you are, on this primitive planet, having come from a world which is itself primitive . . . and you talk of aiding us! It is admirable, but I fail to see what you can do. Still, such courage should be rewarded, if only with information."

He paused as servants brought wine and additional chairs for the others. "This is not very good wine," Deluca said. "But it is all we have here. The Trader has far better on his ship."

"Wine does not make the day," the Archbishop told them. "It is only a vehicle. Look at them, Father Deluca. Barely able to speak the Imperial language, knowing nothing of the capital and its ways, voyaging across space in ships they cannot understand. . . . If the Church could bring men to as much faith in her teachings as these men have in themselves!" He tasted the wine and grimaced.

"You and I have the same mission, my lord Trader," he told MacKinnie. "We are agents provocateur, sent to aid the Imperial Traders Association. The difference is that I know it, and you do not."

"I do not understand."

"I did not expect you to understand. You believe you are here for some other purpose, some great mission to save your own kingdom perhaps, certainly something more important than bringing back gold for your planetary king. And we are here to bring these people back to God. But both of us will serve the ITA as surely as we would if they had hired us."

The room was still as they waited for him to continue. "The Navy will not permit the Traders simple conquest. I am sure that you know that no good military force will fight for a standard of living—their own or anyone else's. It takes God, not gold, to put heart in a soldier. The Navy fights for a cause, for the Emperor and the Church, for New Annapolis, for the Oath of Reunion, but never for the ITA. The Navy will not simply come in here and set up kingdoms for the Traders.

"So they use us. They get us sent here, and prevent the Navy from giving us protection . . . but after we are slaughtered, it will be the ITA delegates who shout the loudest for vengeance. 'Have to teach the beggars a lesson,' they will say. And the same for you colonials . . . back on your planet there is opposition to the Empire. I don't have to know where you come from to know that.

And Imperialism won't ensure much loyalty. The ITA will find them troublesome. But the really troublesome people will be the most patriotic . . . Do you think they will not join when the ITA recruits them for a merchant army to punish this planet? To revenge you? Neatly solving two problems, the conquest of Makassar, and the removal of leaders and soldiers, from wherever you come from. It is an old and tested formula and it works."

"Why do you permit them to use you, my lord?" MacKinnie asked.

"Whatever your reasons, would you have refused to come here if you had known?" the Archbishop answered. "I thought not. Nor could I refuse to bring the Word of God to the heathen." The old man coughed, his thin shoulders shaking violently. "Now go back to whatever plan you have, but remember the ITA. They have large resources, and they have power, but they have no virtue. One day the Navy will tire of being used and kill them all, but others will spring up in their place. There is always the ITA."

"I thank you for your frankness, my lord. Academician, have you anything to say?" MacKinnie added, turning to Longway.

"Not at the moment. I need time to think about all this. I am much afraid the Archbishop is right. You can see the counterparts of the ITA in King David's court. The money-grubbers are everywhere."

"My lord," MacKinnie asked, "if we can aid you in bringing these people to the Church, and yet give the Traders no reason to demand Navy intervention here, can you help us?"

"With what?"

"At the moment, I can't tell you. It isn't my secret, and I'm not sure what you can do in any event."

"I am not unwilling to help you in principle . . . but before you ask it, remember to whom you speak. I am an Archbishop of the Church. I am cynical about some of the Church's officers and many of the Imperial advisors, but do not be deceived. I am a loyal subject of the Emperor and a servant of the Church."

MacKinnie nodded. "I would ask nothing dishonorable. We can talk about these things later; now I had better return to my ship."

The old man stood and offered his hand, and after a moment MacKinnie knelt to kiss the great ring. As they left they saw him raise his hand in blessing, muttering words in a language MacKinnie had never heard.

★15★
THE WAR MINISTER
★ ★ ★

MacKinnie stood atop the high walls of Batav and wished for binoculars. He had bought a primitive telescope, but the lenses were not good and the images were blurred, so that it was better to study the barbarians without optical aids.

He watched for five days, looking out across the low, rolling hills and cultivated fields, watching as the maris rode swiftly from gate to gate. They had camped almost within bow-shot of the city, their tents and wagons contemptuously near the city gates, and constantly they taunted the city's defenders, daring them to come out, shouting insults and obscenities until the Temple warriors were roused to blind fury.

On the fourth day a small party of armored men rode out of the city to attack the nearest enemy camp. The heavy Temple cavalry rode through the enemy, their war-horses trampling the light-armored enemy into the turf, their swords hewing a path through the barbarians, and they shouted triumph. Nothing could stand before them in the charge. But slowly the charge faltered. The great warhorses tired, as did the men. Maris raced to the battle, group after group as the word spread, until the Temple troops were overwhelmed, surrounded. They vanished in a sea of swarthy men, and the sounds of battle died. That night the screams of dying comrades were added to the taunts hurled at the remaining Temple troops.

The day after the disaster MacKinnie asked for audience with the Temple hierarchy, claiming that he had valuable information about the war; information which he could reveal only to a high officer. Meanwhile, Stark drilled *Subao's* crew, forcing them to practice with sword, pike, and shield, marching them in formation to the beat of drums, throwing javelins and firing crossbows in volley, and always marching, holding formation as they quick-stepped about the pier. Their activities attracted notice from the officers of the Temple guard, and on their tenth day in Batav a small party approached the ship.

"We are to conduct you to the Temple," MacKinnie was told. He was ushered to the gates by the officer, then turned over to two gaily clothed attendants who guided him through lavishly decorated halls hung with tapestries and banners. The Temple was a jumble of contrasting chambers and passages, brilliant colors suddenly becoming plain stone walls, rich furnishings and then spartan utility. They climbed stone steps to a row of cells set into the wall high above the Temple courtyard. The officer scratched respectfully at the closed door of one of the cells.

"Enter."

The officer opened the door and stood aside. A black-robed priest sat at a small table, quill pen and inkpot before him. A litter of parchments was strewn about the room, and on the wall behind the priest hung a large map of the city and countryside, roads and villages sketched in detail to a distance of fifty kilometers from the walls.

"Father Sumbavu, the outlander you asked to see," the Temple officer said. "He calls himself Trader Captain MacKinnie." The man stumbled over the pronunciation but managed to say the name correctly.

Nathan had been told that Father Sumbavu served as minister of war for the Temple. There were others who ranked far higher, but few had more power. Sumbavu seemed to care little for the cope and miter of a bishop, and less for other trappings of power, but his men served him without question. Nathan noted the contrast between the sparsely furnished cell and the richly decorated rooms of the Great Hall of the Temple; Sumbavu was concerned with realities, not symbols.

The bare-walled cell was high above the outer battlements, and the narrow window looked across the city, to the wall, and beyond to the barbarian camps. Nathan could see small bands of maris riding endlessly around the gates. They stayed just out of bow-shot. Low, rolling hills, covered with grass and dotted with grainfields, stretched out to the horizon. A few roads crossed the plains, and the ruins of burned villages stood at their crossings.

The priest raised his hand perfunctorily in the ritual blessing, and MacKinnie bowed. Before he could straighten, the priest asked, "Why do you waste my time?"

"But you asked to see me, Father."

"You asked to see a member of the hierarchy. You say you have information about the war. Now you are here. What have you to tell me?"

"Your Worship, I have some experience with fighting these barbarians. In the east, they have been driven from city gates. Although I am but a Trader, I have commanded men in battle against these plainsmen, and I wished to find if our methods have been tried. We drove them from the gates in the south." MacKinnie stood as stiffly as a cadet on parade, waiting for the man to speak again, but there was only silence. Nathan studied the priest at length.

He could not guess Sumbavu's age. The face showed no lines, and there was no gray in the closely cropped hair, but the hands were worn with work, and perhaps with age as well. Sumbavu returned the intense gaze. "Why do you think you can do what we cannot? We have the finest soldiers on Makassar, and they have done nothing against these hordes. We have always beaten them back in the past, but there are too many of them now." He rose and stared out the stone window. His hands were tightly clenched, so that the knuckles turned white.

"It is not the quality of the soldiers, Your Worship, but their manner of fighting. Your guards have excellent discipline, but there are not enough of them. Your lords fight splendidly, but the cavalry is never properly supported to fight against these plainsmen. I have seen little of your cavalry—they have mostly been killed, have they not? I saw fifty of them taken."

"Those not dead live in the city. There were not many

at any time, and they have lost hope. Three times the armored servants of the Temple and the men of the great families rode out that gate. Three times they charged and nothing stood before them. And three times they were defeated, cut off, scattered, driven like straws before the winds, the few survivors riding back into the gates in shame. There are always more of the barbarians, but there are never more of the sons of the great families. And you say that you can do what our greatest warriors could not? Have you perhaps a thousand ships at your back, bringing a new army?" He looked closely at MacKinnie, then motioned to a hard wooden chair. "Enjoy what comforts I allow myself and my visitors," he muttered. "There are few enough. And tell me how the men of the south defeated the barbarians."

MacKinnie sat and chose his words carefully. "It is a matter of combining the foot soldiers and the mounted men so that they support each other," he told the priest. "When they are combined properly, the barbarians cannot defeat them."

"There are not enough soldiers," Sumbavu said. "No matter how clever you may be, you cannot make a few win against thousands."

"Not true, Father. We can make each man do the work of ten. And there are the idlers of the city, the hireling swordsmen, the thieves, the people of the city. They can fight."

The priest shrugged. "If they would. But for each of them you drive into the battle you must have a loyal man to watch him and keep him from running. It is not worth it."

"If they are treated as men, and trained properly, they can fight. We do not need many. But they cannot be treated like cattle or slaves. They must be free soldiers."

"You propose to give arms to the people? You would destroy the Temple?"

"No. I would save it. The Temple is doomed, Father Sumbavu. You are as aware of that as I." MacKinnie gestured toward the window. "The city will fall within the year. I have seen the empty docks, and I am told of the harbors closed against you. I see the people sleeping in the streets while the barbarians harvest the crops. You cannot drive the enemy away until he has eaten everything in your fields. Their supplies will last longer than yours. Your Temple is doomed unless you can drive away the enemy, and quickly."

Sumbavu struggled to keep his icy calm, but his hands moved restlessly across the desk. "And only you can prevent this? You are indeed a man blessed by God. We have held this city for five hundred years. What have your ancestors done? Lived in dirt houses?"

"What I have done is of no matter. It is what we can do."

"And how will you go about saving the city? What is your price?"

"I have no price for saving the fountain of all the wisdom on Makassar. I ask only what I will need. Weapons. Pikes and shields. Authority to recruit men. And I will have to inspect the soldiers, talk to the heavy cavalrymen. I will require a drill field to practice my men. And the men on Temple charity must be brought to it, so that they can be armed. I have no price, but I have much to do. We can save this city and the Temple if you will but listen."

The priest spread his hands and looked intently at his palms. "Perhaps it is the will of God. There is no other plan. It can do no great harm to allow you to train this rabble, for when you and they are killed that will be all the longer our rations will last. I will see that you get what you need."

An army formed gradually on the parade ground outside the Temple. It did not greatly resemble an army. In the first week the men had to be driven to the drill field; they stumbled through their paces, unable to understand orders and unwilling to work. But as they were given weapons and their training continued, a new sense of self-respect slowly pervaded the ragged group. Men who had recently been beggars found themselves alongside sturdy peasants from outside the walls, and mixed among them were younger sons of merchant families ruined by the siege. Under MacKinnie's pleas and Stark's driving, they began to hold their heads higher, to thrust their pikes into the target dummies, even to scream war cries. After the third week of training, MacKinnie called a conference.

"We don't have long," he told the group. "Sumbavu is anxious to know what we are doing, and I have to report to him. You want to be careful of that man. He's a lot sharper than he looks or acts. What's the status of our army?"

"The infantry's so-so," Hal reported. "The Temple troops are fine, but they don't know what to do and they're so sure of themselves they don't want to learn anything new. The people's army can carry pikes and hold up their shields if you don't want them to do it for too long. Weak as cats, most of them. And we'll never get any archers out of that crowd. The Temple's got a fair number, and that's all you'll have."

"Can they hold against a charge of light cavalry?" MacKinnie asked.

"Don't know, sir. They'd never stop the heavy stuff, but they might hold against the plainsmen if they believe in themselves enough. But they have no confidence, Colonel."

MacKinnie noticed Longway's start at Hal's slip, but said nothing. "What of the cavalry?" he asked Brett. "Can they fight in formation? Have they had enough of that cockiness beat out of them to make a disciplined force, or are they going to go charging out into the enemy and scatter?"

"Vanjynk and I have talked to them, Trader," Brett replied. "But their honor is all they have left. Still, these are men who have been beaten before, and after all, it is only barbarians they fight. . . . But it will be difficult to call them back from victory."

"You'll have to," MacKinnie said. "It's the only chance any of us have. Those men have to be taught to charge home, form ranks again, and get back to the shield walls. Any of them that try the grandstand act will be left out there dead. Try to drive that elementary fact through their heads. And add to it the fact that if they're killed their city falls and the whole honor system they're so proud of goes with it. They're fighting to preserve their honor."

"Yes, but by means which to them are dishonorable," Vanjynk said. "They listen to me as one of them, and I have faithfully told them what you desire. I have even come to believe it. But it is strange to them."

MacKinnie nodded. "Strange or not, they'll have to learn. Now what about the commissary department?"

Mary Graham smiled proudly. "That's in good shape," she said. "We have enough wagons now."

"I thought we were short of animals," MacKinnie said.

"We are, but they were hitching them all wrong," Graham said. "They were using leather straps. I had the carpenters make proper collars from wood, and now the horses don't tire as much. We still don't have enough, but the ones we have can carry more."

"Good."

"We have the wagons, but not much grain," she continued. "If you can protect our baggage trains, we can supply your men for a few days. There won't be a lot to eat, but something. After that, we'll have to find forage outside. We might even be able to harvest some grain if our farmers are protected."

"So we have a partially disciplined force of infantry, some cavalry who may be useful and may not, some Temple archers and guardsmen who are our best soldiers but don't understand what's needed, and one whole hell of a lot of barbarians. An interesting situation." He thought for a few moments, staring down at a copy of Sumbavu's map young Todd had laboriously made, then came to a decision.

"We need a demonstration. I'll give each of you a week to select the best men you can, men you think won't break and run and who will obey orders. I'll need provisions for about two days for twice that number of people, and a group of your best-disciplined cooks and camp workers," he added to Mary. "We're going to make a show of force against the enemy. The primary purpose will be to convince our own troops that we can beat barbarians." He stood, dismissing the meeting. "Hal, stay with me for a moment, please."

When the others had left, Stark said, "Sorry about the slip, Colonel. It's too much like a campaign, and I'm not used to being a spy."

"We'll survive. Have you picked the headquarters group?"

"Yes, sir. Using the troops we brought with us as a steadying force we've got a pretty loyal company. I think they'd fight the Temple people for us if they thought they could win. Anyway we can control them. You lead them to a victory, they'll be ours for sure."

"Excellent. We must have that headquarters group, or when this is over there won't be any point to it all. All right, Sergeant, you can go."

Hal stood, grinned for a moment, and saluted. "Old times, Colonel. Different Wolves, but old times."

MacKinnie carefully armed himself before visiting Sumbavu. He struggled into chain mail, threw a bright crimson cloak over his shoulders, donned gold bracelets and necklace, and fastened his surplice with a jeweled pin before buckling on a sword made on Prince Samual's World. The mail and sword were similar in design to Makassar products, but better than anything they had encountered on Makassar. Their possession imparted considerable status to MacKinnie's group. Sumbavu was standing at the battlements above his cell when MacKinnie was brought to him.

"You betray true colors, Trader," the priest said. "You are more the soldier than the Trader, are you not?"

"In the south, Father, Traders and soldiers are the same thing. At least live Traders are. There's little peace there."

"Or here. It was not always thus." The warrior-priest looked out across the great plain beyond the city wall. "There are more of them today. The grain is ready for harvest, and they are formed to protect it from our fire parties. We could burn the crop, but only at the cost of the balance of our knights. I do not think any would return to us alive."

"Yet, there may be a way, Father," MacKinnie said. When the priest glanced quickly at him, he continued, "I wish to take a small party outside the walls. We will not go far."

"You may take as many of your useless mouths as you please. You have made them march with their heads up, but they are not soldiers. They will never be soldiers."

"I need more than my peasants," MacKinnie said. "I will require fifty archers of the Temple and fifty mounted men."

"A fourth part of the archers? And nearly as great a part of the knights? You are mad. I will not permit it."

"Yet, Father, it is worth doing. We will show you how the barbarians can be defeated. And we will not go far from the walls. The archers and knights can seek shelter there if my men do not hold—and there can be no loss of honor if they retreat because others failed them."

"Where will you be?"

"With the spearmen at the van."

"You risk your life to prove these men? You believe, then. Strange."

MacKinnie looked across the plains, to see another band of barbarians approach the walls. There seemed to be hundreds in the one group alone.

"You will take your men into that," Sumbavu said. "You will not come out alive."

"But if we do? It will put heart in the others. Remember, if we do nothing, the Temple is doomed."

"Yet if you slaughter my archers and knights the doom will fall faster. . . ." The priest studied the camps below, watching knots of horsemen dart toward the walls, then turn away just outside the range of the archers at the walls. He fingered his emblem, a golden temple with an ebony-black cross surmounting it, and turned suddenly.

"Do as you will. You are mad, but there are those who believe the mad have inspiration from God. It is certain that I have none." Sumbavu turned and stalked away, age showing in the set of his shoulders.

★ 16 ★
THE WALKING WALL
★ ★ ★

MacKinnie used a week training the picked men for the sally. Finally Hal reported that they were as ready as they could be in the time they had, and assembled them in the marshaling square just inside the gates. His cloak streaming behind him, Nathan mounted the small dais near the gates to address the men.

"You will win today a victory such as has never been seen on this world," he shouted. "There will be no end to the songs of this day. Your homes will be saved, and you will come to glory. Besides, what life is there huddled behind walls? What man hides from his enemies when he can go out and kill them? Today you are all men. You will never be slaves again."

There was a feeble cheer, led by Hal's picked guardsmen scattered through the ranks.

"It'll have to do," Nathan told his sergeant. "They won't believe much of anything until they see they can hold the enemy. But will they fight long enough to find out?"

"Don't know, Colonel," Stark answered. "We've done all we could with them, but most of the spirit was beat out of them before we got here. They might."

"They know what to do," MacKinnie said. "Now it's up to us to make them do it. Get them in ranks and open the gate."

"Yes, sir."

The army was formed as a wedge, spear and shield soldiers at the edges, the cavalry, archers, and supply wagons inside. Picked men held the point, which was rounded to be as wide as the gate would permit. They were to march out in a column, with the sides moving swiftly on the obliques to make the triangular formation they had practiced on the Temple drill field. The crimson uniforms of the Temple archers and the gaily colored armor of the knights formed a brilliant contrast to the drab leather garments of the pikemen as they stood in ranks waiting for the gate to open. Wherever possible, the men in ranks wore breastplates, helmets, greaves, but there were not enough to equip them all. Some had only spear and shield, with a small dagger in their belts.

MacKinnie looked over his force in final inspection. He swallowed the hard knot that always formed in his stomach before action, and wondered if any soldier ever managed to avoid that tension. Then he waved, and the gate opened.

"Move out!" Stark shouted. "Keep your order. Just like on the drill field. Get in step, there."

Young drummers scattered through the reserves tapped cadence as the small force sallied out the gate. When enough of the spearmen had emerged to form a shield wall, MacKinnie sent out the cavalry, then strode swiftly through them to reach his post near the point of the formation. They formed ranks within the protective fire of the archers on the walls. A few of the barbarians charged toward them, but were cut down before they could reach the sallying force. The rest of the enemy stayed well out of range, watching, while thousands more rode swiftly toward the gate.

"Lot of them out there," Stark remarked. "Looks like all of them. Too bad you don't have another sally set up for the other gate."

"There's few enough troops here," MacKinnie muttered. He was grimly watching as the last of the army emerged from the gates and swung across to form the base of the wedge. "All right, Hal, move them out."

Stark signaled to the drummers. The cadence changed, and a drum signal echoed down the line. The men ceased to mark time and slowly marched forward, shields held level, spears thrust forward. Behind each shieldsman were two ranks of pikemen. They marched across the gently rolling plain toward the nearest enemy camp, too intent on looking ahead to know when they had left the range of the protective fire of the city walls.

The maris circled, always keeping their distance, inviting them to come away from the walls. Individual barbarians galloped toward the formation, then wheeled to ride away. They slapped their buttocks in contempt.

The individual riders changed to small groups. Then more gathered just beyond bow-shot. They moved slowly toward MacKinnie.

"Here comes the first bunch," Stark shouted. "They're going right around to hit young Todd's section. Put the archers on them?"

"Two squads, Hal. Let the others fire at high angle to keep the rest away. Todd's men can hold that group."

"Yes, sir."

Volleys of bolts shot from the Temple archers, cutting some of the enemy from their wooden saddles. Then the first barbarians hurtled toward the shield line, not in a wave but in scattered groups.

Before they made contact, Todd shouted orders. The drum cadence changed, and the line of men sank to one knee, spears grounded, the pikemen thrusting over their heads. The maris galloped closer, shouting, cheering.

A barbarian mare screamed as she was impaled on a spear. Other beasts whirled from the thicket of points, getting in the way of men charging behind them, stumbling within range of the thrusting pikes, until the barbarian group was milling in front of the right leg of MacKinnie's wedge. Archers poured fire into the mass of men and beasts. The enemy shouted defiance, broke against the shield wall again, again.

"They flee, they flee!" someone shouted.

"After them!" MacKinnie heard.

"Hold your positions!" MacKinnie shouted. "By the Temple God, I'll have the archers cut down the first man that breaks rank! Brett, keep those damned knights of yours under control!"

"Yes, sir," he heard from among the cavalry in the center of the wedge. The knights were milling about, anxious to give chase to the fleeing enemy. The maris thundered away, wheeled to shout defiance again, then rode off when no one followed.

When calm returned, MacKinnie mounted a wagon.

"You've driven off one small group. It wasn't much of a battle, but you see it can be done. Now don't let them make fools of you. If you break formation or leave the shield wall, they'll be all over you. Stand to ranks and you'll slaughter them. Remember, every man's life depends on each of you. No one may break, not for cowardice, and not for glory. And by God, raise a cheer!"

This time the response was great. As MacKinnie climbed down from the wagon, he saw the driver for the first time: small, dressed in chain mail, and shouting at the top of her lungs.

"Freelady!" he called. "You have no business here."

"You gave me the commissary to organize, Colonel. I have done it. There was no one here fit to command my ragtag group, and I will not have my work undone by incompetents. Your sergeant himself dismissed that oaf from the Temple who tried to drive my men like slaves."

He looked at her and remembered another freelady who had been headstrong, but shook the thought from his mind. Laura hadn't really been like Mary Graham. It was hard to imagine Laura in armor—although she might well have carried a sword. Graham's was on the wagon box next to her. As Nathan studied his ward, one of the commissary troops came up. The cook fingered an enormous meat axe.

"You leave the lady alone," the burly man said. "She's a saint from heaven. You touch her, and commander or not, you die."

"Sumba, thank you, but I don't need protection," Mary protested. "At least not from him."

"That's all right, my lady, we'll watch them all," the

stocky cook said. MacKinnie shrugged and returned to organize the battle.

The group marched forward again, the drums measuring a slow beat. From time to time a group of the enemy would gallop toward them, firing arrows, only to be driven away by the Temple archers. The barbarians' stubby bows were useless against even the leather of the unarmored men until they came to close range, and they did not dare come very close.

"They'll re-form for another try," MacKinnie said softly. "This time they'll try a mass charge with everything they've got."

Stark nodded. "The men have some confidence now, Colonel. I think they'll hold. It was a good thing, their trying a small attack at first."

"Clan rivalry," Longway said from behind them. "I've seen it on South Continent. Each clan wants to be first to remove the insult of your presence. But they'll be back."

"Night's what worries me," Stark said. "We going to stay out here all night?"

MacKinnie nodded. "The whole point of this demonstration is to build up the morale of the troops back in the city. Just moving out and coming back won't do any good. We have to have a solid victory."

"I still do not see what we are accomplishing," Longway said. "Suppose you prove that you can take the field against the barbarians and move about in formations they can't break. All they have to do is avoid you."

"We'll cross that one later," MacKinnie muttered. "Here they come, Hal. Get the men ready."

A flood of the enemy galloped toward them across the low plain.

"Thousands, thousands," someone in the ranks shouted. "We'll never stop that charge!"

"Quiet in the ranks!" Stark ordered. "Beat to arms, drummers!" The tattoo thundered through the small formation. The shieldsmen dropped to one knee again, this time the entire perimeter sinking low, with the pikemen thrusting their weapons over the tops of the shields. A small knot of reserve pikemen stood at each corner of the wedge, while Brett's cavalry milled about. The archers fired into the oncoming horde as the cooks and camp followers struggled to load crossbows and pass them up to the bowmen. Every bolt took its target, leaving riderless horses to run aimlessly, bringing confusion to the enemy charge.

"They don't have what you'd call much formation to them," Stark observed coldly. "They'd do better to all come at once instead of in little bunches."

"Insufficient discipline," Longway said. "They've more than the normal on this world, but that isn't much."

As the drums thundered to a crescendo, the charge hit home. On all sides barbarians plunged and reared, unable to penetrate the shield walls, milling about in front of the wedges, while crossbow bolts poured out.

"Swordsmen! Swordsmen here!" MacLean shouted from his station as commander of the rear section. At his order, a dozen men with shortswords and bucklers ran to his aid, throwing themselves into a gap in the line, thrusting five dismounted barbarians out into the seething mass beyond. A knot of pikemen trotted to station behind them, while the formation closed ranks over the bodies of five shieldsmen, killed when one of their number turned to run.

The maris called to their companions, withdrew a space, and charged the weak spot in the line again.

"They're massing back there against MacLean," Stark reported. "Getting hard to hold."

"Prepare the cavalry," MacKinnie said softly. "I'll go get MacLean ready."

MacKinnie ran across the thirty yards separating the point from the base of the wedge. "Prepare to open ranks, Mr. MacLean."

"Aye, Colonel. Drummers, beat the ready." The drum notes changed subtly. "Fuglemen, pace your men!" The seaman's voice carried through the din of battle, and they heard the orders rattle down the ranks. MacKinnie eyed the situation coolly.

"Now, Mr. MacLean."

"Open ranks!" MacKinnie commanded. The shieldsmen sidestepped, bunching up on each other, leaving a clear gap in the center. The enemy shouted in triumph and poured toward the gap.

The rich notes of a trumpet sounded from the center of the formation. Slowly, gathering speed, ponderously, the heavy cavalrymen trotted across the wedge from their gathering place at the point.

They built up speed, lances were lowered, and they drove into the advancing enemy, using the maris' own momentum to add to their own, sweeping everything before them, riding the enemy down under the hooves of their beasts. Brett and Vanjynk, at each end of the first wave of knights, sounded a cheer as the heavy armor of the iron men proved too much for the light-armed maris. The barbarians scattered and swordsmen poured into the gaps, running alongside the knights, slashing down the enemy, killing the dismounted. The charge pressed onward, the knights scattering to pursue the enemy. The tight formation broke up, and the maris withdrew, formed in tight knots.

"Sound recall," MacKinnie ordered. The trumpet notes were heard again, this time plaintively, disappointed. "Sound it again." He turned to Stark. "This is the turning point, Hal. If Vanjynk and Brett can't control those brainless wonders, we've had it."

He saw his officers shouting to the knights. Slowly they began to wheel, first one, then another, then the entire group. For a moment they paused, and MacKinnie saw that Brett was actually dressing their ranks before they rode in, proudly, contemptuously, in perfect order, their pennants fluttering from their lances, while the shield wall closed behind them over the bodies of a hundred foes.

MacKinnie drove them relentlessly on, across the plain toward the first of the nomad encampments. Twice more they withstood a massed assault from the maris, the column halting to plant spear butts in the ground. The second attack was heavy enough to cause MacKinnie to order the cavalry charge again. The armored knights broke through the concentrations of the enemy before wheeling around to recover their position within the shield wall. In each battle they left a pile of the enemy dead to be crushed beneath the wagon wheels as the column marched on.

They reached the enemy camp, a group of leather tents stretched across wooden frames, a few wagons which the barbarians pulled to safety before the army arrived. A thin wall of men with light shields stood in front of the camp. Brett and Vanjynk rode forward to MacKinnie.

"We can scatter them with a single charge!" Brett shouted. "Open the ranks."

"No. I will not risk our cavalry in a charge beyond the shield walls. There are too few men for that, and we would never return to the city if something went wrong. We march together or we die together. Would your knights abandon us?"

"We would not leave you though you stood alone among a thousand enemies," Vanjynk said quietly. "I have been talking to the knights. Not one of us has ever seen the like of this day. We have left more of the enemy behind us than we number. Each time we fought them before, our charge would carry them away until suddenly they swarmed about us to cut us down. We will stay with you."

The column moved forward, cautiously but inexorably, the drums giving a slow step as the pikemen advanced. MacKinnie rotated the formation until the point was aimed directly at the enemy, then massed his reserve pikes behind the leading men. His archers were silent, their store of bolts nearly exhausted. MacKinnie spoke quietly to the Temple officer who commanded them.

"A full volley on the men to the right of our point. I want a hole driven in their formation. They can't fight as infantry, they aren't trained for it, and they don't like it. We'll break through and roll up their flanks."

As they approached nearer, MacKinnie gave a signal. The archers fired their volley as Todd led a knot of swordsmen forward, cast javelins at the enemy in front of them, and retired behind the forest of pikes. The leading elements of the column struck just behind the javelins, tearing through the thin line by sheer momentum, before the first rank of pikemen fell into a hidden pit behind the maris. Their screams echoed up from below.

"That's what you would have ridden into," MacKinnie told Brett softly. "I thought there was a reason they'd stand like that. They were hoping for a full charge of cavalry."

The barbarians broke and ran, gathering their mounts from hiding places behind the tents and galloping away. Mary Graham's auxiliaries hauled the wounded men from the pits below, leaving five pikemen impaled on stakes set in the ground. She turned pale as she stood looking into the grisly trench, but Nathan had no time for sympathy. "Bury them there," MacKinnie ordered. "It's an honorable enough grave. Send for the chaplain." He moved about the formation placing men in line, setting the shield wall around the perimeter.

A small scouting party entered the enemy camp. They returned with excited reports. "There is much food here," one said. "But we must enter with great care, for they have tethered scarpias on the walls and ridgepoles." The scarpia was a warm-blooded lizardlike creature eight to twenty centimeters long. It faintly resembled the Earth scorpion, and its bite was far more deadly.

"We will camp beyond the enemy tents," MacKinnie ordered. "Use their ridgepoles to add to our stakes, and be sure to set the stakes carefully. They may attack at night. Bring as much food as you can carry for the city."

Under Stark's direction, the battalion built a fortified camp, digging ditches around the perimeter, throwing the earth to the inside and placing stakes at the top of the rampart they formed. They worked in shifts, every other man using his shovel while the rest stood in ranks holding the diggers' shields and weapons, but there was no renewal of the barbarian attack. The maris rode endlessly around the perimeter of the camp, just outside bow-shot, darting in to fire arrows and wheeling away before an answering volley could be launched. MacKinnie ordered the men to ignore the harassment.

"They'll get close enough to fight before the night's over," he told them. "They can't do us much harm from the range they're shooting from. You'll get your chance later."

It was dark before the cookfires were lighted, but MacKinnie would not allow any rest until camp was completed. When the last stake was driven, the sun had set, and a thick overcast obscured the moons. From his command point atop Mary Graham's wagon, MacKinnie could see dozens of fires dotting the plain; barbarian camps, each a band of hundreds of men.

"There are sure enough of them," he remarked.

"I don't see how we can win against so many," Mary answered. "No matter how many you kill, there will always be more."

"Not if there's nothing to eat. They're foraging pretty

wide already. It's only the grain crops that keep them able to stay here. Without those, they'd have to go back into the interior. We'll drive them off all right."

"What were you a colonel of?" she asked. "I thought you were more than just a Trader from the time I met you, and I wasn't very surprised when your man let it slip."

"You've heard of me," he said. Out beyond the palisade, something was moving. The nearest enemy cookfire was obscured momentarily, then again.

"You mean your name is MacKinnie? Let me—" She looked up in surprise. "Iron MacKinnie? The Orleans commander? I should hate you."

"Why?"

"My fiancé was at Blanthern Pass. A subaltern in the Fifth."

MacKinnie climbed laboriously from the wagon, surprised at how tired he was even in the low gravity of Makassar. "The Fifth were good troops."

"Yes. They'd have won against anyone but your men, wouldn't they? I think everyone in Haven hated and admired you at the same time after that battle."

"It's done. Now we're all loyal subjects of King David. I'm sorry."

"Don't be." She moved closer to him, trying to see his face in the dim light from the cookfire. "From these millions of miles away, the big important politics of Prince Samual's World look pretty small. Until today I was sure we'd never get back home. Even now it doesn't seem very likely. But if anyone can do it, you can."

Nathan laughed. "You're beginning to sound like Hal

talking to the recruits, Mary Graham. For now you'd best get the men fed, because we don't have very long before the barbarians try their hand with a night attack. I'll have the troops sent here in shifts so we keep a decent perimeter, and we feed the interior troops last. It's the pikemen and shield boys we want to take care of tonight."

"When do the knights eat?"

"After they've fed their mounts like any good cavalry. And after my pikemen. Your pardon, freelady, I have to see my men."

The night wore on. MacKinnie was relieved when no attack came before his perimeter guards were fed, but did not relax until every man was back in his place, lying at ease with his weapons, while swordsmen stood guard to peer futilely into the darkness.

"They're coming," he told Stark. "I've seen them stirring around, and there's a feel about it. You get it, too?"

"Yes, sir. And like you say, they're moving about some out there. We'll hear from them before morning."

It was nearly midnight when a sentry shouted, then vanished beneath a wave of dismounted men swarming toward the palisade.

"Trumpeter!" MacKinnie shouted. "Sound the alarm! To your feet, men!" He could see a knot of pikemen, kept awake in central reserve, rushing toward the area of the attack.

"To me! To me!" he heard Vanjynk shout. "Leave your mounts and rally to me!" Leading a party of knights with swords singing about their heads, Vanjynk charged to the perimeter, pushing aside shieldsmen struggling to their feet. The iron men stood at the top of the palisades, dealing terrible blows to the enemy attempting to climb out of the ditch. The night was filled with screams and shouts before MacKinnie had his shield wall formed properly and brought the armored men back to a central reserve.

"They're all around the perimeter," Stark told him. "They try one spot and then another, not much coordination to it, but nobody can rest any, Colonel."

MacKinnie nodded agreement. "It's a good tactic. They hope to tire us out and then cut us off from the city. It'll cost them enough."

In less than an hour the battle died away, leaving a quiet shattered at intervals with the groans of the wounded, but the enemy never left them alone. All night there were rushes against one part of the palisade or another, and the whistle of arrows fired randomly into the camp. Morning came slowly, to reveal hundreds of enemy dead and dying filling the ditches, or stretched on the ground where they had crawled away from the battle. Bands of nomads rode slowly around the camp, silently watching the wall of shields.

"Here's the tricky part," MacKinnie said. "But I think they may have had enough for now. They'll want to see what we do next." He carefully moved his men out before the palisade, bringing the wagons and interior troops out of the camp before abandoning the other walls. The enemy watched, but there was no attack as he marched his formation slowly back through the enemy campsite. They burned everything they couldn't carry away. As the maris' possessions blazed behind them, the battalion marched in quickstep back to the city.

★17★
BATTLE
★★★

The war minister was angry as he faced the assembled bishops of the Temple. "He has proved that he can fight the barbarians. He has remained a day and a night outside the walls of the city. He has killed hundreds of them. For this we are grateful. But I say that it is madness to take the entire army into the field. Let him carry on his raids with the troops he used before, not strip our walls of their defenders."

The council muttered approval. Their voices echoed softly in the great room.

MacKinnie rose to speak. He strode forward to the platform before the council table. As he approached he looked again at the council room. Its walls were hung with tapestries; above the woven hangings stone figures, representing heroes of an Empire dead so long its very existence was legend, stared down at them. On his dais high above the council table, His Utmost Holiness Willem XI dozed in starts, interest overcoming senility for moments before his head dropped again. His word was law but the council of bishops wrote his words for him, and spoke them as well more often than not.

"Worshipful sirs," MacKinnie said, "I would do as Father Sumbavu asks if it were possible. But our expedition was a demonstration only. Without sufficient troops to replace the shieldsmen who fall in battle, and more to allow the men rest when they tire, we could never hold against the enemy for more than a day. But with enough men I can destroy their bases of supplies, bring them to battle against us, destroy many of them, and send the rest back to their wastelands. And do not be deceived, worshipful sirs. The plainsmen have studied our methods of fighting. They will even now be devising means to fight us, ways to use their great numbers and speed against us. The next battle will decide the fate of the city. Would you fight it now, or wait until hunger has reduced our ranks to shadows? Will you fight outside the walls like men, or huddled inside waiting to be slaughtered?"

"He speaks well, Sumbavu," the Archdeacon said. He turned his blue eyes toward MacKinnie. "And how do you know you will have success? What manner of Trader are you that you know ways of fighting never seen on this world?"

"Your Reverence, my ways are but those of the Guildsmen of the south and west. We have fought these barbarians before, although never so many of them. As to success, what can be denied the army of God? If we go forth boldly, we must win, for God is with us."

"He was with us before, but it did not save our army," Sumbavu muttered. The old priest glanced quickly about, fearful of having spoken heresy.

"You wish to take all the knights and archers, and your beggars," the Archdeacon said. "This I understand from watching the fighting five days ago. But why do you also demand the swordsmen of the Temple? Of what use will these be to you?"

"The armored swordsmen will guard our camp," MacKinnie said. "They will fight in the nighttime when the shieldsmen are not of such great value. They fight against the barbarians when they leave their mounts and attack us on foot. The citizen army knows only one method of fighting; they are not trained soldiers. We must have a leavening of fighting men if we are to bring the enemy to the final battle."

"And, Sumbavu, what have you to say except that we should not allow this? What reasons have you?" the crimson-robed official asked. "He has done what you could never do." The Archdeacon turned to the others. "For myself, I see the hand of God in this man's coming. Who knows what instruments the Omnipotent may choose for our deliverance?"

Sumbavu measured his words carefully, speaking softly so that they leaned forward to hear him. "I do not know. Yet I do not like this. There is something of this man I do not understand, and I do not think he should be trusted with the army of the Temple."

"Then go with him to command it," the Archdeacon said. "For ourselves, we have heard enough. Let the Trader kill the barbarians, and may God's blessing go with him."

Sumbavu bowed in acceptance, but MacKinnie felt the war minister's intense gaze even as he left the room.

★ ★ ★

MacKinnie used two more weeks preparing for the battle. His entire force of citizens and peasants was trained, with his original group dispersed through the ranks as fuglemen. Stark drilled them relentlessly in the Temple courtyard, taking them again and again through the complex maneuvers which formed squares and columns, opened and closed ranks, brought their pikes to rest and present.

Brett and Vanjynk worked with the knights, shouting and cursing to try to make them understand that their great strength lay in a massed charge, and that they must return to the shield wall to regroup after each attack or they would be split apart and killed. Each evening they discussed the day's progress, talking late into the night, then rising early to drill the men once again.

On the night before the army was to go forth, MacKinnie held another conference. He looked intently at his officers seated at the thick wooden table in front of him, and nodded in satisfaction.

"Mr. MacLean, what of my infantry?"

"Better than when we went out last, Trader. They've seen the way it's done now, and Stark sweated them until they're hardened up. Not like veteran troops, but they'll hold. Doubling the rations didn't hurt any."

"That was the Trader's doing," Mary Graham said. "He found someone who could be bribed at the warehouse."

MacKinnie shook his head. "Stark again, though I thought of it. I've never seen a commissary yet that didn't have a couple of people on the take in it."

"I hope there are none in mine," Mary said indignantly.

"There are, lady, there are," Stark interjected. "Just hope their price is high and they're scared enough of you not to fill up the grain wagons with sand. It's been done to campaigns before."

"And your knights, Vanjynk?" MacKinnie asked.

"They drill well, they wheel to the trumpets, but they still do not like turning from the battle. Nor do I, but I see it must be done." Vanjynk lifted his cup and gulped the wine. "You fight strangely on your world, star man."

"Lay off that talk," Stark muttered. "We have enough trouble with the Temple people without that."

MacKinnie nodded. "Hal's right. But tell me, will the knights obey the trumpets?"

"I believe so," Brett answered. "They have little wish to be killed by barbarians. But there is no fear of death in these men, only of dishonor."

"Aye, so Brett made a song about foolish knights who abandoned their commander and were shamed forever," MacLean said. "Silly thing, but catchy. Seems to have helped."

"If songs help, sing your lungs out," MacKinnie told them. "The key to this whole battle is getting the heavy cavalry to bear on the barbarians while they're bunched up. Nothing on this world can stand up to a charge from those armored ironheads, but as soon as they lose their momentum and scatter, the maris can pick them off with no trouble at all." He turned to Mary Graham. "Do you have all the supplies we ordered?"

She nodded. "We've made thousands of bolts for the crossbows, and the grain wagons are ready. You don't really have very many provisions, you know."

"I know. You're rolling plenty of empty wagons, though. Either we find something to put in them, or we'll come back home for more supplies. This formation's slow enough without heavy transport gear in the square."

"Then we're ready," Mary Graham said.

"Not you. You aren't going," MacKinnie told her.

"Yes I am. It's no safer in here than out there. If your battle is lost, the city is lost as well and you know it." She looked around the room at the other men from her world. "I have a right to his protection, and I choose that he exercise it personally. Don't I have that right?"

"An interesting point," Longway said. "You cannot abandon her without finding a substitute guardian," the Academician told MacKinnie. "And doubtless she is entitled to someone of her own world. Who will you leave with her? Scholar Kleinst remains in the city, but for all his great value he is hardly a suitable guardian."

"I appear to be outmaneuvered, although why you should want to accompany an army in the field is beyond me, freelady." MacKinnie looked at her expectantly.

"I see no reason to stay here," she told him. "There are few enough on this godforsaken place that I can talk to, without being left with the Temple monks. Besides, I can be useful, or can you spare anyone else to manage your commissary?"

"The point is made." Well made, he thought. She's been nearly as useful as Hal. No one else could have organized the logistics half as well as she has. But—

He turned back to the council. "Our whole purpose in this expedition will be to either force plainsmen into battle on our terms, or destroy their base of supply. Either will be sufficient, although I doubt they will let us simply march out and burn their harvests without a fight. . . ." He indicated the map spread out on the table. "As far as we can tell from watching their movements, they've been harvesting the crops for the past three weeks. The nearest big concentration of grain is here, about thirty kilometers from the gates, assuming they use the roads and village structures. I rather think they will. From what I've been able to learn they often do that. We'll make straight for that and burn what we can't load up."

"Then what?" MacLean asked.

"We see if they'll fight. If they won't, we keep marching from place to place until they're short of rations. But they'll fight, all right."

"You may get more battle than you expect," Longway said. "You've hurt their pride with your last expedition, and they'll want to prove it was an accident. Next time, they'll press home their charge with everything they have."

"That's what I'm hoping for," MacKinnie answered slowly. "It will take them time to gather for the battle, and more to decide who leads it. By that time, we should have got to our objective and set up camp. They'll gather troops all night, and probably try to wipe us out in the morning."

"Then you're trying for one big battle," Mary said.

"Yes. One turn of the wheel, freelady. We haven't a lot of time." He glanced significantly at the Makassarians at the table, then stood to dismiss the meeting. "Rest well, and be ready tomorrow. They may not let us get to the first village."

* * *

The army formed outside the city walls after first light. MacKinnie placed his men in a triangular formation again, but this time the broad base of the wedge faced forward, its point to the rear. He doubled the men on the right leg of the wedge, using all the left-handed troops he could find for the forward elements of that line, and placing a large reserve force at the rear point. When he was satisfied with his arrangements, the drums beat their slow march, and the army moved forward.

Clouds of maris rode madly around, darting toward them, withdrawing, waiting for any opening in the shield walls, patient in the knowledge that the city army could never pursue them. The slow cadence continued, wagon wheels creaked and men shouted at the oxen drawing supply wagons, while the knights in the center impatiently led their mounts. Kilometer after kilometer they marched toward the enemy camp, as more and more barbarians joined the forces riding around them. They were completely surrounded.

"Reckon the city can hold with what we've left them?" Stark asked, looking back at the city in the distance. "You didn't leave them much."

"They'll hold," MacKinnie replied. "The enemy has no heavy siege equipment, and as long as the walls are manned the barbarians can't do much. Give them enough time and they could throw up ladders or even stack their saddles against the walls, but the defense can slow that down, and I don't intend to give them any time for stunts like this. We seem to be attracting most of them to us, anyway. What's Sumbavu doing?"

"He's riding with the knights, Colonel. Keeping an eye on those pretty uniformed swordsmen and archers, too. He doesn't trust you much."

"I don't blame him, Hal. I wouldn't trust me much either if I were him. But what else can he do? Keep a sharp eye on him; I can't have him interfering."

"Yes, sir. You didn't make much protest about his coming."

"Maybe I didn't mind him coming. Now watch him."

"Yes, sir."

The march continued, drawing to within a kilometer of the enemy tents. MacKinnie looked closely at the cluster of enemy in front of him: "They're trying to make up their minds. They don't want to give up all that grain without a fight. Watch that group there," he said, pointing. "Here they come! Beat the alarm!"

The drums thundered, then went back to their steady pace. The column continued to advance until the enemy was within bow-shot. "Prepare for attack," MacKinnie said quietly, measuring the distance to the nearest of the plainsmen. "Form the wall." The drums beat again, and the Temple archers rushed to the perimeter, firing into the packed enemy. The charge hurtled toward the broad front of the wedge, then wheeled around to strike the left end of the line. Pikemen rushed to the corner as echelon after echelon of the enemy plunged against the left leg of the inverted wedge.

The shield wall held. A few of the barbarians leaped over the first rank to land among the pikemen, their short-swords slashing, but Temple guardsmen moved forward to cut them down. The battle was short, and when it was finished hundreds more of the enemy lay in front of the column. The men raised a cheer, cut short by the drummers' commands to resume the march.

"Not much of a battle," Stark commented. "Thought they'd try more than that."

"Testing us out," MacKinnie said. "They've found a way to get a few men into our lines now. They'll try that one again. Adaptable beggars."

"They have to be," Brett said from behind him. MacKinnie turned to see the singer walking patiently. "I left my mount with Vanjynk," Brett said. "You understand that there will be many more battles, each different from the last?"

"I understand. But how many more there will be depends on more than their intentions. For now, we take their supplies."

The enemy camp was deserted. They had carried away their tents, but they had left huge piles of harvested grain. The grain piles had recently been covered with hides, but now the food was left to blow about in the wind. They had also fouled some of the harvest with excrement. Graham's commissary workers began the tedious task of bagging and loading the harvest.

The scattered refuse of weeks of enemy life lay about them; there were also signs of what had happened to villagers unfortunate enough to fall into the hands of the maris. Stark sent burial details to dispose of them.

Father Sumbavu examined the remains of a young girl. "Monsters," he said. "Not human at all. They deserve extermination."

"We will hardly be able to do that," MacKinnie said.

"But we may yet surprise them. Your pardon, Father, I must see to our defenses."

Ditch, ramparts, and palisade rose around the campsite while the commissary workers began cookfires. A dozen singers strolled about. MacKinnie moved through the camp, speaking to little groups of his men, encouraging them, testing their morale. It was hard to believe that only months before these had been the sullen slaves and beggars of the streets of Batav. Now they roared lustily at his jokes, shouted defiance at an enemy they could not see, and grimly held their weapons as if half afraid someone would take them. MacKinnie pitied anyone foolish enough to try.

The night was a turmoil. When both moons were high and bright, masses of barbarians stormed forward, some mounted, most on foot, probing to find a weak spot in the perimeter, constantly attacking to keep the men aroused, withdrawing from opposition but coming again and again. MacKinnie sent small detachments of his troops to the center of the camp, replacing them with others, so that each man was able to rest for part of the night. Toward dawn the attacks died away, and he let the men sleep until late in the morning. The Temple swordsmen had borne the brunt of the night attacks, and were most in need of rest. MacKinnie did not call them to breakfast until everyone else had been fed.

A mass of barbarians formed a kilometer from the camp. They were strung out in a vast semicircle between MacKinnie's army and the city, and MacKinnie had never seen so large a group of plainsmen before. Stark joined him as he stood atop the commissary wagon for a better view of the enemy.

"This going to be it, Colonel?" the big sergeant asked.

"Possibly. Let's see if we can get out of this camp. They figure to hit us as soon as there are enough outside the gates to make it worthwhile." MacKinnie shouted orders, formed the men into ranks, then motioned to a trumpeter. The notes rang out, calling his officers to him. Moments later, the main gate opened.

MacKinnie sent a heavy detachment of shieldsmen angling forward and to the left from the camp gate. A second group angled off to the right, while others marched out to form a line between them, its ends anchored with the hard-marching groups of picked men. When the left-hand group had left a large enough opening inside the wedge, the knights were sent forward until they were just behind the shield wall, at the extreme left corner of the inverted wedge the army was forming. Then MacKinnie sent the Temple archers forward, a line down each leg of his triangular formation, leaving none in the center. Whenever the maris approached the two legs of the formation, a shower of arrows greeted them, forcing them away. The enemy clustered around, moving toward the center where the resistance was least.

MacKinnie nodded in satisfaction. "Now comes the hard part," he muttered.

A charge of the barbarians struck the center of the triangle directly in front of the camp gates. The shield wall held, but gradually fell back, stretching thinner and thinner, bowing inwardly toward the gate as the heavier formations at the ends of the line held fast. More troops were sent forward to fill the gaps, keeping a continuous line, but still the enemy pressed forward, forcing them back, back, as more of the maris joined the attack. The formation bowed still more resembling an enormous "U" with its base almost at the palisade. Hundreds, a thousand, four thousand barbarians pressed forward toward the camp gates.

"Now!" MacKinnie shouted. The trumpet notes sounded above the shouts of battle, drums thundered. The knights formed inside their bastion; then, as the formation opened, they charged down the wing, rolling up the flank of the enemy. The shield wall quickly closed behind them; then the ends of the U drew together. Archers faced inward now, firing into the ranks of the enemy, while the heavy cavalrymen thundered over the barbarians, riding them down, breaking up all signs of organization until they rode directly into the camp gate.

MacKinnie signaled frantically to Brett. "Form them up again and be ready to protect the outer flanks!" he shouted. "The archers and spearmen can deal with the ones we've trapped."

The field in front of the gate was covered with blood. Barbarians pressed closer and closer together as the shield wall, bristling with pikes, closed in on them. Temple archers continued the rain of arrows into the helpless enemy, too crowded together even to use their weapons properly, the inner group not able to strike a blow. A few raced frantically out the end of the trap before the heavy knots of men MacKinnie had sent out first made contact with each other and closed all avenues of escape.

The remaining enemy outside the trap attempted to aid their fellows, to be stopped by shieldsmen facing outward slowly moving back as the inner lines moved forward. Concentrations of the enemy were broken up by charges of cavalry, the knights thundering over them and around the ends, wheeling back to enter the camp and regroup, while the Temple swordsmen defended the ramparts of the camp itself. The huge mass of doomed men in the trap could have broken through the thinner lines of the camp, or even the outer defenses of the trap, but they could not escape to fight, while the smaller numbers remaining outside were unable to help them, frantically falling upon the spears of the shield wall or trampled beneath the knights while their luckless fellows were relentlessly cut down.

The slaughter continued until midafternoon. At the end, hapless groups of the enemy threw themselves on the spears or clawed their way up the ramparts to be impaled by the swordsmen at the top, screaming desperately, their courage melted by the faceless mass of swords and the rain of arrows. As the pikemen passed over the dead, camp followers slit each throat and removed the arrows, passing them back to be fired again. Captive beasts were led through the lines into the camp to be tethered with the commissary oxen. The lines came closer together, closer, then touched. There were no more enemies in the trap.

"What do you propose for tomorrow?" Sumbavu asked the council clustered around MacKinnie's campfire. "You have left thousands dead on the field, more cut down in flight by our knights. We can return to the city."

"No." MacKinnie stood, a cup of wine in his hands.

"Until their supply base is destroyed, there is no safety for the city. We must continue to burn their grain."

"It is not their grain, but ours!" Sumbavu snapped. "You cannot burn this great harvest. It must be carried back to the city. Surely this march can be delayed for a time to allow us to provision the Temple! The faithful are hungry, and they should be told of this great victory."

"You forget, there are many more of the enemy than we have killed," MacKinnie reminded the priest. "And we must not give them time to rest. We must pursue them endlessly until they go back to their wastelands in fear."

"I forbid this," Sumbavu said quietly. "We must take these stores of grain to the city. You will not burn them."

"Then I suggest you take them yourself, Your Worship," MacKinnie told him. "Now that we have thinned their ranks, I believe we can do without the Temple swordsmen. I will need some of the wagons to transport grain for the army, but you may have half of them, and three hundred of the camp servants as well. It is only thirty kilometers; each can carry half a hundred-weight of grain. That will leave little to burn."

"So be it. We set forth immediately."

"At night, Your Worship?" MacKinnie asked. "Is that wise?"

"Wiser than being caught by them in the daytime. I see that you will not escort me with your army, though it would involve only a day's march. I will so report to the council."

"Two days' march, Father," MacKinnie said quietly. "One each way. Not to mention the disorganization as each man ran in to tell his fellows of the glorious victory.

We would lose many days, and for what? If the enemy is to be driven from the city, it must be done now."

"What need to drive them away, now that we have means to gather provisions?" Sumbavu snapped. "We could return, and our Temple officers learn to command the soldiers, then set forth again. It would not be so great for you and your outlanders, would it? You must win yourself, for what purpose I do not know. But I tell you again, I know you do not have the good of the Temple first in your heart, soldier of the south. Were I not guarded by the faithful of the Temple, I do not think I would return from this march alive." He stalked off into the night, his bodyguard following him closely.

"Go pick the most useless slaves of your group," MacKinnie told Mary Graham. "The blunderers, the tired animals and those you didn't make new collars for, the wagons ready to fall apart, get them all out of here."

She studied him closely. "I'd almost think that's why you brought all that useless junk. And you added that group of convicts to my picked men . . . . Did you expect this?"

"Freelady, just get them moving," Stark said. "The colonel's got enough problems." He guided her to the granaries, then set men to loading the wagons which were to go back to the city.

Two hours later, Sumbavu was ready to depart. He stood with MacKinnie at the camp gate, watching the sky. "In an hour the moons will be gone. You have not seen the enemy?"

"No, Father," MacKinnie told him. "But they will have men out there."

"There is less chance they will attack me at night than by day," the priest said. "In the dark they will not know that I have only the Temple soldiers, and they will be afraid." He watched the setting moons in silence until darkness came over the plains.

"I leave you my blessing," Sumbavu told MacKinnie. "Perhaps I have misjudged your intentions. May God accompany you."

"Thank you, Father," MacKinnie said. He ordered the gates opened and watched the guardsmen and wagons leave. Each swordsman carried a bag of grain on his back in addition to his weapons, and the carts were creaking under the load. Convicts and slaves, lured on the expedition with promises of freedom and now sent back toward the city with staggering loads on their backs, old oxen, carts with creaking wheels, all filed out with the proud guardsmen. A thousand soldiers and three hundred bearers left the camp before the gates were closed. MacKinnie returned to his tent. After a few moments, Stark and Longway joined him by his fire.

"They'll never make ten kilometers by morning," Stark said. "Not the way they loaded themselves."

"I thought the priest gave them reasonable loads," Longway said. "They did not seem excessive."

"Sure, but the Trader gave them the pick of the loot before they set out. Wasn't a man there wasn't carrying five, ten kilos of junk stripped off the dead or picked up in this camp."

"That was generous of you," Longway said. "Extraordinarily so."

"There will be other loot," MacKinnie told them.

"We'll have plenty chances to get rich, but they won't. They've earned their share."

"Or will," Stark muttered. MacKinnie looked quickly at him, then stared at the fire in silence as Mary Graham joined the little group.

"Best get some sleep," MacKinnie told her. "We start early in the morning, and it's late enough now."

"I don't really need it," she laughed. "I ride a cart, remember?"

"Lady, you can sleep in that cart under way, you'll be the greatest soldier's wife ever lived," Stark observed. "I'd rather walk, the way those things fall into every hole in the ground."

Mary laughed, looked around furtively, then said, "You wouldn't think the Empire would fall if we told them how to put springs in the carts, would you? But I guess it's too late now." She looked around her at the camp. The spear and shield troops were asleep in place around the perimeter, their shields propped up behind the palisade, pikes and spears ready at hand, while guards patrolled outside the perimeter. "I suppose I should start the breakfast fires. No rest for the cooks."

"Don't bother," MacKinnie said. "There won't be breakfast in the morning. Another hour and I'll roust out the men I'm taking with me. You can feed the rest when we're gone if the enemy gives you time. I'll leave MacLean in command here."

"You're dividing your force, Trader?" Longway asked. "That seems unreasonable. How long will you be gone?"

"One day should do it, one way or another. Don't worry about it, Academician, we won't leave you for long."

"What is all this?" Mary asked. "There's something strange going on here! I don't think I like this at all."

"Just get some rest," MacKinnie told her. "Or if you can't do that, please excuse me while I sleep. We'll have to be up early, Hal. Have the guard call me an hour before first light. My apologies, but I can't think clearly when I've had no sleep, and the enemy is still far too dangerous for my mind to be fogged." He strode to his tent and closed the flap. After a few moments, Longway went back to his quarters.

"Hal, what is wrong with him?" Mary asked. "There's something going on, isn't there?"

"Freelady, he doesn't like what he's had to do. I can't say I like it much either, but we didn't see any other way. Now do as he says and go to sleep. I reckon I'd better lie down a couple of hours myself."

★18★
THE PRICE OF LOOT
★★★

"Time, Colonel."

"Uh." MacKinnie struggled to wakefulness.

"Hour before dawn," Stark said. "Here." He gave MacKinnie a steaming cup of tea.

Nathan drank gratefully. "Thanks." He regretted again that there was neither coffee nor chickeest on Makassar. It might have been worse, he reflected. At least there was tea.

The night was dark. Both moons had set, and low clouds obscured most of the stars. The camp was invisible, but MacKinnie heard the men quietly coming awake. They spoke in whispers, with occasional louder curses and orders for silence breaking the low hiss of conversation. Nathan pulled on his boots and went to the cook area. His officers and noncoms were already gathering there.

He spoke to them in low tones. "I'm concerned about Father Sumbavu's group," he said. "We'll take First and Second battalions and the knights out to cover them. The rest will stay here to guard the camp, with MacLean in charge. Be ready to march in ten minutes."

"Is it wise to divide the force?" MacLean asked.

"Wise or not, I'm doing it," MacKinnie snapped. "I'm not accustomed to discussing my orders, Mister MacLean."

"Sir," MacLean answered.

"All right, move," Stark said. He waited until the others had left. "Pretty good troops," he said. "Not much protest at all. 'Course winning a big battle yesterday didn't hurt. Does wonders for discipline."

When the troops were assembled, MacKinnie sent half the spearmen to the walls. The other half, with the knights, were marched out the camp gate. Once outside they turned due east, a right angle to the road to the city. There were mutters from the ranks, but no one questioned him.

When they were a kilometer from the camp MacKinnie turned the detachment toward the city, forming them into two columns of fours with the cavalry inside. They marched in silence without drums, and Stark moved up and down the line to see that each man kept his equipment from rattling.

The sky turned gray, then crimson. When it was light enough to see men fifty meters away, Hal Stark caught up to MacKinnie at the head of the column. "They move pretty fast without wagons and junk," Stark said. "Ought to be able to keep up this pace all morning."

"We'll need to," MacKinnie said. He found it difficult to judge the capabilities of the native troops, and he couldn't use his own abilities as a guide; months on Makassar had softened them, but the Samualites were generally stronger than the natives, and nearly all tasks seemed easier, exactly as Midshipman Landry had predicted.

The sun was nearly up when Stark sent for MacKinnie. When Nathan joined him at the point, Stark showed him deep tracks left by Sumbavu's baggage carts. "Hard to tell how far they are ahead of us," Stark said. "No more'n an hour, I'd say."

"Loaded as they were, they can't be too far," MacKinnie said. "Okay, I want flankers out to both sides. They'll slow us down, but this is good ambush terrain. And let's make tune."

They swung on in silence, now and again changing positions to send fresh men to lead the escorting flankers. It was hard work to break trail in the waist-high grasslike vegetation. The low hills of the plain closed around them, and MacKinnie rushed forward each time they topped a rise. Then, as they approached one low hill, they heard shouts from the other side. When they drew closer, the sounds resolved into the din of a battle.

"Deploy the troops," MacKinnie said softly. "Columns of fours to each side."

The parallel columns split apart, angling out to form two lines, then continued their advance up the hill in silence. The men readied their weapons and helped each other sling their shields properly.

"Draw swords," MacKinnie ordered. "Double time."

They trotted up the final ten meters to the top of the rise. The sounds of battle grew louder. Then they could see the low valley beyond.

A thousand barbarians had swarmed over Sumbavu's column and destroyed it. There were so few survivors that at first MacKinnie saw none at all, but a few Temple swordsmen were huddled in knots of ten or twenty around the makeshift protection of the baggage carts. The maris swept toward them firing arrows and leaping on them with their swords. Even as MacKinnie and Stark watched, another tiny group of scarlet livery vanished beneath a wave of plainsmen.

"Make your charge straight through them," MacKinnie told Vanjynk. "Cut through and go past, then wheel, dress ranks, and charge home again. Don't stop to play with them, stay together as you've been taught. Now go."

Brett and Vanjynk waved the knights forward. The heavily armored horsemen gathered momentum as they rode down the gentle hill, changed from trot to canter, building speed as they rode toward the enemy.

As soon as the knights were in motion the infantry shield wall began its advance. Drums sounded quickstep, then double time as fuglemen shouted frantic orders to dress ranks and keep in line. The wall moved forward.

The maris saw the wave of horsemen plunging toward them and leaped for their mounts, scattering the loot they had been so anxious to gain, but it was too late. The lances came down, and now that they had been seen, MacKinnie waved to the trumpeters. The notes carried easily over the dewy plains as the knights charged home. Lances shattered, swords were torn from scabbards as the knights shouted in triumph. A few remained to fight, wheeling about until they were pulled from their saddles by the lassos of the maris, or their mounts were shot from beneath them. The rest galloped past, riding the enemy down, thundering down the entire line of barbarians before wheeling at the top of the next rise.

The horsemen had broken the enemy when the shieldsmen arrived. Once again the wings of the shield line closed inward, trapping the enemy between ranks, while the knights charged home again, throwing back into the trap any of the barbarians who had attempted to escape, the momentum of their charge crushing all resistance. The plainsmen caught between the lines had no chance. They could impale themselves on the spears of the shield wall, or wait to be trampled by the knights. This time the slaughter was done quickly, for no one attempted to attack the infantry from behind. The plainsmen who escaped were glad of their lives.

They found Sumbavu at the head of the column, a group of swordsmen dead around his body. He clutched a sword with one hand and a crucifix with the other, and his eyes stared at the heavens. There were no more than fifty survivors in his entire command.

MacKinnie grimly formed his troops into columns and marched back to his camp, the carts rattling over the rutted plains, the groans of the wounded sounding over the creak of their wheels.

MacKinnie rested his men through the next day. In the late afternoon, a small party of plainsmen approached, wheeled outside arrow-shot, and waved feathered lances above their heads.

"He wants to talk to you," Brett said. "It doesn't happen very often with city people, but they do have ways of ending wars between clans. He's treating you as the chief of a very powerful clan. The men behind him are family heads."

"How do I meet him?" MacKinnie asked.

"Go outside the gate with a group of retainers. I doubt if he'll trust you not to shoot him if he gets in close range. It's what always happens when they deal with city people."

"Can you talk to him? Do you speak their language?"

"You know I do, star man, and you know why. I'll come with you if you like."

MacKinnie took Brett and young Todd, leaving Stark and MacLean in command. Longway puffed after them, insisting, and MacKinnie invited him along. They walked out from the camp until they were near the extreme range of a crossbow, then halted, still barely within covering fire if it were needed.

Three figures detached themselves from the group, dismounted, and strode purposefully toward MacKinnie. A few feet away they grounded their lances and spread their arms wide. One spoke swiftly in a musical language MacKinnie had never heard.

"He says he comes to speak," Brett said. "He says you fight like a great chief. He says never before have the robed fools fought so well."

"Tell him he has fought well and we admire the courage of his men."

Brett translated. Before the mari chief could answer, MacKinnie said, "Now tell him I am a great prince from the south, and that I have come in a ship. Tell him a thousand more ships full of men like mine are coming, with many horses, and we will cover the plains. Tell him his brave people will kill many of us, but more will come, and soon there will be many dead on these fields."

"It is customary to exchange more compliments."

"Give him a few. Tell him how brave his men are, and how well they fought. Then tell him what I said."

Brett spoke at length, waited for a reply, and said, "He says he is honored to meet a great prince from the south. He says he knew you could not be from the city. He asks how you will catch him."

"Say that we will come to his home in midwinter. We will burn his food and kill his beasts. But we do not wish to do this, for many of my strong men will die, and many of his brave warriors, and all for nothing."

"That ought to impress him," Brett said. He chattered to the plainsman.

This time there was a long pause, then a longer reply from the mari.

Brett listened carefully. "You've impressed him," the singer said. "He's afraid of that walking wall of yours. He can imagine your troops pounding along in the snow, and it bothers him. They don't like to fight in the winter, and he doesn't think you would like it much either. He wants to know why you would go to so much trouble."

"Say I'm a madman," MacKinnie said. "Or will that work?"

"It might. They're familiar with fanatics."

"Good. Then I'm a fanatic dedicated to saving the Temple."

Brett spoke again, listened, and said "He's about ready to believe anything about you. He asks you to speak again. That means he hasn't any reply."

"Tell him any way you want to," MacKinnie answered, "but here are my terms. They can have two days to get out of here. They burn nothing else, but they may carry away whatever they can. At the end of that time, we'll kill every one of them we find. And if they make any more hostile moves after today, we'll follow him to the end of the continent and burn all his villages and kill all his livestock. Make sure he knows that's not an idle threat."

"He's not responsible for all of the maris," Brett said. "Just his own clan. He can't promise for the rest."

"Is this the leader of the biggest group?"

"One of the largest clans, yes."

"Then he'll have to figure out how to drive the others out. He ought to be able to do it, but anyway that's his problem, not mine. Tell him that."

Brett looked pale for a moment. He seemed about to say something to MacKinnie, but Nathan's look stopped him. He turned to the mari chief and spoke at length.

The sinewy chief answered, then another of the attendants shouted. Brett shouted back, and their voices rose angrily before the chief spoke again more calmly. Finally Brett turned back to Nathan. "He'll try. Some of the others have already left. He'll get the rest to go along. They wanted more time, but I told them you really were a madman, that you'd taken an oath never to end the war if it didn't end now. They're still arguing about it, but it's obvious they're afraid of your army. I think they'll go."

★19★
THE HOLY RELICS
★ ★ ★

They entered the city in triumph. Although MacKinnie sent no word ahead, the wagons loaded with grain told enough; by the time the army reached the city gates, thousands had turned out to line the streets. Hundreds more spilled outside the gates and ran emotionally to greet the soldiers. The sound of their cheering was deafening.

It took nearly an hour to march up the winding streets to the Temple's huge courtyard. MacKinnie sent a group ahead to keep the courtyard clear of civilians, and eventually brought the troops and commissary wagons inside. "There'll be celebration enough tonight," he told his officers. "For the moment let's get the men fed and give them some rest."

"We have won a great victory," one of the knights protested. "Now we enjoy the rewards. . . ."

"Certainly," MacKinnie said. "The knights are excused. But we can't totally disperse the army. The maris seem to be leaving, true enough, but we'll need to be able to back up my threats if any of them change their minds. There'll be plenty of revelry right here. I've sent for a whole warehouse of wine. One of you go invite all the Temple soldiers who had to stay behind. They were willing to go, and they ought to share in the fun."

He dismissed the officers, but kept Stark back. "I need the headquarters company now," MacKinnie said.

"Yes, sir. They're ready. It's all planned."

"Good. Send them in. And send a runner for those Imperial churchmen."

"Your reverence," MacKinnie told Casteliano, "you are now in command of this Temple."

The Archbishop was startled. "How is this?" he demanded.

"The only military forces left in this city are a couple of hundred archers, about that many swordsmen, the knights, and my army. Most of them—including the Temple swordsmen—are getting drunk out in the courtyard. The only comparatively sober troops are my headquarters company."

"But—what does this mean?"

Laraine asked. "It means we own the place," MacKinnie said. "Who's to oppose us? The knights aren't any match for the pike-men in a street fight, and the pikes will stay loyal to me for a while at least."

"Surely you do not expect to make war on the Temple," Laraine protested. "We have no wish to wade in blood to the high altar."

"It shouldn't come to that. We've sent a picked force to

the key points. The Temple itself is already ours. Now we've got to tell their ruling council and that Pope of theirs who's in charge."

"Would your men really fight against the Temple?" Casteliano asked.

"Most of them would," Stark said. "Remember who we recruited. They were mostly slaves, and peasants down on their luck. And they've won victories under the—the Trader. They'd fight for him."

"We'd rather not," MacKinnie said. "It'd be hard to control the looting, and there might be fires. Civil wars are never pretty—"

"No. They are not," Casteliano said. He stroked his chin thoughtfully. "And you have not yet informed the ruling council of the changed state of affairs? Good." He turned to Laraine and Deluca. "Go quickly and get vestments. The best we have, and our most ornate trappings. Trader MacKinnie, will you lend us some of your men as attendants? And if you will have your most regal clothing brought to you that would help as well. I believe there is a way this can be done without bloodshed."

"I hope so," MacKinnie said. "Stark will see that you get what you need from us."

"Excellent." Casteliano went to the battlement and looked down at the courtyard. The guards at the gates had left their posts. Civilians, Temple swordsmen, archers, knights, commissary troops all danced in great circles, pausing only to scoop cups of wine from open barrels.

"Look there," MacKinnie said quietly. He pointed to the wide battlemented walls above the courtyard.

Grim-faced pikemen and shieldsmen stood in knots of five at all the crossings.

"I see." Casteliano continued to stare down at the courtyard. "I also see that you brought back none of the Temple swordsmen, and not all of their archers. How did Father Sumbavu die?"

"He was killed with his men in an ambush," MacKinnie said slowly.

"But you were not caught?"

"Sumbavu was bringing supplies back to the city. I went to his aid, but we were too late. We could avenge him, but we couldn't save him."

"I see. A thousand brave men, who served you well. A high price to pay for a city."

"Damned high," MacKinnie muttered. "God help me, there was no other way. You've seen those Temple fanatics. We'd have to kill every one of those soldiers before they'd let us inspect their holy relics."

Casteliano turned away from the wall. "The relics. What is your interest in those?" He inspected Nathan carefully. "Whatever your reason, you have done the Church a service, and we will not forget."

"Thank you."

"And now we must speak to their council. Your pardon, Trader, I must find a room where we can dress properly for the interview—and I would be most grateful if you would bring a dozen of your most loyal men." He paused. "I doubt it will come to battle. Most of those on the council are practical men. As are we. Our demands will not be excessive, and we must be careful not to humiliate them. And of course the maris are not yet gone—"

"Precisely," MacKinnie said.

"Thus we have reason with us," Casteliano said. "And if that fails—"

MacKinnie gestured toward a group of pikemen on the battlements. "Then there is another argument."

Two days later, MacKinnie begged audience with His Ultimate Holiness, Primate of all Makassar, Vicar of Christ, and Archbishop of New Rome. He was led into a small office behind the council room where Casteliano was seated in his shirtsleeves examining Temple records. The Archbishop looked up and smiled.

"It was easier than you thought, was it not?" he said.

"Yes, Your Reverence. I still find it hard to believe that we had no bloodshed. But my men remain on guard, just in case."

"I told you there were few doctrinal differences, and these men are not only realists, but believers. If we had approached them from a Navy landing ship and demanded obedience to New Rome, we would have had to demonstrate our power, but it would have been managed. As it was, arriving in the city like beggars, they would never listen to us. How could they believe we were great lords of the True Church from the stars? But with you at our side, and your soldiers commanding their Temple, they had little choice but to listen."

"You were highly persuasive, Your Reverence."

"As were your actions. It was not difficult to make them see the hand of God in your victory, and His wrath in the death of Sumbavu. Did you foresee that as well?"

"No, Your Reverence."

"It is as well. Now what may I do for you?"

"I don't know how to begin. Yet I must have your help. I see no other way."

"Colonel—do not be surprised, the title is commonly used by your soldiers—you hold this Temple, not me. You could depose me as easily as you created me, particularly if you supported the council against me. What is it I can do that you cannot do for yourself? Do you want to be crowned king of this city? They would do that for you."

MacKinnie laughed. "Nothing that simple. But—but may I speak to you in confidence? Have I earned the right to ask something which, if you refuse, you will not thwart me from attempting another way?"

The Archbishop took a small strip of cloth from the table in front of him, kissed it, and placed it over his shoulders. "My son, for thousands of years the confessional has never been violated. By tradition, by the laws of God, and by the most stringent of Imperial edicts, what you tell me in confession can never be revealed. Have you something to confess?"

Nathan MacKinnie breathed deeply, stared at the old man, and thought for a moment before beginning. "All right. As you surmised, we are from a newly discovered planet which will be a colony world when they get around to classifying us. They won't do that until we have a working planetary government, and King David's advisors are managing to delay that. They won't be able to hold up too much longer. We want to build a spaceship before they make us a colony world."

"A spaceship! Just how advanced are you? What makes you think . . . no, how does this affect me?"

"Father, I came here to get copies of every technical work I can find in that library. Our people think we can do it if we know how. I'm a soldier, not a scientist, and I don't know if they can do it or not, but we've got to try!"

The Archbishop nodded. "You would try. Tell me, Colonel MacKinnie, are you typical of the people of your planet?"

"I don't know. In some ways, yes. Why?"

"Because, and I say it reverently, God help the colonists they send to your world if you are. You don't know when to give up. Yes, I'll help you." He thought for a few moments, then laughed. "And we'll stay within the letter of the regulations. Although I doubt that would impress a Navy court martial if they found you smuggling copies of technical books. Makassar was classified before they discovered the library, and so far they haven't updated it. The classification is 'primitive.' Therefore, any art or craft found here can be taken to any other part of the Empire.

"So, yes, we'll help you and gladly. Think what a splendid joke on the Imperial Traders Association this will make!" He struck a small gong on the desk and told the servant who entered in response, "Go to the holy relics and bring Brother LeMoyne, if you please."

LeMoyne was a small man with sandy hair and flashing blue eyes. He knelt perfunctorily before Casteliano, kissed his ring, and said, "And what may I do for His Ultimate Holiness other than refrain from letting New Rome know his present title?"

The Archbishop laughed. "You can see why he will

never be a bishop. Tell me, can you make the holy relics speak yet?"

"The library is in amazingly good condition, Your Reverence. The Navy technicians fixed much of the equipment when they made copies of the tapes. The Old Empire used nearly indestructible plastics, and everything has been preserved with holy zeal. It only needs a power source to make it work."

"What kind of power?" MacKinnie asked.

"Oh, any good source of current. It doesn't take a lot. Very efficient people, the Old Imperials. They powered the whole palace from a small direct conversion unit taking heat from natural hot springs. That's still working, but the regulators aren't. The unit is putting out so little power now that it won't run much of the system—but we can get a few watts from it, after more than three hundred years! They built better than they knew in those days."

Casteliano nodded sadly. "Their equipment was splendid. But it didn't save them."

"No. Anyway, in addition to the old power unit, we have a hand-powered generator the Navy left. We've got part of the reader working off that, and it won't take long to get everything else in order. Uh, it would be no great trick to build a powered generator, but we couldn't let the natives see it operate."

"I think not for the moment," Casteliano said. "The Church has sometimes evaded the technology transfer restrictions, but that is a serious matter, not to be done without much thought. We need the Navy's cooperation." He paused thoughtfully. "Trader MacKinnie would like to inspect the library if that is convenient."

"Certainly. Now?" LeMoyne asked.

"Yes," MacKinnie said. "And if you could send for one of my people, Kleinst—"

"Oh, he's been down there helping me all morning," LeMoyne said. "Does His Ultimate Holiness care to accompany us?"

Casteliano looked in dismay at the litter of parchment on his desk. "I would be delighted, but this work must be done." He sighed. "Get thee behind me, Satan—"

LeMoyne shrugged and led MacKinnie out of the office. They went down winding stone stairways until they reached massive doorways guarded by four pikemen and a crimson-uniformed Temple officer. The pikemen snapped to attention as MacKinnie approached.

The officer looked doubtful. "He is a layman. Only the consecrated may enter—"

"Who'll stop the colonel?" one of the pikemen asked.

"He has been sent by His Ultimate Holiness," LeMoyne said. "Man, do you not know that if it had not been for the colonel, the *maris* would have the relics?"

"True," the Temple officer said. He took torches from the wall and handed them to MacKinnie and LeMoyne, then stood aside. He did not look pleased.

There were two more guardrooms, but these were empty. Then they went down a broader stairway of marble.

"This is almost certainly Old Empire," LeMoyne said. "After the wars, the survivors built most of the Temple structure over it. Here we are, just beyond that doorway."

They went through. At last, MacKinnie thought. I've come a long way to see this—

The room was not large. It stank of fish oil from the lamps. The walls had been scrubbed innumerable times to remove lampblack, and there was only a tiny suggestion of design or color to them.

There was not much else to see. A small box with crank handles and a seat stood in the middle of the room. Wires ran from that to a small table set against one wall. Above the table was what looked like a dark windowpane. Kleinst, wearing a dark monk's hood, sat in front of the desk. He stood when MacKinnie entered.

Nathan looked around the room in confusion. "Where is this fabulous machinery?" he asked.

LeMoyne chuckled. "Your friend there asked the same question." He pointed at the table. "There it is."

"No more than that?"

LeMoyne nodded. "No more than that. You could put all the knowledge of the human race in four units like that."

MacKinnie did not believe him, but there was no point in arguing. He turned to Kleinst. "Have you made any progress?"

The scholar's eyes gleamed. "Yes! Would you like to see?"

"Of course—"

"The sound units?" Kleinst asked, looking to LeMoyne. When LeMoyne nodded, Kleinst sat again at the console and touched small squares on it.

A tiny voice came from the walls. MacKinnie looked around in amazement.

"And except those days be shortened, there should not be any living creature survive," the voice said.

"Matthew," LeMoyne said, "Whoever was last down here loaded in that. The Temple priests have been listening to it ever since. They don't know how to change record units. The audio unit discharges the accumulators in less than an hour and the power system is so weak that it takes days to charge up again."

MacKinnie shook his head. "Do you understand this?" he asked Kleinst.

"Yes! Or almost. It is a new concept, yet not in principle different from photographic and recording equipment we use at home. Although more compact. And I don't understand everything about it. I don't know if we could read the tapes and cubes if we had them back at the University."

"And if we can't?" MacKinnie demanded. "Then I must learn what we need," Kleinst said. "I have a photographic memory. It is one reason I was selected for this journey."

"There are many blanks in storage," LeMoyne said. "It will not be difficult to copy them. But I fear your friend is correct. The equipment needed to read these records is very complex." He went to a small, ornately carved cabinet near the table and laughed. "They made this into a tabernacle," he said. He opened it and took out a small block. "We could put most of what you need in two or three of these, if only you had means to read it."

"Copying them is simple!" Kleinst exclaimed. "Once we have more electrical power we can copy—and there is everything here! Textbooks for children which tell of physical laws no one at home has understood for hundreds of years. Handbooks, maintenance manuals for equipment I can't describe—look! Sit down there." He pointed to the box with handles. "Sit there, and turn that crank, and I will show you marvels—"

MacKinnie shrugged and did as he was told. The box made a whining noise as he spun the handles.

The dark glass above the table came to light. A diagram of some kind of complex equipment appeared. Then words.

"See!" Kleinst shouted.

"What does it mean?" MacKinnie asked.

"I don't know. But—with time I will. And if not, some of the younger students can be trained. We will learn."

"We have to," MacKinnie said.

"I don't quite understand who you are," LeMoyne said. "But if His Reverence is satisfied, I am."

"How long?" MacKinnie asked. "How long until we can have copies of everything?"

LeMoyne pursed his lips. "How long can you turn that crank?"

"It's tiring. An hour, perhaps—"

"It would be useful to build a powered unit, but that is not easily done down here. If we could move this up to where we could connect water power—"

"Impossible," MacKinnie said. "We hold this Temple, true, but these people are volatile. If we moved the relics they'd be scandalized, and God knows what they'd do."

"Then you had better put your own officers to guard the doors," LeMoyne said. "We can make the copies in four hours, but—"

"But indeed. But how long for you to learn?" MacKinnie asked Kleinst.

"I could study for years and not learn it all—"

"We don't have years. We have weeks at most."

"I know," Kleinst said. "I will do the best I can. And we will make the copies . . . ."

"Which we may not be able to read," MacKinnie sighed. "The winter storms are coming. And we don't know what's happening at home. I know you'll do your best."

★20★
JURAMENTADO
★ ★ ★

Firelight flickered across an old man's face.

Datu Attik's eyes dimmed with hidden tears as he watched two *juramentados* complete their ritual washing. The women came forward to hold high the crimson cloths for the binding. The young men's bodies shone in the yellow firelight.

They sang. Their death chants rang through the darkness around the camp. Otherwise there was silence. Later the others of the band, warriors and women alike, would sing death chants for these two, but for now the tribe had seen too much of death.

Eight hundred of the clan lay beneath the wheat stubble beyond the fire. Eight hundred stiffened and cold in the earth, eight hundred among the thousands who had fallen to the Temple army. How would the clan live without the young men? And now two more would join them, and one the son of the Datu.

Futile. Futile, thought Datu Attik. My son will die, and for nothing, for less than nothing, for worse than nothing.

The Temple is strong. The robed fools have found new strength with their new sultan.

He ground his teeth at the memory. It had been so nearly done! The black-robed ones of the Great Temple of Batav had been defeated, done, were finished, penned into their city to starve while the maris roamed at will, ate the city's crops, rode to the very walls in challenge and laughed at the black robes—

And then came the new sultan from the far west, a giant of a man who made walls march and destroyed the greatest force the maris had ever assembled together.

It was done, it was done, Allah's will was done, and the maris must now return to their barren hills, but first let the city feel sorrow as the maris sorrowed. Let no man say his triumph was complete. Let the Temple mourn as Datu Attik mourned.

"No good will come of this." The voice came from his right side, from where his second son lay at his father's feet. "The sultan cannot be killed. My brother will make new war, and it is war we cannot win."

"Silence. Your brother sings his farewell." But it was true, Datu Attik thought. The sultan has said that if there is more war between the maris and the Temple, the marching walls will come to the fields in winter and pursue the maris to the end of the world.

He will do as he has said, and my sons will die, and my people will die. Why has Allah spared me to watch? Does He hate me so?

The song of the juramentados burst out and struck Attik like a blow, and the old man knew it was too late. These messengers of death could not be turned from their task, not by him or by anyone. Only their death would slow them now.

"O God Thou are Almighty, Allah Thou are Almighty, we witness that God is one God, we witness that Allah is Almighty!

"When the leaves of the Book shall be unrolled, when Hell shall blaze forth, when Paradise is near, then shall every soul know what works it hath made! Witness that Allah is One, witness that Allah is Almighty!"

Veiled women came now to aid the juramentados. They bound the young bodies tightly with scarlet cloths, tightly to hold the blood, scarlet to hide the blood from their enemies. Young, young men, his son was a young man, and now would die, but he would die for the glory of Allah— His second son brought a kriss and Attik raised it to his lips, then passed it to the lips of his first son. "Then shall every soul know the works it hath made," Attik chanted. "So saith Allah, so saith the Almighty, every man shall submit to the will of Allah. Witness that Allah is One, witness that Allah is Almighty."

"Worthy is Allah to be praised."

The death songs hung over the camp long after the juramentados vanished into the night beyond the yellow circle of firelight. They were gone, running toward the city of Batav.

Faint sounds came from the city to the campsite: sounds of song and joy; the sounds of men and women in triumph. Datu Attik heard and shook his fist toward the magnificent blaze of the Temple rising above the city walls.

Temple!

The Temple of God, the Temple which held the very voice of God! The Temple stolen by the black-robed priests of Batav, the Temple which was so nearly in the grasp of the maris. For generation upon generation the false priests of false gods had held the Temple from the faithful. Attik's grandfather was old when he died, and the oldest men his grandfather had known in his youth could not remember when the Temple was not held by the worshippers of the Prophet Jesus.

But Attik knew. Once there had been a time when men flew above the plains of Makassar, flew up to the very stars above. It was a time when God was not angry with men, and in that time the Temple was open so that all men could hear the words of God.

Surely Allah would not forever hold his people from his Word. Surely the juramentados would find the sultan MacKinnie, and then, and then—the maris might yet take the Temple! There were yet enough, and without the sultan to lead them, the black-robes might return to their futile ways of war—

"It shall be as Allah wills," Attik said aloud. "I submit to the will of Allah."

Then, since he was a practical man, Attik ordered the clan to prepare for their journey. It might be well to be far from the city when the juramentados struck. The sultan had ordered them away from the city plains in three days' time, and that time was nearly past.

If the juramentados met success, there would be time to gather the clans and return. Without their sultan the Temple priests would lose battles as they did in the past, and the Temple would fall.

The Temple for Allah, and the city of Batav for the maris. The city, that lovely city—

The sack of Batav could go on for days!

★21★
WAR RECALLED
★★★

The celebrations continued for days. Monks' cells in the hollow of the walls of the great Temple lay empty as even the silent orders found release from their vows. Songs of triumph rose from the massive brooding walls to blend with the Te Deum sung in the Temple Sanctuary.

MacKinnie stood atop the highest Temple battlement and looked up into the night sky toward his home a dozen light-years away. A river of stars ran across the sky, so that it was difficult to locate the star that shone on his world.

The stars belonged to the Empire of Man, and looking up at the myriad of lights MacKinnie could appreciate the problems of the Imperial Navy. How could there be peace among all those and yet each have freedom? The legendary time when Prince Samual's World was united and there were no wars was remembered as a golden age, yet unification had remained a dream and spawned a dozen wars; and that was only one world. The Empire had hundreds, perhaps thousands—he couldn't know. More worlds than there were nations or city-states on Samual.

"Sir?"

He turned at Stark's approach. "Yes, Hal?"

"I brought the shipmaster."

MacKinnie once again marveled at the varieties of man. People on Prince Samual's World were varied enough, but nothing like what he had seen on Makassar. There were the tall, fair men like Vanjynk, and the dark, swarthy men like Loholo; the Imperial Navy even had black men and women. On Samual "black men" were legendary monsters who lived in the hills and ate children. . . .

Loholo stood respectfully and waited for MacKinnie to speak.

"Shipmaster, I must return to Jikar. When can we sail?" MacKinnie asked.

Loholo shrugged. "She is ready now. It will be no easy journey. Much of the time the wind will be in our faces. There is better trading to the east and south . . . and there will be storms."

"Aye." MacKinnie shuddered. Now that they were ashore he could admit that he'd been terrified. But there was no other way. Or was there? "Could we sail east to get there?"

"East? You believe the tales that Makassar is round— but you would know, star man. You would know." Loholo shrugged, jingling the golden ornaments he wore. His curved dagger bore new jewels on the hilt, and there were new rings on his fingers. "I have known of men who believed the world round and sailed east to reach the western shores," he said. "But I never heard of one who arrived. Trader, there are shoals west of Jikar, and there are pirates throughout the islands. *Subao* is faster than they, but there are many pirates. Those are the western waters I know. What else may lay between here and there—" He shrugged again to a jingle of gold. "Only God knows."

God and the Imperial Navy, MacKinnie thought. From the maps they had shown him there was a lot of open water to the east of the main continent. Loholo was probably right. "I had thought as much," MacKinnie said. "So there's nothing for it. We sail in five days."

"So soon? You will hardly have time to buy a cargo. It would be much better to wait until next season."

"No. I must reach Jikar in two hundred days," MacKinnie said.

Loholo chuckled. "Then you will have an uncomfortable voyage. Two thousand klamaters in two hundred days." The sea captain laughed again. "In this season. Well, *Subao* can withstand that—but can you? And why leave Batav at all? You rule here. The priestly star man is Ultimate Holiness, but he came to the throne on your pikes, and did not your pikemen hold the city the old council would elect a new Holiness inside three days."

"And that's a fact," Stark said. "There's some in the new council who'd support Casteliano, but you can't expect all them old Archdeacons to take kindly to the Imperial missionaries movin' in on 'em like that. Mister Loholo's right, there'd be civil war if it wasn't that our troops hold all the strong points."

"Which means I can't take the whole army across the plains," MacKinnie said. "Or if I did, I'd have to take the Imperial missionaries with me—"

"They're not likely to come," Stark observed.

"Exactly. And they won't continue helping us if we take them as prisoners." MacKinnie glanced upward at the stars and thought again of the problems of empire. "So it's by sea. Leave the pikemen here and hope the missionaries know what to do with them. Thank you, Mister Loholo. That will be all."

"Trader?" Loholo made no move to leave.

"Yes?"

"Trader, you promised me *Subao* when we returned to Jikar."

"She'll be yours, Mister Loholo."

"Aye. Then with your permission I'll get back to her. There's still work to be done. Bottom to be scraped, new water barrels, provisions—but if there's a place by water on this world that you want to go to, I'll take you, even if we pass every pirate in the shallows!" Loholo fingered the golden skull ornament at his left ear. "You're the strangest man I've ever seen, Trader. You've shown us how to make ships sail better than we ever knew. You trained an army of city rabble and took them out to whip the barbarians after the Temple people gave up. Now you're in command of the Temple and all Batav, and you want to return to Jikar! Most men would rather stay here as king—and there'd be no nonsense about it, either. You've only to say the word—"

"And you could be my High Admiral, Mister Loholo?"

"No, sir. Your star man Captain MacLean would have that post, and I'm not that ambitious. *Subao's* enough for me, star man. A good ship and open sea's all my father wanted for any of his children."

Loholo began the long descent down the stone stairway to the street below, and MacKinnie turned away to lean on the ramparts. Batav was a blaze of lights, with bonfires in all the public squares. Every one of the city's thirty thousand souls seemed to be reveling in the streets, their numbers swollen by another thirty thousand peasants who had sought refuge within the city walls. The peasants would soon go back to their fields, and the remnants of Batav's great feudal families, all those who survived the futile charges against the maris before MacKinnie arrived, would return to their great halls and tournaments—

And then what? "Getting control of that damned library was easier than letting loose," MacKinnie said. "I'm concerned about the missionaries. Can they hold on after we leave?"

"I doubt it. Not without a good commander who knows how you fight."

"Could Brett hold the Temple?" MacKinnie asked.

Stark shrugged. "He's maybe smart enough, but they'd never trust him. He was raised a mari, sure enough, and it shows. Nobody's going to put him in command."

"Then who can do it?"

"You."

"And no one else, Sergeant?"

"Not that I know of, Colonel. You built this army, and you know what it can do. The others don't think like you."

"And that worries you?" MacKinnie asked.

"Don't get paid to worry," Stark said automatically. "Except—"

He's in a strange mood, MacKinnie thought. He really is worried. I haven't seen him that way since—

"You know," Stark said, "Mister Loholo's got a point, Colonel. A year ago we was down to it, looking for a place fightin' in some petty war on South Continent and wonderin' how to pay the rent on a flophouse until we found something. We never expected to find anything as good as we've got now."

"I gave Dougal my word, and I swore allegiance to King David," MacKinnie reminded him.

"After Haven used the goddam Empire to bake half our Wolves, Colonel! They'd never have took Orleans without the Imperial Marines . . . and then they turned you out like an old dog! What do we really owe Haven, Colonel? What do we owe anybody?"

MacKinnie turned to his sergeant in surprise. "We're soldiers, Hal. It's all either of us has ever been—"

"Soldiers for who, Colonel? You owe Haven any more'n you owe Batav? If it wasn't for them peasant kids we trained we'd never have beat the maris. Them boys would follow you to hell, and what's goin' to happen to 'em if we pull up stakes and leave? And when we get back to Haven, that Dougal's likely to slit our throats to shut us up. What use are we to him after we bring back them books or whatever it is Kleinst has got? There's not much for us back on Samual, and that's the size of it—" Stark turned quickly and grasped the hilt of his sword. "Watch out, Colonel, there's somebody comin' up the stairs."

"Go see who it is." There were guards posted at the foot of the stairway to MacKinnie's penthouse, and from the sounds there was only one person approaching. Hal could deal with any single man. Nathan turned back to the battlements.

The revels continued in the city below. Drunken apprentices staggered from shop to shop, demanding that lights be placed in all dark windows on pain of having the building itself burned to provide light. Barrels of wine and ale stood at street corners, open to all comers. But through the drunken reveling MacKinnie's peasant pikemen stood in grim, disciplined knots at the strategic points, waiting for their relief before joining the festivities. . . .

Follow me to hell, MacKinnie thought. Why not? I found them not much better than slaves and now they've just defeated the worst threat this city's ever faced.

Why the hell shouldn't I be king? Because of another duty. . . .

All his life MacKinnie had lived under a soldier's code and like most dueling societies Prince Samual's World held honor higher than life . . . but what was the honorable course now?

Who owns my loyalty? he wondered. Dougal, who had a dozen men and women killed to protect the secret babbled by that drunken Imperial officer? Casteliano, who's Ultimate Holiness courtesy of my pikemen? Or those lads out there? It's obvious what Hal thinks.

"It's Freelady Graham, Colonel," Stark announced.

Mary Graham had taken off her armor and had let her long brown hair fall in waves and curls to below her shoulders. A blue linen gown with tight bodice set off her small figure, and she was much lovelier than she'd been the first time MacKinnie had seen her.

"Nathan, you're missing the party," she said accusingly.

"Can't you ever relax, even for one evening? Let's have some fun!"

MacKinnie was surprised by the possessive tone in her voice. Had he imagined it or—Great Saints, he thought. She's a real beauty tonight. And with her hair let down she looks a lot like Laura. Nearly as headstrong, too. And she's twenty-four, you're fifty, and she's your ward. But—

Unwanted the memories poured past his guard. There had been another girl, once. A freelady, not one of the innumerable camp followers any military commander would know. She was no more than thirty, and it was no more than three years ago. . . .

A bleak picture formed in MacKinnie's mind. Haven, defeated at Blanthern Pass, was on the march again, invading Orleans with inadequate troops and a dangerously thin supply line. And Iron MacKinnie's Wolves were ready, this time ready to end Haven's threat to Orleans forever and aye. When this battle was done, the Orleans Committee of Public Safety could dictate any terms they wanted to David Second!

The Wolves lay in ambush at Lechfeld. Two battalions waited, enough troops to force Haven's invading force to deploy and fight. Lechfeld couldn't be bypassed or the Haven army would be without any possible supply line. Twenty kilometers away, in dense forest, a regiment of Orleans Dragoons moved swiftly through the forest gullies, leading their horses until they reached open country. Above, behind rolling hills overlooking the Lechfeld plains, MacKinnie waited with the balance of his Wolves to close the trap—and the Haven army was moving into it.

The Committee had protested the battle plan. Converging columns were too dangerous. There was no reliable way to communicate between them, even if the University professors did believe they would have reliable wireless soon. The timing of the battle needed great precision or the Orleanists would be defeated in detail.

The Committee had protested, but MacKinnie had won that fight. He knew the capabilities of his troops to the last small unit, and his scouts would cover the battle area. There would be no surprises for Orleans; only for Haven—and the Wolves would not fight at all until Haven was in the trap.

And now they were marching in, and they were doomed. Freelady Laura waited with him in the hills above Lechfeld. He had tried to send her to the rear before, but she came back—and except for Stark there wasn't an officer or a noncom in his command who'd disobey the colonel's lady even on his direct orders. Still, it was safe enough. The losses today would be Haven's! But she was in a place of danger, and that wouldn't do.

"Go to Lechfeld while the road's still open," MacKinnie had told her. "Major Armstrong is well dug in and his position won't be exposed until the battle is over. Meet me in Lechfeld."

She protested, but he needed a message carried, and finally she agreed to go. "We'll be riding at the charge all the way, Laura," he'd said. "You can't keep up with that! We'd be separated anyway. If I can't make you go to the rear—damn your father for letting you out of the house! —I want you safe."

"All right. I won't have you worrying about me when

you should be directing the battle." She sat proudly in the ambulance. The escorting cavalry saluted. Cornet Blair mounted with a flourish, proud to be chosen as protector of his colonel's fiancée.

"And we'll see the chaplain when the battle's ended," MacKinnie promised. "Ride out, Blair."

"Sir." Ambulance and escort rode away in a thin cloud of dust and MacKinnie gave his attention to the Haven forces below. In an hour their advance units appeared. They weren't surprised to meet resistance at Lechfeld and fell back to wait for the rest of the column.

The Haven army deployed skirmishers, then formed a main battle line for attack, their artillery moving forward at the gallop. Trumpet calls rang across plowed fields as Haven's last army prepared for a set piece battle.

It worried Nathan. Haven had better soldiers than that! They'd walked into a classic military trap, and they hadn't even put out guards to their flanks and rear! But MacKinnie's hard-riding scouts, their horses lathered with flecks of white foam, had circled the enemy. They had seen nothing. There were no significant reinforcements, no support at all for the forces moving so blindly into MacKinnie's trap. Haven was doomed.

Why? MacKinnie wondered. It hardly mattered. Perhaps they had planned some clever counter-coup, but there was nothing, nothing at all that they or anyone could do now. . . .

The Orleans Dragoons took the field within minutes of the time MacKinnie had set for them. They advanced and dug in, closing off the Haven column's escape route, forming a solid anvil against which the charging Wolves would crush their enemy, and bow, now it was time! "Mount 'em up, Hal! Move 'em out! Fox and Dragon troops will charge those batteries on the right flank. The rest dismount at five hundred meters and advance on foot. We've got them, Hal, we've beaten everything Haven can put into the field!"

The Wolves charged down the hill, whooping like South Continent barbarians, while the youthful trumpeters blew every call in the book. It was done. The Wolves were in perfect position to roll up Haven's flank—and death fell from the skies. A sleek black shape roared overhead and, as it passed, Lechfeld was turned into a blackened cinder.

And again, again that thing passed overhead, and blinding beams of light stabbed out to burn the Dragoons! Now it hovered over the battlefield, playing its deadly beams across MacKinnie's army.

"Dismount! All troops fire on that thing! Troop Commanders, fire troops in volley! Trumpeter, orders to artillery! Where the hell are those field pieces? Gunners, get those goddam cannons in action!"

Somehow they'd done it. The black shape fell from the skies, settling hard into the cornfields, and when the gray-coated troops in the sky machine came out, the Wolves cut them down and howled in triumph!

Too late. Haven's army was still intact. The Dragoons were dead or running, Lechfeld was gone, and the Wolves had taken terrible casualties. The Haven force wheeled to face right, and for the first time in his life Nathan MacKinnie had known defeat. When the trumpeters sounded recall it was the end of his career, and the end of everything else. Laura had been in Lechfeld. . . .

"Colonel." Stark took his commander by the elbow. "Colonel, it don't do no good to think about it."

"Uh?" The bright fields of Prince Samual's World faded. Awkwardly he turned away from the battlements and let his hands relax. The knuckles were white. "Your pardon, Mary. I was—somewhere else. You're right, let's go join the revels."

★22★
GRACE AND ABSOLUTION
★★★

Mary Graham watched the mad light fade from Nathan MacKinnie's eyes. I know, she thought. I know what he saw. When Hal tells that story, it's like being there.

MacKinnie's voice came from the bottom of a well of emotion. Mary tried to smile reassuringly, but that was impossible.

What must it be like, she wondered. To feel that much for someone? And what was she like, that girl he was thinking about? Hal wouldn't say much about her. I don't even know her name. What was she like, to make a man like MacKinnie feel that way? I'll never have that kind of devotion from anyone.

Have I that much to give?

Yes. I do. I've always been sure of that, that somewhere, somehow—

A little girl's dream.

No. Not that at all. When I was little I thought of a handsome, rich lord and now, well, yes, I've usually thought of him, whoever he'll be, as rich and handsome, but mostly he'll be a man who'll let me be more to him than my father ever let Mother be.

She stared up into the star-studded darkness. That tiny dot is my sun, she thought. One dot among thousands, tiny, insignificant, and yet it was my whole world for all my life until just last year—

A world she no longer cared much for. She had resented the restrictions Haven society put on her, but that had been a formless resentment, almost unconscious. Now she knew better. There were other ways to live, other cultures on other worlds, worlds without end, worlds after worlds, and what was Prince Samual's World, or anyone on it?

We are what we make ourselves. And we can change whole worlds. We're doing that now. Isn't it enough?

She had felt the magic touch of command, of knowing that others depended on her judgment. MacKinnie had won the battles, but without her cooks and supply wagons he couldn't have taken the field. He'd known that, and he'd trusted her, trusted her with the lives of all his men, and his troopers were more important to him than his own life—

"Your turn to be in a blue daze," Nathan said. "What we need is some company."

She nodded and let Nathan and Hal lead her down the stairs to the streets below, but still the pensive mood pursued her. Do we need company? she wondered. Maybe we have too much already. Hal would be happy enough to go join the revels without us. . . .

She almost laughed aloud. A year ago that thought

would have shocked her. Or at least she would have pretended, even to herself, that it did. Properly brought up young ladies didn't have any doubts about what was proper.

Proper young ladies had dull lives.

The streets were alive with people. Where there had formerly been beggars and empty shops there were shouting throngs drowning the bitterness of months of defeat in wine and ale. The barbarians were driven from the gates!

Those who hadn't pawned their finery during the siege now wore it. Several pawnshops had been looted, so that many others were gaily dressed in bright woolens, silks, even cotton prints. A riot of color wove complex patterns through the streets. It seemed the entire city had turned out. Even the saffron-robed members of the Temple minor orders, the gray deacons, and the black-robed full priests joined in the revelry. Only MacKinnie's on-duty pikemen held aloof, and many of them quaffed hastily offered beakers of wine and beer.

"Seems different without them Temple swordsmen," Hal said. "I see the Temple people are already recruitin' more to replace the ones we lost out on the field—"

"Yes." MacKinnie would rather that subject were dropped.

"It was terrible," Mary said. "Father Sumbavu and a thousand swordsmen killed after our victory . . . I can't understand how it happened."

"It always happens," MacKinnie said. "There's always a price."

But what really did happen? she wondered. Had MacKinnie understood Sumbavu so well that he could deliberately use the priest to destroy the Temple army? That was a bit frightening. If he knew Sumbavu that well, how much does he know about me?

What if he did send Sumbavu and all his men out to die? Was there any other way to get control of the Temple? Probably not. Was it worth the price? That's the real question. What are we doing here? What am I doing? From what I've seen I'd rather live in Imperial society than my own—

But Imperial society has no use for me or any of us, women and men alike. Haven does. This mission is important to Haven, and I'm important to the mission, and that ought to be enough. It's more than I ever dreamed of. Except that now my part of the job is done. . . .

MacKinnie found a goblet of wine and gave it to her. It was strong, heady stuff, and she knew she shouldn't drink all of it, but the festive mood of the streets was hard to resist, and she drank more than half. Nathan took a beaker of ale from one of his off-duty troopers. "Thanks, Hiaro," he said. "What'll you do now that the war's over?"

"I don't know, Colonel." The little pikeman stood tall, and Stark's merciless drillfield exercises showed in his muscles. Mary remembered when she'd first seen him: when Hiaro had joined MacKinnie's army he was an emaciated ghost living on Temple charity, sleeping in a gutter and waiting to die. "My farm is burned, my wife and children are dead . . . the lord of my fields wants us to return to the land, and it seems I must do so for I am not tall enough to join the new Temple guards."

MacKinnie drank and turned away but the fugleman pursued him. "Colonel—Trader—sir, it is rumored that you will march west with an army. There are many like me who would go with you. Some talk of remaining together and seeking employment as soldiers for another city, but we would rather go with you."

"Thanks, Hiaro. I'll remember," MacKinnie said. What is there about him that wins loyalty? Mary wondered. Not just Hiaro. Hal Stark. The other guardsmen. It's like a tangible force. I can feel it, too, but I suppose that could be something else, something more physical. Heaven knows he's attractive enough. And sometimes he looks at me— She drank the rest of the goblet. Someone stepped out of the crowd to fill it again.

They wandered through the brightly lit streets. Wind chimes with a Temple replica as centerpiece tinkled in every doorway. They rounded a corner, and she slipped on the rough cobblestones. MacKinnie caught her, and she leaned against him for a moment. She felt his warmth, and she leaned against him for a moment. She felt his warmth, and she didn't want to move away. Gently he set her back on her feet, but she thought he took his time doing it, as if the physical contact wasn't unpleasant for him.

"The pikemen could do all right as mercenaries," Stark commented. "They can beat anything on this planet exceptin' heavy cavalry, and with the right battle plan they might even do that. No leaders, though, so they'll probably hire out to some idiot who'll waste them. Nobody on this end of Makassar appreciates good infantry. Be a pity what's goin' to happen to them lads after all the training we gave them. . . ."

"I got your message before, Sergeant," MacKinnie said. His voice was cold.

"Yes, sir."

"What message?" Mary asked.

"Hal thinks I ought to stay here as king of this city rather than return to Jikar."

"But you can't do that! Haven is depending on you, all of Prince Samual's World—Nathan, you wouldn't really do that!"

But we could, she thought. We could stay. She thought of Hiaro as she'd first seen him. And the children of Batav. The Empire wouldn't help them. Someone should. But not us! We've our own world to save, and even if I don't like Haven as much as I once did, it's my home, and this is my duty.

"Wouldn't I? Who's to stop me?" he asked.

She drew away from him, then began to laugh. "Why, *you* are, Iron Man! I suppose you really could get away with it. The Imperial Navy wouldn't like that, but with their Archbishop on your side you'd be all right." She spoke tauntingly now. "Go on, Your Majesty. Forget your oaths. Why don't you take me into the nearest building and ravish me while you're at it? Who's to stop you? I have no protector here. No one but you." MacKinnie turned away.

They were approaching a large group, peasants, soldiers off duty, knights in mail, all gathered around a cart in the center of a public square. One mailed warrior in bright surcoat stood atop the cart, his head tilted back in song. "Look, there's Brett," Nathan said. "Let's go listen." Two pikemen saw MacKinnie approach and efficiently cleared a way through the crowd to the wagon.

★ ★ ★

"In the public house to die, is my resolution,
Let wine to my lips be nigh, at life's dissolution!
That will make the angels cry, with glad elocution,
'Grant this drunkard, God on high,
grace and absolution!'"

Brett ended his song and seized a flagon of wine. As he drained it he saw MacKinnie. "Ho, lads, it's the colonel and his lady, our Lady Mary who brings food and drink and takes care of the wounded. A song for the real winner of our battles!"

"Oh mistress mine, where are you—"

He had hardly begun when he broke off and straightened in horror. "Hal! Behind you! Guard the colonel!" Brett tore his sword from its sheath and leaped from the cart.

It all happened so fast that Mary had no time to react. A short, brown man rushed through the crowd. He brandished a heavy curved knife. A bedlam of shouting erupted, but the intruder ran in deadly silence. When a pikeman moved to intercept him the kriss flashed, lopping off the soldier's arm at the elbow. There were more shouts, of warning and terror. The kriss swung again and again, and more of MacKinnie's warriors fell to the wine-soaked cobblestones.

"Haigh!" A soldier flung his javelin from somewhere behind her. The meter-and-a-half dart took the charging warrior below the chest, but the man plucked the javelin from his body and charged on, still dealing terrible blows to everyone in his path. Then there was no one but Stark between him and the colonel.

Hal had no time to draw his sword. Instead, he moved in front of Mary and MacKinnie. The kriss flashed again. It caught Stark on the right shoulder and battered him to the ground, but he'd bought MacKinnie time enough to draw his own weapon.

And the brown man was still coming forward, directly toward her, toward Nathan, the great curved knife held high. Nathan took his stance, his face determined but calm, no fear at all as he held the point of his sword leveled at the enemy—

And the man, impaled on the sword, still ran forward down the blade toward MacKinnie. The kriss lifted high and Mary saw death descending.

"Haigh!" Brett shouted a curse similar to the assassin's, His broadsword flashed, catching the descending wrist to cut it off. Brett lifted his weapon again and cut viciously at the head, then again. The stocky warrior slumped, his weight tearing MacKinnie's sword from his hand.

"Haigh!" Brett shouted again. "In time! Hal, do you live?"

"Yeah." Stark eased himself gingerly to his feet and clutched his right shoulder with his left hand. "Man, he swings that thing hard! Caught me more with the flat than the edge, damn good thing I didn't take off my mail after duty today. . . ." he tested his arm. "Gonna be stiff for a week."

"Better that than to lose the arm," Brett said quietly.

The crowd was milling about the square, and men and

women were shouting. "The colonel lives!" Brett leaped to his wagon and shouted it again. "He lives. The colonel lives!"

"Glory be to God!" Someone screamed. A Temple priest began to pray loudly.

It was only then that the reaction took her. She was still shaking when MacKinnie climbed onto the wagon to show himself unhurt. He was just in time. Already his pikemen were advancing with leveled weapons, ready to avenge their commander's death with a massacre. . . .

Nathan climbed down from the cart. A near thing, he thought. As near as ever I came to buying it.

Now that it was over he'd get the shakes. It almost always happened. When there was work to do, danger only made him calmer, but when it was over. . . . He found Mary in the crowd. She seemed calm enough, but subdued, and he took her hand.

A hastily assembled squad of pikemen escorted them back to the Temple compound. They walked in silence to MacKinnie's rooms, then Mary went to find the Temple physicians, while Brett and MacKinnie assisted Stark in removing his armor and the thick woolsh-hide padding beneath it. The shoulder was swollen and discolored.

"It don't feel broke," Stark said. He moved his arm gingerly. "But it sure don't feel too good, either. Could you pour me some wine, Colonel?"

"Sure." MacKinnie got the bottle and goblets. "We could all use some. Brett, who was that man?"

"A mari fanatic," Brett said. "Sent to kill you. The juramentados are usually very high-ranking members of the clan, and they never come back alive. You should feel complimented. They think killing you is important."

"They're right, too," Stark said. "Without the colonel—"

Brett nodded. "They'll have the Temple within a yir. Probably sooner."

"Damn it, now both of you are after me," MacKinnie said. "And what am I supposed to do?"

"Nothing you can do, Colonel," Stark said. "You took on a job, and you wouldn't be who you are if it was in you to throw off your duty. Still, it's a pity. Those are good lads."

There was a long silence. Hal broke it at last. "Maybe Brett and I, between us, could hold onto this place."

"But—"

"You won't be needing me to get home," Stark said. "Not really. MacLean and Todd and Loholo can handle the ship. And there's nothing much for me after we get back."

Nathan still didn't say anything.

"Damn it," Hal said, "I don't like splitting up any better than you do. But— Colonel, we made soldiers out of those peasants. Don't we owe them?"

"It could be our salvation," Brett said. "I know the maris. As you suspect, although I was not born one of them, I grew up in a mari clan, and I know them. When they hear that you are gone, they will return, and who can fight them? I cannot. Nor can Vanjynk. Yet we can control the knights, and if Hal commands here—for you, of course. We must say that we hold for you, until your return, and let Hal command in your name."

Stark grinned wryly. "Like old times. It's what I've

always done. All I ever wanted to do, for that matter. And we'd have a good chance."

"You might have time to build a good military force," Nathan said. "Good enough to hold the maris. But what about the politics? Sergeant—"

"Colonel, don't order me to come with you."

I don't think he ever interrupted me before, MacKinnie thought.

"I'll take care of these new Wolves for you," Stark said. "Just until you come back for us. Let's leave it like that."

Except we both know I'll never get back, MacKinnie thought.

He looked at Stark, then looked away. There had always been the possibility that Stark would be killed in a battle that MacKinnie survived, but after Lechfeld it hadn't seemed likely. After Lechfeld, Stark was all that was left of his former life. He had never considered what it would be like to be alone.

I guess now I find out, he thought.

Mary came in with two yellow-robed priests. They looked at Hal's shoulder and exchanged glances, then bent to feel it gingerly. "I do not think it broken," one said. "It will heal. But it may be dislocated. We will have to wrench it into place, then bind it up. That will be painful. If you will come with us—"

"I'll go, too," Brett said. "Just to be certain."

MacKinnie got up as well.

Stark shook his head. "No need for you to come, Colonel. I'll see you in the morning."

And you'd rather I didn't watch, MacKinnie thought. I've seen the Temple medical people work, they're good at their job—and Hal won't want me around when they start yanking at that shoulder. It's easier to yell bloody murder if your friends aren't around. "Right." He watched as the priests led Hal and Brett away.

Nathan went to the door and closed it. When he turned back he saw Mary was still there, still lovely, making no move to go—

"Freelady, you shouldn't be—"

"Don't be silly," she said. "You're shaking—"

"Yes, damn it. I—"

"So am I." She held up her hands.

MacKinnie laughed wryly. "You're not in my line of work. It's always been like this, after the action is over—"

"And you wonder if I think less of you?" she asked. "Because your hands tremble?" She shuddered.

Why is she here? MacKinnie wondered. Right here, two steps away, all I have to do is—

She's your ward and you're fifty and she's half your age. And damned beautiful. And what do I do now? "Do you want a drink?"

"If you're having one—"

He poured two goblets of wine.

There was a long silence while they drank. Then Mary laughed.

"What?" Nathan asked.

"Us. You were almost killed tonight. You could be killed tomorrow. Or we both could be. And we're standing here in the middle of this room, when—Nathan, this is foolish!"

"But—"

"But nothing! Guardians. Never be alone with a man.

Nathan, that's another world. A world so far away I can't even imagine it—and you stopped looking at me like a daughter a long time ago. . . ." She moved closer to him and put her hand on his arm. "We're here, Nathan. We're here and tonight we're alive. Tomorrow we might not be."

Gray dawn gave just enough light to see when MacKinnie woke. He lay still for a moment, half remembering a dream. Then he sat upright. He was alone in the bed—

But not in the room. Mary sat in a big chair, her knees drawn up to her chin. She had covered herself with a large fur robe.

"You're awake," she said.

"So are you—why are you sitting there?"

"I couldn't sleep, and I didn't want to disturb you."

"Are you—are you all right?" he asked.

She laughed, a soft tinkle in the gray light. "You silly goose, of course I'm all right." She laughed again. "Why, did you think I was brooding over lost innocence? If you must know, I was thinking of how much time we wasted before tonight."

"So was I."

She smiled and stood. She was naked except for the fur robe, and she threw that aside. "Then let's don't waste any more. There won't be a lot of privacy on *Subao*."

It was fully light outside when he woke again. MacKinnie moved carefully and gently kissed her. She smiled and opened her eyes lazily.

"Good morning," Nathan said.

"Yes. It is a good morning." She stretched lazily. "It would be a better one for some coffee. Or chickeest. Or even that horrible tea they have here."

"I'll just send for some, shall I?"

She drew away in mock horror. "And scandalize your guards?"

"They would be. Or would pretend to be," Nathan said.

"Don't be so serious."

"Someone has to be."

"I suppose. And we've both work to do. We'd better get up."

"To hell with the work—"

"You don't mean that," she said.

"Maybe I do. The harder I work, the quicker we go back. Assuming Kleinst can do anything useful to begin with, and I'm not at all sure he can. Mary—we really could stay here."

"You're not going to start that again, are you? Nathan, I don't really know why we're here. It has something to do with the library, I can guess that. And Lord Dougal said this was the most important mission in the history of Haven, important to the whole planet."

"It is," Nathan said. "And it's time I told you what we're doing here. All of you should know, so you won't let something slip to the Imperial Navy people." He explained the mission to her. "But I've come to think it's senseless," he finished.

"Why?"

"Why? You've seen their ships. How can we build anything like that?"

"What does Kleinst say, now that he's seen the library?"

"Humph. He's so enraptured by all the new scientific laws that he isn't even thinking about building ships. And he doesn't know if we can read copies of the records on Samual, even if we can take copies back. He could learn, he says. But in how many years? I think we've been chasing a dream, Mary. A noble dream, but nothing more than that."

She stared at patterns of sunlight on the wall. When she spoke she was very serious. "Dream or not, we have to try," she said. "Not just for us. For everyone. The Empire is wrong, Nathan. Their policies. Look at what they're doing to this world. With what little we know we could save them from so much misery."

"Or destroy them," MacKinnie said.

"That's strange, coming from you."

"Oh, I've no love for the Imperials. I just don't know how to do their job."

"You don't have to. All you have to do is your own."

"But—"

"There really is something wrong, isn't there?"

He nodded. "Hal won't be coming back with us."

"Are you certain?"

"Yes. He's going to stay with Brett. He thinks he has an obligation to these peasant lads he trained. So do I."

"He's been with you a long time, hasn't he?"

"Since I was a junior lieutenant," Nathan said. "Mary, how can I leave him here? And for what? It's not my job any longer. It's all up to Kleinst, and he doesn't know how to build a spaceship either."

"Iron MacKinnie gives up," she said. "The terrible

warrior—no, I won't mock you. I don't suppose I'll ever know the kind of friendship you and Hal have. But the mission isn't finished until we get home, and Nathan, be honest, what are our chances without you?"

"Not as good as if I come." It was as if the words were wrenched from him, as if they said themselves without his willing it. "But what good are we doing?"

"Nathan, we've got the library. When we started even that didn't look possible. Now we just keep on doing what we can."

"Why is this important to you?" MacKinnie asked.

"They trusted me," she said. "For you that's nothing new. But for me—Nathan, I can't betray that trust." She moved closer to him. "I hope—"

"What?"

"I'm selfish enough to hope you won't make me choose," she said.

There were tears at the corners of her eyes. Nathan knew she was fighting to hold them back, that she wasn't acting.

Duty and honor and love. He'd sacrifice all three no matter what he did. But when he looked at her, he knew he had no real choice at all.

★ PART THREE ★
PRINCE SAMUAL'S HOPE
★ ★ ★

★23★
ARINDELL'S CASTLE
★★★

Angus Volker, fourteenth Regent of Prince Samual University, looked at the invitation and sighed. It was a simple card written by someone with beautiful handwriting, and the message seemed harmless enough. "David II, by grace of God King of Haven and Grand Duke of Orleans, Mayor of Halmarch, Prince-Magnate of Startford, requests the honor of your company at an audience to be held at the residence of Lord Arindell at 1664 hours on Wednesday next."

Certainly the card was formally correct. It was not a command.

But it might as well have been. Academician Volker looked around his richly furnished tower office and sighed again. When the faculty elected him rector it seemed likely that he would preside over the University's celebration of its two-hundred-fiftieth anniversary of independence. Now it was likely that celebration would never happen. The very titles King David chose to have placed on the invitation were significant: Orleans, Startford, and Halmarch had all been prominent in the alliance of free states which by treaty guaranteed the independence of Prince Samual University. Now they were merged into Haven, as were several more so thoroughly subjugated that they had not even the shadow of existence in David's titles.

I could refuse, he told himself. I could send polite regrets. . . .

But the next invitation would not be so polite. It might even be accompanied by Haven guards. The University proctors couldn't keep armed Haven troops from entering the campus. Some of the students would undoubtedly riot, but the end of that was inevitable. The University's independence had never depended on anything as weak as its power to defend itself. And now the alliance which had been its real defense was a hollow shell.

No. Better to accept an invitation. So long as David was being formally correct, there was a small chance that the University might retain independence. If the gloves came off there would be no chance at all.

Volker turned the matter endlessly in his mind as his chauffeur drove him toward Lord Arindell's palace.

Arindell. Was the meeting place significant? Arindell was a prominent socialite, and it was not unreasonable that the king might host a social gathering at his residence— but Arindell was also Minister of Justice. There were stories about him and the Haven Royal Police; of how suspected enemies of King David had vanished without a trace. There had always been such stories, but lately there seemed to be more. Was it merely because no one understood the role of the Imperials, or was there more to it? Volker didn't know.

But surely they would not so openly arrest the Rector of Prince Samual University! The University was the most important institution on Prince Samual's World, above petty national politics, older than most nations and subject to none of them. Surely he need not worry. He told himself that again, then carefully folded his pudgy hands in his ample lap and with an effort of will made them stay there as the car drove on through uncrowded cobblestone streets.

Lord Arindell's palace had once been a fortress. The moat had long ago been filled in, and the cannon on the terraces were obsolete, purely decorative, their mouths stuffed with fresh flowers. Banners and streamers fluttered from high battlements. Yet despite the festive decorations there was an air of foreboding about the place, and Volker was reluctant to leave his steam car. He wanted desperately to tell the chauffeur to take him back to campus where he felt safe. But if he did, how long would the campus be a place of refuge?

"One step at a time," he told himself. Then, louder, he told the chauffeur, "Go back to the University. Mrs. Volker will have errands for you. And send another driver for me. Have him come here and wait."

"I don't mind waiting, Rector. I could send a telegram to have Andrew help Lady Volker."

"No. Please do it my way." He hesitated. "I'm not unhappy with you, Felix. I've got reasons."

The chauffeur looked up at the massive stone walls. "I guess you have, sir. If I was going in there, I expect I'd want somebody to know what time I went in. Somebody outside."

Volker smiled wryly. "I hadn't known I was that obvious. I'm certain nothing will happen."

"Be more certain with me back on campus," Felix said. "I could stop by the provost's office on my way to help Lady Volker . . . I've got a cousin who's a proctor."

"It won't be necessary," Volker said. "Thank you."

He waited until the steam car was out of sight before he went down the rose-lined path to the great gates.

A hundred of Haven's most glamorous people were gathered in the ancient palace ballroom. Angus was announced by a butler and greeted by Lord Arindell. The gathering seemed purely social, but Volker remained watchful.

"The king's upstairs," Arindell told him. "He'll join the party presently. Enjoy yourself." He bowed and left Angus to his own devices.

Curious, Volker thought. It seemed a pleasant enough party. But why had he been invited? I'll find out sooner than I like. . . .

Most of the guests' conversations were confined to two subjects: the war of unification, which was going well, and the economy, which was booming but which might be hurt by the consequent inflation, and which was also made uncertain because no one knew what the Imperials would do. Imperial trade would make some rich, others poor, and no one knew which. Yet even these subjects were but lightly treated. There was no serious discussion at all. A number of the people present had sons at the University, and Volker knew of most of them; the University might be independent, but it was only prudent to be wary of students from Haven's great families. He set himself to the task of being charming, telling anecdotes about student pranks, and acting as if he enjoyed the opportunity. It was an easy act; much of the rector's job was concerned with obtaining donations.

He had been in the palace for half an hour and refilled his cup at the punchbowl twice when a man in butler's livery approached. He didn't look at all like a butler. He stood too straight, and he was too young to be a retired soldier. . . .

"If you would come with me, sir," the servant said. "You have an appointment—"

"Certainly," Volker said. He followed the butler out a side door and up back stairways to the third floor. At the end of the hall was a door, and three more liveried servants, all young and very military in appearance, stood outside it. They opened the door for Volker.

"In here, sir," his escort said.

The room was a large, book-lined study. King David, Sir Giles Og, and a man Volker didn't know were seated informally near the fireplace. Volker bowed to the still-seated king. David wasn't *his* king, but it cost nothing to be polite. By rights, they should meet as equals. They were both sovereigns. It didn't escape Angus that King David must know that as well as he did. "Your Majesty."

"You are kind to come," David said. "You've met the

Prime Minister, of course. And allow me to present Citizen Dougal, a minister without portfolio."

They stood, and Volker acknowledged their bows. That, at least, was protocol, and Angus felt better.

"Won't you be seated?" the king asked. "Would you care for grua?"

"Yes, please—" Volker had expected the king to ring for a servant, but Dougal went to the small table to bring Volker's drink. "Thank you."

"This meeting is confidential," David said. "I want your assurance on that."

"Certainly," Volker said. "Although of course any discussion of importance to the University must be reported to the Regents. . . ."

"That's why you're here," Dougal said. "Let's be open about this, Professor. You want to preserve the University's independence. Well, you may get that, but there are conditions."

"But the Regents—"

"Nothing said here will be reported to the Regents," Dougal said. He sounded like a man accustomed to being obeyed. "If it comes to formal meetings with the Regents, we'll have an entirely different conversation. One you and they won't much care for. Better we settle matters here."

"Honesty is important," Sir Giles said. "But we can remain polite. However, we stray from the subject, which is your word on the secrecy of this meeting."

That wasn't a hard decision to make, for the same reasons that had brought him here in the first place. He could guess Dougal's next move. He'd already hinted at it by addressing him as "Professor." The title was used by the faculty in addressing their rector, but others generally employed more honorific phrases. Angus sighed and submitted to the inevitable. "You have my assurance. This meeting will remain confidential."

"Excellent," Sir Giles said. "Now. Let us sum up the situation. Prince Samual University has been an independent institution since just before the Plague Years. You have your own laws and courts and you set your own policies, and you share knowledge equally with all. That's worked well. We don't want to change it, even if you are in the middle of Haven. God knows there have been times when your privileges of sanctuary were dreadfully abused, but we've always put up with it.

"But times have changed. When there wasn't any unity to Prince Samual's World it made sense to have supernational entities like the University and the Brotherhoods, but we're putting an end to national entities. Haven's treaties granting you independence were for the large part with states that are now part of Haven. The rest will be soon. So it's time to talk about the future of the University under the new order here."

"I see," Volker said. "We have expected this, of course. But I do not see why you have not come to the Regents. . . ."

"Because we need your help," David said. "And we've agreed that you can be trusted."

"And it is very much in your interest to work with us," Dougal said. "You can negotiate with us. We understand each other. Your alternative is the Imperials—and they won't leave you a damned bit of independence."

Imperials. Interesting, Volker thought. Certainly they

would have something to say about Haven's rule of Prince Samual's World. Curious that they'd never told anyone their intentions. Even more curious that a Haven cabinet officer would speak that way. . . . "They are your allies, not mine," Volker said. "Of course you probably know that the Regents have granted the Imperial officers the privileges of visiting scholars. They often come to use the library."

"We know," Dougal said. "What you don't know is why they're here."

What's wrong with the man? Volker wondered. He looks like he's about to be executed. That's not a happy thought, given where I am. . . . "No, of course I don't know. We have always assumed Imperial intentions to be a Haven state secret."

"I think there's no choice but to tell him, Sire," Dougal said.

"We agreed on that some time ago," King David said. "There's no real choice in the matter."

"No. I suppose not," Dougal said. "Very well . . ."

Volker listened with growing amazement. There was a lot to think about here. Did he believe the part about the Empire's intentions for Prince Samual's World? But why shouldn't I? he wondered. It's almost reasonable. They have been damned secretive about the way their government works, and they've studied our science but given our people very little in return. . . .

"I see," he said when Dougal finished. "But what has this to do with me?"

"Everything," Dougal said. "I won't say how, but we expect to have a lot of their science and technology soon.

Books and books of it. Much of it so far advanced over what we have that most of us can't even comprehend it. Yet we *must* comprehend it. If anyone can understand, it will be your people at the University—but we have to keep everything secret. We even have to conceal the fact that we *have* a secret to keep."

"How shall we do that?" Volker asked.

"Some of your scholars can be trusted," Dougal said. "You'll help us choose them. But we'll need others even though they can't keep secrets. Those will have to transfer to one of His Majesty's research stations. To our naval facilities, or elsewhere. They'll have to go willingly— or seem to, at any rate. Some of your best students will be cloistered, kept away from the others, so they can study this new science. And—"

"My God, man, that's the end of the University!" Volker protested.

"Do you see another way?" Sir Giles asked. "If our world is colonized, what do you think will become of the University?"

A good question, Volker thought. I wonder if the Imperials would bargain? Would it be worth something to them to learn of this plot? But that, he decided, was not likely. What use independence for a University on an enslaved planet? With Imperial agents watching his faculty, suppressing discoveries—

And there was the new knowledge itself, new discoveries that Haven was somehow to steal from the Empire. That alone was a deciding factor. But first—

"There remains the matter of confirmation of the University's ancient privileges," Volker said.

"You'll get that. Most of it," Dougal snapped.

"All," Volker insisted.

"If we succeed," King David said. "If we succeed, I will reconfirm your privileges."

"And if we fail?" Volker asked.

"Then we all fail," Dougal said. "You can deal with the Imperials, for all the good it will do you. But we won't fail."

"I wish I were certain," Volker said. "I have seen the Imperial landing boats. We've never built anything like them." And that struck a nerve, he thought. In Sir Giles at least.

"Nothing is certain," King David said. "Yet we must try. Will you help us?"

This might go well, Volker thought. The University might come out of this very well indeed. King's promise or not, once Haven governs the entire world, the University will never keep *all* its ancient privileges, but we'll have a good bargaining position when that's accomplished. And we'll have all their new science. . . . "Of course, Your Majesty."

★24★
PROMOTIONS
★ ★ ★

There was a large map of Prince Samual's World on Malcolm Dougal's office wall. It had to be changed at frequent intervals.

Too frequent, Dougal thought. The unification war—if you could call desultory mop-up actions a war—was going all too well. There was very little fighting now. There hadn't been a lot since the fall of Orleans, although for the first year it had been necessary to march Haven's armies to the border of a state before it was willing to commit political suicide. Now, though, many of Haven's victims were ready to negotiate without a visible show of force at all.

It was hardly surprising. For over a century Orleans had been the rock against which Haven's expansionist ambitions had foundered; with that republic out of the way it was to be expected that a number of other states would surrender. Even so, the speed at which Haven's Sunburst and Cross spread across the planet was astonishing.

Not that Dougal could blame the others for capitulating. A major point of treaties of unification put each absorbed state's military forces at Haven's disposal. Most had to be disbanded, but there were professionals in every army, and they could be recruited. And there was always the military equipment, the artillery and warships. . . . It was an effective way to build power.

The treaties were drafted by the Imperial High Commissioner's staff. Of course they were only being helpful—but their help was impossible to refuse. Malcolm's plan to buy time by delaying the final unification of Prince Samual's World simply wasn't going to work.

Haven's forces were now so large that no one could resist. If that weren't enough, the Imperial Marines stood ready to break any major center of opposition. Lechfeld had its effect; in the years since then, the Imperials had seldom fired their space weapons. The example of Lechfeld was more than sufficient.

Pacification of the barbaric South Continent would probably take a generation more, but within two or three years Prince Samual's World would be effectively unified under King David.

And thus under the Empire. Dougal looked again at the map and cursed. It was all happening too fast.

There were advantages, he thought. There was plenty of money now. The secret research center in the Corliss Grant Hills, and the others, the shipyards and Magnate Vermuele's foundries, got plenty of support. There was also money for the University, and that institution was invaluable.

Dougal nodded in satisfaction. In the months since they'd recruited him Angus Volker had kept his bargain.

Haven's research centers were well staffed. They didn't dare launch big rockets, but they'd fired several models. Static tests of larger motors continued satisfactorily. The shipyard facilities had developed airtight compartments and now worked to make them lighter. They could *almost* build a ship which would keep men alive in space.

Almost.

Almost meant anything from three to thirty years, depending on who you talked to. Three might just be enough—but Malcolm had had too much experience with eager engineers to believe that estimate. And more than five years would certainly be too late. He would not have that long. When the Imperials first arrived, they seemed in no hurry; lately, though, they were anxious to finish unifying the planet. At the same time, there were fewer Imperial civil servants at Government House. Sir Alexei Ackoff was as affable as ever, but he seemed distracted, as if Prince Samual's World had lessened in importance—but he was also in a greater hurry than ever.

We need either time or help, Dougal thought. And we can't get time, so it's got to be help, and that's MacKinnie.

It had been a year since they heard that MacKinnie and all his people had set out to cross Makassar in a small ship. They'd gone against the Navy's advice and despite plentiful warnings. The Imperial High Commissioner had been emphatic about that. It wasn't the Empire's fault that the expedition had been lost. . . .

Malcolm didn't believe the expedition was lost, but it was difficult to wait.

Difficult or not, there was nothing else to do. Weeks passed.

★ ★ ★

The large, square, metal box in Malcolm Dougal's office squawked unintelligibly. Irritated, Dougal got up to adjust the small dial set on its front. He didn't really know what he was doing, but they'd shown him how to operate the thing, and as he turned the dial slightly the words became clearer.

"Calling Citizen Dougal, calling Citizen Dougal. Answer, please."

He leaned close to the wire grill on the front of the thing and shouted, "Dougal here."

Nothing happened. He cursed and pushed the button on top. "Dougal here."

"Navy reports Makassar expedition returning. Will land in twenty days," the box said.

This time Malcolm remembered to push the button. "Thank you. Send details by messenger. Anything more?"

"That's all, sir."

"Thank you." He returned to his desk. Probably the communications man knew more details, but Malcolm didn't want them discussed on the wireless. The Imperials might not be listening, but certainly they could if they wanted to. Dougal laughed mockingly at himself. The only way anyone could learn that the expedition was returning would be from the Imperials; they'd know anything Malcolm could learn from a messenger. It was wise to be cautious, but it could be carried too far.

Not that it mattered. He'd learn nothing really important until MacKinnie's people were down and safely hidden.

Details. MacKinnie's crew would be a sensation. Everyone would want to see them. Parliament, the newspapers, the University; hundreds of opportunities for one of them to let something slip, the merest hint that would warn the Imperials and end their chances.

Something would have to be done about that. But first there were other preparations. He took a speaking tube from the wall behind his desk and whistled into it.

"Sir."

"Send Captain Gregory to me."

"Sir."

Dougal waited impatiently for the knock on the door. It was only a few minutes, but it seemed hours, and Dougal cursed himself for his impatience.

Hans Gregory was a middle-aged officer, nondescript and harmless in appearance; a man much like Malcolm Dougal. He stood in front of Malcolm's desk. "Yes, sir?"

"You look well," Dougal said. "I had meant to see you anyway, but now it may be more urgent. Please be seated."

"Thank you, sir—"

"I take it that all is well and there is no difficulty in your friendship with Citizen Liddell?"

"None, sir. I see him at least weekly now that I had him elected to my club. He very much appreciated my sponsorship."

"Excellent. It is now time for him to repay the favor. Things have reached a critical stage, and we will need a great deal more information about the Imperials. How well do you know Elaine Liddell?"

"Fairly well, sir. She's friendly enough. I used to see her when I called on Liddell—we play Go fairly often. Unfortunately, as I've reported, lately she's out as often as not."

"So you don't know if she would work with us?"

"No, sir." Gregory shrugged. "She certainly fancies herself in love with that young Imperial. If it came to a choice of loyalties, I wouldn't bet either way."

"Even if the king himself asked her to help?"

"I just don't know, sir. They're pretty thick, those two." He gave Dougal a knowing look. "You've seen the reports."

Dougal nodded. "If she's not in love with Lieutenant Jefferson, she ought to be. I do not understand how her father tolerates the situation."

"He has very little choice, sir," Captain Gregory said. "He could hardly challenge an Imperial officer. And of course Freelady Elaine does speak—privately—of Lieutenant Jefferson as her 'fiancé.'"

"But not publicly. Does Jefferson acknowledge the relationship?"

"That's more complicated than you would suppose," Gregory said. "He has made no objection to being called that by Elaine in the presence of Citizen Liddell. However, he cannot officially become engaged to a local without permission of his commanding officer—or says he cannot."

"Sounds as if Jefferson has found a good thing," Dougal said. "Privileges without obligations."

Gregory nodded agreement.

"I can't think the girl would much care for the situation."

"No, sir. I know her father doesn't," Gregory said.

"You're certain of that."

Gregory smiled. "Oh, yes. Laurence Liddell and I are very good friends—in fact, I am the only one of his friends who knows the situation."

"But why does he tolerate it?"

"He has little choice, sir. When Elaine began seeing Jefferson privately, Liddell was horrified, of course, but when he tried to do something about it, she threatened to get a job working for the Imperials and move into an apartment on their compound. He'd have had no control over her at all if she did that—".

"Is that still possible?" Dougal asked.

"I suppose so."

"We might get a lot of information—no, of course that can't work. Liddell would have to disown her. We'd never see her." Dougal looked thoughtful. "But we do need her cooperation. Have you suggestions for how to approach her?"

Captain Gregory held his fingertips together under his chin and looked up thoughtfully. "Have you considered how she must feel?" he asked. "She has thoroughly compromised herself, but she has no commitment whatever from Jefferson. If under those circumstances she found he was unfaithful to her—"

"Umm. And Jefferson has certainly been known to be interested in tavern girls. A good suggestion, Captain. Keep it in mind. Better—perhaps before we speak to her directly, we should have, uh, evidence—"

"I can arrange that."

"Excellent. And Jefferson himself might be vulnerable," Dougal mused.

"I can't think his superiors don't know of his adventures. One more wouldn't make a difference."

"I wasn't thinking of his rather libertine ways with tavern girls." Dougal said. "Tell me, Captain, have you any reason to believe that Freelady Elaine is sterile?"

"No, sir—"

"Yet if she has obtained a birth control device, she has been exceedingly discreet. Might Jefferson have given her what the Imperials use? Something called 'The Pill' is mentioned prominently in the novel we found. If he has given her Imperial technology, he may be in violation of one of their regulations."

"Isn't that a lot to deduce on little evidence?" Gregory asked.

"Some of it isn't deduction, Captain," Dougal said. "I have a number of agents watching those two. One is the concierge at the apartment Jefferson keeps in the suburbs."

"Even if you're correct, he would probably report any approach from us to his superiors," Gregory said. "From what I've seen of him he is rather admirably loyal to the Empire."

"Yes. Unfortunately. I suppose you're right, it was only a thought. Now, to return to the matter of Citizen Liddell. Will he cooperate?"

"Yes. He's very loyal. Favors the unification wars and all that. And this business with Jefferson hasn't made him love the Empire."

Dougal looked thoughtfully at the dossier on his desk. "Roads and public works," he mused. "Good recommendations from his superiors. Fairly senior civil servant—tell me, do you think he's competent to be one of the roads commissioners?"

"Yes."

"Good. He'll have that." Dougal made a note on the memo pad in front of him. "Sir Giles Og's political managers aren't going to be too happy about losing that appointment, but that can't be helped. Time to show Liddell he has friends who appreciate his talents—make sure he knows it was your influence that got him promoted. What else does he want?"

"A knighthood on retirement, but he has no reason to expect it—"

"Offer him that, too. If his daughter will cooperate with us. If not—" Dougal shrugged. "If not, a Haven knighthood won't be worth a lot anyway, but we can't tell him that. Captain, Elaine Liddell is potentially one of our best sources of information about Imperial policies, and I need that information badly. Especially now."

"Yes, sir. I'll do my best."

"I know you will. That's all."

"Sir." Gregory stood.

"Your very best, Commandant," Dougal said.

Gregory was halfway to the door. He stopped and turned in surprise. "Commandant?"

"Yes. I've just promoted you. See that you deserve it." Dougal made another note on his memo pad.

This is dangerous, Dougal thought. The expedition is returning and we will need information on Imperial activities. Elaine Liddell is potentially invaluable, our only real source, but she could also arouse Imperial suspicions.

But, he thought, there is nothing else to do. It is worth the risk, but that risk will have to be minimized. He took a report from his desk and scanned through it. Freelady Liddell and Lieutenant Jefferson liked sailing. They often went out alone in small craft, but only in the daytime. They did have *some* sense of discretion. . . .

He continued to scan the report. Citizen Liddell owned a pair of Mannheim pacers, and Jefferson took Elaine riding at least weekly. Mannheims, he thought. Very spirited horses. Took controlling. You could break your neck falling off a horse. The Imperial High Commissioner would be saddened by the loss, but what suspicion could be attached to a riding accident? He nodded to himself. Best see Inspector Solon. Just in case the interview with the girl went badly.

And there were endless other details to be attended to before the expedition returned. Dougal's fingers drummed on the polished wooden desk, and a thin smile came to his lips. The waiting was over. Now they could get to work.

★25★
DECISION FACTORS
★★★

The small boat skipped across the water, running directly downwind and going like a corkborer chased by an eagle. She had a nasty tendency to roll, and it took all of Jefferson's skill to keep her heading straight. He stood in the cockpit, his legs spread wide, the tiller behind him, feeling the following seas as they lifted the stern, throwing his weight against the tiller to correct any deviation from center, careful not to overcorrect and let her fall off the other way. It would be easy to broach, and in these seas the boat might swamp.

"You look like you're having fun." Elaine leaned against the forward cockpit coaming with her knees drawn up to her chin.

"I must be. I'm grinning a lot," Jeff said. He glanced thoughtfully at the boomed-out spinnaker, then down at the wake. "We must be making twelve kilometers! I've never gone this fast before. . . ."

She laughed. "You travel in starships, and you're impressed by a small boat?"

"It's not the same," he said defensively. Now why did she have to remind him of starships? And how was he going to tell her? Maybe now was as good a time as any. Just say it. "And I may not have many more opportunities."

Her look was enough to wrench out his heart. "Why?" she asked. But she knew.

"Something's happened out in Trans-Coalsack Sector," Jefferson said. "Something big. They discovered an alien civilization."

She frowned. "But you told me yourself there aren't any intelligent creatures other than humans—"

The boat took a rogue wave and he struggled with the tiller for a moment before he could answer. "It's a big universe. We were mistaken. Actually, they were discovered some time ago, and the news is only just getting here."

"But how does that affect us?" she asked.

"They sent an expedition to the alien planets," Jefferson said. "I don't know what they found, but they're ordering a main battle fleet to Trans-Coalsack."

"War?" She shuddered. "We have stories about the last wars. And those were with humans."

"I just don't know," Jeff said. "It might be. Why else would they want a fleet?" A big fleet. To be commanded by Kutuzov! Kutuzov the butcher, Kutuzov the hero . . . it depended on your point of view. "They're sending a lot of ships out there, so the rest of us have to cover more territory. I don't know where *Tombaugh* will be sent. Maybe even to Trans-Coalsack."

"Is that far?" she asked.

"Yes. Very far. And behind the Coalsack that's a mass of

interstellar dust so thick it hides the stars behind it. You can't see the sector capital from here."

"I knew it would happen," she said. "My father told me not to—not to fall in love with a Navy man. So now you're leaving me."

"Hey, I haven't left yet," he said.

"Can you stay?"

"I don't know." Possibly, he thought. I'd have to resign from the Navy and go into civil government. Do I want that? Oh, damn. He thought of *Tombaugh* ordered away, his shipmates leaving without him. Would that be harder than leaving Elaine?

He'd been planet-bound for two years except for brief tours aboard the orbiting *Tombaugh*. It was a pleasant relief from ship duty. But if he resigned to stay here, he'd never go to space again except as a passenger. He'd known he'd have to face this decision one day, but not so soon, not so soon. He tried to imagine his life as a civil administrator building an industrial civilization. He'd have honors enough. Possibly a barony. Almost certainly a barony on retirement. Another title in the family. His father would be proud of him. And he'd have Elaine.

Would that be enough?

Certainly he'd thought so when he first met her. But now he wasn't sure. That frantic need to be with her was gone, and while he didn't go looking for other women, he no longer felt repelled by them. Like that tavern girl he'd met the other night, the really friendly one—he pushed that thought away. Jeff didn't believe in telepathy, but Elaine had surprised him before.

She was her loveliest today. The wind brought a bloom

to her cheeks, and her hair, tied with bright ribbons, blew wantonly in the gusts. His eyes met hers and he smiled, and her answering smile was warm and trusting.

Trusting. Certainly she was that. Far too much so by the standards of this world.

You owe her, Jefferson thought to himself.

Not really. Happens all the time. Why make such a big thing out of it?

Because she does, and her father does, and all her friends do, and you knew it all along, and—

Another rogue wave threatened to swamp them, and he tried to force his worries and doubts from his mind to give all his attention to the tiller.

He almost succeeded.

Jefferson looked at his crowded "work-to-do" screen and frowned. It was all trivial stuff, but it took time to process, and it was hard to keep his mind on his work. Remembering last night's stormy scene with Elaine after they got ashore didn't help. She'd sensed his uncertainties, and although she hadn't accused him of not caring for her, she'd thought it. Worse, it was true. Or almost true. Or partly true. He cared for her, but enough to abandon his shipmates, his whole career? It came to that. She'd never fit into Capital social life.

And the choice would have to be made within the year. Just now High Commissioner Ackoff was trying to recruit naval officers for his civil service, and Navy policy was to let him; but if *Tombaugh* got war orders it would be too late. Captain Greenaugh would never let one of his officers resign under those circumstances.

He was keying in data on platinum production—surprisingly high on a world so poor in copper—when his door opened and Lieutenant Adnan Clements came in. "Got a minute?"

"Just that," Jeff said. "What's up?"

"Blivit, of course. Old man's got a new job for you."

Jeff gestured toward the screen. "I've got plenty of jobs—"

"So now you have another one. That Makassar expedition's coming in. Somebody's got to give Navy clearance for passengers and cargo. You're elected."

"Oh, hell. Why me?"

"Because the skipper's not about to do it, and I'm being sent down to South Continent to bust up a pirate fleet, that's why."

"Hey, that sounds like fun—"

"Sure, if your idea of fun is shooting up wooden boats that can't shoot back." Clements's face showed his distaste.

Jeff nodded agreement. "Guess I'd rather look for contraband at that." He turned to the keyboard and punched in the assignment. The schedule screen looked more cluttered than ever. "Get me a coffee?" he asked.

"Sure," Clements said. "Back in a minute."

Might as well see what the job involves, Jeff thought. He went back to the keyboard. "Let's see," he mused. "Keywords 'MAKASSAR' and 'EXPORT CONTRABAND.' Now the library search function. . . ."

"MAKASSAR EXPORT CONTRABAND: NO ITEMS LISTED" appeared on the main working screen.

"Aha," Jefferson said.

"Coffee time." Clements came in carrying two plastic

cups and set one on Jeff's desk. "I just remembered, you've been to Makassar. Job's a natural for you." He glanced at the screen. "Looks like you drew an easy one."

"Maybe. It's for sure there's not much there." He typed in "CONTINUE DETAIL TRADE/TRAVEL POLICY" and waited.

"MAKASSAR IS CLASSIFIED 'CLASS 5 PRIMITIVE' WITH NO SIGNIFICANT TECHNOLOGY NO EXPORT RESTRICTIONS. SUFFICIENT SAMPLINGS INDICATE NO EPIDEMIC DISEASES. FULL SPECTRUM IMMUNIZATIONS REQUIRED FOR LANDING OR EXIT FROM PLANET.

"THREE ADDICTING DRUGS ARE KNOWN TO BE PREPARED ON MAKASSAR BUT THEY ARE UNATTRACTIVE AND THERE IS NO MARKET FOR THEM. FOR FURTHER DETAILS SEE 'MAKASSAR-GENERAL.'"

"IMPORT RESTRICTIONS: SEVERE IM—" The flow of words was cut off as Jeff touched more keys.

"See?" Clements said. "An easy job."

"Still takes time I don't have."

"Poor you. How's your romance going?"

Jefferson shrugged. "I told her about the Moties," he said. "And the possible alert."

"I gather she wasn't pleased."

Jeff snorted. "You could say it that way."

"So what *are* you going to do?"

"Hell, Adnan, I don't know. I like the Navy."

"Five hundred hours ago you couldn't talk about anything but resigning. Get married and become a colonist. Found a new dynasty, to hear you talk."

Jeff nodded. "Yeah, but now we really have to decide—"

Clements laughed. "What's the problem, laddie? Afraid to admit you're just another sailor feeding bushwa to his girl? Hell, I knew you were never going to resign."

"Maybe you're right," Jeff said. "But damn it, this girl's different—"

"Sure. They all are," Clements said. He drained his coffee. "My screen's not like yours, but it's full enough. Best get at it."

"Yeah." Jefferson turned back to his work. More reports. Mining and refining capabilities. Steam generation facilities. All important, he knew, but—

If I give up the Navy, this'll be my career, he thought. God Almighty, how could anyone spend his entire life at this? Better a naval battle. Better a long, dull patrol. Better almost anything!

The days passed, and Jeff was no further ahead. As soon as he finished one task they'd give him another. He had five locals gathering data, and they brought it in faster than he could code it into the machines.

Twice he'd sent memos to the High Commissioner's office explaining the desirability of hiring and training locals for elementary clerical work of this type. It wouldn't harm this planet for some of its people to learn how to produce machine-readable data. He'd had no answer.

Which, he thought philosophically, is better than a definite "No."

And Elaine was—strange. They'd patched up their quarrel. He didn't tell her how soon he'd have to make a decision, and she didn't bring up the subject. She did encourage him in his work, and seemed interested in what he was doing. She hadn't cared before, but now of a sudden she encouraged him to talk about his work, as if—

"Landing boat's on final approach now, Lieutenant."

"Ah. Thanks, Hawley." He went out onto the pier to wait. In moments he heard growing thunder and the sharp clap of a sonic boom. He shaded his eyes to stare over the water and made out a small speck just at the horizon. It was coming directly toward him, angling in a long glide path toward the water.

"There it is!" Someone shouted from behind him. Jeff grimaced. There were a thousand civilians out there, all eager to see the locals who'd been off-planet. They weren't allowed on the pier itself, but they were close enough. A lot of them were shouting now.

The landing boat settled onto the water. Jeff nodded approval. It was a smooth landing. Two small local steam tugs went out to tow it to the pier. They'd be a while doing that. Jeff wondered whose idea it was. The landing boats were hard to maneuver, but they weren't so difficult to handle as to need local assistance. Some boondoggle to employ locals? Maybe the local harbormaster was worried about the big landing craft losing control and smashing up the docks. He tapped his foot impatiently as he waited.

Finally the craft was alongside and the gangway lowered. Three naval officers got off first. Junior lieutenants, very young. Just up from middle, Jefferson thought. Proud as peacocks. He remembered when he'd sewn that stripe on his sleeve. It had been a good feeling.

They looked around uncertainly and Jeff went over to them. Although they were nominally the same rank as

Jeff, two of the newcomers saluted him. Jeff grinned. "Assigned here?" he asked.

"Yes, si—. Yes, thank you. Were you sent to meet us?"

Jeff laughed. "Hardly. But wait around and I'll see you get to headquarters. Know anything of what you're supposed to do?"

"Not really," the spokesman said. "What's this place like?"

"Takes a bit of getting used to, but not bad," Jeff said. "Oops, excuse me, that's my crew." He left them and went to the gangway.

The group getting off had to be native to Prince Samual's World. Jeff wasn't sure how he knew that, but they had the look about them. They were led by a tall, broad-shouldered man with straw-colored hair going to steel gray. Distinguished, Jefferson thought. The files said Trader, but that man had obviously been a soldier.

He examined the others. The girl was all right, but no raving beauty; there were plenty of prettier ones in Haven. She looked self-possessed, though, more poised than Elaine, and that made her attractive. There wasn't much to notice about the others.

"Trader MacKinnie?" he said to the leader.

"Yes, sir."

Sir. A word *that* man doesn't mean. Not to me. "I'm Lieutenant Jefferson, sir. I've been assigned to conduct your landing interviews and inspection."

"Will this take long?"

"I shouldn't think so," Jefferson said. "Just formalities. Shall we go inside?" He led the way into the building to the interview room and ushered MacKinnie inside. "Have a seat, please." He turned on his recorder and put his pocket computer on the desk. "Here, I've got your records on here somewhere—ah. 'Jameson MacKinnie, Trader, citizen of Haven. Expedition leader.' Successful trip?"

MacKinnie shrugged. "Moderately. I expect the cargo we brought will cover the expedition costs, but there won't be a lot of profit."

Jefferson nodded. "I don't recall seeing much there I'd want to buy," he said. "Where did you go on Makassar?"

"Well, we landed at the Navy base at Jikar and went on from there," MacKinnie said.

Man's nervous, Jefferson thought. *Is there a special reason? Or does he just dislike Imperial officers?* "The report from the Makassar garrison says you went to Batav."

MacKinnie nodded.

"I was there once. Did you see the Temple?"

"Certainly. Most prominent building on the whole planet."

"It is, isn't it? Get inside?"

"Not beyond the courtyard," MacKinnie answered. "It's a holy place, and the unconsecrated don't get into the inner buildings."

Jefferson grinned to himself. "Right." *It had been that way when Jefferson visited. Of course other Navy people had been inside, all the way to the crypt where they kept the remains of the old library. What might this chap have done if he'd known what was in there? Or did he?* "Why is the place holy?" Jefferson asked. "I didn't stay long enough to find out."

"Relics, they say," MacKinnie answered. "The building's very old. We ran into a party of Imperial missionaries in Batav, and they said something about stuff left over from the First Empire."

Jefferson glanced down at his computer. There it was. A note from the commander at Jikar. 'Archbishop Casteliano found this group helpful and sent a note of commendation.' So. They had friends in the Church. Might as well get this over with. "Any injuries or diseases?" he asked. "And I'll need your cargo manifests. . . ."

★26★
HOMECOMING
★ ★ ★

When MacKinnie saw Lieutenant Jefferson waiting for him at the gangway his first reaction was panic. Somehow they must have found out. . . .

But the only armed Marines in evidence were a pair of sentries looking very bored, and there was no evidence of suspicion at all. Jefferson acted as if he'd never seen MacKinnie before. Given his condition the only time they'd been in the same room together that was hardly a surprise. And his greeting was polite. Everything seemed routine.

For all that, it was unnerving. Nathan followed the Imperial officer into the stone warehouse the Imperials had converted into their customs office, and tried to act relaxed about the interview. It seemed to go well enough, and Jefferson's interest in the Temple was natural. The real test would come when they inspected the cargo. The carefully copied library records were concealed inside handcrafted statuary. It wouldn't take a lot of ingenuity to find them, but Nathan could think of no other place to conceal them. He'd almost left them behind, but Kleinst had said he couldn't rely on his memory, and that left few choices.

MacKinnie found he needn't have worried. The cargo inspection was cursory. Jefferson had a couple of the crates opened, but mostly seemed curious to see what they'd brought.

"Copper statues," Jefferson commented. "I didn't see anything like this on Makassar."

MacKinnie laughed. "Nor did we. But copper is cheap enough there, so we had artists copy their work in it."

"Clever of you," Jefferson said. "Should fetch a good price here." He continued to look through boxes. "Ah. I should have picked up one of these myself," he said. He held up a tusked sea creature carved in one of Makassar's ultra-hard woods. "What's your price for it?"

MacKinnie shrugged. "We'll have to hold auctions. How else can you establish prices on rare artworks? But that's yours if you like."

"I should pay for it—"

MacKinnie shrugged. "Set a price, then."

"I don't suppose I could afford what you can get for it here—"

"Probably not. It's still yours if you want it."

"I'd better not. Thank you for the offer." He made notes on his pocket computer. "You're cleared," he said.

MacKinnie was surprised and looked it. "Thanks."

"That's Navy clearance," Jefferson said. "You'll get a customs bill later." He glanced at the small screen on his pocket computer. "Since this expedition was owned by a sovereign ally, that won't be very high. May even be waived. Have you arranged for a crew to transport?"

"No, but I expect His Majesty's government has."

"Good."

"What's next?" MacKinnie asked.

"Immigration," Jefferson said. "Nothing to that. Just identification. To be sure you're the same people who left. Are you all here?"

"Not quite. Barstonic and Danvers and Stark were killed on Makassar." He was surprised at how easy it was to say that. Of course Hal wasn't dead. Or wasn't when they left Batav.

"Sorry to hear that." Jefferson glanced at his pocket computer. "Stark was your guard leader?"

"Yes. Your people there took a full report—"

Lieutenant Jefferson sighed. "They don't seem to have sent it along," he said. He did things to his pocket computer and looked at it again. "No, I'm afraid not. You'll have to tell that story again. Unless— Just a minute." He used a small stylus to write something else on the machine's face. "Aha. They did send it after all. Illustrated with satellite photos." He read for a moment, then looked up at MacKinnie. "You seem to have fought a proper little war at Batav."

"There were a few barbarians," Nathan said.

"Yes." He read more. "No superior weapons—"

"Of course not. Look, we were inspected when we landed on Makassar."

"I know."

What else do you know? MacKinnie wondered. "What's the problem?"

"Just wondering if tactical innovations come within the limits of the technology transfer laws," Jefferson said. "Well, that's not my business. If the Makassar garrison didn't have a complaint there's no reason for me to raise the question." The frown faded and he smiled at MacKinnie. "Forgot to say it. Welcome home."

There was a large crowd outside, with a dozen reporters in front. They all shouted questions at once. Then, suddenly, they fell silent.

Inspector Solon came through the crowd. His black uniform opened a way as if by magic. "Welcome back, Trader. Freelady. Gentlemen." His voice was cold even though his smile was broad. He turned to the crowd. "His Majesty requests that he be given the first interview," Solon said. "Surely that is reasonable? You will all have your opportunities, but I am commanded to bring the members of the expedition to the palace."

There were murmurs from the reporters, but no one actually protested. Solon led them across the broad avenue to waiting steam cars. "We will go directly to the palace," he said.

It was as if Stark had come up behind him. Nathan heard him as clearly as if he'd been there. "Bets on our ever gettin' out of there alive, Colonel? That guy gives me the creeps. So does his boss."

There were three cars. "Trader, you and Freelady Graham and our scholars will ride in the first car with me," Solon said. He held open the door.

Nathan and Mary climbed into the vehicle. It was new, a model he hadn't seen before, and the interior was luxurious. When they were inside, Solon handed each a sheet of paper.

"SPEAK ONLY PLEASANTRIES. DO NOT DISCUSS THE EXPEDITION UNTIL YOU ARE TOLD IT IS SAFE."

MacKinnie read it and nodded. Solon waited until each one acknowledged the message, then collected the papers and put them in his pouch. "Was it a pleasant journey?" he asked conversationally.

"Return trip was dull," MacKinnie said.

"Yes," Mary said. "There were no other passengers. Just three young naval officers, and they stayed forward in the crew area. We were left to our own devices."

"Not like the trip out," Longway said. "The Navy craft we returned on had few luxuries. Not even windows to look out of."

Kleinst had been silent. Now he said wistfully, "I saw Prince Samual's World from space when we left. Magnificent! And Makassar when we arrived there. Worlds so different—I think of what we could learn about weather and climate by observing different worlds from space. It is no wonder the Imperials are able to predict weather accurately. They know so much—"

Solon gestured with an upraised palm. "I'm certain they do," he said. "Well! You will have much to tell His Majesty."

MacKinnie glanced back through the rear window. The other cars were following. "The Navy released our cargo," he said. "Arrangements must be made to move it—"

"At once," Solon said. "When we reach the palace I will go myself. Thank you."

The palace was hidden in a maze of scaffolding. That,

too, was new. They were taken inside, and quickly led to the living quarters in the rear of the building. "I am sure you will wish to wash and change your clothing," Solon said. He gave them more papers with instructions.

MacKinnie nodded agreement.

The clothes were his own, but they felt too large. As he had expected, there were no weapons. He dressed quickly and followed the guide upstairs to a small sitting room.

Malcolm Dougal was alone in the room. He stood when MacKinnie entered, and his smile of welcome seemed genuine. "So. You returned," Dougal said. "Were you successful?"

"You'll pardon my suspicions, but where are the others?" MacKinnie asked.

Dougal frowned and looked genuinely puzzled. "Changing their clothing, of course—ah. You are concerned because I had Inspector Solon bring you here? How else could I have extracted you from that crowd?"

"We were told we would be meeting King David."

"As you will, when all are ready," Dougal said. "Your guardsmen will not be needed. They will be entertained by some of my men."

"Entertained how?"

"With whatever they want," Dougal said. "Why are you so suspicious? Are you expecting punishment? Did the mission fail?"

"Not exactly. But I've been wondering what you had in mind for us. You had a dozen people killed to protect your secret—and you don't need me and my troopers any longer."

"That was then," Dougal said. "Since you left there are many who know our plans. We've had no choice but to tell them. As a matter of fact, two of your former officers are now part of the security force at our research station. Which is what I had in mind for you and the guardsmen. You disappoint me, Colonel. I am neither bloodthirsty nor evil. Simply determined not to fail. Now, what success have you brought me?"

MacKinnie spread his hands. "I honestly don't know. We secured the library, and Kleinst read a number of the old books. We made copies of many of them—but Kleinst wasn't sure we could make them readable with anything we have on Prince Samual's World. And once we left Batav—that's the city the old library was in—we couldn't discuss any of this among ourselves. Too many locals aboard our ship. It was worse when we got to the Navy's base at Jikar, and on that spaceship. I thought Kleinst was going to burst for lack of someone to talk to."

"I see. And you don't know if we can build a ship?"

"I know damned well we can't build anything like their ships," MacKinnie said. "Dougal, you can't imagine what their equipment is like. Even the library. A box no larger than that sideboard there—we were told that could contain every book on Prince Samual's World with room to spare. The things we brought home are about this big." MacKinnie held up thumb and forefinger to indicate the size. "And each one holds a whole library. If we can read them."

"So you learned nothing?"

"It wasn't my job to learn," MacKinnie said. "I was hired to get them there and bring them back. I did. All but two guardsmen."

"So we must rely on Kleinst."

"Kleinst and Todd. They spent days in the library. Not as long as they'd have liked to, but I didn't dare wait any longer before starting back. As it was we only had five days to spare before the ship left, and I gather there won't be another for a while. Something strange is going on in another part of the Empire. They wouldn't tell me what, but they take it seriously."

"Indeed?" Dougal looked thoughtful. "We will have to see if we can find out," he said. "It may affect us."

He's a good liar, MacKinnie thought. But he knows something he's not telling me. I wonder if it's important. . . .

"As for this audience," Dougal said, "there will be many present who know nothing about your true purpose in going to Makassar, and we suspect the Imperials can listen to conversations in the audience chamber. You will continue the pretense of a simple trading mission."

"You didn't even tell the king?" MacKinnie demanded.

Dougal laughed. "His Majesty knows all," he said. "But many in the government do not. We intend to keep it that way. Come, let's get this over with. I am anxious to talk to all of you, and I will not feel really comfortable until we are out of Haven."

"Where are you taking us?"

"We have a large military research post in the Corliss Grant Hills," Dougal said. "Most of what goes on there is weapons research, which the Imperials know all about. But it is a large place, and much goes on that we do not tell them."

"I see. You've organized well," MacKinnie said.

"As best we could. But now it all depends on what you have brought us. And we are running out of time."

Their quarters in the Corliss Grant research station were comfortable, but they were prisoners.

"I prefer you do not think that way," Dougal told MacKinnie. "You have weapons. You are all housed in the same building. All of you, including your soldiers. From time to time one of you—I prefer Academician Longway, he has a knack for talking—will go to Haven to be seen and speak to the press. But think, Colonel. You will be recognized if you are seen often. And if there is no one to tell your secrets to, you will not reveal them." He threw up his hands as if in dismay. "I have given you every possible assurance of your safety. I make no doubt that with your skill and the number of men I have left you, you could escape at any time. I rely on your word, Colonel. You have sworn to Haven and Prince Samual's World. Can I not trust you?"

There wasn't any answer to that, as MacKinnie later told Mary.

"So we're our own jailors," she said.

"It comes to that," MacKinnie said. "He even has me in the security department. I don't really blame him. I'd do the same thing myself. But as Hal would say, this spy business gets old pretty fast." He tried to laugh, but the sound was unpleasant.

"Are you sorry?" she asked.

"Sorry I lost Hal? I'll always be sorry."

She moved closer to him, and he held her, clinging to her. They stood for a long time. Finally he let her go. "But

I'm not sorry I found you. Which reminds me, I have to speak to your father—"

"No."

He frowned. "What do you mean, 'no'?"

"You don't *have* to do anything," she said. "That's not what either of us wants. Haven is ruled by customs and duties—we don't need them with each other."

He was silent for a moment. "All right, let's say I want to speak to your father. It's time I made an honest woman of you—"

"Or an honest man of yourself."

They lived in luxury, but there was nothing to do. The research station was isolated, far from any town, sealed from the rest of Prince Samual's World, and keeping it "secure" required no effort at all.

Since no one objected, Nathan went to technical conferences. Much of the discussion involved forces, and specific impulse, and other meaningless terms. He did understand that Kleinst had no way of reading the cubes they had brought back.

"It's enough to drive me mad," Kleinst said. A dozen older engineers seated around the conference table nodded sympathy. "It's all right here." He held up one of the small plasticine cubes. "And if I had nothing else to do, I might, in ten years, be able to read this. I know the theory—"

"We're working on it," Academician Taylor said. Taylor headed a group who worked on long-distance communicators and other electrical matters. They thought they had a method of reading the Makassar data, but so far it had not worked.

"But I have to spend time on the ship also," Kleinst said. "And I fear that is hopeless."

"We've got your liquid oxygen," Todd said. He looked pleased with himself, and MacKinnie thought he had a right to be. In his days in the library on Makassar, Todd had found books on ancient technology—methods ancient even in the days of the First Empire—and studied how they'd done things. MacKinnie had never thought of air as something that could be made liquid, but Todd had done it by putting oxygen under high pressure, then rapidly letting it expand and cool. It all seemed simple once it was done—

"Yes," Kleinst said. "But we can't build pumps. And the stabilizing mechanisms." He shook his head sadly. "We have large gyroscopes, but every attempt to make small ones with electrical connections to guide the ship has failed. Everything we can make is large, too large—"

"In time we can make it smaller," Douglas Starr said.

"Time is what we don't have," MacKinnie said.

Starr glared at him. "My mechanics are working themselves to death now. I can get no more from them. There are no more hours in the day!"

"I know. I meant no disrespect," MacKinnie said. And I shouldn't even be here. But what else do I have to do? Every day he examined the political maps. Haven's reach extended far to the east, all the way to the eastern ocean. In one memorable four-day period seven city-states capitulated to King David. One large kingdom on the eastern coast of the continent was holding out, and even though it looked as if it would take only a short campaign to conquer it, MacKinnie had asked for a command in Haven's army. Of course Dougal refused to consider his request.

"Go back to first principles," Todd said. "We can't build true spacecraft. We can't even build anything like the Empire's landing boats."

"So we must build rockets," Kleinst said. "And large liquid rockets are very complex—"

"Why rockets?" Todd asked.

Kleinst frowned. "What else is there?"

"It largely depends on what you mean by a spaceship," the midshipman said. "Or rather, what the Empire will accept as a spaceship. . . ."

"If it will take us to space, it is a spaceship," Kleinst muttered. "We have no time for senseless debate on definitions. What have you in mind?"

"There was an ancient document," Todd said. "I hesitate to say how ancient—" He saw the intense interest of the others and laughed self-consciously. "Before the second millennium of the Christian era," he said. "In the time of the first spacecraft, on Earth."

There was a long silence. Earth, MacKinnie thought. Before the Empire, before the CoDominium, before space travel. Those times were no more than legends, yet Todd had seen copies of works written then.

"The first spacecraft used rockets," Kleinst said firmly.

"Yes, but they had another concept," Todd said. "It was not used, but it might have been. And it is something we can build. . . ."

★27★
WITNESS
★★★

Lieutenant Jefferson tapped nervously at the door to High Commissioner Ackoff's office. Jeff could think of no reason why the Imperial governor would want to see him. In the past few months he'd worked on a dozen assignments, all routine and all dull, and as far as Jefferson knew he'd done them all satisfactorily; Ackoff couldn't be unhappy with him. On the other hand, he'd done nothing outstanding either. Jeff didn't like economic intelligence work, and longed for a space assignment.

"Come."

Commissioner Ackoff's office might have been used as a textbook example: office, one each, governor's, minor colonial planet. There was the large wooden desk and leather chairs; conference table and more chairs; conversation group with couch and soft chairs off to one side; computer screens and input console discreetly hidden in the desk; portrait of the Emperor draped with the flags of Empire; shelves of curios including models of ships Ackoff had served in; large sideboard filled with liquor—

Ackoff was seated at his conference table. So was Captain Greenaugh.

"Come in, Jefferson," Ackoff said. "Have a seat."

"Thank you, Your Excellency—"

"Haven't seen you for a while," Sir Alexei said. "I miss those government seminars. Really ought to start them up again. Only time I get to meet my officers." The Commissioner shook his head slowly. "Too much work, no one to do it. I'm afraid we've an additional job for you."

"Sir?" Jeff looked to Greenaugh for some hint of what was happening.

"Not in space," Greenaugh said. He laughed at Jefferson's expression. "Tired of this place already? I'm told you're practically engaged to a local girl—"

"Not yet, sir," Jeff was emphatic.

"But you still see her," Greenaugh said. It wasn't a question.

"Yes, sir."

"Quite often."

"Yes, sir," Jeff said. Often, and the relationship was certainly one that Elaine might take as "practically engaged." Certainly her father had a right to think so. The less said about that the better.

"Not trying to pry into your private affairs," Greenaugh said. "But I take it you do not intend to apply for transfer to the civil service."

"No, sir," Jeff said. "I'm ready for space duty whenever there's an assignment—"

Greenaugh chuckled. "And you'd like to know when that will be. So would we all, Lieutenant. So would we all. But I'm afraid not even Sir Alexei knows that. Meanwhile, we've a job to do here. Know anything about Haven's military research establishment?"

"Well, a little—"

"A lot, I'd say," Ackoff interrupted. "It was your economic analysis that got us interested. Haven has a big research station in the Corliss Grant Hills. From what we can see it siphons off a good part of their budget and a lot of their technical talent. We can't think why."

"Any ideas?" Greenaugh asked.

"Not really, sir," Jefferson said. "Frankly, I can't see any need for a big military research effort. Haven has just finished the consolidation of this continent, which effectively means the whole planet. They'd have finished the job sooner if they hadn't dragged their feet. They've no one to fight."

"Precisely," Greenaugh said. "Which is what disturbs us. One, they did drag their feet. From what we know of their history, unification of the planet has been Haven's dream since the present dynasty took over. We gave them the chance to do it, and they went very slowly. Then all of a sudden they speeded things up and finished with a bang. Two, they're spending a lot of money and sending the cream of their engineering talent to a military research station that's working on weapons they'll never need. Quick-firing cannon. War rockets—big ones, too; *Tombaugh's* radar tracked one six hundred kilometers. Balloons, for Christ's sake. And that's just what they tell us about. What else are they doing out there?"

Jefferson frowned. "I don't know, sir—"

"No, and we don't expect you to," Greenaugh said. "But we do want to find out. You get along with the locals. Come to that, you've got more purely social contacts in Haven than most of us."

"Yes, sir, but Elaine's father is a roads commissioner. He wouldn't know about the Corliss Grant station."

"Didn't expect him to," Ackoff said. "But you go to social gatherings. What's the mood here? Officially they love us, but what do they really think?" He spread his hands helplessly. "Are they mad enough to be working on weapons to fight us?"

"I've heard no hint of *that*," Jefferson protested.

"Nor would you," Ackoff said gently.

"Christ," Greenaugh snorted. "Aliens in Trans-Coalsack. Half the fleet sucked off to *that* godforsaken corner of the Empire. Outies not twenty parsecs from here, and nowhere near enough ships to deal with them. All we'd bloody need is some kind of abortive revolt just when we're ready to report this place pacified." He shook his head grimly. "Christ, what would we do? We don't have enough Marines to occupy the place—"

"They're hardly a threat to the Empire, sir," Jefferson said.

"They are if they've linked up with the outies," Greenaugh said.

"But—do you have some reason to believe—"

"No," Ackoff said. "We've no reason to believe anything at all. But the fact remains that they're spending enormous sums for no reason we can determine, and their explanations don't make sense."

"I wish we'd never found this damned place," Greenaugh said. "But that's neither here nor there. This whole conversation is about to be mooted. Apparently they're going to tell us what they're doing out at Corliss Grant."

Jefferson looked puzzled. "Sir?"

"They've requested an official observer," Ackoff said. "An Imperial officer as official witness to some important test they're going to conduct."

"But why would they want a witness?" Jefferson asked.

Ackoff shook his head. "We haven't any idea. Of course colonials do strange things."

"I admit enough curiosity to consider going myself," Greenaugh said. "But the governor won't let me."

"Not without sufficient escort," Ackoff said. "And since our best guess is that what they're doing is harmless, it would be impolitic for the captain to arrive with a company of fleet Marines."

Whereas, Jeff thought, lieutenants are more expendable than captains. "Surely they know the Empire's policy on negotiating with kidnappers," he said.

"They ought to. We told them often enough," Greenaugh said.

Imperial policy on the subject was simple. The hostages were counted as dead from the moment they were kidnapped. Imperial forces might storm the place the hostages were kept in, or they might bomb it. The one thing they wouldn't do was negotiate for their safety. The policy was supposed to take away any incentive for kidnapping Imperial officials, and Jeff had always approved of it. Now he wasn't so sure. . . .

"It's possible they don't believe us, of course," Greenaugh continued. "But I don't think so. It's too raw. Invite an Imperial officer out to their most secret place just to kidnap him? Easier to grab one of you chuckleheads in a local bar after a long night. Also, there's the matter of the weather."

"Weather?" Jeff asked.

"Yes," Greenaugh said. "They want an observer as soon as possible, but only on a day that we can guarantee will have clear weather, no storms or high winds, in the Corliss Grant area." The captain shrugged. "No difficulty this time of year, of course."

"But no explanation given?" Jeff asked.

"None."

"Whatever they intend," Ackoff said, "this is an opportunity to find out what they're doing out there. I will give you credentials—meaningless, of course—certifying you as an official witness, and you'll be sent in answer to this request. The computer says the weather down there ought to be fine for at least another five or six days, so you can leave tomorrow."

"Take a couple of Marines, lad," Greenaugh said. "And keep an open communication line to headquarters. I'll have someone listening in, just in case. We'll get you out if we possibly can."

The Corliss Grant Hills were located on a long peninsula jutting southward nearly a thousand kilometers from Haven City, the most southerly portion of the Kingdom of Haven. Jeff sat in the first-class compartment of the surprisingly fast train and watched the countryside roll past. There was little else to do. The palace equerry assigned to escort him was not talkative. Unfortunately, there wasn't much to see, either. This part of Haven was mostly farmland dotted with patches of swamp. Once something large and dangerous-appearing reared out of the swamp, but it didn't challenge the train itself, and they were moving too fast for Jeff to see what the beast really was.

After a while the rail line cut inward through rolling brown hills cluttered with low brush. Jeff shook his head in perplexity. The compartment grew hotter with each kilometer they traveled southward; now it was downright uncomfortable. As a location for a secret research station, the Corliss Grant Hills had nothing to recommend them except isolation. Why, he wondered, why would the government of Haven choose to send a large part of their budget and increasing numbers of their all-too-scarce trained personnel to this godforsaken area?

The train slowed with screeching of brakes and hiss of steam. Jefferson collected the two Marines Greenaugh had sent with him and allowed himself to be led off the train. There was a small group led by an officer of the Haven Royal Army waiting on the platform. The officer—a colonel by his insignia—seemed vaguely familiar. Jefferson frowned, trying to recall him.

"MacKinnie," Jefferson said. "Trader MacKinnie. I hadn't known you were in the Haven army." Although, he thought, I might have guessed. "Does this mysterious event you want us to observe have something to do with the expedition to Makassar?"

MacKinnie's smile was noncommittal. "Less than we'd like," he said. "But I suppose you could say so. Welcome to Corliss Grant, Lieutenant. Our transport is just over here—"

The steam car was luxurious. Jefferson declined a drink from the built-in bar and tried to question MacKinnie, but the Haven officer wasn't answering questions.

"All in due time," Jeff was told. "All in due time. Fortunately the weather is perfect—"

"As you knew it would be," Jefferson said.

"Yes. Thank you."

Four times they passed through guarded gates. The soldiers on duty seemed quite alert, and were highly deferential to MacKinnie. Curiouser and curiouser, Jeff thought. "I take it you're not in charge of this show?"

MacKinnie shook his head. "No, you'll be meeting some of His Majesty's ministers shortly. I'm just supposed to get you on post and feed you lunch."

"Skip the lunch," Jeff said. "Let's get to why I'm here."

"Can't skip the lunch," MacKinnie said. "Timing's rather critical, I'm afraid."

MacKinnie's half smile was irritating. There was something else, too, an air of tension. Colonel MacKinnie's worried about something, Jeff thought. Worried and trying not to show it. I wonder—

There was a series of loud explosions. Jeff sat bolt upright. His hand flew to his sidearm before he noticed that MacKinnie hadn't moved. "Put it away, Donivtsky," Jeff told his Marine escort. "I will say I'm pleased to see how fast you can draw that weapon."

"Sir."

"Colonel, what the devil *was* that?"

"Experimental cannon. Fires several hundred rounds a

minute," MacKinnie said. "They're testing it. You'll see it soon enough."

"Did you drag me down here in this heat to look at a *cannon?*"

"Not exactly. Ah. Here we are."

The car pulled up in front of a large wooden building. There were armed sentries on duty outside it, and more soldiers waiting to open the car doors for them. Again Jeff had the impression of tension, of something about to happen, but there was nothing definite, and certainly nothing threatening.

He was led inside to an ornate dining room where white-uniformed mess stewards served an excellent meal. Jeff declined wine, but was persuaded to have a small glass of grua after he ate. Conversation was minimal, and once again MacKinnie avoided answering his questions.

When they finished, MacKinnie stood. "And now it is time to meet my lord Dougal, His Majesty's cabinet officer in charge of this establishment. If you'll come with me—"

They didn't have to go far. Jeff was privately amused. It wasn't unknown for colonials to show their importance by insisting on elaborate rules of precedence. Obviously a mere lieutenant wasn't important enough for a cabinet officer to have lunch with.

There could have been a scene at the office door. Jeff's Marines didn't want to be separated from him. "My apologies, Colonel," Jeff said. "The sergeant has been ordered to protect me—"

"Surely not from us," MacKinnie said. "On this post that's my job."

And he looks plenty insulted, too, Jeff thought. Oh, hell. "I'll be right out, Sergeant," Jeff told Donivtsky. "Please wait for me here."

The Marine wasn't pleased. His "Sir!" made that clear. Jeff went into the paneled office musing on just how much expression a senior NCO could put into a monosyllable.

The man seated at the large desk certainly didn't look dangerous. Jeff remembered meeting him briefly at some palace function or another.

"My lord Dougal, minister without portfolio," MacKinnie said. As Jeff shook hands with Dougal, MacKinnie closed the door.

"Very kind of you to come," Dougal said. "Please have a seat. Thank you. Grua?"

"I've been entertained well, my lord," Jeff said. "If you'll pardon me, I'm overcome with curiosity about why I'm here."

"Yes, of course you are," Dougal said. "If you could please give me your credentials as an official observer for the Empire?"

Jeff handed over the documents. They were studded with seals. "Dazzlers," Ackoff had called them. Since there wasn't any such office as "official witness" the text had been cobbled up by Ackoff's secretary. It was possible that the locals could read some of the Imperial language—their own wasn't all that different from Anglic—so the documents stated, in flowery terms, that Lieutenant Jefferson was empowered to observe and make an official report.

Dougal examined the papers, then put them in his desk. "If you'll excuse me one more moment?" He lifted a small tube from the desk and put it to his ear, listened, then spoke into it. "Excellent. Please ask H. M. to be ready to come in." He put the tube back on the desk and turned back to Jefferson. "Indeed, it is time we had a long discussion, Lieutenant. I would rather your government had sent a more senior officer, but you'll have to do. First, though, I must make a strange request. Would you allow me to lock your sidearm in my desk?"

MacKinnie spoke from behind him. "No sudden moves. Please."

"I regret that the colonel is armed," Dougal said. "As am I. And of course this office is under observation by several of my agents. Believe me, Lieutenant, you are not being kidnapped. No demands will be made on you, and your weapon will be returned to you shortly. But I must insist that you surrender it. You see, we have a silly law that only the king's officers may be armed in his presence, and His Majesty is waiting to come in."

And Colonel MacKinnie is behind me, Jeff thought. These blithering idiots are going to get themselves in trouble. Already have. He could imagine what was happening at headquarters. The duty officer listening would have sent for Greenaugh—if Greenaugh weren't already there. Jeff hoped he was. He didn't really need to be rescued.

"No problem," Jeff said. "You didn't have to be so dramatic. A simple request—"

"Which is all we have done," Dougal said.

Jeff carefully drew his pistol and held it out. MacKinnie stepped forward and took it.

Dougal lifted the speaking tube again. "All clear," he said pleasantly.

The door opened and King David came in.

★ ★ ★

Dougal stood when the king entered, so Jeff did also. And what's the protocol for a disarmed Imperial officer meeting a colonial king? Jeff wondered. Can't hurt to be polite. "Your Majesty," Jeff acknowledged, and bowed.

"This is not an official audience," David said. "Please be seated."

Jeff waited until both the king and Dougal were seated before he resumed his chair. As King David took his seat, Jeff studied him. Not a bad-looking fellow, he thought. And not an idiot, from everything Greenaugh says. This is a pretty stupid move, but they'll never know just how stupid. By now Greenaugh himself is certainly listening—

As if he were reading Jeff's thoughts, King David said, "My lord, you are convinced we are not being overheard?"

"Nearly certain," Dougal said. "All through lunch the technicians detected some kind of radio wave. After the lieutenant came in here and the door was closed they couldn't detect it any longer. I suppose it's possible they have some other kind of secret communication we can't stop, but I doubt it."

"How long have we?" King David asked.

Dougal shrugged. "As best we know, we're duplicating that signal exactly. At this moment, three actors who sound very much like myself, MacKinnie, and the lieutenant are exchanging meaningless pleasantries."

"What the devil does this mean?" Jeff demanded.

"Please," King David said. "Lieutenant, you have my word that no harm will come to you and that you will shortly be given your weapon and taken to a place where you can communicate with your superiors. Indeed, we will *insist* that you communicate. All we want is to be certain you will not interfere with our test."

"Then may I suggest that Your Majesty conduct his test and not interfere with an Imperial officer on duty?" Jeff said.

"Please," Dougal said. "If you'll listen for a moment all will be clear. We have one question we need answered." He looked sourly at MacKinnie. "The colonel insisted we find this out before we allow the flight. Lieutenant, we know your spaceship is in orbit around this planet. We've been tracking her."

Jeff stood abruptly. "If you damned fools fire some kind of rocket at *Tombaugh* you really are stupid—"

"Sit down." Colonel MacKinnie stood close to Jeff. "Now you've been blunt, let me. We're not trying to hurt your goddam warship. What we want to know is, if we launch someone into orbit can your ship rescue her?"

"Rescue? What—Your Majesty, just what *do* you contemplate doing here today?"

"Surely that is obvious from the question," King David said. "We are launching a spaceship. Our only problem is that it cannot return to Prince Samual's World. Thus we need to know how long it will take your ship to rescue our helmsman."

"Helmswoman," MacKinnie said.

"The colonel's fiancée," King David said. "He is understandably worried about her."

"I see." Jeff sat down. "May I take out my computer?"

"Please do," Dougal said.

Jeff scrawled numbers across the screen. "You're launching due east?"

Dougal nodded. "They tell me that's best, although I confess I don't know why."

"I do." Due east from this latitude . . . what orbit was *Tombaugh* in just now? Not true polar, but highly inclined. No problem to intercept a ship coming up from Prince Samual's World, but to match orbits . . . "Your Majesty, you must not do this. *Tombaugh's* defenses will be on automatic, and they might shoot down your ship—"

"We've timed our launch pretty carefully," Dougal said. "Your ship will be on the other side of Prince Samual's World precisely because we supposed something like that. Once our ship is up you can warn your people."

"I see." Jeff scrawled more numbers. "Assuming your craft actually makes orbit—which I doubt, that's tougher than you can possibly know—then *Tombaugh* should be able to match orbits in a bit more than three hours."

"You see," Dougal said. Jeff noted the cabinet officer was speaking to MacKinnie. "Plenty of margin."

"I suppose," MacKinnie said.

"If Your Majesty will forgive a blunt question," Jeff said, "I really would like to know why you're doing this."

"But surely that, too, is obvious," King David said. "As of last week I am in effective control of this planet. Presumably we will now be admitted to the Empire. Since we are about to demonstrate that we can construct a spaceship, we wish to apply for a status somewhat higher than that of a colony."

"Jesus Christ on a crutch," Jeff said.

★28★
LONG PAST THUNDER
★★★

There were a dozen officials waiting on a platform behind the office building. It had been too hot inside the office, but at least there had been air motion provided by fans. Outside there was not a breath of wind, and Prince Samual's bright sun stood high overhead. Instantly, Jeff felt sweat running down his chest inside his tunic.

He fingered his sidearm to be sure it was still there. As soon as he was outside the building he spoke. "Whoever's on duty, get Captain Greenaugh at once."

The acknowledge symbol appeared on the screen of his pocket computer. Moments later the computer spoke to him. "Greenaugh here."

"Captain, there's a lot happening. First thing is that they're about to launch a one-way spaceship."

"Lieutenant, what have you been drinking?"

Jeff patiently explained. "And they're about to launch it now," he finished. "I haven't seen the ship yet, but any moment now—"

"I don't suppose you could delay this launch?" Greenaugh asked.

"There are about five hundred of their troops here, and the three of us," Jeff said.

"Yeah." Greenaugh was silent for a moment. "And their king is there," Greenaugh said. "I'd better get His Excellency brought up to speed. What the hell kind of spaceship have they got, anyway?"

"They haven't told me, sir. I assume it's some kind of primitive rocket. I don't see any ship, but everyone's acting expectant. They're coming back now; they went off to give me privacy—although nothing's private about it; they know what kind of communications I've been using. They're probably listening."

There was another long silence from the other end. Then, "We didn't even know they suspected. What else don't we know?"

Jeff was tempted to say they hadn't known anything about a spaceship, but decided not to.

"Look just over there," Dougal told Jeff. "Just at that hillside."

There was a roar of thunder, a series of explosions so close together it was impossible to distinguish between them, but still it seemed like many explosions because it went on far too long to have been just one. It did not at all sound like a large rocket.

The ship that rose above the hill was like nothing Jeff had ever imagined. It looked like an artillery shell mounted above a large inverted cup. Impossibly bright flashes came downward from the cup. They were so close together they appeared to be one long tongue of flame, yet once again Jeff had the impression of many small explosions rather than one continuous burn. He cringed involuntarily. There was no protection at all if the—ship?—exploded. He wondered why they would expose their king to so much danger. "What *is* that thing?" Jeff demanded.

"A piloted spaceship," Dougal said proudly.

"It doesn't *look* much like a spaceship," Jeff said. "It doesn't even look like a rocket."

"It's not a rocket." The newcomer's voice was high-pitched and almost querulous, but filled with pride.

"Allow me to present Academician Kleinst," Dougal said.

"Kleinst," Jeff said aloud. "You were also on the Makassar expedition."

"I had that privilege," Kleinst said. He turned to stare after the rapidly rising ship.

Jeff watched it also, and willed it to succeed. There was something highly dramatic about this ship rising on a thunder of fire. "If it explodes we could be killed," Jeff said. "Didn't you think of a bunker for the observers?"

"Your pardon," Dougal said. "His Majesty thought that as the pilot was willing to take the risk, we should all share it. Perhaps we had no right to assume you would feel the same way. It is not your ship—"

"It's academic now," Jeff said. "How does the ship work, then?"

"For God's sake," Greenaugh's voice interrupted. "Call it a goddam craft, or a probe, or anything else, but don't be on record as calling it a ship! His Excellency almost excreted bricks when I told him what your colonial friends are up to."

"Craft," Jeff corrected himself. "How does it work if it's not a rocket?"

Kleinst preened. "There is a rapid-firing gun, a multi-barreled gun that fires explosive shells downward. The shells explode in the hemispherical chamber beneath. The explosion drives the ship upward."

"I never heard of anything like that," Jeff said. "Captain, have—"

"I'm looking it up," Greenaugh's voice said. "Primitive spacecraft, propulsion by explosive—Jesus Christ!"

"Sir?"

"The earliest known reference is 1899."

"Sir, did you say *1899?*"

"I did. We don't have the text, but the reference is here. And in 1957, Goddard applied for some kind of license to build such a ship. Dyson experimented with them, too."

Goddard. Dyson. Names from ancient history, people who'd lived in legendary times. Jefferson had been aboard a luxury liner named *Goddard,* and thought he recalled a scout survey ship named *Freeman Dyson* as well.

The ship was almost out of sight now. Its thunder was muted as it plunged eastward and rose into the ultra-deep blue of Prince Samual's skies.

"How are you stabilizing it?" Jefferson demanded.

"It's largely self-stabilizing," Kleinst said. "From the geometry of the explosion chamber. We also have peroxide rockets to correct the heading."

"And your pilot's a girl—"

"A freelady," Colonel MacKinnie said coldly.

"The gyroscopes do most of the steering," Kleinst added.

MacKinnie was staring toward the east at the spot where the oddball ship was now almost invisible. Jeff didn't care much for the expression on the colonel's face. "Captain, you'd better alert *Tombaugh* not to shoot it down," he said.

"Already done," Greenaugh said.

"Colonel," Jeff said, "am I being too personal in asking why you sent your fiancée as pilot?"

"Weight," MacKinnie said through clenched teeth.

"Mass," Kleinst corrected. "We needed a pilot who had experience in no gravity. Of those few available, Freelady Graham and I mass the least. I was needed on other duties."

"And what's your plan now?" Jefferson demanded.

"There is a transmitter aboard," Kleinst said. "When the ship achieves orbit it will be turned on to provide a signal so that *Prince Samual's Hope* can be located in space. We had hoped your ship would be able to assist."

"No reentry capability," Jefferson said.

Kleinst looked puzzled for a moment, then nodded. "Correct. We were unable to provide for a return from orbit within the time limits available."

"And you call that a spaceship?" Jefferson demanded.

King David had been listening quietly. "That, I think, is a matter to be discussed between your superiors and my advisors, is it not, Lieutenant? *Prince Samual's Hope* has carried one of my officers to space. Does that not make it a spaceship?"

"Don't answer," Greenaugh's voice said. "Don't even discuss the matter with them!"

"Yes, sir," Jeff said.

He tried to remember Mary Graham's face, but he couldn't. It had been too long ago that he inspected the Makassar party. She's one hell of a lady, Jeff thought. I wouldn't have got in that gun-powered coffin for an earl's coronet. Hope she makes it.

He turned and like the others stared at the empty indigo skies.

★29★
S.O.S.
★ ★ ★

The ship rose in fire and thunder.

Mary Graham lay on the leather-strip couch, unable to move, her face drawn into a rictus grin by the acceleration. Despite the couch and its shock mountings, the vibration was fierce. She felt sharp, stabbing pains in her abdomen.

For all that, she felt better than she had while she was waiting for the launch. That had been a time of real terror, an hour stretched into years of waiting and wondering and remembering.

You wanted to be important, she told herself. Well, lassie, you've managed that, if you haven't got yourself killed. But I wish it didn't hurt so.

The noise gradually died away as the ship rose above the atmosphere. The vibration was no better, and the acceleration continued to increase. With the cannon's roar muted she heard other sounds. The clatter of the feed mechanism pushing an endless stream of heavy shells into the rotary feed hopper. The steady whirr of the big gyros. Clicking sounds as punched steel ribbons fed through the clockwork mechanism. The ribbons controlled the gear mechanism that controlled the gyros; they might call her a pilot, but she knew better. Those steel ribbons were the actual pilot, and she was no more than a passenger.

How long does this go on? I can't stand a lot more of it. What am I doing here?

Finishing a job.

Maybe. And maybe not. Even if I live through this, there's no guarantee the Empire will accept this thing as a real spaceship. But it's all we have, and they certainly wouldn't accept it if there were no passengers at all. Somebody had to ride *Prince Samual's Hope, and she was the most logical choice. Young, strong, with experience in space . . .*

It had made a lot of sense at the time she proposed the idea. First to Kleinst, then to Malcolm Dougal. She hadn't convinced Nathan, but there hadn't been much he could do to stop her. She wasn't married to him yet.

Would she ever be? Did he want her? He'd been furious, and could he live with someone he couldn't control? That's silly, he's known since Makassar, and he's always wanted me as much as I want him, and O God, do I want him now.

She felt dizzy, and the acceleration and vibration increased constantly. She couldn't open her eyes.

O God, make it stop!

She woke to silence and the sensation of falling. The silence wasn't complete. The gyros continued to whirr, but the cannon was silent. She unbuckled the straps holding her to the couch.

Her body ached. Not just the dull ache she'd expected from the acceleration. This was stabbing pain, pain so intense it was like a bright red veil across her eyes, pain all through her lower abdominal region, pain made worse when she touched herself or moved her legs.

I've got to get up. I've got to turn on that—transmitter. Or what Kleinst called a transmitter. Nothing like the box Lieutenant Farr kept at Navy House in Jikar.

But first I've got to know. Are we in orbit, or—

She floated to the viewport. A river of stars swung past, then Prince Samual's World. The ship was rolling, not fast enough to create artificial gravity, but definitely rolling.

Once each minute her world was below. Not a whole world, only a large disc. She wedged her head against the port and waited, cautiously experimenting with her legs to see if she could find a position that might alleviate the pain even a little.

Gradually she detected motion. She was moving across the Major Sea, and if anything she was drawing *away* from Prince Samual's World.

Later she'd get out the sextant and take angles, but it looked good. The *Hope* was in orbit. Maybe. Time for the transmitter. She pushed away from the port and over to the bulkhead. The transmitter was nothing but a vibrator, some coils, and a gap across which a fat electrical spark jumped when she pressed the keys.

Dit dit dit. Dah dah dah. Dit dit dit. Which stood for S.O.S., which stood for something so ancient that no one knew what it might be. Did the Empire still use S.O.S. as a distress signal? The First Empire had. Longway was certain of it. So why wouldn't the present day Imperials?

Not that it mattered a lot. The Empire knew she was there. Nathan had arranged that. Their observer would tell the Imperial Navy ship all about her, and what kind of signal she'd be sending, and they'd come get her. She wound the clockwork that controlled the spark gap. An endless tape fed through it. Dit dit dit. Dah dah dah. Dit dit dit. A thick wire from the spark gap led through insulators to a mess of fused quartz, through that to outside the ship. She tried to imagine the signal going through space, reaching out to *Tombaugh*. Dit dit dit. Dah dah dah. Dit dit dit.

Now they'd hear it and come get her—

But there was nothing to do but wait, and time passed slowly.

If only I didn't hurt so bad. We didn't expect this. What's wrong with me? Acceleration? Vibration? Something awful. God, it hurts. . . .

Gradually, though, the pain lessened. It wasn't as bad if she stayed curled into a tight ball. She pushed herself to the couch and drew a strap loosely across herself and lay there.

Time passed slowly. There was a counter on the tape mechanism driving the transmitter. Not a very accurate clock, but the best she had. It told her that thirty minutes had gone by. She stretched her legs experimentally. Not too bad. Painful, but she could stand it. And there was something wrong with the gyros. Batteries weakening. They were slowing down.

If they slowed enough, she'd have to try to control the

ship herself. There were big wooden levers by one of the ports, and she could use them to control the jets mounted in a ring around the ship. If they didn't run out of peroxide for the jets, she might be able to control tumbling. She hoped she wouldn't have to. Kleinst wasn't sure she—or anyone else—could do it by eye with nothing but the viewports to guide her.

The stars were still rolling past, first the stars, then Prince Samual's World. The ship was rolling, but it wasn't tumbling yet. She wondered if she should cancel the roll motion. Kleinst hadn't been sure about that. It might be difficult, and the Empire surely had ways to stabilize the ship.

No, damn it, she thought. We'll do as much of this ourselves as we possibly can. She took off the cords that held the control levers in place, and experimentally moved one of them. There was a subdued sound, more a rushing than a roar, and the stars swung more slowly.

Not so hard, she thought. Not hard at all. She moved the lever again, held it a bit longer, then waited to see what that did.

Three more times, and she had almost done it. Now the ship rotated very slowly. Prince Samual's World visible for long minutes at each of the three viewports. Good enough, she thought. No point in taking chances. There still didn't seem to be tumbling, although the sound of the gyros was definitely weaker.

If she listened carefully, she could hear the hiss of the air tanks. Five hours of air. Then—

Don't think about that.

What should I think about?

It's beautiful up here. Prince Samual's World is lovely, a big saucer with wispy clouds, and the stars above, rivers of stars, and—

Where is that ship?

Dit dit dit. Dah dah dah. Dit dit dit.

★30★
DEFINITIONS
★ ★ ★

There were three senior civil servants with Ackoff and Captain Greenaugh when Jeff arrived at the High Commissioner's office. The massive conference table was littered with overflowing ashtrays and dirty coffee cups.

Ackoff was preoccupied and his introductions were perfunctory. That was telling; Ackoff was generally impeccably polite. "Lieutenant, you know our First Secretary, Dr. Boyd? And Madame Goldstein and Mr. Singh. I presume you've completed your inspection of that colonial craft?"

"Yes, sir."

"An official inspection," Greenaugh said. "By our official observer."

Jeff winced at the irony in his commanding officer's voice.

"Report says the pilot's not in good shape. Is she all right?" Greenaugh asked.

Boy, and how! Jeff wanted to say. "She was shaken up

rather badly, sir. They have her in *Tombaugh's* sick bay. She's cheerful enough. I think she's rather flattered by all the attention. . . ."

"Hardly surprising," Goldstein said.

"We will need your observations, Lieutenant," Commissioner Ackoff said. "We have a problem. What do we do with this?" He held up a parchment. "As you suspect, it's King David's formal application for admission of Prince Samual's World as a second-class space-faring planet. I expect it comes as no surprise to learn it begins with great professions of loyalty to the Empire. . . . He's got his prerogatives right, too. Self-government under Imperial defense and Imperial advice on extra-planetary policy. Official observers at Court. Representative in the lower house of Parliament. Willing to accept reasonable trade restrictions. And while this doesn't ask for it, you can be certain the next document we get will be a request for technological assistance. I would be interested in knowing how they learned so much about Imperial politics."

Dr. Boyd was a tall man, well rounded, going to fat but not quite there yet. "To be precise, about the structure of Imperial government as it existed before the last Reform Act," Boyd said. "They obtained excellent information, but much is somewhat out of date. A deficiency I think Mr. Soliman's people will remedy shortly."

Jeff muttered something.

"Yes, Lieutenant?" Ackoff asked.

"Nothing, sir. It doesn't seem to me that Trader Soliman's firm would be too happy at losing a colony world since they've got the trade concession."

"On the contrary," Dr. Boyd said. "Trader Soliman's on-planet factor has already attached a letter recommending that this application be approved."

"I don't understand," Jeff said.

Ackoff smiled grimly. "The situation is rather delicate. . . . Tell me, Lieutenant, how much of that craft represents imported technology?"

"It's hard to say, sir," Jeff answered. He spoke carefully, knowing his career was at stake in this meeting. *And not just mine,* he thought. *All of us. We let them do this right under our noses, and someone's going to pay—* "The, uh, craft is unbelievably primitive. I wondered why they were so mass-conscious, but it's obvious as soon as you board the thing. Take the gyros for instance. They're huge. They have to be, because they're mechanically coupled to the attitude jets."

"Mechanically coupled?" Rosa Goldstein said. Her voice was incredulous. *"Mechanically?"*

"Yes. They didn't know how to do it electronically. The whole craft is that way. Good ideas, but very primitive in implementation. Some of the workmanship is splendid, but it was all done by handcraft."

"It was implemented well enough to get to space," Ackoff said.

"It's ridiculous on the face of it," Third Secretary Singh said. "A tiny handmade capsule able to put one person in orbit is *not* a spaceship!"

"Have you found a technical definition of a spaceship?" Ackoff asked.

Singh looked chagrined. "No, Your Excellency."

"Nor have I. I suspect there is none," Dr. Boyd said.

"Therefore we may accept their definition or not, as we choose. If we do not, they will certainly appeal." He paused thoughtfully. "I wonder just how we'd look pleading this case before a high tribunal?"

"Fairly silly," Goldstein said. "Some of the Lords Judges have a sense of humor. And of course we would have to explain how we let it happen."

"Not to mention the time and trouble involved in preparing the case," Boyd continued. "Transportation of witnesses. Investigations. Depositions. The cost would not be trivial."

"Returning to my previous question," Ackoff said. "Lieutenant, would you swear that ship was locally designed without benefit of knowledge obtained on Makassar?"

"No, sir. I'm certain it's not. Do they say it is?"

"No," Greenaugh said.

"Which is why this is no small matter," Ackoff said. "And why Trader Soliman's firm will provide them with the best possible legal assistance if it comes to trial." He smiled thinly. "Very clever, that Lord Dougal of theirs. He pointed out to Soliman's factor that if Prince Samual's world is admitted as a Classified Member, then their importation of space-flight technology is quite legal. If not— then we've all failed in our duties. Especially Soliman."

"And the Navy," Greenaugh said. "We inspected their cargo on return."

Jeff nodded. He'd been ready for that one. "To be exact, I did."

"Not that you'll be the only one with his arse in a crack," Greenaugh said. "I'll have to stand up with you."

Dr. Boyd cleared his throat. "I really see little to discuss," he said. "If we accept their application, we will look slightly ridiculous, but it's not likely to become a notorious decision. Few families have been selected as colonists, and no important ones. The ITA won't be troublesome. Quite the opposite; it's very much in Soliman's interest to keep things quiet. The church has never approved of colonization, and I understand King David is preparing the documents submitting his state church to New Rome, which cannot displease His Holiness." He ticked off points on his fingers. "Thus if we accept, there is little opposition to our decision. If we reject their application, we will be subject to well-financed appeals, including, I should fancy, a personal appeal from King David to the Royal Family itself." He spread his hands wide and brought them together. "QED. Lieutenant, are you not prepared to testify that Prince Samual's World has launched a spaceship and therefore technically qualifies as a world with limited space-faring capabilities?"

"Sir, I'd hate to defend calling that thing a spaceship," Jeff said. "At least not in a courtroom."

"With any luck, you won't be in court," Ackoff reminded him.

And it's obvious what answer they want, Jeff thought. How the devil did I get in this mess? But there sure as hell doesn't look like but one way out. "I just don't know."

"Let's see how to put it," Goldstein said. She looked thoughtful. "The supporting documents ought to be signed by Captain Greenaugh as well as the lieutenant. Captain, will you accept this: 'In the absence of challenge by any interested party, we conclude that the craft qualifies as a spacecraft of marginal performance characteristics, and may be accepted as evidence of limited space-faring capability existing on Prince Samual's World at the time of application for membership.'?"

Greenaugh thought for a moment. "Yes. I can sign that. Jefferson?"

"Of course, sir."

"Then are we agreed?" Ackoff asked. "Good. Madam Goldstein, if you would be so kind—"

There was a slight whirring, and a paper emerged from a slot in the end table next to Ackoff. He took it and scanned it quickly, then passed it to Greenaugh.

Greenaugh signed and handed it to Jeff.

"If you please, Lieutenant," Ackoff said. "Thank you." He took the document and laid it carefully on top of King David's parchment. "That's settled, then."

"There's another matter," Greenaugh said.

"And that is?"

"We've been made fools of. Someone's going to pay for that."

"I shouldn't be too hasty," Ackoff said.

"Allow me, Sir Alexei," Dr. Boyd said. "Captain, while your desire is understandable, have you thought through the consequences? What end would be served?"

"You can't let colonials make fools of the Navy and get away with it," Greenaugh said.

"It is hardly a situation likely to arise again," Boyd said. "As to being made a fool, I'd rather be thought a generous fool than a mean and petty one."

Greenaugh stood and bowed coldly to Ackoff. "I see there's no point in my being here," he said. "With your permission, I'll leave." He turned and stalked out of the room.

"That could be a problem," Goldstein said. "He wants someone's blood."

"I'll speak to him later," Ackoff said. "After all, we are the ones who must live with the consequences of what he does." He looked thoughtful for a moment, then turned to Jefferson. "Lieutenant, I don't think it would be wise to repeat anything you've heard in this room today."

"No, sir."

"Also, you will probably want to put your affairs in order. I doubt that your ship will be in this system much longer. Given the changed state of affairs here, we will need a somewhat different sort of naval assistance."

"Yes, sir."

"Thank you for coming."

"Yes, sir," Jefferson said. "If you'll excuse me—" As Jeff left the office, Boyd was saying. "It does seem possible to comply with the captain's wishes and at the same time solve another pressing problem—" Jeff let himself out of the office. By the time he reached the stairway, he was whistling to himself.

Regular Navy not needed, he thought. Colonists not needed. Well, that's one decision made for me, not that I really needed help making it. They won't be accepting transfers from the Navy to the civil service. Particularly not mine!

Now how am I going to tell Elaine?

Tell her any damned way you like, he told himself. You're going to space again!

He took the steps three at a time.

★ ★ ★

An octopus of wires stretched upward to a bewildering array of dials and buttons. At one end the octopus terminated in electrodes attached to Mary's abdomen; its other end vanished into a bulkhead of *Tombaugh's* sick bay. She'd already learned to call it a bulkhead rather than a wall.

The Navy physician removed the last of the electrodes from her belly. "You can put your clothes on now," he said. He seemed quite impersonal, although he'd been friendly enough in the wardroom two hours before. He held a shadowy photograph to the light. She'd heard him call it an X-ray, and he'd told her it showed a picture of her insides. She would have liked to study it, but she didn't quite know how to ask.

"How am I doing?" Mary asked.

"You'll be all right," Lieutenant Commander Terry said. He looked at the X-ray again. "That treatment should do it. If it doesn't, we'll need to do some slicing." He saw her look of dismay. "Didn't mean to scare you. Routine, actually. You're a standard chromotype. Regeneration stimulators work fine on you. Problem is, sometimes it's easier to remove something and get it to grow back than to fix the original parts. Either way, you'll be fine."

"But what was wrong?"

"Vibration. Enough to tear some intestinal mesentaries. They'll grow back, but I'm worried about adhesions."

"That sounds serious."

"Not really. You'll have to take it easy for a bit, that's all. Nothing strenuous."

"I—" She was embarrassed, but it had to be said. "I was hoping to be married. Quite soon."

"Hmm. Honeymoon wouldn't be very interesting for a while," he said. "But we'll get all that fixed, too. You'll be fine."

"You're sure?" The honeymoon could wait. It wasn't as if they were impatient virgins. But— "Are you really sure?"

"Yes, ma'am." Commander Terry's smile was reassuring. "I may not have had a lot of experience treating women's problems, but yours is quite simple. Nothing wrong with the reproductive system. Just intestinal tissue. I'll have you right in a few weeks."

"I didn't think you could treat colonials," Mary said.

"We can't, as a usual rule, but of course the rules don't apply to prisoners."

"Prisoners? But—"

"Didn't you know? Sorry," he said. "I thought they'd told you. Captain Greenaugh sent up an arrest order three hours ago. You've been charged with interfering with the orderly development of Makassar."

★31★
HORSE COLLARS
★ ★ ★

The Imperial Marine officer was polite, but very insistent. "Colonel MacKinnie, I have my orders. You are to accompany me to Empire House immediately." He looked around Dougal's office, then at Dougal. "I have a squad of Marines outside, and I am in communication with Marine Barracks."

"Calmly, calmly," Dougal said. "We have offered no resistance. I merely asked what Colonel MacKinnie is charged with. I assume he is under arrest?"

"I'd rather not put it that way," the officer said. "But I could."

"But what am I charged with?" MacKinnie demanded. The officer shrugged.

"What should I do?" MacKinnie asked.

Dougal looked grave. "I would prefer that you go with him. Until this matter is settled, we should be prepared to go to any lengths to show how well we cooperate with the Imperial authorities."

MacKinnie shrugged. "All right."

"We will protest to the High Commissioner at once," Dougal said.

"While you're doing that, get them to set Freelady Graham free," MacKinnie said. "We've got a wedding scheduled."

"We will do our best," Dougal said. "I'll talk to the King immediately."

Nathan sat in an ornate chair in the study at Government House. A cheerful fire burned on the hearth, but he hardly noticed it.

Where is Mary? Have they brought her here, or is she still up in that ship? Damn them, damn them to hell. They'll have to let her go. They can't hold her. She's the most famous person on Samual, better known than King David.

That thought was disturbing. Dougal would see that, too. What would Dougal do about it? He can't have one of David's subjects more popular than the king, not if he plans to control the development of this planet.

Wonder if he'll get that control? He's certain the Empire is going to approve his application for Class Two status. He seems to know a lot about Ackoff. Or says he does, and I've no evidence one way or another.

Suppose he's right, they approve David's application and bring Samual into their Empire. What happens then? What have they done with Mary?

The door opened and a large man, formally dressed, came in. "Colonel MacKinnie? I am Dudley Boyd, First Secretary. His Excellency will see you now." MacKinnie stood, remembering that it was in this room that he'd first met the Imperials. That seemed like a long time ago.

And it is interesting, MacKinnie thought as he followed the diplomat down the hall. The First Secretary for escort. I've come up in the world. . . .

Mary was in the High Commissioner's office. He went to her without waiting to be introduced to the Commissioner, but then he stood self-consciously. He wanted to hold her, but old habits die hard. "Are you all right? You look pale."

"I'm fine—"

"The Navy's surgeon says she will recover," Boyd said. "There was internal bleeding, and perhaps an intestinal adhesion may need minor surgery."

MacKinnie looked shocked. Boyd's voice was gentle as he said, "What did you expect? The vibration in that—" He hesitated a moment over the word. "The vibration in the ship must have been fierce."

"Was it bad?" Nathan asked.

She grinned lopsidedly. "No worse than the carts on Makassar." Her reserve broke, and she stepped toward him. He opened his arms and held her.

Boyd cleared his throat. "Your Excellency, may I present Colonel Nathan MacKinnie. Colonel, High Commissioner Sir Alexei Ackoff."

"Your servant," MacKinnie said automatically.

"Hardly," Ackoff said. "Have you any idea of how many man-hours of planning you two have wrecked? No, I wouldn't suppose you would. Sit down, Freelady, Colonel. We have much to discuss." He led the way to the comfortable couches arranged at the far end of his office. "Would anyone care for a drink? This will be quite informal."

"Informal but official," Boyd warned. "Colonel, you and Freelady Graham have been charged with interfering with the orderly development of a primitive world, to wit, Makassar."

"But we didn't interfere," Mary protested.

Ackoff waved impatiently. "Don't be nonsensical. There's *always* interference when an advanced people move among primitives."

"I see," MacKinnie said. "You were embarrassed by our ship, and you've chosen us to pay for it."

"Pronouns," Dudley Boyd said.

"I beg your pardon?"

"Wrong pronouns," Boyd said. "You said 'you,' meaning us, and that's not true. You've been arrested by Navy orders, not ours."

"Makassar is under Navy jurisdiction," Ackoff explained. "There is no civil government there. Captain Greenaugh is within his rights, and he could try you by court martial. You would then have the right to appeal to civil authority, which is to say, to me. We're trying to save time by dealing directly with you."

"But what did we do?" Mary asked.

"Captain Greenaugh is still building his case," Ackoff said. "But as it happens, I can put one precise specification to his charge. Horse collars."

"Horse collars?" MacKinnie frowned. "I hadn't thought the Empire concerned itself with trivia."

Ackoff laughed. "Trivia? Colonel, the horse collar

effectively ended slavery on Earth in pre-atomic times. I see you don't understand.

"Consider that if you harness a horse by fastening a strap around its neck, the poor beast can't pull very hard because when it pulls it strangles itself. Improperly hitched horses can do about five times as much work as a man. But a horse *eats* five times as much as a man. Given the choice between a horse and a slave there isn't much in it.

"But. Add the rigid horse collar so the load goes on to the shoulders, and the horse can do ten times as much work as a man—and it still eats only five times as much. Horses are then clearly preferable to humans for heavy work. Prior to the invention of horse collars there were as many slaves as free people on Earth. Afterwards, slavery became fairly rare and only imposed on people thought inferior. And I see I am indulging my tendency to lecture.

"My point is simple. I know from the reports—from your own admissions—that you introduced rigid horse collars. Probably a lot of other seemingly minor innovations will have a profound impact. Privately, I expect you did them far more good than harm, but if we want to charge you, we have all the evidence we need."

"And you can't say you weren't warned," Boyd said. "Captain Greenaugh is adamant on that point. He warned you himself."

"But—" Graham protested.

Nathan shook his head. "They've obviously got more to say. Let's hear them out."

"A good attitude," Ackoff said. "Colonel, you know very little of Imperial politics. I can be certain of this, because it's true of everyone on this planet. That's going to change, of course. Once Prince Samual becomes an actual member world, there'll be travel and trade. And intrigue. I doubt that King David and Lord Dougal have any suspicion of what's in store for them, of how hard it will be for them to maintain control here when new technology begins to flow unrestricted.

"Have you any place in that struggle?"

"Not much," MacKinnie said. "I'd thought of that already. Even that Dougal might see us—" He took Mary's hand. "Might see us as a threat."

"Discerning," Ackoff said. "And actually the situation is more complicated than I described it." He pointed upward, out the arched window above his desk. "Out there in Trans-Coalsack Sector they've discovered aliens. The fleet's being sent there. Sparta's attention will inevitably follow. There won't be a lot to spare for Samual. My staff will remain, and we will bring in our intelligence people, but this will be, after all, a rather minor provincial world for some time to come. You two have won King David the right to a measure of independence, and he'll have to endure the consequences."

"I don't see where we come in," MacKinnie said.

"Think upon it," Boyd said. "The contest for power on this planet is hardly over. You two will shortly be the best-known people on Prince Samual's World. You cannot avoid being drawn into politics."

"That's not my game," Nathan said.

"It is tempting," Mary said. "We could—"

"To be blunt," Boyd said, "you can work with Dougal or be killed; and it will be difficult to fit into Dougal's plans. Also, understand that there's no way we could protect you even if we wanted to. Pardon the interruption, but were I you I would think of few *less* tempting alternatives."

"Nor could we allow you to raise an army of your former soldiers for protection," Ackoff said. "We will not permit a civil war on this planet."

"You're working up to something," MacKinnie said. "Make your offer."

Ackoff nodded. "You are admirably direct. But then you're a soldier, not a diplomat. There is one other point of background you ought to be quite certain of. Captain Greenaugh does not like you."

Mary Graham laughed. "We hadn't expected him to."

"The matter is serious," Dr. Boyd said. "The Navy has great influence, and Captain Greenaugh is adamant. Someone must be punished—visibly punished—to assuage his embarrassment."

"And we're elected," Mary said.

"It seems that way," Boyd said.

"The Navy arrest warrant is quite genuine," Ackoff said carefully. "It cannot be ignored. But we would very much prefer to avoid a trial."

"Why?" MacKinnie asked.

"No one would win," Ackoff said. "Your King David would defend you, but I doubt his heart would be in it. He'd want us to win, and thereby prove that we are tyrants. We, on the other hand, would prefer to lose the case and thus demonstrate the fairness of Imperial justice. If Greenaugh insists on a court martial, then you will appeal. If we grant that appeal, Greenaugh will insist the case be opened at a higher level. A waste of time all around, with no profit for anyone—and unpleasant for you in the bargain. Fortunately, there is an alternative. You can plead guilty and ask for Imperial clemency."

"Why should we do that?" Mary asked.

"Because *we* would then determine the sentence, which would be permanent exile."

"Exile?" Nathan said.

"Yes. To Makassar."

"Makassar?" MacKinnie asked. "I don't see—"

"Simple, actually," Boyd said. "If you accept voluntary exile on Makassar, Greenaugh will be satisfied. You made fools of the Navy, and you paid for it. But of course there are side benefits. You will also be removed as a factor in this world's politics." The First Secretary examined his fingertips. "That makes our task just a bit easier."

"And Makassar could benefit as well," Ackoff added. "If we can't give much attention to Prince Samual's World, what have we to spare for that place? A world of no importance. But there are nearly a million people there, people as human as you and I."

"You really want us to go back?" Graham asked incredulously.

"Precisely," Boyd said.

"You impressed the churchmen," Ackoff said. "And now that you are a citizen of a classified world, it would be legal for you to hold an official appointment. As, say, civil advisor to the Archbishop. His memorandum makes it clear that he would welcome your assistance."

"You could do a lot of good," Boyd said. "No one will govern Makassar for a long time. Certainly not with the resources we can spare. But Makassar will inevitably fall into Prince Samual's sphere of influence, and someone must see that the ITA doesn't absolutely plunder that unfortunate world until it is capable of protecting itself. You might make a difference in their development."

Mary and Nathan looked at each other in amazement. Were these two actually pleading with them?

"It's quite a logical position for you," Ackoff said. "You know as much about Makassar as anyone in the Empire. You even had access to the old library." Ackoff smiled thinly. "Not that I expect you to admit it, but your ship rather proves that, doesn't it? And while you don't know a lot about modern technology, Makassar's not likely to *get* much modern technology. What's needed is someone who knows how to make do."

"How can you trust me?"

"We don't have to," Boyd said. "No matter what you do, you'll be no threat to the Empire." He shrugged. "Assume the worst, that you make yourself king of all the barbarians. The ship that takes you there will remove most of the tapes from that Old Empire library. What can you do to us? And Makassar is unlikely to be worse off with you than without you."

"And if I refuse?" Nathan asked. Ackoff shrugged. "We'd have to consider our other alternatives."

"The threat isn't needed," Mary said. "We want to go back. Nathan never wanted to leave."

MacKinnie nodded agreement. "I left some obligations back there. But—Mary, are you certain you want this?"

"What makes you think you're the only one who wants to be needed?" she demanded. "For a moment I was mad enough to suppose that because I was a passenger in Dougal's ship I could be a match for Dougal, but that won't work. And—I was needed on Makassar too, Nathan MacKinnie. Not just by you."

"We'll give you time to think about it," Ackoff said.

"We won't need it," Mary said. She turned to MacKinnie. "Will we, Your Excellency?" She made no attempt to hide her laughter.

Ackoff nodded. "If it were done, 't were best done quickly. We'll arrange transportation in a ship with proper medical facilities. You should be as good as new when you arrive on Makassar." He cleared his throat. "Uh, I can see there's a chaplain aboard also. I understand congratulations are in order. . . . That's settled, then."

Ackoff smiled warmly, then turned to his computer screen. That was one problem solved. There would be others. There always were.